D0108455

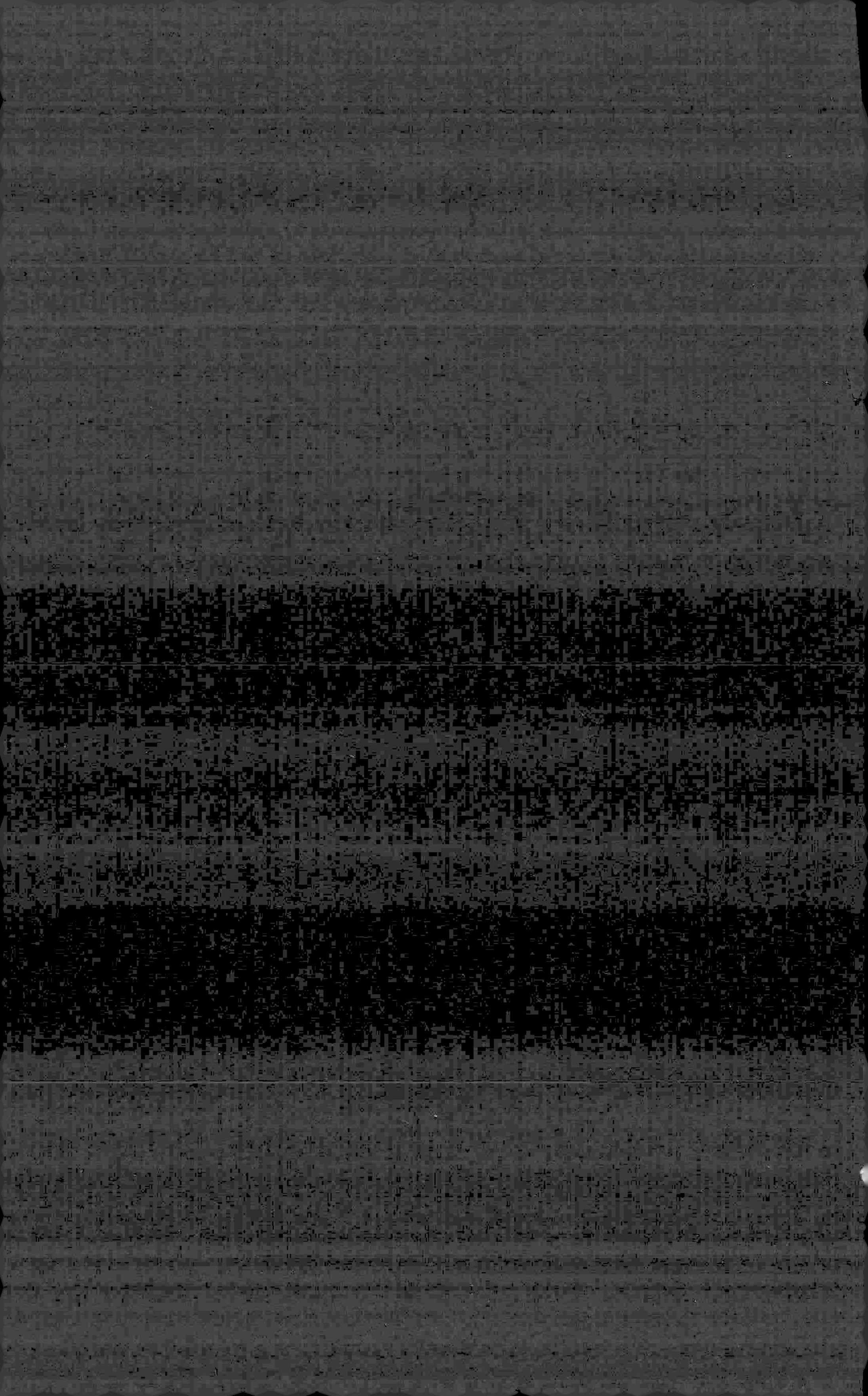

Backstabber

By the same author

Billie Jo
Born Evil
The Betrayer
The Feud
The Traitor
The Victim
The Schemer
The Trap
Payback
The Wronged
Tainted Love

Backstabber

Kimberley
CHAMBERS

HarperCollins*Publishers*

HarperCollins*Publishers*
1 London Bridge Street
London SE1 9GF

www.harpercollins.co.uk

Published by HarperCollins*Publishers* 2017
1

A catalogue record for this book is available from the British Library

ISBN: 978-0-00-752180-7

Typeset in Sabon LT Std by Palimpsest Book Production Ltd, Falkirk, Stirlingshire

Printed and bound in Great Britain by Clays Ltd, St Ives plc

MIX
Paper from responsible sources
FSC C007454

FSC™ is a non-profit international organization established to promote
the responsible management of the world's forests. Products carrying the
FSC label are independently certified to assure consumers that they come
from forests that are managed to meet the social, economic and
ecological needs of present and future generations,
and other controlled sources.

Find out more about HarperCollins and the environment at
www.harpercollins.co.uk/green

In memory of Bradley Arthur
Taken far too soon
1990–2015

A loving son, brother, father, grandson,
friend and fellow Spurs fan

RIP Brad

ACKNOWLEDGEMENTS

A massive thank you [illegible] hard work and [illegible]

[illegible]

And last, but certainly not least, a big thank-you to all of my readers. Thank you so much for all your loyalty and support. Means the world to me x

ACKNOWLEDGEMENTS

A massive thank you to the team at HarperCollins for all your hard work and belief in my books – a truly brilliant publisher. I count my blessings daily to be working with you all.

Much love to Kimberley Young. You are such a joy to work with Kim, and as an editor – SIMPLY THE BEST!

Special mentions to my awesome agent Tim Bates. My lovely publicist Felicity Denham – another joy to work with. The fantastic Sue Cox. Unforgettable and wonderful Rosie de Courcy. My mad-as-me mate Mandasue Heller. The brill Laura Meyer. The finest and most supportive CEO ever Charlie Redmayne. My second mum Pat Fletcher. And all my gym pals from down the Y who help keep me sane while writing each book. Love you guys x

And last, but certainly not least, big gratitude to all of my readers. Thank you so much for all your loyalty and support. Means the world to me xx

'The devil is a gentleman'

Anon

PROLOGUE

It was a cold February evening. So bloody cold, the car windscreens had started to freeze.

Beads of sweat forming on his forehead, the man wanted to take off his crash helmet, but daren't. How had it come to this? he mused, even though he already knew the answer. His brother had a screw loose, wasn't right in the head. He'd never been sane, truth be known. That was obvious, and it should have been dealt with.

There had been some good times, brilliant in fact, but the bad outweighed those massively now. His brother was a ticking time bomb that exploded every now and then, leaving a trail of carnage and sadness. Well, this time he had gone a step too far. Which was why a decision had been made to stop him in his tracks, for ever. There was no other option.

The man's heart rate went into overdrive as he heard the distinctive sound of an approaching vehicle. He knew without a doubt it was him, could hear the sleek diesel engine, and the song 'Jealous Guy' blaring out the speakers. His brother had always been a big fan of Roxy Music, reckoned Bryan Ferry's voice was second to none.

Sporting the number plate VB1, the black Range Rover

screeched to a halt and a tall suited man leapt out. He looked the part, as always. Thick black hair greased back, expensive watch and shiny shoes.

'Bruv! You shit the life outta me then. Where's your motor? I'm pleased you called.'

Hands trembling, Michael Butler lifted the gun. 'I'm sorry, Vinny, I really am. But . . . '

PART ONE

'I'm not upset that you lied to me,
I'm upset that from now on I can't believe you'

Friedrich Nietzsche

CHAPTER ONE

2001

The envelope was one of those extra-large brown padded ones, and as Eddie Mitchell opened it the putrid smell engulfed his nostrils with enough force to make him gag. 'What the hell! Vinny, Vinny!' he bellowed.

Having recently acquired premises along the A13 that would soon be opened as a casino, Vinny Butler strolled towards his and Eddie's office. 'What's up with you? You look like you've seen a ghost. And what's that terrible smell?'

'Have a look for yourself. I ain't going back in there.'

Vinny looked in disbelief at the bloodstained box and the two dead rats inside. Both rodents' throats had been cut. 'Who the fuck sent that?'

'I don't know, do I? Have a look at the postcode and see if there's a note.' Eddie was petrified of rats, even dead ones, but he wasn't about to admit that to his new business partner.

Vinny put his hand inside the envelope and pulled out a typewritten note:

DEUTERONOMY 24:16

FATHERS SHALL NOT BE PUT TO DEATH BECAUSE OF THEIR CHILDREN, NOR SHALL CHILDREN BE PUT TO DEATH BECAUSE OF THEIR FATHERS. EACH ONE SHALL BE PUT TO DEATH FOR HIS OWN SIN.

Eddie could not but help stare at it in total horror. He and Vinny had only bought the gaff less than a fortnight ago and hadn't overly broadcast their purchase yet.

'Perhaps it was meant for the previous owner? Not got our names on the envelope, has it?' Vinny said.

'Don't talk bollocks, Vin. Three days ago it was posted, from poxy Romford. You had grief with anyone recently you haven't told me about?'

'Don't ya think I've had enough bleedin' grief with all the incest bollocks and murder of my sacred aunt? I've been too busy holdin' my grievin', messed-up family together to be gettin' up to no good.'

Rubbing the stubble of his chin as he usually did when deep in thought, Eddie Mitchell apologized. 'I'm sorry, mate. It's just worrying that we've already got grief and we ain't even open yet. It's obviously a quote from the bible or something. But who would send shit like that – and why?'

Vinny poured two large Scotches and handed a glass to his pal. 'Your guess is as good as mine. Probably some jealous bastard who wishes they were us. Best put it to the back of our minds, eh? I'm not being funny, but we've got enough on our plates as it is. Besides, if somebody was truly gunning for us they wouldn't be sending us warnings. I had something similar happen to me donkey's years ago. Funeral flower arrangement shaped as a gun, delivered to me mum's with a card sayin' "You're next". Sod-all came of it. Was probably that wrong 'un Ahmed trying to wind me up. And that's all this is, a wind-up, so put it out of your mind, OK?'

'Get rid of them rats and I will. Can hardly forget about it with that stench,' Eddie complained.

Vinny chuckled, picked up the box, and eyed the dead rats. 'You're not scared of ickle rodents, are you, Mitchell?'

'Leave off. It's the smell. Making me feel queasy, it is.'

When Vinny sauntered out the office with the deceased Mickey and Minnie, Eddie sprayed some air freshener around before sitting on one of the luxurious leather chairs. Vinny had better not be telling him porkies, because if he was, he'd regret it.

'You little squirt, what you think you're doing?' Harry O'Hara demanded menacingly. Harry and Georgie had been raised by their gypsy father, had only known their little brother for a matter of months, and Harry hated him with a passion.

Petrified of Harry, who was four years his senior, seven-year-old Brett averted his eyes and stared at his lap. If he had one wish in the world it would be that Georgie and Harry had never come to live with him. 'I'm playing on my PlayStation Two.'

'I'm playing on my PlayStation Two,' Harry mimicked in a whiny voice. 'Gis it 'ere. I wanna have a look.'

Too scared to say no, Brett's hand shook as he handed over the controls.

Grinning like a Cheshire cat, Harry kicked the controls around the room like a football.

'Stop! You'll break it,' Brett pleaded, his eyes welling up.

'Stop. You'll break it,' Harry repeated, in an even sillier voice.

'What's all that racket up there? We're going out in a

minute, boys, so get yourselves ready and downstairs, please,' shouted Frankie Mitchell. The eldest daughter of Eddie Mitchell, Frankie felt much older than her twenty-nine years just lately. She was elated Georgie and Harry were home, but they were bloody hard work. Her once long, glossy, dark hair was now dull and lifeless, her complexion was sallow, everything about her looked worn out. She'd never expected instant harmony, but neither had she expected daily battles and arguments. It was tiring, to say the least.

Grabbing Brett around the neck, Harry warned, 'You tell Frankie I did anything and you're dead meat. Got me, cry baby?' Harry found it hard to believe Brett had the same parents as he and Georgie. The boy was such a wuss which was obviously Frankie's doing. Brett would've been knocked into shape had their dad raised him.

Brett Mitchell nodded. Not for the first time since his brother moved in, he actually wished he was dead.

'How's it going? Sorry I couldn't get here any earlier. Something cropped up with Eddie,' Vinny Butler explained.

Queenie Butler stood on tiptoes to kiss her eldest son. Both her sons were six-foot-plus strapping, handsome men who wore their hair Brylcreemed and dressed in the finest designer suits and handmade shoes. Everybody always commented on how immaculate and well turned out her boys were, and that made Queenie swell with pride. 'That's OK, boy. Your brother and me have got most of the boxes unpacked already. I'll put the kettle on now.'

Vinny closed the lounge door. 'How's she doing?' he asked in a hushed tone.

'OK. Better than we expected. Slept well, by all accounts, and she's already fallen in love with her new garden. Reckons there's loads more birds to feed round 'ere,' Michael Butler replied.

'D'ya reckon it's an act?'

Michael shrugged. 'Hard to tell with Mum, but she seems chirpy enough whichever way you look at it.'

Having lived the whole of her life in Whitechapel, seventy-four-year-old Queenie Butler had been forced to up sticks thanks to the brutal cold-blooded murder of her beloved sister, Vivian. Vinny had found his mum a nice bungalow in a quiet road in Hornchurch, and both he and Michael were keeping a close eye on her.

'Talking about me, are ya?' Queenie snapped, as she walked in the front room. Vinny was her eldest. He'd be fifty-six soon. Roy, her middle son, was six feet under. Michael was fifty-one.

A doting mother, Queenie could not be prouder of her boys. She'd encouraged them to make something of their lives from a very early age, and they had. Notoriety and wealth were wonderful attributes for a man to have, especially if they had the looks to go with it. Both Vinny and Michael oozed charm, and looked much younger than they should.

'I was just saying to Michael, that couple opposite seem nice. Spoke to me again, they did. Said you're to knock there if you need anything,' Vinny told his mother.

Queenie pursed her thin lips. 'Don't like the look of 'em. Remind me of those notrights who had the bungalow next to us down at Kings. Perverts, they were. Swingers.'

'You don't know that for sure.' Michael chuckled.

'Well, I very much doubt the couple over the road are perverts or swingers. You gotta give people a chance round 'ere, Mum. You don't want to alienate yourself,' Vinny said sensibly.

'I am quite capable of choosing my own friends, thank you. And I'm hardly gonna be bothering to socialize until I've given our Vivvy the send-off she thoroughly deserves.

You spoken to them bastards any more about releasing the body?'

'I rung the nick again this morning, but that DI Cater weren't around. I've left another message for him to ring me back. I'd rather speak to the organ grinder than any of his two-bob monkeys,' Vinny explained.

'I don't know what the hold-up is if they've got the lads who attacked Auntie Viv. Do you want me to go down to the station and make some noise?' Michael offered.

'I'll tell you what the hold-up is, shall I? Our name is Butler. Always hated you boys since you made something of yourselves. Jealous bastards, because you earn far more money than they can even dream of,' Queenie said bitterly.

'Nah. Leave it, Michael – I'll sort it. And don't worry, Mum. Auntie Viv'll have the best send-off the East End's seen in a long, long time,' Vinny vowed.

Turning away so her sons couldn't see her misery, Queenie sniffed then put on her bravest voice. 'I should bloody well think so an' all.'

'Harry, we're in a restaurant now. Use your knife and fork, love,' Frankie Mitchell urged.

'Harry don't know how to use a knife and fork,' joked Georgie O'Hara.

'Shut up, you tart,' Harry said, grinning at his sister.

'Please, Harry,' Frankie pleaded.

Unlike Georgie, who had nice straight teeth and dark hair like their father, plus a cute button slightly turned-up nose like their mum's, Harry O'Hara looked menacing. His mop of strawberry blonde hair rarely came into contact with a comb or brush, his nose was squashed like a boxer's thanks to fighting, and he had a missing tooth at the front. He glared at his mother. He could not stand her; the way he saw it, she had ruined his once idyllic life. 'Nah, prefer eating like this, Frankie,' he told her. He never called her 'Mum' and knew that made her sad.

'Do as your mother says, boy,' Stuart Howells ordered. Stuart had been in love with Frankie long before they had got together, but she'd been so scarred by her relationship with Jed O'Hara, it had taken her ages to trust him.

'Nah. You ain't my dad, you can't tell me what to do,' Harry spat, his voice raised. In a lower voice, he added, 'Dinlo.'

Realizing her fiancé was about to argue the point, Frankie squeezed his arm. People were already staring at them, like they usually did when they went out as a family. Frankie knew this was because of her children's unruly behaviour and unusual accents. She'd often seen couples move tables, mumbling the word 'gypsies'.

'He's been home nearly six months now, Frankie. You can't keep allowing him to get away with the way he treats you,' Stuart hissed, looking daggers at the child he loathed so much. Stuart had come to rue the day Georgie and Harry had been snatched from the gypsies and returned to Frankie. Their arrival had turned everybody's lives upside down.

'Leave my brother alone. Harry's right. You ain't our dad and you never will be,' said thirteen-year-old Georgie. She was fiercely loyal when it came to Harry.

'Now, let's stop all this. I don't want any arguing today of all days. This is Harry's special day, and I want it to be perfect,' Frankie said, smiling at her son, who was currently gnawing a lamb chop like a starving animal.

'Special day. Silly old rabbit's crotch,' Harry whispered in his sister's ear.

When Georgie whispered something back and both children burst out laughing, not wanting them to see she was upset, Frankie excused herself to go to the toilet. Once inside a cubicle, she pulled down the toilet seat, sat on it and allowed the tears to flow. How the hell had it come to this?

Harry had been a loveable four-year-old when Jed O'Hara and his family had disappeared into the night taking Frankie's children with them. At the time, Frankie was residing in Holloway Prison due to stabbing Jed, and he had custody of the kids. Jed was an English gypsy who originated from Cambridgeshire, and his community stuck together like glue, so finding Georgie and Harry was never going to be easy, even for someone with Eddie Mitchell's resources. Seven long, excruciating years it had taken until a tip-off from a traveller Frankie had met in prison reunited her with her children. It was one of the best days of her life, but also the worst. Georgie and Harry loathed her on sight and made it clear they didn't remember her. Frankie had cherished every memory of her precious children and it broke her heart that to them she was no more than a stranger.

As Frankie dabbed her eyes and stared at her unhappy face in the compact mirror, she couldn't help but think about the last birthday she'd spent with Harry. He'd been such a good little boy as a toddler. Gentle and sweet-natured. Now he was an uncouth, unrecognizable piece of work. But Frankie could not give up on him, or Georgie. It was her duty as a mother to love her children no matter what.

'Mummy, where are you?'

Her youngest son's voice snapped Frankie out of her depressive thoughts. Brett was Jed's child also, had been born while she was in prison. But thankfully, unlike her other two, had been spared ever meeting his arsehole of a father, or sharing his surname.

Plastering a smile on her face, Frankie unlocked the cubicle and held Brett close. Georgie and Harry's homecoming had turned his little world upside down as well. So much so, that lately Brett preferred staying with her dad and stepmother, Gina, who lived nearby. 'How's my favourite boy?'

'Can I go to Granddad's now please, Mum?'

'We haven't had our dessert yet, darling. Granddad is picking you up from our house later.'

'I don't want no dessert. I don't like Georgie and Harry. They're nasty and they scare me,' Brett said, his lip wobbling.

Frankie crouched down. 'Your brother and sister can't help the way they are, love. Unlike you, who was brought up in the correct manner, poor Georgie and Harry were dragged up by not-so-nice people. It isn't their fault, and even though I know this is difficult for you, we must all try to be patient with them and get along. Can you do that for Mummy?'

Knowing it would upset his mother greatly if he told her Harry regularly punched him in the ribs and broke his toys, Brett Mitchell simply nodded sadly.

Vinny Butler sauntered back from the bar. After a hard day's graft with their mother ordering them about like a pair of skivvies, both he and Michael felt they deserved a drink.

'Cheers, bruv. I reckon Mum'll be happy there ya know, in time. Such a nice area, compared to Whitechapel. And with her arthritis, being in a bungalow'll make life so much easier for her,' Michael said.

'Early days yet, but fingers crossed. Any more news on the boys or Roxanne?'

'There is actually, but I don't think we should tell Mum

until after the funeral. I got a letter in the post from Lee this morning. He's gone abroad to start afresh with Daniel. Reckons he won't be coming back to England. He must've posted it on the way to the airport or something.'

'Whereabouts are they?'

Michael shrugged. 'Didn't say. Gutted, I am. It's not quite sunk in yet, but it looks like I've lost my sons for good.'

Vinny sighed. He'd been really close to Daniel, and hoped his nephew would stay in contact. It was all such a mess, it really was. Daniel had thought Roxanne was the girl of his dreams; he was so in love with her that when she told him she was pregnant, he'd asked her to marry him. He'd been about to slip the ring on her finger when Michael's ex, Nancy – who everybody thought had committed suicide years earlier – ran into the registry office screaming, 'He's your brother!' It turned out Roxanne was fifteen, not eighteen as she'd told Daniel, and nobody bar her deceitful mother had known she was Michael's daughter – and Daniel's little sister. Vinny shook his head. 'I still can't believe everything that's happened these past few weeks. Even a zonked-out soap writer could not make it up. You spoken to Nancy since it happened?'

'A couple of days ago. There's still no word from Roxanne, and Nancy's worried sick. Nancy mentioned involving the Old Bill again, but I managed to talk her out of it. No way do we want our kids splashed all over the front page of every newspaper. The press would have a sodding field day.'

'Too right they would. Let's hope Roxanne's seen sense and got rid of the baby by now, else it'll be too late to abort it. What'll you do if she bastard well keeps it?'

'Cheer me up, why don't ya, Vin? Nah, she won't keep it. What sort of bird chooses to raise their own brother's child? I know she lied about her age, but you gotta remember Roxanne didn't have a clue she and Dan were related until Nancy showed up.'

'I wouldn't bank on her getting rid of the kid. If you ask me she takes after her mother: a nutjob and a compulsive fucking liar.'

Eddie Mitchell handed his least favourite grandson a card. 'Happy birthday, boy. I didn't know what to get you, so thought if I got you vouchers your mum could take you to Lakeside and you could pick something out yourself.' Eddie hated calling the child Harry. He knew who he'd been named after and why, and that made him feel sick to the stomach.

'Ta. Can me and Georgie go outside now?' Harry asked his mother.

'Yes. But put your jackets on. It's nippy out there.'

'Not if you were brought up as a traveller it ain't. We don't feel the cold like you gorgers. Come on,' Harry ordered, grabbing his sister's arm.

'And if them blokes come anywhere near us I'm gonna kick 'em in the balls. You can't keep us here like prisoners for ever, you know,' Georgie yelled, before slamming the back door.

Eddie glanced at Stuart. They'd been pals long before Stuart had got together with Frankie and both were uncomfortable with the current arrangement. It just wasn't right.

When Eddie had first snatched the kids from a gypsy site in Scotland, Frankie and Brett had been happily sharing a house in Brentwood with her pal Babs, and Babs' son, Jordan. The arrival of 'the devil's spawn', as Eddie sometimes referred to Georgie and Harry, soon changed all that. They led poor Jordan a dog's life, so much so, Babs moved out with her son within a month of their arrival. Frankie couldn't cope on her own, so Stuart moved in to help out, but every time their backs were turned, Georgie and Harry tried to do a runner. Brentwood station was the last place Eddie had found the banes of his life. They'd been about to board a train when he'd grabbed hold of them from behind.

Frankie had pleaded with her father to find them somewhere more secure, so Eddie had rented a big gaff not far from him. The house had acres around it, and was surrounded by CCTV and six-foot metal railings and gates. He'd also hired a security team and had a little office built near the entrance so the kids could not escape.

'Georgie does have a point, babe. Reminds me of Colditz, and the lease runs out in eight months. This was only ever meant to be a temporary measure. You're gonna have to trust 'em at some point. They need to go to school and mix with other kids if they're ever gonna turn out half normal,' Eddie advised.

'No way! Georgie hated school when she was little and ran away even back then. If I send them to school they will just disappear again, I know they will,' Frankie's voice was panic-stricken.

Stuart put an arm around his wife-to-be. He'd proposed three months to the day he and Frankie had first got together. They'd been friends for a long time beforehand, but because of all the upheaval surrounding Georgie and Harry, they'd yet to set a date or even discuss the actual wedding. 'Frankie wants to hire a tutor and teach them from home, Ed,' Stuart said, raising his eyebrows to show his displeasure.

Eddie was desperate for his daughter to see sense. 'Ruined everyone's lives, that pair of little fuckers have. Why d'ya think Brett is upstairs in his bedroom as we speak, Frankie? And why do you think he wants to stay at mine and Gina's all the time? Because the poor little sod is desperately unhappy, that's why. Brett's a shell of his former self and it's about time you started putting him, yourself and Stuart first, girlie. Let the little bastards run away and see how far they get. The O'Haras no longer live on that site near Glasgow. A desolate piece of land, that is now. And before you ask how I know, I had someone check it out for me. You got to be cruel to be kind sometimes, so if Georgie and Harry think the grass is greener in Scotland, let 'em have a mooch up there. They'll soon come back with their tails between their sorry legs. You mark my words.'

'You don't know Jed like I do. He'll never let them go. He'll be waiting and watching in the wings, then as soon as an opportunity arises he'll snatch Georgie and Harry and take them away. I know you said he'll never bother me again, Dad, but I'm telling you he will. He's pure evil.'

Eddie and Stuart shared a knowing look. Nobody bar those present on that fateful night knew exactly what had happened, but perhaps now was the time to let Frankie into a little secret. 'Jed's dead, Frankie. So's his old man,' Eddie said bluntly.

Frankie looked at her father with an incredulous expression. 'When? How? Who told you? Why didn't you tell me?'

Eddie moved over to the sofa and put an arm around his daughter's shoulders. 'Because you'd only just got the kids back and had enough on your plate at the time.'

'Did you kill them?' Frankie bellowed.

'No,' Eddie replied honestly. 'But I can assure you they're both dead.'

Tears of anger streaming down her face, Frankie pummelled her father's chest with her fists. 'Why did you only tell me you'd scared them away for good? Don't you know how many nights I've laid awake wondering if and when Jed might come back? I will never believe another word that comes out of your mouth. You're a liar. A wicked, evil liar.'

Eddie grabbed her wrists. 'Got some front, you have. Talk about pot calling kettle! Slipped your mind to tell me that evil toe-rag you were shacked up with brutally murdered your grandfather, didn't it?'

'I explained why I never told you, and you said we'd never mention it again,' Frankie screamed.

Eddie's father Harry Mitchell was a legend in East London, and a notorious underworld figure. Until 1988, when he'd been battered to death whilst tucked up in his bed. His killer had never been caught and it only came to light on the day Jed died that he was the one responsible. Frankie knew, by all accounts. She'd heard Jed and his cousin Sammy joking about it. That's why Frankie had stabbed Jed and ended up in prison. She knew at that point Jed was beyond evil and she needed to get him away from her children. She'd meant to kill him, but unfortunately failed. Frankie hadn't told her father the truth at the time because she was worried for his safety. She was also scared her dad would get locked up for life and Georgie and Harry would be taken away from her by the authorities. Looking back now, Frankie cursed her stupidity. Even if the authorities had stepped in, her children could not have turned out any worse than they had. And her father was more than capable of looking after his bloody self.

'You mustn't tell anybody about Jed and Jimmy, babe. Only I'll be in trouble too. We all will,' Stuart warned.

'Joey was there, wasn't he? He saw Jed and his old man die.' Frankie's twin brother hadn't been the same person since that night. Though he'd refused to confide in her, she'd known something must have happened to him. 'No wonder he gave up his bloody job. He's haunted by what he saw, I bet,' she cried.

Eddie and Stuart shared an awkward glance. Joey had been the one who pulled the trigger and killed Jed and Jimmy, but Eddie would take that piece of information to his grave with him. So would the other men who'd been there that night: Stuart, Raymond, Terry and Eddie's eldest son, Gary. His second eldest, Ricky, was already dead when Joey turned up, and the rest of them were tied up and about to die. Joey had saved them all, and saved the day.

'Joey never saw sod-all. None of us did, OK?' Eddie growled.

Frankie was about to interrogate her father some more, when Georgie's screams stopped her. 'What's happened?' she asked, leaping up off the sofa.

'Longtails! Loads of 'em. Hate 'em, I do. Nanny Alice says they're evil and a curse like magpies. She's frit to death of them,' Georgie gabbled.

Eddie was bemused. 'What's she on about?' he asked Stuart.

'Longtails are a gypsy word for rats. The kids have a phobia of them,' said Stuart, 'I saw one yesterday. Think there's a family of 'em living under the decking.'

Harry put his hands on his hips. ''Orrible, they are. Granddad Jimmy once put a dead longtail in Old Man Macca's bed when he knocked him for a horsebox. Nanny Alice said the curse of the longtail would rub off on Old Man Macca and it did. A week later the old shitcunt crashed the horsebox and died.'

Eddie felt his complexion change colour. Given that Vinny Butler had more skeletons in his closet than a full-to-the-brim graveyard, he'd been sure the dead-rat delivery had been aimed at his partner. Now that seemed unlikely. Too much of a coincidence. Perhaps the remaining O'Haras had tracked him down and sent the rats to the casino?

'You all right, Ed?' Stuart asked. At thirty-four, Stuart

often got mistaken for Eddie's younger brother. Both were tall, dark and broad-shouldered. Eddie had taken Stuart under his wing in prison. A strong friendship had developed which had since resulted in Stuart becoming a part of Eddie's firm.

Rubbing the stubble on his chin, Eddie nodded. 'Yeah. I was just thinking about what Frankie said earlier. That home-tutoring lark might be a good idea after all. For now, at least.'

'Why the sudden change of heart?' Frankie snapped, her tone as cold as ice.

Not wanting to worry his daughter, Eddie casually replied, 'I just want what's best for the children. That's what we all want, isn't it?'

CHAPTER TWO

Gina Mitchell was awoken by her husband's naked arm and leg entwining with her own. She rolled over. 'Not again. I'm sure you have a sex addiction,' she smiled.

Eddie Mitchell kissed Gina on her naturally luscious lips. 'Never. I'm just more hot-blooded than most men. Don't knock a good thing, darlin'. You don't know how lucky you are. Women are queuing up to be in your position,' he joked, tantalizingly circling Gina's vaginal lips with his middle finger.

Gina chuckled, then sighed as Eddie's finger finally made contact with her clitoris. He was a joker, her man, but as loyal as a guide dog. He'd never cheated on his previous wife Jessica, and Gina knew he would never betray her either. Eddie Mitchell was a one-woman man, that was his finest attribute, as well as being permanently horny, charming, funny and incredibly handsome.

Eddie entered Gina then allowed her to take charge by riding him. His wife was forty-two, seventeen years his junior, but nobody ever guessed there was such an age gap. Gina was of Irish origin, had a mass of dark wavy hair, the longest legs Ed had ever seen in the flesh, and was incredibly beautiful. He, however, did not look a day over forty-five. Many people told him so. He'd started training while serving time in prison and had kept the gym sessions up on the outside. His body was lean, and the only sign of Eddie's true age were the grey hairs that now mingled with his dark-brown.

Gina quickened her movement and ran her hand down Eddie's battle wound. The scar ran from the outside of her husband's left eye to the corner of his mouth and Gina had always found it quite a turn-on. It was a reminder of what he'd once been. Before they'd got together, Ed had run a pub protection racket and been a loan shark, and this particular scar had been given to him back in the seventies by Jimmy O'Hara. There were few secrets between them. A lot of Ed's past had come to light in court, and the rest he'd told her in person.

'I love you,' Ed whispered, his orgasm nearing.

'I love you too,' Gina responded, running her fingers through her man's hair to smooth it down.

Eddie still had a full head of hair and wore it in a short-back-and-sides style. It was a standing joke between him and Gina that once it got to a certain length it would start to curl, and it was in desperate need of a cut at present.

'I'm nearly there. You?' Eddie mumbled, his face reddening with desire.

Before she could reply, a voice said, 'Mum, why are you sitting on Daddy's tummy? Get off, you're hurting him.'

'Rosie! You mustn't creep about like that.' Gina rolled off Eddie and was horrified to see Aaron standing next to his sister in the doorway. She pulled the cover over her body to hide her nakedness. Rosie was only two, but Aaron was six now and had already started to ask questions about the birds and the bees. 'Why do boys have a winkle and girls don't, Mum?'

Eddie sighed. 'Talk about pick your moment.' His own winkle had just shrunk.

'Why don't you knock first? I've always told you to, haven't I?' Gina scolded.

Rosie's eyes filled up. 'Because I thought you were hurting my daddy.'

Aaron put an arm around his little sister's shoulders. 'It's OK, Rosie. They were making us a brother and sister.'

Eddie chuckled. 'No chance of that, I'm afraid. You two are enough to put a sperm donor off having any more kids.'

When her children leapt on the bed, Gina couldn't help but laugh. She turned to Eddie. 'The wonders of bloody parenthood, eh?'

Vinny Butler breathed heavily as he threw Felicity Carter-Price on to the bed, then forcefully tied her legs and arms to the posts. She was face downwards, just the way he liked his women.

'Get off me. Who are you?' Felicity shrieked, while trying to wriggle out of Vinny's grasp.

Lifting his hand, Vinny whacked it as hard as he could against Felicity's bare buttocks. 'You'll find out soon enough, slut.'

Felicity begged for mercy until, unable to move, she lay on the bed defeated. Seconds later, she screamed in agony as the huge vibrator was shoved up her backside without as much as a smear of KY Jelly.

Vinny grunted and groaned when he replaced the vibrator with his pulsating penis. He'd met Felicity earlier that year when she'd started working at his Holborn Gentleman's Club as an exotic dancer. He preferred to think of her as that rather than a stripper or plain old lap-dancer. *Exotic* had a certain ring to it, and she was certainly exotic in the sack. Fliss, as he called her, was as keen on wild sexual role-play as he was. Vinny liked her to pretend she was a stranger and he was a rapist. Not once had Fliss complained. Anything he suggested they try, she was up for.

Vinny's orgasm was powerful and, once over, he untied Felicity and lay on his back, sweating. That was another thing he liked about this particular relationship. She wasn't demanding. Vinny wasn't one to go down on women, he didn't even like kissing them, truth be known. Sex was all about what he got out of it. In Vinny's eyes, a woman was born to please a man. Although that didn't apply to his close female family members, of course. He always wanted the best for those. His mother had deserved far better than his drunken bum of a father. And one day he hoped Ava would meet a wealthy bloke who wasn't cut from his cloth. He wanted his daughter to be with a man who had a decent, law-abiding career and who would treat her like a princess.

Felicity snuggled up to Vinny. He was a selfish lover, but so good to her in other ways; she was willing to overlook his faults. She was also seeing more and more of him, which pleased her immensely. She knew she was Vinny's first proper girlfriend in years, and that he was a hard nut to crack because of his past. It was only recently he'd started opening up and Felicity could tell he was warming towards her. He'd even kissed her properly and passionately on a few occasions of late.

Feeling more relaxed around a woman than he could ever remember, Vinny planted a kiss on Felicity's forehead. He'd had his heart broken as a teenager by Yvonne Summers and he'd never really recovered from that. The few relationships he'd had since were based solely on sex or payback. The only reason he'd snared Joanna Preston was to get even with her father. Johnny Preston had shot his brother Roy, and it appealed to Vinny's warped mind to impregnate his daughter, especially as the bullet had been meant for him in the bloody first place. As for Little Vinny's mother, Karen, she'd been a stripper at his old club and he'd only been using her for the odd shag.

'What are you thinking?' Felicity asked.

'I was thinking it's about time we went public. Not to my family, yet, but we will soon. First, though, I'd like you to meet my new business partner and his wife. You'll like Eddie Mitchell, he's good craic. And Gina's OK too. I'm sure you'll have lots of girlie stuff in common. Shall I give 'em a bell, see if they're free tonight? I'll book a restaurant, take us somewhere nice.'

Felicity pecked Vinny on the lips. 'I'd like that very much.'

Gina Mitchell was none too enthralled by the evening ahead. She'd met Vinny Butler on a couple of occasions in the past, but had yet to form any kind of connection with the man. Unlike her Eddie, who was a loveable rogue who liked a laugh, she could sense Vinny had more of a sinister serious side to him and little respect for women in general.

'Cheer up, for Christ's sake. We rarely go out on our own these days, so let's make the most of it, eh? Vinny's footing the bill an' all, so make sure you order the most expensive champagne and food on the menu,' Eddie Mitchell joked.

'What's Vinny's girlfriend like? You told me in the past that he was destined to remain a bachelor for the rest of his life,' Gina reminded her husband.

'Well, he was. But a bit like me and you, I suppose, darlin', love sometimes smacks you in the chops when you're not exactly searching for it. I don't know that much about Felicity, but Vinny's definitely taken with her. She's a lot younger than him – mid-to-late twenties, I think. Oh, and she used to work for him as a dancer at his Holborn club.'

When Gina turned to look out the car window, Eddie

squeezed her hand. 'Don't be worrying about the kids, they'll be fine. You know how they adore Joey and vice versa.'

She wanted to bellow, *I am not worried about our children, Eddie. I'm more concerned about trying to hold a conversation with your strange friend and his young stripper*, but instead Gina bit her tongue. Her husband wasn't a fool and if he deemed Vinny Butler to be a good enough man to go into business with, Gina knew she must make an effort for his sake.

'Who is it?' Queenie Butler shouted, her voice full of suspicion. Even though her new home was in a much nicer area than Whitechapel, after what had befallen Viv, no way was she taking any chances.

'It's me, Nan.'

Queenie opened the door and smiled at the sight that greeted her. Her grandson was holding a large bouquet, his wife a beautiful potted plant and her eldest great-grandson had a balloon with *WELCOME TO YOUR NEW HOME* scrawled across it. 'This is unexpected. To what do I owe this pleasure?'

Little Vinny was Vinny's eldest child and Queenie's first grandchild. He put his free arm around his nan and kissed her on the cheek. 'We're neighbours now, aren't we? Dad said he wasn't about tonight and Sammi-Lou thought we'd surprise you. I'll treat us to a takeaway.'

'I'm not fond of that Indian or Chinese rubbish, as you well know. A nice bit of fish and chips'll do me,' Queenie said, hugging Sammi-Lou. Her grandson's wife was, in Queenie's eyes, a godsend. Though she was no ravishing beauty – she'd put on quite a bit of weight since having the children – she had a pretty enough face, but it was her personality that had won Queenie over. The girl had a heart of gold and Queenie only wished her own sons would take a leaf out of Little Vinny's book and date an average-looking girl instead of the bloody glamour model types they seemed to go for. There'd been a time when Queenie had worried and despaired over Little Vinny's future, but meeting Sammi-Lou and becoming a father had been the making of him.

'It's a nice bungalow, Nan. I like your kitchen. When you going to invite me round for a Sunday roast? Mum's isn't as good as yours,' Oliver Butler said, winking at his mother.

Queenie gave her favourite great-grandson a hug. He was sixteen now, a proper little man. Unlike his father, who was a typical Butler male, tall and dark-haired, Oliver had the trademark Butler bright green eyes but was blond. 'Where's your brother?' Queenie asked. Oliver had two brothers: Regan, the youngest, was currently serving a sentence for stabbing his school teacher; it was the middle child Queenie was referring to.

'Calum's gone round a pal's to play *Pokémon*,' Oliver replied.

Little Vinny raised his eyebrows. 'How times have changed since I was a lad, eh, Nan? Kids don't want to breathe fresh air or do much bar play computer games these days.' The truth was, Calum had been in a foul mood and refused to visit Queenie, but Little Vinny didn't want to hurt his grandmother's feelings by telling her that.

'Oh well, at least if Calum's indoors playing games he can't put you through what you did me. Little bastard, you were, out street-raking with that Ben Bloggs. Surprised I never went grey.'

Seeing her grandson's relaxed expression change, Queenie grabbed him by the arm. 'Your father and uncles were bastards an' all. Now, come and look at the garden. I've decided to do a memorial fence in honour of Vivvy.'

Little Vinny followed his nan outside. She pointed to the right-hand fence and told him of her plans to put a plaque up, plus a framed photo of Viv. 'I'll plant a rose bush in her honour too. She loved a garden, did Vivvy, boy, and I can't see myself going to that cemetery much. Be too upsetting, especially as it's all still so raw. If and when those bastards finally decide to release her body, I'll go to the funeral then remember her here for the time being. You and your dad can drive over there once a week to make sure the grave's tidy, can't you? Leave some fresh flowers an' all. Vivvy's going in the same grave as Lenny. Be nice, pair of 'em resting in peace together. It's what she wanted.'

Little Vinny couldn't speak. Lenny's grave was very close to Molly's and he hadn't been able to visit that cemetery for years. How could he, after the atrocious crime he had committed? The guilt wouldn't allow him to. It wasn't right. But neither had he been, back in the day. Not right at all. In fact, he'd been evil.

Having dreaded the evening ahead, Gina Mitchell was pleasantly surprised. Vinny had been thoroughly charming and his pretty young girlfriend was adorable, rather posh and extremely good company.

Vinny clicked his fingers. 'Another bottle of champers over 'ere, guv,' he shouted, well aware that he and Eddie were the focus of the rest of the diners. With their swagger and sharp suits, they looked what they were: top-class villains. Both had evaded the law and had their fingers in many pies over the years while hiding behind legit businesses.

'You still got the salvage yard, Ed? Not heard you mention it for yonks,' Vinny asked.

'Sold it a while back. I thought I told you. No need to hang on to it any longer. Everything's above board for the first time in my life,' Eddie chuckled. Unlike Vinny, who'd always owned a club or two, Ed's enterprises, aside from the salvage business, had all been dodgy. Earnings from pub protection and loan-sharking weren't exactly something you declared to the taxman. He'd made plenty of dosh over the decades, but these days Gina and the kids came first and he didn't want to take unnecessary risks so he'd knocked everything bent on the head. He was looking forward to getting his teeth into the new venture, and had put the nasty surprise received yesterday to the back of his mind. He'd yet to tell Vinny that he thought the gypsies were behind it, but he planned to when the time was right.

'Found a new number plate earlier: VB1. Gonna treat meself to it, put it on the new Range Rover. Arm and a leg job the price, mind,' Vinny bragged.

Eddie burst out laughing. 'You bell-end. I remember you telling me private number plates were a waste of wonga and a curse, 'cause every bastard clocks where you are. You'll stand out like a sore thumb with that one, pal.'

Vinny shrugged. 'As you said, we're all above board now, so why not? I certainly haven't got any enemies, so if you have, best you speak up now.'

Eddie gave Vinny a warning look. He had told him earlier that under no circumstances was he to mention the dead rats to Gina as he didn't want to worry her. 'Oh well, each to their own, mate.'

Aware that Vinny wasn't very amused, Gina chuckled falsely and punched Eddie on the arm. 'Don't be taking no notice of him, Vinny. He made me go for a test drive in a Rolls-Royce with him the other day. A bright red convertible, I kid you not.'

Vinny put his arm around Felicity's shoulders and leaned back in his chair, rolling up. 'You prick! Don't tell me you bought it, Ed?'

'Nah. Gina reckoned it wasn't suitable for everyday use

with the kids. She has got a point, I suppose. I was bloody tempted though. You should've seen the interior. It's the bollocks of a motor and a dream to drive.'

When the men started chatting and bantering about motors, Gina moved next to Felicity. She was very beautiful, classy and reminded Gina of a younger version of Bella, Michael Butler's other half. Gina knew that Vinny had once had a fling with Bella when she and Michael weren't together. They'd even produced a child, and Gina could not help wonder if that was what had attracted Vinny to Felicity in the first place. She could remember Eddie telling her a while back that Vinny had once had a fixation with Bella.

'Is it always like this, people looking over? I know when I worked at the club, Vinny was seen as some kind of god, but I didn't expect him to be so well known in a restaurant in Ongar,' said Felicity.

Gina smiled. Smith's restaurant was a favourite haunt of hers and Eddie's, and it was her husband who'd suggested coming here when Vinny rang up earlier. 'You'll get used to it. I think Eddie and Vinny are reasonably well known wherever they go. It can be a pain in the butt at times, especially if the children are with us. I remember going to a restaurant in Brentwood a few years ago and Eddie got pestered left, right and centre. Aaron was only young then and the attention scared him.'

'Vinny doesn't take me out much, to be honest. You're the first friends of his I've dined with. That lady with the short blonde bob we spoke about earlier is looking over again at your Eddie. Does that not bother you, Gina?'

Gina laughed. 'Not at all. For a start, Eddie is well aware I'd chop his testicles off if he even thought about messing me around. And secondly, there are some sad, lonely women in this world. The amount of times I've seen women try to chat Eddie up or pass him their phone number is far too many to count.'

'Really! I don't think I would like that at all. It's very disrespectful to do such a thing in front of you.'

Having been half-earwigging, Vinny turned to Felicity. 'What's disrespectful?'

'Nothing important. We're just having a girlie chat.'

'Come on, I wanna hear it. Otherwise that's disrespectful, isn't it? To be sitting on the same table as your bloke, who's treated you to a top night out, and whispering behind his back.'

Gina glanced at Eddie while Felicity spilled the beans. She knew her husband wouldn't be bothered about anything they'd spoken about, so why was Vinny?

Eddie moved seats and kissed Gina on the cheek. 'Can't help being a handsome bastard who regularly attracts menopausal old birds, can I?' he joked.

Aware of the angry glint in Vinny's eyes as he grilled Felicity over something she'd said, Gina leaned towards her husband's ear. 'I know he's your business partner, but I feel sorry for that poor woman. Vinny's not like you. He's possessive and arrogant.'

'More like nosy and pissed. Vin's OK, Gina. He's got a good side, very loyal – he's offered to watch my back many a time if I needed him to. You'll get used to him in time. He's just not used to being with a woman. Jo died years ago and this dating lark is all new to him,' Ed whispered back.

Gina wasn't a big drinker as a rule. She was devoted to being a mother these days, an odd glass of wine occasionally once the children were in bed was all she consumed. Forgetting to whisper, she blurted out, 'I don't care what you say, Felicity won't be happy with him.'

Vinny smashed his glass against the table. 'Sorry, Gina.

I didn't quite catch that, love. If you've got something to say to me, I'd prefer you to say it to my face.'

Eddie Mitchell leapt out of his chair, grabbed Vinny by the arm and marched him out to the toilets.

'Don't be getting bolshie with me, Ed,' Vinny spat, his eyes blazing. 'It's your old woman you want to be having a word with. I heard every fucking thing she spouted,' he added, releasing his arm from Eddie's grasp like a petulant child.

Once inside the men's a furious Eddie Mitchell grabbed hold of Vinny's lapels and pushed him against the wall. 'You need to man up, you do, and start acting like a gentleman. We've all had a skinful tonight, but that doesn't excuse your lack of respect. Gina isn't a "love", as you so nicely put it; neither is she an "old woman". Gina is a Mitchell. My wife and the mother of my kids – and don't you ever forget that, Vinny. Because if you do, me and you are gonna fall out big time. Under-fucking-stand?'

CHAPTER THREE

'I think it might be three, six, four, Harry. Keep those numbers firmly in your head and as soon as we get a chance, we'll try them,' Georgie O'Hara said.

Desperate to return to the family that had raised her, Georgie O'Hara had been racking her brain for weeks trying to remember her boyfriend Ryan's phone number. She knew it started in 07973 and ended in 187, but the middle numbers she could not seem to fathom.

'I reckon Dad and Granddad Jimmy are dead ya know, Georgie. They would have come and rescued us by now if they were still alive. Eddie telling us they went back to Scotland is a load of bollocks. No way would Dad go back to Scotland without us.'

Eyes welling up, Georgie squeezed her brother's hand. She feared the same but prayed she was wrong. She knew her father and Granddad Jimmy had followed her and Harry on the day they'd been abducted because she and her brother had heard the mumblings of Eddie and the others. 'I've got a plan. Why don't we say sorry to Mum for being bad yesterday, then beg her to take us to Joycie's birthday party. We can't use the phone here 'cause the numbers will show up on the bill and we'll get into trouble like we did before.

But we can use Joycie's. She must have a phone upstairs. Most gorgers have phones in their bedrooms.' Joyce Smith was their great-grandmother, their dead Nanny Jessica's mum, but neither Georgie nor Harry really remembered her from the past. Neither did they like her very much, which was why they called her 'Joycie' rather than 'Nan'.

Harry shrugged. 'I ain't saying sorry to Frankie though. I wish she'd die.'

Backcombing her dyed-blonde hair into a bouffant, Joyce Smith repeatedly yelled her husband's name.

Stanley Smith puffed out his cheeks as he ambled up the stairs. Today would be the first time he'd been forced to socialize with the man who had murdered his daughter since she'd died, and Stanley was dreading being in close proximity to Eddie no-good Mitchell.

Jessica's death had been a tragic case of mistaken identity, but that didn't lessen Stanley's hatred towards the man who'd snuffed out her life. Eddie had thought it was Frankie's gypsy boyfriend hiding under the bed in a trailer in Tilbury when he'd manically fired that machine gun. Jessica had been pregnant at the time with her and Eddie's third child, so Mitchell had two lots of blood on his hands. In Stanley's eyes, a judge and jury should have locked Eddie up for life, but they didn't. He got found guilty of only the firearms offence and was let out of prison far too soon.

'You're not wearing that, Stanley. You look like a bundle of shit tied up ugly. Go and put your blue suit on, and wear that new tie I bought you.'

'I'm not wearing a suit and bloody tie indoors. I'll look like a poxy doctor's clerk,' Stanley complained.

'I bet you wore a suit for the old slapper. Now go and get changed. Chop, chop.' Joyce had been equally appalled and devastated when Stanley had once left her and moved in with that brazen old bag, Pat the Pigeon. To this day, Stanley insisted they'd been just good friends and their relationship was platonic, but Joyce wasn't a forgiving woman. Most days she would remind her husband of his infidelity, especially when she wanted her own way, or jobs around the house doing.

Mumbling obscenities, Stanley took his suit out of the wardrobe.

'Answer that phone. I'm doing my make-up,' Joyce shouted out.

Stanley did as he was told, then relayed the message to his wife. 'That was Eddie. He said Frankie's bringing Georgie and Harry with her, but you're not to worry as he's invited some other kids to keep them occupied.'

Dropping her make-up brush, Joyce looked at her husband in despair. 'But they can't come. I've invited Rita and Hilda now, and Jock and your pigeon club mates. We can't have the monsters running riot amongst friends, Stanley. Whatever will they think?' Joyce wasn't a big fan of her gypsy great-grandchildren. They were terribly behaved and reminded her of all the bad things that had happened over the years. If Frankie hadn't got in with that Jed O'Hara, her Jessica would still be alive today.

Stanley shrugged. 'Eddie better not be bringing his kids by that other woman. He's not, is he?' Eddie Mitchell was remarried now to a woman called Gina and Stanley had no wish to meet her or her children.

'No. Eddie's coming with Vinny Butler and his mum, Queenie.'

'Vinny Butler! Jesus wept, Joycie! I know you love mixing with the criminal fraternity, but you're asking for bleedin' trouble inviting those Butlers to our home. They're rotten to the core, you silly woman.'

*

'That was my dad. Vinny Butler's son is coming and bringing his kids, so Georgie and Harry will have some company. I do hope they don't start performing, Stuart. I can tell my nan don't like them very much.'

Stuart held his pretty fiancée in his arms and stroked her long dark hair. Frankie had changed since Georgie and Harry's return. She'd lost a lot of weight and her once happy persona had all but disappeared. 'Today will be fine. Kids will be kids – there's no point worrying about it, babe.'

Frankie clung to Stuart, taking in the smell of his familiar aftershave. What she would have done without him these past six months she did not know. He was her rock and she could never have coped alone.

In Queenie Butler's opinion, she looked bloody good for her seventy-four years. Her shoulder-length straight hair was regularly dyed blonde and she wouldn't be seen dead without her make-up on. She was still the same ten dress size as when she'd got married and, considering she was short, Queenie classed that as an achievement. Both herself and Vivian had loathed the thought of ever letting themselves go.

'You look beautiful, Mum,' Vinny told her. His mother hadn't wanted to attend Eddie's ex-mother-in-law's birthday bash, but Vinny had managed to talk her round by pretending she was doing both he and Eddie a big favour. He was desperate for his mum to make friends in Essex and was hoping that she and Joycie would hit it off. Like most people, including Eddie, Vinny always referred to Joyce as Joycie.

Queenie picked up her handbag. She and Vivian had always had a passion for dressing up in nice clothes and it felt weird getting glammed up without her sister's presence.

'I'm as ready as I'm ever going to be, but I'm not staying long, Vinny. It doesn't feel right, not with Vivvy still lying on a slab. In fact, I think I might get changed, wear black instead.'

'No, don't. That green really suits you and Auntie Viv wouldn't want you walking around for weeks on end wearing black. She liked bright colours, and she'd want you to try and enjoy yourself today, wouldn't she?'

'Fat chance of that happening. Come on; let's go before I change my mind.'

'Hurry up, Sammi. The boys are ravenous and so am I,' Little Vinny urged.

'I can't do my jeans up and I look like an elephant. You go with the boys and I'll stay here.'

Little Vinny opened the bedroom door. His wife had put on a stone and a half since they'd first met, but he had no issues about her weight at all and wished he could convince her how stunning she was. 'You've got to come, Sammi. I want us all to go as a family.'

'But we don't even know the woman whose birthday it is, Vin. No way am I turning up at someone's party without a present. We'll have to stop at a florist's on the way.'

'OK. We'll get a bouquet and a card if it makes you happy. And you will look beautiful in whatever you wear, so just put a spurt on,' Little Vinny ordered, playfully squeezing Sammi-Lou's backside. Meeting Sammi had been the best thing that had ever happened to him. They had three sons whom they doted on and couldn't wait for their youngest Regan to be allowed home. He was currently serving a bit of juvenile bird for stabbing his school teacher with a screwdriver, but had behaved himself since and all being well would be released in the next few months.

When her husband locked the bedroom door, Sammi-Lou

scolded him as he began kissing around her neck. He knew she found that a turn-on. 'I thought you was in a rush. We can't, not now. The boys will hear us.'

Little Vinny grinned as he put his wife's hand on his erect penis. 'Nah, they won't. We'll be extra quiet.'

The four-bedroomed house that Joyce and Stanley now lived in had once been Jessica and Eddie's marital home. Eddie had signed it over to Joyce whilst in prison, insisting it was what Jessica would have wanted. Stanley saw it as a guilty gesture and blood money, but instead of telling Eddie where to stick his unusual offer, Joyce, being the boastful show-off that she was, could not wait to collect their belongings from their old house in Upney and up sticks for good.

Panicking at the thought of her great-grandchildren embarrassing her, Joyce was running around like a blue-arsed fly to keep herself busy. 'Tidy up that corner again by your armchair. The guests will be arriving soon,' she shrieked.

'Stop getting in such a two and eight, woman. And they're not guests. They're friends and family – well, apart from the notorious underworld figures you've invited. They're guests, unwanted ones.'

Brett Mitchell stared miserably out of the window of Stuart's motor. He had been really looking forward to seeing his granddad and great-grandparents, until Harry had threatened to drown him in the swimming pool earlier. Now he didn't want to go to the party. Water scared him and he couldn't swim very well. 'I feel ill, Mum. Can I go to Granddad's house instead? I have a bellyache and want to lie down,' Brett lied.

'Bellyache! What's that when it's at home?' Harry

taunted, grabbing his little brother in a none-too-gentle headlock.

'Stop that, Harry. Leave your brother alone, love,' Frankie ordered. 'Brett, you must come to the party. Nanny Joycie will be upset if you're not there, and you don't want to spoil her birthday, do you? You can lie down on her bed until your tummy ache has gone.'

Stuart watched surreptitiously through the interior mirror. He was sure that little bastard Harry had been picking on Brett, but he'd yet to catch him in the act. He'd even asked Brett in a roundabout way, but Brett had denied there was any issue.

'Tummy ache,' Harry said in a silly voice. A warning nudge and look from his big sister stopped him from saying anything else.

Stuart kept half an eye on the mirror and finally saw Harry pinch his prey. Brett winced, and Stuart angrily slammed his foot on the brake.

'What's the matter?' Frankie asked.

'I'm taking Brett round your dad's. He looks a bit peaky to me. Gina will look after him.'

Feeling a sense of relief wash over him, Brett's heartbeat returned to normal.

When Jessica was killed, Joyce swore she wanted nothing more to do with Eddie Mitchell, but time was a healer and she knew how much Ed had loved her daughter. Apart from a few minor ups and downs, they really had been the perfect couple until that fateful evening in Tilbury.

'Eddie, thank you so much. They're beautiful,' Joyce gushed, waving the bouquet in the air so her old neighbours Rita and Hilda could see her lovely flowers. She knew they were jealous of her closeness to Eddie. He was a somebody and their children had married nobodies.

'Joycie, this is Queenie, Vinny's mum. Queenie, this is the wonderful woman who I will always class as my mother-in-law. We're very close,' Eddie grinned, winking at Joycie. Not many mothers would have forgiven him for the major mistake he had made and Ed would always be grateful to Joyce for reuniting the family in more ways than one. Little did she know it, but Joycie's interference had actually saved his life. It was all her doing he and Joey were back on speaking terms in the first place.

The two women looked one another up and down, and neither particularly liked what they saw. Joycie thought Queenie was extremely hard-faced and nobody of her age should be wearing a skirt slightly above the knee. As for Queenie, she thought Joyce was an ugly old cow. Her teeth were far too big for her mouth, her nose slightly hooked and that bouffant hairstyle had gone out with the ark.

Queenie smiled falsely. 'Nice to meet you, Joycie.'

'Likewise, Queenie. Would you like me to give you a tour of the house and grounds?' Joyce asked, in her poshest voice.

'No, thank you. I have just lost my sister, so not an awful lot impresses me at the moment.'

Eddie and Vinny shared an awkward glance. This certainly wasn't going to plan.

Georgie and Harry O'Hara were bored, miserable and felt like fishes out of water. They'd sneaked upstairs earlier and tried the number Georgie had thought was Ryan's, but some silly old lady had answered.

'All right? Shit party, ain't it?' Calum Butler voiced, plonking himself on the grass next to Georgie and Harry.

Harry eyed the boy suspiciously. 'Who are you?'

'Big Vinny is my granddad and Little Vinny's my old man. Are you Eddie Mitchell's grandkids? I heard you were gypsies.'

Georgie O'Hara glared at the boy. 'So what if we are?'

Fourteen-year-old Calum smiled. He'd fancied Georgie the moment he'd laid eyes on her. She had dark hair and green eyes like he had, and she had big knockers and a very pretty face. 'Wait 'ere and I'll steal some booze. I won't be a tick.'

Loving nothing more than bragging and showing off her wealth to her old neighbours, Joyce dragged Hilda and Rita upstairs to view her newly acquired bedroom furniture. 'Look at the quality of the pine,' Joyce urged, stroking the chest of drawers as one would a tiny puppy.

Hilda and Rita pretended to be interested, then nudged one another, raising their eyebrows as soon as Joyce turned her back. Joyce had always thought she was the bee's knees when she'd lived a spit's throw away from them in Upney, and since moving up in the world had become ten times worse.

About to start gushing about her new en suite, Joyce was stopped in her tracks by an out-of-breath Stanley. 'Get your backside downstairs now, Joycie. One of your Butler guests has just knocked Jock in the swimming pool – on purpose. Never will I invite my friends round here again. This is all your fault, you senile old bat.'

The sight of Stanley's best mate spluttering and mumbling obscenities while fully clothed in her swimming pool appealed to Joyce's warped sense of humour. She tried to keep a straight face, but when she locked eyes with Queenie, who was laughing like a hyena, Joyce did the same.

Arriving amidst the drama, Joey Mitchell was none too surprised to learn that his nephew was at the centre of it. He had done his utmost to bond with Harry, but the child was bloody hard work and so was Georgie.

'Where's Dom?' Eddie asked his son.

'He's not coming. We had words earlier, you know how it is. He's on my case constantly to go back to work and I just don't feel ready. To be honest, I don't know if I want to go back to my old job at all. It's too stressful and I don't think I could cope with it now.'

Eddie felt guilty. Joey had been earning bloody good money at the Stock Exchange before that fateful night with the O'Haras. An unlikely hero, Joey had never returned to work since.

'Where's Frankie?' Joey asked. He and his twin were extremely close, but looked nothing alike. Frankie had his dad's dark skin, hair and features, whereas Joey was fair-skinned and blond like his mum had been.

'I think she's gone round the side of the gaff to give the devil's spawn a talking to.' As Joey made to set off in search of his sister, Eddie laid a hand on his arm. 'There's something you need to know: I had to tell her Jed and Jimmy were brown bread.'

'You what! You said you wasn't going to tell her. You didn't let her know—'

Eddie interrupted his son. 'Of course not. What happened that night stays between those present. Nobody else will ever find out, so don't panic. As far as Frankie knows, none of us were there when the deed was done, me included. But I had to tell her something, son. She was out of her mind with worry that Jed would come back and snatch the kids. Stuart said she hasn't been sleeping properly for weeks. Well, it's done and dusted now, but she was interrogating me about you. Reckons you must have witnessed something because you've changed since that day. If she starts questioning you, tell her she's talking bollocks. Make something up about you and Dom if you have to, eh?' Eddie had been mortified when he'd first learned his son was gay and in a relationship with Dominic.

Time was a healer though and even though he still wished Joey was straight, he'd managed to finally accept the situation.

'I'll tell Frankie me and Dom are on the rocks and that's the reason I've not been myself lately. It's partly true anyway. He knows something went on that evening and I can never tell him the truth, can I? He would disown me.'

'You saved your family's bacon, boy. That's something to be proud of, not ashamed. But no, the less people that know what really happened, the better. Listen, how d'ya fancy being mine and Vinny's assistant manager at the casino when it opens? Keeping your mind occupied might do you good, and if you don't like it you can always go back to the Stock Exchange at a later date.'

Joey toyed with the idea. The thought of working in the City again filled him with dread, and he couldn't be unemployed as he and Dom had a mortgage to pay. He was on the sick, his father had sent him to a bent doctor who had lied and informed his employers he'd had a nervous breakdown.

'I'll pay you good dosh,' Eddie promised.

Joey held out his right hand. 'You got yourself a deal, Dad.'

Having never met before, Sammi-Lou Butler and Frankie Mitchell were getting along famously. Frankie had few friends these days, and it was good to speak to another mother whose children were problematical.

'It's awful having to keep Georgie and Harry under lock and key. But I'm at my wits' end and have no other option. Would you do the same, if you were in my position?'

Sammi squeezed Frankie's arm. 'Probably. I can't begin to imagine the heartache you went through when their dad took them away. All those wasted years when you could have been watching them grow up. But you've got them back now and that's all that matters. Things will improve, but it's bound to take time.'

Frankie looked towards her children and smiled at her new-found friend. 'They seem to be getting on well with your Calum, so that's a start. They've had no interaction with other kids since they came home. It's a relief to know they can mix, to be honest.'

'I have an idea. Why don't you bring the children over to ours for the day so they can hang out with Ollie and Calum? We have a big garden and while the weather's still nice, we can have a barbecue.'

'That would be lovely. Our men seem to be getting on like a house on fire too, so I'm sure Stuart will be up for it. But please be forewarned, Georgie and Harry can be awfully behaved at times. They swear like sailors and I'd hate you to think badly of me and Stuart. It's the way they were dragged up in the travelling community.'

'Mine weren't dragged up and they're no better. Oliver is an angel compared to Calum and Regan. Little bastards they are. I seriously don't know where me and Vin went wrong. We're decent parents, I know we are. Worst moment of my life was when they sent Regan away. I miss him so bloody much, even though he drives me insane.'

Frankie offered words of comfort to Sammi before asking, 'When would you like us to come over then?'

'How about tomorrow? Shame to waste this nice weather, and we have nothing planned.'

'Brilliant. OK, tomorrow it is.'

Having been raised by travellers, Georgie O'Hara was far more savvy than most children her age. 'Go and nick some more booze and we'll meet you round the side of the house. Hide it behind those plant pots again,' Georgie ordered Calum, before dragging her brother away.

'You fancy him, don't ya? I saw the way you were looking at him,' Harry said accusingly.

Had she not promised to marry Ryan one day, Georgie might have fancied Calum. He was a bit wild, a bad boy, which was her type, but she had other plans for him. 'Of course I don't fancy Calum, you dinlo. I'm just playing him to get us out of the house. He could be our perfect opportunity to escape.'

'How? Frankie don't let us out of her sight, the slag.'

'She will if she thinks we can be trusted, Harry.'

Vinny Butler handed Eddie a cigar. Neither smoked cigarettes any more, but liked the odd cigar on special occasions.

'I wonder if we've got any more nasty surprises in the post today? Got a feeling I know who sent the last one,' Eddie announced, before telling Vinny the story about the rats, Jimmy O'Hara and what Harry had told him.

'But Jimmy ain't about no more, is he?' Vinny enquired. Eddie had ended up with a broken arm, leg, and ribs after his confrontation with the O'Haras. Ed had told Vinny the feud had been sorted at the time, and Vinny hadn't wanted to pry too much.

'Jimmy's out the picture and so is Jed, but they have other relations. Breed like flies, those bastards, don't they?'

'Yeah, but we can handle ourselves, mate. We'll have plenty of back-up at the casino an' all. I've hired new doormen at my club, so Pete and Paul can run the door, and you're bringing muscle in an' all. The pikeys are no threat to us.'

'You're right. We'll have enough brawn to deal with any chancer. Ray, Tel, Gary and Stuart are no mugs either,' Eddie replied, referring to his own firm. 'Is Carl gonna still be working at the Holborn club?'

Vinny nodded. 'Carl and Ava will run Holborn for me.

Not long now, me old mucker, and we'll be greeting our first punters. The Butlers and Mitchells unite, eh?'

Eddie dotted out his cigar. 'That's if Joycie and your mother ain't murdered one another. Come on, let's go see the damage.'

After initially hating one another on sight, Joyce and Queenie bonded over Jock nearly drowning, and now decided they did rather like one another after all. Both were strong characters, with similar views on family and life in general.

'So, was your son Raymond here today?' Queenie asked Joyce.

'Nope. He's abroad. Married a posh tart, Raymond did, and you can bet your bottom dollar that it was she who booked the holiday so they wouldn't have to come to my party. As for their daughter, that's an absolute replica of its mother. Want, want, want, it is. Spoilt as arseholes.'

Queenie smiled. 'I've got a grandchild like that an' all. My Michael's youngest, Ellie. I can't take to her. Don't like her mother either. Trapped my Michael, did Katy. Gold-digging whore.'

With all the guests now gone, Vinny poked his head around the door. 'You OK, Mum? Let me know when you want to make a move.'

'I'm OK, love. You can top mine and Joycie's drinks up, though, if you want to make yourself useful.'

'Bring us in a bottle of Baileys. Do you like Baileys, Queenie?' Joyce asked.

'My favourite. Where's your husband? Has he gone to bed?' Queenie enquired.

'Stanley'll be out in the shed, playing with his cock,' Joyce chuckled.

'I beg your pardon.'

'The old goat keeps pigeons. Spends hours in that shed, he does. Suits me. I don't have to look at him. Left me once for another woman, he did. Right old trollop she was. I mean, who'd look at Stanley twice? Bald-headed, short old bastard.'

Queenie laughed out loud. Today was the first time she'd properly laughed since Vivian had died. Joycie sounded just like her and Viv. She was certainly a 'Say it as it is' type.

Vinny did the honours by pouring the Baileys, then walked into the kitchen shaking his head. 'Women, eh? Getting on like they've known one another all their lives. I'll never understand the female species.'

Eddie raised his eyebrows. 'Me neither. I'm thankful there won't be any bloodshed though.'

As Vinny and Eddie carried on chatting, neither had a clue that plenty of blood would soon be shed. In the most atrocious way imaginable.

CHAPTER FOUR

Michael and Vinny Butler met in a café near their mother's bungalow. The Old Bill had got in touch this morning and were now ready to release their darling aunt's body.

'Where you been staying?' Vinny asked his brother. Like himself, Michael was looked up to and respected. He was also classed as a big underworld figure, although it was common knowledge Vinny ruled the roost. The name Butler tended to put the fear of God into people with bloody good reason. Many a man had his life ended prematurely after falling foul of Vinny especially.

'I stayed at Bella's again last night, but your son has some serious issues and I can't be doing with 'em,' Michael snapped.

In 1980, Vinny had indulged in a one-night stand with a woman he had met in a nightclub up town. It only came to light many years later that the woman in question was Bella, who was now Michael's girlfriend. Vinny then learned he'd fathered her son. This had caused ructions between the brothers, and he and Michael had only been on speaking terms again since the brutal attack on their aunt. 'Antonio needs to man up and fend for himself. Leave it with me. He's nineteen, not fucking nine. It's about time he got a job and moved out.'

'He hates me being on the scene again. Just acts like a spoilt brat, banging and crashing about, spewing insults. Makes me wonder if I'm doing the right thing. If Katy finds out, there'll be murders,' Michael said miserably. He had a son and daughter with Katy and spent a couple of days a week with them in Tunbridge Wells. In Katy's eyes, they were still a couple, but Michael only visited to see his kids. Occasionally he'd still sleep with her out of duty, and to stop her moaning. Anything for a quiet life.

'Don't let Antonio rule your life. You and Bella are made for one another. Have you told Mum you're giving it another go with her?'

'Not yet. Mum's got enough to deal with at the moment. I'll tell her after the funeral. Better coming from me than she hears it through the grapevine. I also need to tell her Daniel and Lee are living abroad. I popped round to see Lee's old woman yesterday. In bloody bits, she is. Says she can't afford the mortgage. I bunged her a couple of grand, but I ain't offering to pay no mortgage. Not like her and Lee have kids, is it?'

'Beth ain't your problem, bruv. I'd stay well out of it, if I were you. Any more news on Roxanne's whereabouts?'

'Nope. Probably still up the spout with her own brother's child. Jesus wept! What a fucked-up family we are. That Jeremy Springer geezer would have a field day with us.'

Little Vinny put the meat in the fridge, then turned to his wife. 'Ollie wants to go round his mate's. He wasn't overly keen on Georgie and Harry, reckons he'll be bored.'

Sammi-Lou called her eldest son. Oliver had recently left school and was now at college. Calum and Regan were ringers for their father, but Oliver was like herself. He even had her slightly turned-up button nose. Handsome, polite and charming, Oliver had never caused her and Vinny any worry. He was a special lad with a good heart.

'What's up, Mum?'

'Instead of going round your friend's, can't you invite a few of your pals around here?'

'Georgie and Harry are kids, Mum. They'll have far more in common with Calum than me and my mates. Anyway, I'm meant to be meeting a girl later.'

'Oooh, tell me more. What's her name? Where did you meet her?' Sammi-Lou asked.

'Her name's Emma and she went to my school. I bumped into her recently and she looked . . . well different. She's working in an office now.'

As his wife began to ask more questions, Little Vinny crept up behind her and put his hand over her mouth. 'Let the boy get on his way. He's on a promise, eh, Ollie?'

Oliver blushed. 'Shut up, Dad.'

'Yes, shut up, Vinny. That's our baby you're talking about. He doesn't do things like that,' Sammi-Lou laughed.

Grabbing Oliver in a playful headlock, Little Vinny messed his son's perfectly styled hair up. 'Look worse than this when your bird's had her way with ya later,' he goaded.

Sammi-Lou smiled broadly. She had a big house, three healthy, handsome boys, a wonderful husband and, apart from Regan being locked up, life truly could not be better.

'One in a million, my sister, therefore I want the full works for her. Finest black horses in their full regalia and a stunning glass carriage,' Queenie told the funeral director.

'We also want three of my aunt's favourite songs played. "Pal of My Cradle Days', "Spanish Eyes" and "You Are My Sunshine",' Michael added.

Vinny felt his stomach churn at the mention of 'You Are My Sunshine'. That had been the favourite song of his young daughter Molly, who'd been abducted back in 1980, then strangled and buried in a shallow grave. Twenty-one years on, her death still felt so raw at times. Not a day went by when Vinny did not think about her. She'd been such a little superstar, and so very beautiful.

'I don't want "Spanish Eyes",' Queenie informed her sons. 'Doesn't seem right, seeing as your father was crooning it as Viv took her last breath. I don't want that old bastard at the funeral either.'

Michael looked at his mother in disbelief. In the last few years, Albie and Viv had grown very close, though they'd kept their relationship a closely guarded secret, knowing the trouble it would cause if Queenie ever found out. Vivian had regularly sneaked round to his father's house in Barking, and Michael knew how fond of her his old man was. Albie would be distraught at not being allowed to say a goodbye. 'Don't start being silly now, Mum. Dad is coming to the funeral, end of.'

'No he ain't,' Queenie spat viciously.

In Vinny's eyes, his father was a loser, a tosser and a pisshead, so he waded in to defend his mother. 'It's gonna be a tough enough day for Mum as it is, bruv. We must respect her wishes.'

The funeral director jumped out of his skin when Michael leapt up and punched the wall of his parlour. 'I'm telling you now, if you don't allow me dad at the funeral, then I won't be going either.' Adding the words, 'Fuck the pair of ya,' Michael stormed out of the building.

'I nicked us some booze and stashed it in my bedroom,' Calum Butler informed Georgie and Harry.

Georgie grinned. 'Let's go to your room then. What we waiting for?'

'Where do you think you're going?' Frankie shouted out.

'Calum's got a computer and he's gonna show us how to play games on it,' Georgie replied shirtily.

'I locked the front door from the inside, just in case,' Sammi-Lou informed Frankie.

'You got a phone up here I can use?' Georgie asked Calum. She'd never had intercourse, that was a sin for a travelling girl before marriage, but she was alert sexually for her age and knew Calum fancied the pants off her. That's why she had worn a low-cut top today. She enjoyed the attention her breasts drew from boys and planned to reel Calum in. In the travelling community, girls tended to dress and act flirtatious from a young age to potentially attract a future husband. Lots of girls Georgie knew had met their boyfriends at fourteen or fifteen, then married them as soon as they turned sixteen.

'Who you ringing?' Calum enquired.

'Her boyfriend,' Harry replied.

'Take no notice of him. I ain't got a boyfriend,' Georgie said, glaring at her big-mouthed brother.

Juggling the numbers around, Georgie tried but failed again to connect to Ryan. 'Gertcha you miserable old rabbit's crotch,' she screamed at a woman who had a go at her as she'd mistakenly rung her twice.

'Rabbit's crotch. That's well funny,' Calum chuckled.

'You ain't never gonna remember the number, so we need to resort to plan B,' Harry sulked.

Having warned Harry not to mention plan B in front of Calum, Georgie glared at him again. 'Who's that in the photo?' she asked. The lad standing with Calum reminded her of Ryan. He had the same shaped face and a similar smile.

'That's my brother, Regan. He's banged up at the moment. Stabbed his teacher, he did.'

Harry and George were both suitably impressed. 'Did he kill the teacher?' Harry asked.

'Nah,' Calum responded, before bragging about many of his and Regan's scrapes with the law.

Georgie giggled, while forming plan B in her head. She would use Calum to help them escape, then dump him like a bag of old rubbish. She and Harry didn't belong in the gorger world. Being part of a close-knit travelling community was all they knew.

With her sons' brotherly relationship only recently back on track, Queenie Butler decided to swallow her pride for once in favour of not upsetting the apple cart. She had been devastated all those years Vinny and Michael were estranged, and blamed Bella wholly for everything that had happened.

'Let's have a bit of lunch before we order the flowers, eh? Then I'll show you how the casino is coming along. It'll look amazing once it's finished,' Vinny said.

'We've got to think of another song an' all. I don't mind your father being there, but "Spanish Eyes" is his party piece and I am not having that played for Viv,' Queenie insisted.

Michael stared gloomily out of the window. If his mother ever found out his father regularly sung that song for Viv, or that she'd been visiting his dad in hospital on the night she was attacked, it would cause mayhem.

Having only had two true friends in his life, Little Vinny was thoroughly enjoying a bit of male bonding with Stuart. Apart from Sammi's parents, he and his wife never socialized with other couples and it was nice to have made new friends.

'Lovely bit of steak, Vin. And that potato salad is handsome,' Stuart said, grinning at Frankie. It was lovely to see her having a little tipple and looking so relaxed. Even the brats seemed to be behaving themselves for once.

Scoffing a chicken thigh, Georgie winked at her brother. 'Mum, me and Harry want to go for a walk with Calum. We won't go far, I swear.'

'Nope. You'll run off again,' Frankie replied.

'We won't. We promise. You can't keep us locked away for ever, it ain't fair. How can we be happy if we can't even go out?' Harry piped up.

Stuart put his hand on Frankie's knee. 'He has got a point, babe. It's not very fair on 'em.'

Frankie could feel her heart beating rapidly in her chest. 'But say they don't come back?'

'I'll look after Georgie and Harry,' Calum piped up.

Harry glared at Calum. He wasn't much older than him, the dickhead.

'Of course we're coming back. We ain't got no money, so where we meant to go?' Georgie stated.

Looking at Frankie for approval, Stuart turned to the children. 'We'll start trusting you on one condition.'

'What?' Harry asked.

'That you be nice to Brett in future. And don't lie and say you are nice to him, because I've seen you do stuff with my own eyes. Have we got a deal?'

Georgie and Harry reluctantly nodded.

'One hour you can go out for and if you're not back, I'm calling the police,' Frankie warned. Her stomach was in knots, but what could she do? She was sick of living in a virtual prison, and Georgie and Harry needed to start mixing with other kids at some stage. Apart from Harry pushing Jock in the swimming pool, they'd behaved themselves impeccably yesterday and today.

'Just going to the toilet,' Calum said.

'Are we coming back?' Harry whispered to Georgie.

'Of course, you dinlo. And we're gonna keep coming back until Mum really trusts us and allows us to go out for a whole day – that's when we'll escape for good. And Calum is gonna help us.'

'Is he?'

'Shush. He don't know it yet. But yes, he will. I'll make damn bloody sure of it.'

The hand-delivered package was lying on the doorstep of the casino.

'You expecting a parcel, love?' Queenie asked her son.

The handwriting on the label was the same as the previous package. Capital letters in thick marker pen. 'Go inside and have a gander. Eddie was expecting a delivery,' Vinny lied. He knew what a worry-pot his mother could be, and didn't want to scare the living daylights out of her.

Vinny gingerly lifted the lid off the box. The smell was horrific and so was the sight of the dead snake with its head chopped off. Vinny stared at the verse.

DEUTERONOMY 32:35
VENGEANCE IS MINE, AND RETRIBUTION.
IN DUE TIME THEIR FOOT WILL SLIP;
FOR THE DAY OF THEIR CALAMITY IS NEAR
AND THE IMPENDING THINGS ARE
HASTENING UPON THEM.

'Jesus wept,' Vinny mumbled, glancing around to check nobody was watching him. No way was this the work of gypsies. Most couldn't read, let alone spell. This was the work of some serious nutjob. But who? And why?

The hour it took Georgie and Harry to return seemed like ten to Frankie Mitchell. She'd cursed her decision to allow them out, and cried at the thought of them not returning.

'I told you they'd come back, didn't I?' Sammi-Lou beamed.

'Get off me. What ya doing?' Harry complained, as his mother tried to hug him. Didn't the stupid bitch realize he loathed her?

Knowing she and Harry were finally getting somewhere, Georgie smiled sweetly and shared the first proper hug with her mum since she'd arrived home.

'We're going back upstairs now to play on the computer,' Calum said.

Georgie lay on Calum's bed and stretched out so he could see her belly button. She knew she had a good body, which was another reason she liked to flaunt it. 'Harry, go back downstairs and grab us a bottle of Coke. Get some crisps as well.'

'Can't you go?' Harry mumbled, staring at Calum's computer as it burst into life. He had never seen anything so weird, yet fascinating. No travellers he knew owned a computer. Neither did they have Sky TV with all those stupid channels. The life of a gorger was a whole new world to Harry and he couldn't get his head around the way they lived.

'No. You go. Go on,' Georgie urged in a raised voice.

As soon as Harry left the room, Georgie sat up and put her hand on Calum's knee. 'Thanks so much for helping me and Harry today. Do you think you could invite us around again soon so we can all go out together? My mum trusts you.'

Feeling Georgie's hand move towards his thigh, Calum Butler thought he had died and gone to heaven. ''Course I will. I'll invite you round loads.'

CHAPTER FIVE

Queenie Butler stared dismally out of the window. The weather had taken a turn for the worse this past week or so, and today it was teeming with rain. There was nothing sadder than watching a coffin being lowered into the ground in such weather, but God had rarely been kind to her family over the past few decades, Queenie thought bitterly.

It was the 1970s when the Butler curse had originally struck. Roy, Queenie's middle son, was the first on God's hit list. He'd been shot, paralysed, and left wheelchair-bound. Roy had hated his life from that moment onwards, which was why he'd ended up killing himself. Then there had been the car crash that had wiped out the life of Vivian's son, Lenny. Vivvy had never forgiven Vinny for driving home inebriated, but what had happened was no more than a tragic accident. Vinny had adored his younger cousin. Lenny was 'special needs', and Vinny would've never intentionally put his life at risk.

'You OK, Mum?' Vinny asked, putting his strong arms around the woman he adored so much. She was tiny in comparison to him, but what she lacked in height she made up for in strength.

'Why is life so unfair, boy? Roy, Lenny, Molly, Adam,

Brenda and now Vivvy, all taken before their time. I don't know any other family that's suffered such bad bastard luck as us. It's a cruel world, it really is.'

Picturing his Auntie Viv's face, Vinny felt incredibly sad. Vivian had been attacked in Whitechapel High Road by a gang of mixed-race hoodies. They had punched her and she had hit her head against the kerb. She'd never woken up, had been in a coma until she passed away. 'Those lads will pay for what they did, Mum. I will be waiting at the prison gates for 'em, and will personally gouge their eyes out and chop their fucking hands off. You can rest assured of that.'

'When can we see Calum again, Mum?' Georgie O'Hara asked. It was so boring being stuck at home all day. She and Harry hated it. Travellers had outdoor spirits.

'Soon. I'll call Calum's mum later.'

'Can't you call her now?' Harry asked.

'Sammi's got a family funeral today, so I won't be able to get hold of her at present.'

'I suppose I'd better make tracks meself. I hope your dad don't wanna stay at the wake for hours on end. I'll be bored shitless if I'm not drinking,' Stuart said, kissing Frankie goodbye. He'd never met Vivian Harris, but Eddie thought it respectful they attend and show moral support for Vinny.

'I think we'll have a takeaway tonight. Try not to be too late,' Frankie said.

Little did Frankie know as she waved her doting fiancé goodbye that Stuart would not be returning home, ever.

Little Vinny straightened his eldest son's tie. 'Auntie Viv'll come back and haunt you if you wear that wonky,' he said, trying to make light on such a horrid day. Auntie Viv had always been a permanent fixture in his nan's house, had only really used her own place to sleep in.

'There's lots of people outside the house, Dad,' Oliver commented.

'Auntie Viv lived in Whitechapel all her life, boy. Last of a dying breed. You can guarantee a lot of people who've moved away will turn up today to pay their respects. It used to be a close-knit community round 'ere. Well loved and respected, Auntie Viv was,' Little Vinny explained. His sons' only memories of Whitechapel were the shithole it now was and he liked them to know their roots. When he was growing up the community spirit in the East End was awesome.

Thinking how grown-up and dapper her sons looked in their smart black suits, Sammi-Lou linked arms with her husband. Obviously she had no inkling of what the day had in store for her. If she had, she'd have run a mile.

'He's not getting in the first car. Let him go in the second,' Queenie informed Michael, glaring at her ex-husband.

Feeling desolate, Albie Butler averted his eyes. He might have been a drinker and a womanizer back in the day, but Queenie had never really wanted him. He knew in his heart he'd married the wrong sister. Due to their age, his and Vivvy's relationship had been purely platonic, but there'd been a lot of love and laughter. That was something he'd never had with Queenie. She'd been all for their sons, Vinny especially, and Albie knew without a doubt that it was she who'd turned them into notorious underworld figures.

Michael Butler led his father away. The poor old sod was eighty now, and had been so upset when Michael picked him up earlier. 'Take no notice, eh? You know what Mum's like. Her bark is worse than her bite.'

'No, it isn't. Her bite is far worse than her bark, son. Like a pit bull.'

As the striking black horses took Vivian Harris on her final journey, the sun made an appearance through the clouds.

Lots of old neighbours who'd moved away to areas such as Kent and Essex returned to pay their respects, and the church was soon full to the brim. The vicar Queenie and Viv had known since childhood had recently suffered a stroke, so Queenie had appointed the young Reverend Johnson to conduct the service. He was a local chap, and both she and Viv had known his mother for years.

Flanked either side of their mother, Vinny and Michael Butler looked a formidable force. Both wore their thick black hair Brylcreemed, Vinny's combed back and Michael's parted and smoothed to the side. Their expensive suits, shoes and Crombie coats were part of their image. Neither would dream of being seen out in anything less than a top-of-the-range suit. 'You need to look the part if you want others to respect you,' their mother had told them from an early age.

Queenie fought desperately not to crumble as the vicar gave a glowing eulogy. He described Vivian as a vivacious, humorous, good-natured pillar of the community who would do anything to help the less fortunate. The last part wasn't exactly true, but his words were lovely nevertheless.

'Morning Has Broken', Vivian's favourite hymn, was played, then Michael stood up and gave a heartfelt tribute to his aunt. Vinny had wanted to give a eulogy, but Queenie decided to honour her sister's wishes. 'If I croak it before you, don't you dare let that murdering bastard of a son of yours speak at my funeral. Disobey my wishes and I swear I will come back and haunt you,' Viv had insisted.

Sitting in the front row next to his father, Little Vinny

felt his body stiffen and the colour drain from his face. 'You Are My Sunshine' was the song that had been played at Molly's funeral, and as an image of what he'd done to her flashed through his mind, he felt the bile rise to the back of his throat. Her eyes were bulging with sheer terror and the look of confusion on her face as he'd pressed against her windpipe would haunt him for ever. He was so sorry, but nothing would bring Molly back. He had to live with what he'd done.

'You OK?' Vinny asked. Little Vinny put his hand over his mouth and ran from the church as rapidly as his shaking legs would allow.

Annoyed by his son's departure, Vinny squeezed his mother's hand. 'You sure you want to speak? I can say something on your behalf if you like?'

'I'll be fine,' Queenie answered, somehow maintaining a stiff upper lip. She walked up the front and turned to face the mourners. 'My Vivvy. Where do I start? She was an angel, she really was. The best sister I could have wished for. She was kind, loving, funny, charming and so loyal. She always had my back. As kids we would play along the Waste for hours on end. Hopscotch was our favourite pastime. Then as adults we'd get dolled up and spend our Saturdays mooching along Roman Road market. So many happy memories of the good old days, that's all I'm left with now.'

Pausing to blow her nose, Queenie bravely continued. 'I never used to believe in life after death, but that's the only thing I can hold on to now. I've got to make myself visualize Vivvy in heaven with her Lenny and cling on to the hope that one day we will be reunited. I wouldn't be able to get out of bed in the mornings otherwise. My heart is broken – beyond repair, to be honest. But my Viv was a tough old cookie and she'd want and expect me to carry on with my life. It's so difficult, though, as she was such a big part of it and I feel like I've lost my right arm, I really do. We were inseparable, as most of you know, and some days I kind of forget she's not here and pick up the phone to call her. Like the other day, for instance, when the news broke that a bloke had been found dead floating on top of Michael Barrymore's swimming pool. Loved Barrymore, Vivvy did. Me and her used to roll up at *My Kind of People*. We'd take the mickey out of all the notrights on there.'

Dabbing her eyes, Queenie's expression turned vicious. 'A natural death I could've coped with better, but not this. Scum, they are, the ones who did this to my Vivvy, and I hope they rot in bastard hell. She didn't deserve to die like that. Cunts, that's what they are, who did this to her. Wicked, despicable cunts.'

In shock that the C word had been used not once but twice in the house of God, the vicar quickly took over. 'Let us pray,' his voice boomed.

The service ended with Vera Lynn's 'We'll Meet Again', and there was barely a dry eye in the house. Albie Butler was a broken man, shoulders hunched, sobbing into his handkerchief. Ava, Vinny's daughter, was in pieces. Queenie's obvious pain could probably be heard as far away as the Mile End Road, and even Vinny and Michael had tears rolling down their faces.

Vinny put an arm around Michael's shoulders. 'Come on, we'll have a cigar and look at the flowers. We've done Auntie Viv proud, eh?'

Michael nodded. Some of the floral tributes had been spectacular. He and Vinny had a beautiful white angel made with AUNTIE VIV spelled out in pink roses. The neighbours had all chipped in to buy a big LADY OF THE MANOR display and the Frasers had sent a beauty that simply said LEGEND, which was very apt. Vivian Harris had received the kind of send-off a legend like herself truly deserved.

Little Vinny was crouched around the back of the church, head in hands. How he could have done such a detestable thing to his own flesh and blood he did not know. But he had, and he'd had to live with it ever since.

Growing up, Little Vinny had issues. His mum had died when he was very young and his dad was too busy running the club to take proper care of him, so he'd ended up living with his nan. At school he wasn't popular, and his only real pal was another loner, Ben Bloggs. Little Vinny would call the shots and Ben would dance to his tune. It was when they got into the skinhead scene that Little Vinny's behaviour went from bad to worse. He was a lost soul back then and had a ruthless, evil streak. Sniffing glue, getting drunk and smoking cannabis became the norm to him, and he was paranoid and eaten up with jealousy that his father doted on his little sister. So he'd planned three-year-old Molly's abduction, enlisting Ben's help, and then callously strangled her – dumping the body in a shallow grave near Hackney Marshes.

'There you are! Are you OK? You're shaking. I've been looking everywhere for you. Did you find the service too upsetting?' Sammi-Lou asked, her kind face full of concern.

Panic attack in full flow, Little Vinny took deep breaths like the doctor had once told him to, and nodded his head. What else could he do? Admit that he'd murdered his beautiful little sister and the police had locked up the wrong person?

The sun continued to shine for the actual burial, then the rain lashed down again.

'Gawd stone the crows! That has to be a sign from Vivvy, boys. She wants us to know she's OK. I mean, come on, it's not stopped raining this week, has it? Not up until the hearse arrived.'

Vinny and Michael glanced at one another. Neither were big believers in the afterlife, but they agreed with their mother, offering words of comfort. If it made their mum feel better to think that Viv had the power to change the bloody weather, then so be it.

'The caterers have done us proud. I belled Nick when I popped to the loo, and he reckons they've laid on a feast fit for a king. The seafood display is the bollocks, by all accounts,' Vinny said.

Relieved that the funeral was over, Queenie managed a smile. 'Loved her seafood, did Vivvy. She'd eat winkles like they were going out of style, bless her.'

Wanting to laugh at his mother's innocent turn of phrase, Michael instead put his arm around her. 'Ted's gonna sing all of Auntie Viv's favourite songs. I've given him a list, and I'll put money on it she's looking down singing along with us all, sweetheart.'

'I'll second that. Gonna be the best wake ever. One that people will still talk about in years to come,' Vinny insisted.

Little did Vinny know at that point that the wake would turn out to be the worst in living history. It would be spoken about for many years to come, mind. But for all the wrong reasons.

CHAPTER SIX

Vivian's wake was held at a restaurant in Stratford that Vinny part-owned. His pal Nick ran the gaff and had rearranged the furniture to accommodate the many mourners.

'Ted's not singing until later. I thought it best that people have a chat and something to eat first. I've given him a list of songs that Auntie Viv liked,' Vinny informed his mother.

'I love that photo of Vivvy. Who got it blown up? She looks so beautiful and radiant, doesn't she?' The huge framed photo on the wall had been taken in Queenie's back garden a couple of years ago.

'Michael sorted it. He said you're to take it home with you later. Her smile lights up this joint, eh? I'd put money on it she's here with us in spirit. I can sort of feel her presence, can't you?' Vinny said kindly. He knew it was what his mum wanted to hear.

Queenie nodded, then received a hug from the handsome Eddie Mitchell. Vivvy would be thrilled he'd attended her funeral. She'd always had the hots for Eddie.

'A lovely send-off for a lovely lady, Queenie,' Eddie gushed.

'Thanks, Eddie. How's Joycie?'

'You've got yourself a fan there. Not stopped raving about you since her party. She tells me you're going shopping together soon.'

'Yes. We're going to Lakeside. I'll give her a bell tomorrow. I couldn't concentrate on shopping beforehand, not with the funeral looming over me. Will cheer me up no end to see Joycie again.'

'Great stuff. Joycie's a one-off, like yourself, Queenie. What you see is what you get with her. Be good for you both to pal up and get out and about a bit. Stanley drives her doolally indoors.'

Spotting a white feather stuck to her shoe, Queenie grabbed Vinny's arm. 'Look! Another sign.' Viv had always believed in the myth surrounding white feathers.

What neither Queenie nor Vinny realized was there was one almighty sign heading their way, and it was by no means pleasant.

Mehmet Malas studied the photograph of Vinny Butler. It had been taken many years ago, but Vinny was very distinctive looking and shouldn't be too hard to pick out of a crowd. 'How long till we arrive?' he asked his brother.

'About thirty minutes. No hanging around. Straight in, do the business, then we leave immediately.'

The Turks continued their journey in silence. All three had been good pals with Ahmed and Burak Zane and it was obvious what had happened to them. Vinny Butler had had it coming to him for a long while, and now he was finally going to get it. If you live by the sword, expect to die by it.

'Slow down a bit, Vin. You haven't half been knocking them back,' Sammi-Lou advised her husband. Little Vinny didn't usually touch alcohol and wasn't the best drinker in the world on the odd occasion he did.

'Don't nag me, babe. I need a drink today. Spent a lot of time with Auntie Viv when I was young. I miss her,' he replied. The real reason he was knocking them back was to recover from the trauma he'd suffered at the church, but he could hardly admit that to Sammi-Lou.

'I think I'll make a move with the boys if you're going to get plastered. You can get a cab home later.'

'Stay 'ere and chill. The music's starting now.'

Teddy Chapman was a legend on the East End pub and club circuit. He'd once worked at Vinny and Michael's old haunt in Whitechapel, and kicked his set off with Sinatra's 'Fly Me to the Moon'.

'Vivvy loved this song, boy. She would've much preferred this played inside the church than Vera bloody Lynn. She didn't even like Vera,' Albie informed his son, before knocking back another straight brandy. He'd been drinking like a fish again since Viv had died.

Michael put an arm around his father's slumped shoulders. 'I've told Ted you'll be singing "Spanish Eyes" later. It's what Auntie Viv would've wanted, so bollocks to Mum and Vinny. They start kicking off, they'll have me to deal with.'

Tears in his eyes, Albie managed a weak smile. 'Thanks, boy. Means the world to me, and I know it would've meant the same to Viv.'

Psyching himself up, Mehmet Malas ran his fingers gently along the barrel of the machine gun. He'd been sentenced to a hefty stretch inside for supplying a large quantity of heroin around the time Ahmed and Burak had disappeared, hence his delay in getting revenge for his dear friends. 'Brothers', he liked to refer to his compatriots as. Ahmed and Burak were the real deal, had always been there for him and his family.

Deniz was driving and had been instructed to wait outside the restaurant with the van's engine running. 'We'll be there in fifteen minutes,' he informed Mehmet and Hassan.

The two men glanced at one another, then smiled. 'Allahu Akbar,' Mehmet mumbled. He was a big believer, and knew Allah would be on their side.

'I've got something to tell you, Nan. Dad said I wasn't to say anything until after the funeral, but I've finally got myself a job. I'm manageress of Dad's Holborn club, and will take care of the business for him when he opens the casino,' Ava informed her grandmother.

Queenie Butler looked at her granddaughter in astonishment. Ava was twenty now and Queenie had virtually brought the child up after her mother died. She was a stunner, with long black hair, and piercing green eyes like her father. Unfortunately, she also took after her father in being a law unto herself and full of surprises. 'You can't work there. It's a knocking shop! No way is that a place for a young lady like yourself to work. It's absurd! Disgusted with your father, I am!'

Ava hadn't been herself lately. She'd been very close to her cousin Daniel and had formed a bond with Roxanne, so it had knocked her for six to find out they were related. She'd also been upset that neither had contacted her since their doomed wedding. On top of that, Auntie Viv's death had been terribly upsetting. But now the funeral was over, Ava was determined to move on with her life and enjoy every second. 'We're not in the sixties now, Nan. It's the twentieth century, and I assure you I can handle a few strippers. It's the family business, remember? Puts food on all of our tables, yours especially.'

*

When his father started to sing, Vinny stormed out the back rather than take his anger out on his brother. Eddie Mitchell followed his new business partner. 'What's up, pal?'

'Just this fucking song. It's the old man's party piece. He was singing this to Viv when she croaked it, so the nurses reckon. Bound to upset my mum. I don't wanna kick off, though, as it's obvious Michael's given Ted the nod for the old bastard to ruin Al Martino's street cred.'

Eddie chuckled. 'Families, eh? Can't live with 'em or without 'em. So, how's it going with Fliss? Gina thought she was top drawer,' Eddie said. Vinny had apologized profusely after they'd had words in the restaurant. He'd said he was drunk and sent Gina a beautiful bouquet. Eddie wasn't one to hold grudges over something so trivial, so their flare-up was now forgotten. Unless Vinny stepped out of line in the future, of course.

Vinny smiled. Though no one would have suspected, he'd been celibate for years until Felicity had come on the scene. The reason being, he was a brutal bastard in the sack and had a habit of terrorizing women, especially prostitutes. He'd accidentally killed one bird and ended up having to set the body on fire to dispose of it. 'It's going quite well, Ed. She's a cracker. Never thought a bird would reel me in again, but she seems to be doing just that. She's ballsy, but not demanding. Very intelligent too.'

Eddie Mitchell was glad Vinny had finally found love. Rumours were rife in the underworld, and Eddie was not impressed by the way Vinny had treated prostitutes back in the day. In his eyes, those poor girls were only trying to earn a crust and did not deserve to be violated and treated brutally. 'You told your family about her yet?'

'Little Vinny met her briefly when he popped round unexpectedly yesterday. Other than that, the only one I've told is Michael. Too embarrassed to tell my mum or Ava, to be honest. It's the age gap, ain't it? Neither will be impressed. Ava had an inkling a while back and called me a nonce-case.' Felicity was half Vinny's age.

About to ask Vinny if he was going to move in with Felicity, Eddie was interrupted by his sidekick, Stuart. 'I don't know how long you're planning on staying, Ed. But I'm gonna have to leave soon. Just had a phone call from Frankie – Harry is playing her up big time.'

'Today isn't about Harry or Frankie, Stu. We are here to remember and pay our respects to the lovely Vivian Harris. For once in her life, my daughter is going to have to cope without our help. Serves her right for stabbing me in the back and getting involved with the O'Haras in the first place, eh, lad?'

Stuart sighed. Eddie had been on the Scotch today and it had a tendency to make him argumentative and arrogant. Harry had apparently smashed to pieces the new computer he had paid a lot of money for only yesterday, and Frankie was incredibly upset about it. 'OK. I'll give it another hour or so. Tired, I am, to be honest though, Ed.'

'Always remember, I call the shots, Stu. It ain't the other way round, kiddo,' Eddie cockily reminded his employee.

Aware of Vinny smirking, Stuart said no more and stormed back inside the restaurant.

Still reeling that her granddaughter would soon be running a club that was no more than a knocking shop, Queenie Butler had just received some more shocking news. 'Abroad! What do you mean, they're not coming home?'

'I got a letter from Lee, but didn't want to tell you until after the funeral,' Michael explained. 'It was only a short note, he just said that he was going abroad to start afresh with Daniel. Dan must have jumped on a plane soon after the wedding fiasco, I imagine.'

'But what about Beth? Lee's got responsibilities, and a mortgage. He can't leave that poor girl in the lurch.'

'Well, he has, Mum. Between me and you, since they found out Beth couldn't have kids, the marriage was on the rocks anyway. Drove him up the wall, she did.'

'So where the bloody hell are they living?'

Michael shrugged. 'The letter didn't say, but my guess would be Spain. They're bound to be in touch again soon. Once the dust has settled.'

'That's not good enough, Michael. I love my grandsons and I'm certainly not getting any younger. I want you to find them and bring them back home where they belong. You can find Roxanne as well, while you're at it. You might have chosen to forget that poor girl is your daughter, but I bloody well haven't. She's fifteen years old and all alone in this world. Poor little cow must be petrified, and for all we know she might still be carrying Daniel's baby. Doesn't bear thinking about, does it? So best you get your head from up your arse and do something about it.'

Michael nodded dumbly. He'd been planning on dropping the Bella bombshell today as well, but the mood his mother was in, that would just have to wait.

Mehmet handed Hassan the rubber Bill Clinton face mask. His own was that of Colonel Gaddafi. Both men were broad, tall, dressed in black tracksuits and trainers, and looked terrifying enough without the masks on, let alone with them.

Mehmet and Hassan's sister, Asli, was a professional make-up artist and she'd done a wonderful job of disguising Deniz, who was driving. She'd reinvented his face in such a way that he still looked human, but like a completely different man.

'How far away are we?' Hassan enquired.

'Five minutes, if the traffic would move. We're at a standstill. I hope there has not been an accident,' Deniz replied.

Feeling beads of sweat forming on his forehead, Hassan rubbed frantically at his mask. This was all going wrong. He could feel it in his bones.

Ava Butler tapped her father on the shoulder. 'Nan's got the right hump. She was none too happy when I told her about my job at the club, then Michael said something to upset her even more. They looked like they were arguing, Dad.'

Excusing himself to Eddie Mitchell, Vinny walked over to the food area. His mother was standing alone, eating a bowl of jellied eels. 'This was one of Auntie Viv's favourite songs, eh, Mum?' he said jovially, referring to Teddy's rendition of Jim Reeves's 'He'll Have to Go'.

Spitting an eel bone into a piece of tissue, Queenie wasn't in the mood for pleasantries. 'Disgusted with you, I am – and your brother. What sort of fathers are you?'

Trying to shift the focus off himself, Vinny replied. 'Told you he's back with Bella then, I take it? I knew you wouldn't be pleased. But Michael's a grown man and if Bella makes him happy, so be it.'

Queenie looked at her eldest in astonishment. 'You've got to be kidding me! How could he? After everything that Italian whore has done to this family. Where is the silly bastard? I'll give him "back with Bella"!'

'He's outside. I'll go get him. Sorry, Mum. I thought he'd already told you.'

'What's up now?' Eddie Mitchell asked, grabbing Vinny's arm as he went to walk past him.

'I've just put me foot in it that Michael's seeing Bella again. Best he deals with it himself now. Let him pander to my mother's wrath and we'll get out the way. There's a boozer nearby. She's proper on the warpath, me mum.'

Eddie Mitchell smirked. 'And I thought my mob were the most dysfunctional family ever to step out of the East End of London.'

Having battled through the traffic, the Turks finally arrived at their destination.

'I cannot park outside. There are no spaces,' Deniz informed his partners in crime, who were seated in the back of the van.

Urging Deniz to drive past the venue, then turn the van around, Mehmet leaned across to peep out the passenger's side window. It was dark now, so he wouldn't be spotted. 'There's a shop nearby with a space on the pavement. Reverse on to that and we'll leap out there. Make sure nobody blocks you in though, OK?'

Feeling slightly nauseous, Hassan began mumbling a prayer in his native Turkish.

Standing with a few of her and Vivvy's old neighbours, Queenie Butler was well and truly on her soapbox. Albie was singing another of Vivian's favourite songs, this time Engelbert Humperdinck's 'Please Release Me'; annoyed by the attention he was getting, Queenie was doing her utmost to redress that by slagging off her absent grandchildren. 'I can fully understand Camila not being here as she is appearing in an important West End musical at present, but Tommy and Tara should be bloody ashamed of themselves. Spent plenty of time with Vivvy when they were young. It's rude and so bloody wrong, that's what it is. Selfish they are, just like their mother was.'

Their mother was Queenie's only daughter, Brenda, who'd been an alcoholic and an embarrassment to the family in more ways than one until her untimely death. In her heart, Queenie would always love Brenda and her kids, but it annoyed her greatly that Tara, who'd recently had a baby, had never bothered visiting her grandmother. She'd even posted a lovely present for the child and not received as much as a thank you card. Both Tara and Tommy lived in Leeds now and seemed to have forgotten their nan existed.

'Were Daniel and Lee at the church, Queen? I didn't see them,' Mouthy Maureen enquired.

Big Stan discreetly nudged Maureen. Rumours had been rife about the fiasco that had occurred at Daniel and Roxanne's wedding. The Butlers had of course denied they were brother and sister, saying it was all a terrible mix-up. But Queenie wasn't in the best of moods and Stan didn't want to rile her further.

Treating Mouthy Maureen to a look of pure hatred, Queenie was just about to tear into the trappy tart when she heard a kerfuffle going on behind her. People were screaming and Queenie thought a fight had broken out until she spotted a man in a Bill Clinton face mask waving a machine gun. 'What the hell! Are they armed robbers? Where's my Vinny?' she shrieked.

'Get down!' Big Stan bellowed, grabbing hold of Queenie and Maureen and shoving them to the floor. His disabled wife had attended the funeral, but he'd taken her home before coming to the wake. As he crouched behind a table, he whispered a prayer. He was thankful that if the worst happened and he didn't make it out of this, his wife would still be around to watch their grandkids grow up.

Teddy Chapman was too wrapped up crooning Tony Bennett's 'I Left My Heart in San Francisco' to realize exactly what was occurring, but at the sound of the first gunshot, he dropped his microphone and literally ran for his life.

'Billy! My Billy's been shot,' a woman screamed.

Waving his gun in the air, Mehmet ran over to Hassan. 'That's not Vinny, you fucking fool,' he spat. Billy, the guy who'd been shot, was Fat Brenda's son. Though he bore a passing resemblance to Vinny, he was a lot shorter.

Hassan could feel his heart pounding in his chest as he bellowed, 'Where is Vinny Butler?' He prodded his gun into the chest of a terrified woman. 'Fucking answer me, otherwise this lady dies.'

When his mother screamed, Michael Butler instinctively darted towards her, positioning his body on top of hers to try to protect her. Placing his hand over her mouth, he whispered, 'Shhhh.' He could see his father hiding under a table, and knew Vinny had sloped off somewhere with Eddie.

'Nan, Nan! Where are you?' Ava cried. She was petrified, couldn't believe what was happening.

Fearing for the life of the woman being held at gunpoint, Big Stan stood up and bravely wagged his finger at the lunatic in the mask. 'You'll rot in hell for this, you no good bastard.' Seconds later, he was shot with such venom, the bullets seemed to push him backwards before he fell to the ground in a bloodied, crumpled heap.

'Not Stan. Noooo,' a voice shrieked.

People were sobbing and screaming. Some fled in terror; others stayed rooted to the spot, unable to move through sheer fright. The masked men had only been in the restaurant for a matter of sixty seconds, but for the terrified mourners it felt like sixty minutes.

'Someone has to do something,' Little Vinny spat.

'No, Vin. Stay here,' Sammi-Lou pleaded.

Ignoring his wife's sound advice, Little Vinny crept towards the figure wearing the Colonel Gaddafi mask. The bloke had his back to the table Little Vinny had been sitting at.

Desperate to stop her husband from doing something daft, Sammi-Lou leapt out of her chair.

'Don't, Mum. Come back,' shrieked the terrified Oliver Butler.

Little Vinny lunged at the guy and all hell seemed to break loose.

Mehmet fired a shot at the ceiling. 'You tell Vinny Butler we'll be back for him. This is for our brothers Ahmed and Burak,' he shouted, before spraying the room with random gunfire.

Calum Butler screamed as he was splattered by a huge amount of blood. 'Ollie, Ollie,' he wept helplessly. He immediately knew his brother was dead; his face was all but obliterated by the bullet. He didn't even look like Oliver any more.

Instinct told Calum to duck under the table, and as he did so, a man's body fell on top of him. It was Stuart. He'd been shot too. 'Mum! Dad!' Calum screamed in absolute terror. Stuart was a dead weight and Calum could barely breathe, let alone move. He was crushed.

Overcome by sheer fright, and unable to breathe properly, the last thing Calum Butler heard before he lost consciousness was his dad scream out his mum's name and a man's voice shout, 'They've gone. Call the police and an ambulance. Hurry up, for fuck's sake!'

CHAPTER SEVEN

Eddie Mitchell plonked his drinks on the table. He looked extra suave today in his black Armani suit and he'd finally got around to having his hair cut yesterday. 'The barmaid wouldn't stop talking. She's got the hots for me,' he chuckled. 'Nice-looking sort. But you know me, Vin. Only got eyes for my Gina.'

When his phone started to ring again, Vinny turned it off. 'Me and my big mouth. It's deffo all kicked off at the wake. Five missed calls from my mum in the space of two minutes. Michael's probably on the warpath, searching for me as we speak. Let's hope he don't get his hands on a cricket bat again, eh?' Vinny joked. When his brother had originally found out about his fling with Bella, Michael had stormed inside the Blind Beggar and taken a cricket bat to his head.

'Did you tell Michael you'd put your foot in it?' Eddie asked.

'Nah. I said Mum needed to speak to him urgently. We'll shoot back there in half an hour or so. Hopefully, he might have calmed down a bit by then.'

Every head in the place turned as the pub door crashed open and a white-faced man staggered in. 'There's been a shooting,' he stammered, 'down the road. It's carnage out there – loads of people dead.'

Vinny leapt up. 'What's happened? Where?'

'Nick's restaurant – two masked men ran in there and started shooting. Ring the police and call some ambulances,' he told the barmaid. 'I'm going back there to see if I can help in any way.'

Vinny's face turned a deathly shade of white. So did Eddie's. Seconds later, the two of them bolted from the pub.

'Sammi! Talk to me. Open your eyes. Please, keep awake, babe.' Little Vinny's tears dripped on to his wife's cheeks as he gently cradled her head while pleading with her to speak to him. She'd said his name just now, and whispered Oliver's, so she'd definitely been alive then. But now her eyes were shut, and as much as he pleaded, she wouldn't open them again.

'Move out the way. I'm a first aider,' a female urged.

Little Vinny did as he was told. Punching the wall in frustration, he sank to his haunches, put his head in his hands and cried. He already knew Oliver was dead. His handsome first-born's face now resembled something out of a horror movie. Nobody could have survived that, let alone a sixteen-year-old lad. As for Sammi-Lou, she'd been shot twice, in the chest and arm. This could not be happening, surely? Was it a bad dream? A fucked-up nightmare?

'The police are here,' a voice yelled.

'Cover Oliver up. Put a coat over him or something. I can't bear to look at him like that,' Queenie wept, trying to comfort Ava at the same time. Her granddaughter was in trance-like shock, most people were. The atmosphere was completely surreal and Queenie was petrified that Vinny had also been caught up in the crossfire. She hadn't been able to hear much with Michael lying across her as a human shield, but she'd caught enough of what the masked men had said to know they were after her eldest's scalp in some warped form of retribution for Ahmed Zane.

'The paramedics have arrived. Move away from the injured,' a male voice bellowed.

Mouthy Maureen sobbed as Big Stan was covered over. He'd been a great neighbour, so kind, and Whitechapel certainly wouldn't be the same without him. His family would be devastated, especially his poor wife, who was completely dependent on him due to her own health problems. She struggled to walk these days.

Totally beside himself, Calum Butler repeatedly smashed his forehead against the wall.

'Stop that. You'll hurt yourself,' Michael said, grabbing hold of the distraught lad and wrapping his strong arms around him. Like everyone else, Michael was stunned by what had happened but was trying to hold it together for the sake of the family. He was also relieved his own children weren't present. Camila had had an important audition for a show, thank God. And Nathan and Ellie hadn't known Viv that well.

'Ollie's dead and now my mum's gonna die. I need to be with Regan. They'll have to let him come home now, won't they?' Calum gabbled, clinging on to Michael. He'd always been closer to his younger brother than he had to Oliver, but he'd still loved him a lot. Now he didn't have an older brother any more. A disfigured corpse was all that was left of Ollie.

'The professionals are working on your mum now. Fingers crossed, she's gonna be OK, boy. Let's both say a prayer for her, eh?'

'Nah. God's a fucking wanker. I don't believe in him anyway.'

'Dad! Nan, there's Dad,' Ava shrieked, the relief in her voice clear to hear.

Shocked at the horrific sight that greeted his eyes, Vinny scanned the room for his mum and dashed towards her, throwing his arms around her, then Ava. 'Thank God you're both all right. Where's Little Vinny, and Michael? Is all the family OK?'

'Little Vinny and Michael are, but Oliver and Sammi-Lou both got shot. He's gone, boy. Ollie's dead,' Queenie sobbed. It was only recently her great-grandson had visited her in her new home. Laughing and joking, he'd been, telling her all about his college course. She couldn't believe she'd never see him again. His life had been wiped out in front of her very eyes, in an instant.

Vinny looked at his mother as though she had lost the plot. 'Ollie? Where is he? He can't be dead.'

The gaff was now swarming with police and paramedics. Tears rolled down Queenie's cheeks as she pointed towards where Oliver lay. The once-clean carpet was soaked in blood and gore. And most of the blood was her great-grandson's.

Vinny ran over to the lifeless body of his first-born grandchild. 'Move out the fucking way,' he demanded.

A police officer grabbed hold of Vinny's arm. 'You can't go near the victims, sir. We're doing everything we can, as are the paramedics.'

Vinny pushed the copper out of his way. 'I wanna see my grandson. I've got every right to.'

Another police officer stepped in. 'I'm so sorry, but your grandson is a fatality. Now, can we clear this area? Move everybody outside. This is a crime scene,' he yelled at his colleague.

Stunned, Vinny couldn't move. He could remember holding Oliver in his arms as a baby for the very first time, and had felt great pride in watching him grow into a charming young man. The lad had his whole life ahead of him, how could it be wiped out in a split second?

Vinny was jolted back to reality by Eddie Mitchell's voice. 'Stuart's in a proper bad way. Been shot in the gut and shoulder. I'm going in the ambulance with him. He's unconscious.'

'Jesus wept! I hope he's gonna be all right. They reckon Oliver's dead. He can't be, surely? We only went to the pub. Who would pull a stunt like this at a wake? And why?' Vinny mumbled. The carnage around him was dreadful, and he just couldn't take it all in at present. How the hell was his son going to cope if Oliver was dead? That boy had always been the apple of Little Vinny's eye. As for Sammi-Lou, she'd been the making of his son. No way would he be able to carry on without her.

Looking around for Little Vinny, Vinny heard the blood-curling scream come from his mouth before he saw him:

'You can't die, Sammi-Lou. Me and the boys love you. We need you. Wake up, sweetheart. Please, I beg you. Wake up . . . '

Eddie Mitchell paced up and down the hospital corridor. Stuart was currently undergoing a life-saving operation and the doctors had already warned Eddie that his chances of pulling through were no higher than fifty–fifty.

'I'll go and get us some coffees. Anyone hungry?' Raymond asked. Not many men would still be pals and employed by a bloke who'd ended their sister's life, but Raymond had been employed by Ed since he was a teenager and wasn't a man to hold unnecessary grudges. Eddie Mitchell was a good person, Jessica had idolized him. What had happened was no more than an accident, a horrific case of mistaken identity.

Gary Mitchell, Ed's eldest son, shook his head. He and Raymond had been out collecting a few debts when they'd heard through the grapevine about the shooting. News travelled fast amongst the underworld and as relieved as Gary was to learn his dad was unscathed, he was gutted that Stuart had copped it. Stu was a good bloke and since he'd taken up with Frankie, he'd well and truly become one of the family.

When Raymond walked away, Eddie plonked himself on his chair. 'I'm such a cunt when that Scotch gets in my veins, ya know. Stu wanted to leave the wake, but I weren't having none of it. Spoke to him like a piece of shit, I did. If only I'd listened to him. Poor bastard's fighting for his life now because of me.'

'Don't beat yourself up, Dad – you weren't the one who went loopy with a poxy gun. Any idea who's responsible? Gotta be somebody who's got it in for Vinny, surely?'

'I heard a murmur as I left that they were Turks. Someone said they shouted out Ahmed's name.'

'Ahmed who?'

'Ahmed Zane – you must remember him. Used to be Vinny's business partner, and pal. Slimy shitbag, he was. I never liked him. Well, he wronged Vinny, him and his cousin Burak, so Vinny made them vanish. Years ago now, though. Why wait all this time for revenge?'

Gary sighed. 'It'll all come out in the wash, I dare say. I bet you wish you'd never got involved with Vinny bloody Butler now?'

Eddie shrugged. 'Even if it's true that it was revenge for Ahmed, it ain't exactly Vinny's fault. Ahmed had it coming to him and disappeared years ago. Whoever is responsible must be the same sickos who sent us the rats and snake.'

'What rats and snake?' Gary asked.

Eddie explained about the unwanted gifts that had turned up at the casino.

'Why didn't you mention that before?'

'Didn't seem important. I thought it was something to

do with the pikeys, if I'm honest. Something Harry said pointed towards those bastards.'

'Stu better pull through, Dad. Frankie'll go to pieces without him by her side. No way will she be able to manage the devil's spawn on her own.'

About to reply, Eddie was stopped from doing so by the appearance of a stony-faced doctor. 'I'm so sorry, Mr Mitchell. We really did do everything we could, but Mr Howells's injuries were far worse than we could have imagined. The bullet was lodged only a centimetre from the heart and as we tried to dislodge it, he went into cardiac arrest.'

'He's dead?' Eddie mumbled stupidly.

The doctor nodded.

Little Vinny Butler felt like his whole world had collapsed, and it had. He'd been sick and couldn't stop shaking, and as an image of Molly flashed through his mind once again, he shut his eyes and rocked to and fro. He could see his little sister clearly, she was smiling at him, laughing almost, and he knew without a doubt this was retribution for his past sins. To lose a much-loved child was an excruciating feeling, and Little Vinny now knew how his dad must've felt when Molly died.

'I think the doctor needs to sedate him, love. He looks grey and can't stop trembling, bless him,' Queenie muttered in Vinny's ear. They were currently in Newham General Hospital. Against all odds, Sammi-Lou had been resuscitated after her heart had stopped. However, the doctors weren't overly hopeful of a full recovery, as her heart had stopped for a good few minutes.

'I wanna go home. I need to phone Regan,' Calum spat. His tears had turned to anger, and he hated the world.

'I'll ring Regan's social worker in the morning. Once the authorities know what's happened, they should allow him home,' Vinny replied, rather coldly. He had never particularly been a granddad type. Pipe and slippers were not his style, and he'd tended to treat his grandsons like little mates. He remembered how he'd once ordered young Oliver to call him 'Vinny' rather than 'Granddad'. How he wished he could change that now. Oliver could call him 'Granddad' every minute of every day, if only it would bring him back to life.

Queenie squeezed her eldest's hand. Ava hadn't wanted to come to the hospital, had chosen to go back to Albie's house in Barking with Michael. No way would Queenie leave Vinny's side though. She could see in his eyes how hard this had hit him, and even though she was still in a state of shock herself, she needed to remain strong. It was her duty as a mother.

'Tell me again what the bastards said, Mum. See if you can remember the exact words this time.'

'It was all such a blur, Vin, I really can't think straight at the moment. But they definitely spoke with Turkish accents, and I'm ninety-nine per cent sure I heard them mention Ahmed's name. They said something like "This is for Ahmed." It was the one in the Bill Clinton mask, I think. No, it might've been the other one. So scary, those awful masks were. I thought they were armed robbers at first, I really did.'

'I'll find 'em and fucking make 'em wish they'd never been born, I promise you that much. When I get my hands on the bastards, I'll—'

'Shut up! Just fucking close that big mouth of yours for once, will ya?' Little Vinny screamed, stopping his father mid-sentence. 'My beautiful wife is fighting for her life. My son is dead. And all this is your fault. You playing the big man is what has brought on this tragedy in the first place. How dare you sit there, planning your revenge at a time like this? Piss off home, and take him with you an' all,'

Little Vinny said, poking Calum on the arm. 'None of yous are bothered about Sammi-Lou. All he's bothered about is Regan. As for you and Nan, you're two of a fucking kind. All you care about is each other.'

About to jump to his mother's defence, Vinny Butler was stopped from doing so by the arrival of Sammi-Lou's father. Vinny and Gary Allen had never seen eye to eye, and when Gary started insinuating that what had happened was his fault, instead of arguing the point, Vinny blanked the man and stood up. 'Come on, Mum, and you, Calum. We'll leave Sammi's family in peace and pop back later.'

The last thing Vinny heard as he stomped down the corridor was the scathing comments from Gary Allen: 'Leave us in peace! I've never had a decent night's sleep since my Sammi became a Butler. A disaster waiting to happen, this was. And it isn't your son's fault, it's yours.'

'Don't let him talk to you like that,' Queenie hissed.

Unusually for Vinny, he chose to ignore his mother's advice. Oliver was dead; Sammi-Lou, even if she did survive, would probably be brain-dead. So for once, Mouth Almighty Allen did have an extremely valid point.

Albie Butler was sitting in silence in his favourite armchair. It was full of cigarette burns, and worn out in places – and that's exactly how Albie felt at this moment. Old, stained and faded. Albie had hoped, even prayed that the wonderful Vivian would get the send-off she truly deserved, but it wasn't to be. Her funeral would go down in history for many years to come, but for all the wrong reasons.

Michael grabbed the brandy bottle and topped his father's glass up, then his own. 'You got any food in the fridge? You didn't eat at the wake, did ya? I'll make you something.'

'I'm not hungry, lad. But thanks anyway. Be turning in her grave, will Vivvy, and truth be known I hope I don't wake up tomorrow. I've had enough of this world, Michael. I'm tired, I'm old, and I want to see Vivvy again. And our Roy, Adam, Oliver, Brenda and Molly. Got more family up above now than down 'ere.' He shook his head sadly. 'Your mum's always blamed me for Molly's death, seeing as it was my bastard son that did it. But I had nothing to do with the way he was brought up – I never even knew the kid existed. It wasn't me that made him a killer. So I reckon your mother has far more blood on her hands than me. I've often wondered if Vinny was born evil, but I don't believe he was. It's your mother's doing, the way he's turned out. Queenie was determined to mould her first-born into a crime lord to match the bloody Krays. I remember how she used to look up to Violet Kray back in the day. She'd see the way shopkeepers would let Violet jump the queue and make a big fuss of her, how everyone kowtowed to her, and she was jealous. That's what your mother craved: notoriety and adulation. And with no way of achieving that in her own right, she was determined yous boys would do it for her. It's her that's evil, boy, and she has blood all over her hands after today's shambles. Lovely lad, our Oliver. What a waste of a bloody life. And I've always thought the world of Sammi-Lou. Why is it always the good ones that suffer and not the bad souls? The devil certainly looks after your mother and Vinny,' Albie spat.

Shocked by the viciousness in his usually mild-mannered father's words, Michael was taken aback. 'Mum ain't evil, Dad. She is what she is. Today wasn't her doing. As for Vinny, we all know he's got a streak, but he has calmed down of late. I bet he's as shocked as anybody. Ahmed and Burak vanished years ago – why wait until Auntie Viv's wake to turn up, hell-bent on revenge? It just doesn't make sense.'

'Of course it makes bleedin' sense! They were gunning for your brother and, as per usual, he got away unharmed while others weren't so lucky. How you can stick up for Vinny or your mother after that Bella turnout, I will never know. Your mother moulded Vinny into the money-grabbing power-loving fruitcake that he turned out to be, and Vinny chose to pal up with Ahmed in the first bloody place. Had he chosen his friends more wisely, Oliver would still be alive and Sammi-Lou would not be at death's door. You need to wake up and smell the coffee, boy. The evil in this family will outlive you, if you're not very careful. You mark my words.'

Head bowed, Eddie Mitchell felt desolate as he leaned against the wall and lit a cigar. Stuart's motor was parked up in Stratford, but no way could he face travelling back to Essex in the vehicle the two of them had been laughing and joking in only this morning. He got all choked up just thinking about the way he'd been taking the piss out of his future son-in-law's girly-looking air freshener and his rubbish taste in music.

'I'm gonna have to get off in a bit, if that's OK?' Raymond stated and asked at the same time. His wife's parents were coming over to theirs for dinner and Polly would have his guts for garters if he did not turn up. It was her mother's birthday.

'Yeah – you get off. And you, Gary,' Eddie muttered. He'd originally met Stuart in prison. They'd shared a cell together and bonded almost instantly. Stu was far more than a pal or employee to Eddie. The lad was like another son to him.

'I haven't got to be anywhere. I'll come to Frankie's with you. Have you switched your phone back on yet? Frankie isn't silly, ya know,' Gary reminded his father.

'I rang Joey. She's been trying to ring me and Stu, but she don't know anything yet. Joey took her out for something to eat, like I told him to. I couldn't even tell him on the phone Stuart's dead, so fuck knows how I'm gonna explain that to Frankie. She's bound to blame me. So will Stu's mum, I bet. Best I pluck up the courage to pay her a visit tomorrow an' all. It's what Stuart would've wanted me to do.'

Gary put a comforting arm around his father's shoulders. Life had toughened him up to the point that not much fazed him these days. 'Let's call a cab, eh? I'll do the talking when we get to Frankie's. We need to be strong, Dad. Frankie's gonna need us more than ever now. Poor little cow ain't destined to find happiness, is she? Perhaps those bastard gypsies cursed her after all.'

Meg Allen darted along the hospital corridor with her youngest daughter by her side. She and Millie had been spending a relaxing day being pampered at an Essex health farm when Meg had checked her phone messages. Gary had left one, telling her there'd been an incident and she needed to make her way to the London Chest Hospital in Bethnal Green as soon as possible.

'Whatever's happened? And why haven't you been answering your bloody phone? We've been worried sick,' Meg Allen screamed at her husband. She and Millie had thought of every scenario possible and panicked throughout the journey. Meg had come to the conclusion her husband must have endured some kind of heart failure, but here he was, fully dressed, and apart from looking a bit peaky he seemed as right as rain.

Gary Allen was not a man who shed tears easily. Even when he'd buried his dear old mum last year, he'd managed to keep a stiff upper lip during his moving eulogy. However, Sammi-Lou was his first-born and he'd doted on her since day one. As for Oliver, unlike the other two horrors his daughter had given birth to, he truly was *the* perfect grandson. Gary had idolized the lad, even as a baby.

Having never seen her dad cry before, Millie was frightened. 'Where's Sammi-Lou and the boys? Is it Little Vinny? Has something bad happened to him?'

Gary Allen put one arm around his wife, and the other around his daughter. 'There was a shooting at the wake. Two masked men burst in. Oliver didn't make it, and Sammi-Lou is critical. Her heart stopped, and . . . '

Meg Allen pushed her husband away. 'Oliver didn't make what? A shooting at a wake! Where is Sammi now?'

'Surely you don't mean Oliver's dead, Dad? That's ridiculous. And Sammi's heart can't have stopped,' Millie Allen shrieked.

When Little Vinny suddenly appeared, his white shirt covered in blood and a doctor in tow, the realization suddenly hit Meg and Millie Allen full in the face. It was then Meg became hysterical.

Frankie Mitchell wasn't daft. She knew when Joey had turned up out of the blue earlier, demanding to take her and the kids out for something to eat, that her father must have told him to do so. No doubt her dad had enticed Stuart to get rat-arsed at the wake and now he was feeling guilty, trying to put her in a good mood so she wouldn't bite Stuart's head off when he rolled home. Or at least, that's what she'd assumed.

'No. Don't put the TV on,' Joey shouted, snatching the remote out of Brett's hands.

'But Mum says I'm old enough to watch *The Simpsons* now,' Brett complained.

Frankie snatched the remote out of her brother's hand. 'You've been acting bloody weird ever since you got here. I reckoned Dad sent you because him and Stuart are bladdered, but you're so twitchy it's starting to freak me out. So come on, Joey, tell me: what's going on?'

All Joey knew was that there had been a shooting at the funeral his father had attended, and Stuart had been wounded. When his dad had rung back again, about an hour or so ago, he'd offered no more information. His orders were to keep Frankie away from the TV and radio; Eddie promised he would explain all when he arrived at Frankie's himself.

'I'm not acting weird. It's just me and Dom. He went mad when I told him I'm going to be working for Dad. Stormed out, and I think it's all over between us, for good.' Joey was telling the truth to a degree. Dominic had gone ballistic when he broke the news he was giving up his high-flying career as a broker to go and work for his father.

Harry nudged Georgie. In the travelling community, homosexuality was extremely frowned upon. Rumour had it that Old Man Macca's grandson had been gay, and he'd disappeared without a trace. 'Uncle Joey, can I ask you something? I know I don't call Frankie muvver, but it's OK to call you my uncle, ain't it?'

Knowing whatever the horrible child said was bound to be crude and also a dig at him, Joey's response was, 'Call me whatever you like, Nephew.'

'I wanna know if it hurts when Dom sticks his cory up your bum? Only, sometimes when I have a crap it's painful – and that's going out the normal way, ain't it?'

Frankie was speechless for a moment, but when Georgie burst out laughing she turned on her children and yelled: 'Get back upstairs now, the pair of ya. I've had enough of you two for one day and if you don't get out of my sight, I'll swing for you. No way are you going out with Calum again until you learn how to behave in the correct manner. And I bloody well mean that!'

Georgie giggled as she playfully pushed her brother up the stairs. 'We'll be nice to her tomorrow, behave ourselves. Bet she does let us see Calum.'

'Yeah. The dinlo will fall for it an' all, she's that desperate,' Harry grinned.

'Mum, if Stuart doesn't come home, can I sleep in your bed with you tonight?' Brett asked Frankie. The last couple of mornings Harry had crept into his room and been really nasty to him before anybody else in the house had woken up.

'Stuart will be coming home, love. But if Granddad has got him very drunk, we'll make him sleep on the sofa, shall we?' Frankie replied jovially. So far, Brett hadn't picked up on the terrible sayings and language Georgie and Harry used, but Frankie was worried he would in the long run. Brett certainly wasn't his usual self lately, and that did concern Frankie immensely. Her youngest had always been a bubbly little chap before Georgie and Harry came on the scene.

'Nooooo,' Joey yelled, snatching the remote off Frankie and turning off the TV the second she turned it on. His dad had said there was bound to be something about what had happened today on the news.

Frankie put her hands on her hips. 'Right! Tell me the truth now. What the fuck is going on, Joey?'

The buzzer sounded in the nick of time. Joey Mitchell was relieved to fling open the front door and see his father and Gary step out of a black cab. He ran outside to greet them. 'Frankie knows something's up. Have they kept Stuart in hospital? He's going to be OK, isn't he?'

One look at his father and half-brother's sombre expressions told Joey all he needed to know.

Minutes later, Frankie Mitchell's screams of unbridled anguish could be heard half a mile away.

CHAPTER EIGHT

It was ten p.m. when Michael and Albie Butler arrived at the hospital in Bethnal Green. Little Vinny had rung up in a terrible state, and aware that Vinny had left the hospital, Michael had insisted his nephew needed some family around him.

'They won't tell us anything,' Little Vinny bellowed, eyes bulging with a look of sheer terror.

Gary Allen glared at Michael and Albie, mumbling, 'I'm going to find Meg and Millie,' before stomping off. Unlike his wife, who'd been quite at ease with Sammi-Lou's relationship with Little Vinny from the very beginning, Gary had always seen the danger signs. He was a self-made millionaire through pure hard graft, and a family of notorious gangsters did not impress Gary in the least. Especially one that seemed to have a personal bond with the Grim Reaper.

'You sit with your granddad and I'll see if I can find out what's going on,' Michael said.

'Gary hates me now. He's blaming me for what happened. I only went to Auntie Viv's funeral, so how is all this my fault?' Little Vinny told Albie. 'Dad's the one to blame, if anybody. It was him they came to shoot. Why did they have to turn the gun on Ollie and Sammi? Why would anybody do that to an innocent woman and child?'

Albie had no answers, all he could do was put an arm around his distressed grandson's shoulders. Little Vinny had lived with him when his father had gone to prison, and they'd been extremely close ever since. It was an awful feeling to lose a son; Albie could remember Roy's death as though it were yesterday, and all he could do was say a silent prayer that Sammi-Lou would pull through. With Sammi by his side, Little Vinny would cope with the loss of Oliver in time, but without her Albie feared for his grandson's future. Sammi was the strong one in their relationship. It was she who had turned Little Vinny into the good man he was today.

'Gary upset Meg and she stormed out. He was really nasty to her, said some proper shitty stuff. Aimed at me being a Butler it was. He was insinuating that our family is rotten to the fucking core. I've always been a good dad and husband, haven't I? The man's a cunt, Granddad.'

'Don't be taking no notice of Gary, boy. It's grief and worry making him say such stuff. Michael will have a chat with him – put him straight, so to speak. What happened with your father? Did you two have words?'

'He's a cunt an' all. All him and Nan are bothered about is themselves, so I told 'em where to go. They make me sick. How dare they discuss fucking revenge when I've just lost my son and I don't even know if my wife's gonna pull through?'

Albie shook his head in disgust. Queenie and Vinny never failed to disappoint him.

'Where's Calum?' Little Vinny asked.

'Round your nan's with your father. We dropped Ava off there before coming here. In a right state of shock, she is, bless her. She sends her love to you and Sammi.'

'Sammi's gonna need more than love. The first doctor we spoke to said her heart had stopped for a few minutes. Then the Indian quack said it was longer, and hinted if she wakes up she might be brain-dead. What am I gonna do, Granddad? I love her so bloody much.'

'I know you do, lad. She's a fighter is Sammi. Let's hope she—'

Albie never got to finish his words of comfort. The doctor appeared at that moment and the look on his face spoke volumes.

'I'm so sorry. We did our utmost, but Sammi-Lou didn't make it, I'm afraid.'

Little Vinny picked up the chair and threw it down the corridor. 'Nooooo. Not my Sammi-Lou. This ain't happening. It can't be. Sammi, Sammi,' he screamed.

Georgie and Harry O'Hara were in an extremely upbeat mood. Neither child had liked Stuart. He was far less of a pushover than their mother, and they were delighted he was now out of the picture.

'She's wailing again. Hark at her. Sounds like that Jack Russell I used to torture,' Harry chuckled. He, more so than Georgie, was getting a real buzz out of his mother's pain. It served her right.

'I think we should say something to her. We can pretend to be sad, can't we?' Georgie suggested. She and Harry had been earwigging earlier when their granddad and Uncle Gary had delivered the shocking blow to their mother. She'd screamed like a nutter, then locked herself in her bedroom and had not stopped making weird noises since.

'I ain't saying nothing to her. And why should you? The bitch took us away from our family. Now she knows how it feels to be apart from someone you care about. Poor old Stuie. I wonder how badly he suffered before snuffing it?'

'Oh, don't say that, Harry. He did buy us loads of stuff. I'm gonna knock on Mum's door and tell her we're sorry for her loss.'

'Go on then, crawler. And while you're at it, ask the slag when we can go and visit Calum next.'

Michael Butler glared at the unfeeling police officer. 'The lad's in no fit state to talk to you mob. Would you wanna chat if you'd just lost a son and your wife?' he hissed.

'No. But I will need to take a statement from him soon. How about tomorrow?'

'How about you go catch the killers instead of pestering us? I've already told you everything that happened. I ain't telling you again,' Michael snarled.

Little Vinny pinched himself on the arm to check he was actually awake. He felt so numb, he doubted he was capable of stringing a couple of words together, let alone a full sentence. His mind kept replaying the first time he'd laid eyes on Sammi-Lou. He might have only been a teenager back then, but he'd known immediately that one day he would marry her. People question whether love at first sight exists, but he and Sammi were living proof that it did. Or they were up until this morning. Now his beautiful wife was dead, and he was about to say his goodbyes to her. Surreal didn't even scratch the surface.

'One of the nurses will be with you in a minute,' the doctor told Little Vinny.

'Do you want me to go in with you? Or would you rather be alone?' Michael asked his nephew.

'Alone. I want to be alone – with my wife,' Little Vinny replied. Even his voice didn't feel like it belonged to him. It sounded flat and dead, which was exactly how he felt inside.

'I'll make up the spare bed. You can stay at mine for as

long as you like. With Calum, of course,' Albie said. He really did not know what else to say. On a day like today, there were simply no words.

'I'll go home.'

'Me and Granddad'll come and stay with you then,' Michael stated. Little Vinny was understandably shell-shocked and no way was Michael leaving him all by himself.

'Nah. You go back to Barking. I need my own space.'

Michael and Albie shared a worried glance. Both were thinking the same thing. Little Vinny had endured problems with drink and drugs in the past. Would this send him spiralling out of control again?

'Mummy! Mummy, please open the door. I want a cuddle,' Brett Mitchell wept. He had loved Stuart and seen him as the dad he'd never had. They'd played lots of games together, had fun days out, and Stuart had bought him toys and games. Now he was gone for good and Brett knew his life was about to get a whole lot worse. His mum would be sad all the time, and Harry would pick on him even more.

'Move out the way, Brett,' Eddie ordered. 'Frankie, unlock the door, darlin',' he bellowed. After hours of constant wailing, it had all gone worryingly quiet inside the bedroom.

'Do as Dad says, Sis. I know you're upset and want to be alone, but Brett needs his mummy,' Joey added. Being twins, he and Frankie had always been exceptionally close. His heart went out to his sister, it really did. Even though his own relationship was rocky at the moment, he'd still managed to find and hold on to love. With Stuart, Frankie thought she'd finally found love too.

Unable to stop himself, Harry O'Hara burst out laughing. 'Brett needs his mummy,' he mimicked.

Georgie giggled. 'Shhh. They'll hear you.'

'Go shut that pair up, Gary. If I go in there, I'll strangle both of 'em,' Eddie ordered his son.

Georgie and Harry insisted on sharing a bedroom, and as Gary flung the door open, Harry scowled at him. 'You're meant to knock first. Says so on the sign outside. Georgie might've been getting changed. Hoping to see her titties, was ya, you perv?'

Seeing red, Gary raised his right hand and whacked the cheeky little shit around the head. He didn't feel like an uncle to these kids. They were vermin, just like their father had been.

Harry O'Hara was stunned as he fell to the carpet.

'Leave him alone, you bastard. Touch him again and I'll beat the granny out of ya,' Georgie O'Hara screamed as she flew at Gary, scratching at his face like a wildcat.

Gary held both of Georgie's wrists and glared at Harry. 'We could hear you, taking the piss. Your mum's fiancé has just been murdered. Have you no fucking heart?'

'We've lost our family an' all, you know,' Harry spat.

Letting go of Georgie, Gary Mitchell wagged his forefinger at both kids. 'I'd watch my back if I were you two. Me and your granddad are on to ya, big time.'

When Gary slammed their bedroom door, Harry O'Hara stuck both middle fingers in the air. 'Go fuck your grandmother,' he mumbled. In the travelling community, that was the worst insult there was.

Little Vinny stared at his wife's pretty face. It didn't have a mark on it. Sammi looked as though she was sleeping and would wake up any second. She truly was beautiful, even in death.

Sammi's body was covered over, but unable to stop himself, Little Vinny lifted up the cover to hold her hand.

It was still warm. 'I love you, babe. I'll always love you. Forever soulmates, eh?'

As he continued to pour his heart out to Sammi-Lou as though she could hear him, tears flooded down Little Vinny's cheeks. 'I won't let you down, I won't fall to pieces, I promise you that. It's your job to take care of Ollie now, and mine to look out for Calum and Regan. I'm going to get in touch with Regan's social worker tomorrow, fight tooth and nail to get him an early release. That's what you would've wanted, eh? And Calum's gonna need his brother now he hasn't got you or Ollie, isn't he?'

For a split second, Little Vinny could have sworn he felt Sammi-Lou's hand slightly squeeze his, but he guessed that was only wishful thinking. 'I want you to tell our Ollie how much I love him, babe. I can't go and see him, not with his face like that; I'd rather remember him how he looked this morning. Smart and handsome in his suit and tie. Tell him he will always be my number one son, no matter what.'

Little Vinny carried on chatting to his deceased wife until a nurse opened the door and informed him the Allens wanted to see Sammi-Lou. He stood up and kissed Sammi tenderly on the forehead. 'Goodbye, princess. Wait for me in heaven.'

Little Vinny's final memory of visiting his dead wife would be of Meg Allen as she was taken inside the room. 'My baby. My beautiful little girl. Sammi-Lou. Sammi-Lou. You can't leave me. Wake up,' Meg screamed.

Shuddering, Little Vinny ran towards the hospital exit.

'You've got thirty seconds to open this door, Frankie, before I break it down,' Eddie Mitchell threatened.

'Go downstairs a minute, Brett. Mum'll be down in a tick,' Gary said, ruffling his nephew's hair. Unlike the other two horrors, Brett was a lovely little boy. So much so, it was hard to believe Jed O'Hara's sperm was involved in his creation.

'You don't reckon she's done something stupid, do you?' Gary whispered, as soon as Brett was out of earshot.

'Only one way to find out,' Eddie said, taking a step back then aiming his right foot at the door.

The door finally splintered at the third attempt and Joey was first to burst into the room. 'She's not here.'

Eddie peered out of the open window. Frankie had obviously made her escape via the garage roof, but there was no sign of her. 'What the fuck am I paying these so-called security men for, eh? Gary, you stay here and look after Brett. Joey, me and you will find your sister.'

Ten minutes later, Joey Mitchell found his sister in the summer house. She was sitting on the floor, her knees huddled to her chest, shivering. 'Dad, Dad! I've found her,' Joey yelled, before taking his jacket off and putting it around Frankie's shoulders.

'What you doing out here? You had us worried sick. You could've broken your neck jumping off that garage roof,' Eddie Mitchell told her.

'I wish I had. I don't want to live any more. I've had enough. First Mum, now Stuart. He didn't even want to go to that fucking funeral you know. Said he didn't know the dead woman. Why did you have to drag him there? Were you not content with just killing my mum? Did you want me to lose my fiancé as well?'

Tears pricking his eyes, Eddie crouched to his haunches. The day he'd accidentally killed Jessica had been the worst of his life, but today was right up there with those dark days when his father and his son Ricky had been brutally murdered, that was for sure. 'I loved him too, Frankie. Stu was like a son to me, you know he was.'

'But he was more than that to me, wasn't he? Stuart was my future, my everything. And now he's gone, thanks to you. You're gonna have to take care of Georgie and Harry for me now. I can't manage. Harry's evil, just like Jed was. You should've heard what he said about Stuart earlier. He was laughing, I heard him. That's why I had to get out the house. I couldn't take any more. I just want to curl up and die. That's why I brought these in here with me,' Frankie screamed, waving a packet of tablets in the air.

Joey snatched hold of the packet in panic. 'How many have you taken, Frankie?'

'None! I forgot to bring a drink. But if I had, I would have swallowed every single fucking one of 'em. Other than Brett, I have nothing to live for now. Nothing whatsoever.'

Queenie Butler switched the bedroom light on. 'You hungry, Calum? You need to eat something. I've got burgers, sausages, bacon. Can cook you whatever you fancy.'

'Not hungry. I just wanna sleep,' came the muffled reply. Calum had been under the quilt for hours and had no intention of getting up. All he could think about was his mum and Oliver. Not being able to see, talk, laugh or even argue with them again seemed so unreal. Their deaths hadn't sunk in, and Calum doubted they ever would. He'd stared at his nan in a state of disbelief when she'd informed him: 'Your mum's gone to heaven to look after your brother, boy. Your dad, me, and the rest of the family will take care of you and Regan from now on. A promise that is, an' all. You'll want for nothing; I'll make sure of that.'

'Na-night then, love. If you wake up later and need anything, just give me a shout. Even if you just wanna chat, OK?'

Calum didn't bother answering. How could his great-gran

even say 'You'll want for nothing' when his mum and brother had been shot to smithereens right in front of him?

'How is he? Silly question, I know,' Vinny asked solemnly, his arm draped around Ava's shoulders. His daughter was usually as strong as an ox, but today had knocked the stuffing out of her. It had all of them. Everybody seemed to be running on autopilot, but Ava in particular was acting weird. She was clingy, childlike almost, and it reminded Vinny of days gone by when she'd been a little girl. Not the stroppy teenager she was most days now.

'Still under the quilt. I dunno what else to say to him. I'm not the greatest with words at times such as these. Suffered too many tragedies in the past, that's bloody why. Will you talk to him, Vin?'

'I dunno what to say to him either. Molly, Auntie Viv, Roy, Champ, Adam . . . You just run out of words in the end, don't ya?' He purposely left his sister Brenda out of his list of deaths because he hadn't really liked her that much. When Queenie offered no reply but continued to look at him expectantly, he turned to his daughter. 'Go chat to Calum for us please, Ava? You're much better at saying the right things than me and your nan are.'

Imagining how dreadful Calum must be feeling, Ava reluctantly made her way upstairs.

'I feel so ill, Vin. Must've aged ten years recently. And there was me thinking moving home would change my luck. Cursed, this family is, I'm telling ya. Him up above hates us. I wouldn't mind if we were bad people, but we have hearts of gold. Do anybody a good turn if we can. Why us?'

'None of it makes any sense, Mum. Why wait all these years then decide to turn up waving guns on today of all days? I will start making enquiries tomorrow and when I find out who's responsible, I'll personally hack their limbs off while they're still alive.'

Queenie's eyes welled up. 'But say they find you first? If anything happens to you, it'll be the end of me. I couldn't live without you, Vin. I love you too much.'

Vinny held his mother in his arms trying to soothe her fears. In truth, he was a very worried man. If the Turks were capable of the chaos they'd caused at the wake, then he'd better watch his back very carefully indeed.

'No way is Ava going to work at your club with those loonies on the loose. I won't allow it,' Queenie insisted.

'I know. I'll talk to Ava tomorrow. I don't want you going out alone either. Not until I've sorted this mess.'

For all the conviction in his voice, Vinny had no idea how he was going to sort this particular mess. Turks were like travellers: a closed community who stuck together like glue, so finding out who'd pulled such a stroke was not going to be easy. But money talked and, like all communities, the Turks were bound to have one or two backstabbing traitors living amongst them.

'Now go give Little Vinny a ring,' urged Queenie. 'What that lad must be going through doesn't bear thinking about. My first great-grandchild dead, and poor Sammi-Lou. I feel numb, truly can't get my head around it. The look on Big Stan's face as they shot him will haunt me for the rest of my days. We said we was gonna give Vivvy a send-off that the East End would remember and talk about for years to come, but we didn't mean like this.'

CHAPTER NINE

Eddie Mitchell felt his heartbeat accelerate as he clocked the parcel sitting on the step. Even without even opening it, he knew what would be inside. Same packaging, same printed writing, and delivered by hand like the last one was.

Two weeks had passed since Vivian Harris's funeral, and for once the police had come up trumps. An anonymous phone call had led them to a garage in Forest Gate. The van was inside, and when the Turks came back that very same evening, they were immediately surrounded by armed police. They'd since been charged and sent to Belmarsh prison to await their trial. The Old Bill reckoned it was a foregone conclusion they'd get a 'Guilty' verdict as their DNA was all over the vehicle, and they'd even recovered the masks.

Eddie had breathed a massive sigh of relief on hearing the news of the arrests. With the new casino due to open soon, he hadn't wanted a war on his hands. Especially a war he'd had sod-all to do with in the bloody first place. Stuart's death still needed to be avenged, mind, and Eddie was hoping he could pay somebody to do the dirty work for him. He had a lot of contacts in Belmarsh, and was sure there would be an opportunity in the future to get at those Turkish bastards. He would make it his mission in life, if need be. That, and keeping the rest of his family safe from now on. You only got so many reprieves in his world, and his close brush with death earlier this year had forced Eddie to see life in a whole new light. It was a gift, something sacred, and he was now determined to see all his kids grow up and get married.

He was about to open the dreaded parcel, when his phone rang. 'Everything all right, Joey? How's she doing today?'

Gina was having none of it when he'd suggested Frankie and the kids stay at theirs for a while. His wife had told him that Brett could stay for as long as he wanted, but under no circumstances would she ever allow Aaron and Rosie to sleep under the same roof as Georgie and Harry. Frankie was currently struggling to look after herself, let alone the devil's spawn, so Joey had stayed at hers since Stuart's death. There was no other solution at this moment in time.

'We had plenty of tears again this morning, but thankfully she seems to have perked up this afternoon. Little Vinny rang earlier, and invited Frankie and the kids over to his tomorrow. She didn't want to go at first, but I managed to talk her into it and she called him back. It'll do her the world of good to talk to somebody who is going through the same thing as she is. Even worse, in Little Vinny's case, as he lost Oliver as well. When I spoke to him, he said he was worried about his lads. One of his sons has just come out of some youth detention centre, and both boys are understandably missing their mum and brother. He seems to think the brats' company will perk them up, which I can't quite understand,' Joey Mitchell explained.

'Little Vinny's youngest stabbed his teacher, so I'm sure

he and Harry'll get along just fine,' Eddie replied sarcastically. 'Did Frankie drink again last night?'

'Yes, but only about a bottle and a half of wine. No vodka, which is an improvement on last week. I can't stop her, Dad. She reckons it's the only way she can sleep. We have to hope that, now the funeral is over, she'll knock it on the head.'

'The devil's spawn been playing her up?'

'Nope. Been in their bedroom most of the day. Georgie has even offered to cook us dinner one evening. Although I might pass on that for fear of her poisoning me.'

Eddie managed a weak chuckle. 'Cheers for staying with her, Joey. Dunno what I'd do without you at times. You truly are a star.'

'Thanks. But as I told you at the funeral, I can't stay here forever, Dad. Dom needs me too. We spoke last night, sorted a lot of stuff out, and I promised him I'd go home next week.'

Alarmed, Eddie Mitchell rubbed the stubble on his chin. 'But Frankie can't be left on her own, son. How's she meant to cope? It's far too soon.'

'Perhaps you can stay with her for a while? Or let Gary take his turn at playing the caring brother? I'm not being funny, Dad, but I'm not going to balls-up my life while everybody else seems to be getting on with theirs.'

'You know what a needy notright Gary's married to. She ain't gonna let him stay at Frankie's now they've got their first nipper on the way. And Gina needs me at home. Aaron and Rosie are a handful at times. Can't Dominic stay at Frankie's with you? She likes him and that might cheer her up.'

'No, Dad, he can't. You know what a piss-taking, homophobic piece of work Harry is. I'm not putting Dom through any more of his snide remarks. I suggest you put your foot down with Gina. Either tell her you to have to stay with Frankie, or insist Frankie and the kids stay at yours. Frankie should come before Gina. She's your daughter.'

Mumbling, 'And you're her fucking twin,' Eddie ended the call and opened the package. As he'd thought, it wasn't a 'Good Luck with Your New Venture' present from Harrods. Instead he found two dead pigeons and another bible quote:

DEUTERONOMY 19:18–21

THE JUDGES SHALL INVESTIGATE THOROUGHLY, AND IF THE WITNESS IS A FALSE WITNESS AND HE HAS ACCUSED HIS BROTHER FALSELY, THEN YOU SHALL DO TO HIM JUST AS HE INTENDED TO DO TO HIS BROTHER. THUS YOU SHALL PURGE THE EVIL FROM AMONG YOU. THE REST WILL HEAR AND BE AFRAID, AND WILL NEVER DO SUCH AN EVIL THING AMONG YOU. THUS YOU SHALL NOT SHOW PITY. LIFE FOR LIFE, EYE FOR EYE, TOOTH FOR TOOTH, HAND FOR HAND, FOOT FOR FOOT.

Bemused, Eddie put the lid back on the box. If the Turks were locked up, it couldn't be them sending this weird shit. So who the hell was it?

Firing up the ignition, Vinny Butler turned to his son. 'You did Sammi-Lou and Oliver extremely proud. Your speech was phenomenal.' Today Sammi-Lou and Oliver had been laid to rest, and Vinny was so proud of the way his son had behaved since their deaths. He hadn't fallen to pieces as Vinny had feared, and it was his son who'd contacted him to apologize for the silly argument they'd had at the hospital.

'Cheers, Dad,' Little Vinny replied, before ordering his sons to fasten their seatbelts. The authorities had cut the rest of Regan's sentence. He'd been due home soon anyway, so it was no big deal to them. It was to Little Vinny though. He'd achieved something Sammi-Lou had long craved.

Being banged up had changed Regan somewhat. He'd matured whilst away, shot up in height and acted far older now than a twelve-year-old. Vinny Butler liked the new Regan. Suddenly he saw him as a chip off the old block. 'You OK, lads?' Vinny asked. Both his grandsons had cried briefly today, but considering the dreadful circumstances, they'd held their emotions in check brilliantly. Regan had even stood up and bravely read a poem he'd written himself about his mum and brother.

'We're OK. Can me and Cal order a pizza when we get home? We're starving now,' Regan replied. There would have been plenty of food at the wake, but because it was being held at Sammi-Lou's parents' house, his father hadn't wanted to go. Granddad Gary had been acting arsey lately; it all came to a head at the vigil when he told Regan: 'You've been a terrible son. Put your mother through hell, you did.' Little Vinny had flipped and punched Gary Allen in the face. 'Ever talk to my boy like that again, you'll have my dad to answer to, cunt,' he'd yelled, before storming out, dragging Regan and Calum with him.

'How did you leave it with the Allens?' Vinny asked his son. 'I saw you chatting to Meg outside the church.'

'I told her she's welcome to see the boys whenever, but Gary needs to calm down before I'm allowing him contact with 'em. Ball's in their court now. Calum and Regan are Butlers, whether Gary likes that or not, and I won't allow him to drag our name through the mud. I know he's upset and angry, but aren't we all? I dug you out at the hospital, but soon realized the error of my ways and apologized. Best Gary does the same, eh? He needs to treat me and the boys with a bit more respect if he wants to be part of Calum and Regan's future.'

Vinny put the palm of his hand on the back of his son's neck. 'I can't tell you how fucking proud of you I am these days. Whatever happened to the skinhead delinquent that used to knock about with that muppet Ben Bloggs, eh?'

Shuddering as he thought of Ben, then Molly, Little Vinny turned the volume on the radio up.

Queenie Butler put the kettle on. Sammi-Lou and Oliver had been laid to rest together. Queenie had been dreading the actual funeral and had cried buckets. She still couldn't believe she would never see Ollie's handsome face again or hear that cheery voice of his, but he and Sammi had been given a nice send-off and thankfully it had gone off without a hitch.

Plonking Michael's mug on the coffee table, Queenie pursed her lips. 'So what's happening with your love life, Don Juan?' She'd been fuming on learning he was seeing Bella again, but because of everything that had happened since, had been unable to give her son a hard time about it. She'd had more important things on her mind.

'Do we have to talk about my love life? I'm a walking car crash when it comes to women. The one thing I do know is, I do not and have never loved Katy Spencer.'

'Should of thought of that before you shoved your dingle-dangle up her and got her pregnant twice! I hope you're popping back to Tunbridge Wells still. You can't abandon Nathan. That boy needs a father.' Queenie purposely didn't mention her granddaughter Ellie. She had very little time for that spoiled brat. Its mother's double, that one was.

'I saw Nathan and Ellie last week, and I'm gonna drive down to Tunbridge Wells again tomorrow. I tried to tell Katy me and her were over, but she'll do anything to keep me trotting back there once a week and staying overnight. Including turning the kids against me, blackmailing them to make me feel guilty, and threatening to move to France with them to live with her parents, who she doesn't even get on with.'

'She knows a good thing when she sees it, that's why. Once a gold-digger always a gold-digger. And what about the other one? Still Alfie-ing it up round there, are you?' Michael had always been one for the ladies, even at an early age. That's why Queenie had many years ago nick-named him after Michael Caine's character in the film *Alfie*.

'It's complicated, Mum. I know you hate her, but I will always have feelings for Bella. We were truly happy once, and we're both so proud of Camila. There's a lot of water under the bridge though, and Antonio to contend with. No way will I be jumping in feet first. I'm just gonna take things slowly and see how it goes.'

Coughing at the same time she said the word 'Slut', Queenie asked after Camila before chatting about the funeral. 'Hope I'm never forced to be in that Gary Allen's company again. See the face on it? Needs a stocking of hot shit slapped around his clock, he does. I mean, Little Vinny fell over backwards to accommodate his and Meg's wishes. He even allowed the dead bodies of Oliver and Sammi to be gawped at by all and sundry at the Allens' house. And we had to listen to all that Catholic claptrap today, being sprayed with that bastard holy water. That boy was a Butler, should be buried alongside our family.'

'Little Vinny did what he thought was best. Meg Allen wanted Sammi to be buried near her nan, and Little Vinny was adamant Oliver be buried with Sammi-Lou.

That cemetery isn't exactly a million miles away, Mum. I'll drive you over there whenever you want.'

Queenie shook her head vehemently, and in a flippant tone replied,'Nah. Don't bother. I'm not a Catholic. Would rather stick with me own.'

Vinny Butler was stunned to say the least. Neither he nor Eddie had expected to receive any more unwanted parcels. They'd put the earlier ones down to the Turks. 'I dunno what to say to you, mate. I'm just as gobsmacked as you. Perhaps you were right in the beginning? You know, about the pikeys sending 'em.'

Eddie Mitchell was in a Scotch-fuelled, extremely bad mood. 'Nah. What if there are more Turks queuing up to shoot us, Vin? Just because those three fucktards are locked up doesn't mean to say we're in the clear. And this shit has sod-all to do with me in the first place, does it?'

Vinny ran his fingers through his dark Brylcreemed hair. 'No, it doesn't, Ed. But who's to say this crap we keep getting sent was anything to do with the Turks in the first place? Could be any nutter sending such shit, and those bible quotes get more wacky by the fucking delivery. Not knocking you, but neither of us have been angels in our time, so it could be aimed at both or either of us. What I suggest is that tomorrow, we get some cameras put up outside. CCTV will catch the bastards.'

Eddie slammed his glass against the table. 'Bar the O'Haras, I've kept myself out of the firing line for years. I really don't need agg like this at my age, mate. I've got young kids and a wife I adore. I would never have agreed to our business venture in the first place had I known we'd be having this conversation now. I've just lost one of my best men thanks to you, Vin, and I don't intend on losing any more. I'll tell you what I'm gonna do, shall I? I will insure this gaff up to the hilt and, on my kids' lives, any more grief, I will set fire to the cunt personally. Get my drift?'

'Mum, what was I like when I was little?'

Frankie Mitchell managed a weak smile. Georgie had certainly warmed towards her since Stuart's death, even though she still spent most of her time holed up in the bedroom with Harry. 'You were always headstrong, wasn't she, Joey? Do you remember that time she ran away from that pub? You gave us a real fright.'

Georgie giggled. 'Where did I go?'

'You were found up a tree, if I remember correctly,' Joey informed his niece.

'And you were such a fussy eater, you'd turn your nose up at most things. The one thing you would always eat though were those tinned sausages with baked beans. They were your favourite.'

Georgie shuddered. 'Nanny Alice says you should never eat meat out of tins. She says the animal needs to be recently killed.'

Frankie topped up her glass of wine. Alcohol had become her friend these past couple of weeks, helped to lessen the feelings of pure panic that would wash over her. The police had refused to release Stuart's body immediately; therefore his funeral had only taken place yesterday. It had been terribly sad, and without drinking half a litre of vodka beforehand, Frankie would have been unable to attend.

'You look sad again, Mum. You thinking about Stuart?' Georgie enquired.

Frankie plastered a fake smile on her face. 'No. I'm thinking about our day out tomorrow. Calum's dad rung up earlier and invited us over. You'll get to meet Regan,

Calum's brother, too. And if you promise to come back and look after Harry, you can go out and play there.'

Georgie wanted to laugh at her mother's use of the word 'play'. How old did she think she and Harry were, five? Instead, she smiled sweetly. 'I promise, Mum.'

Georgie O'Hara could not help but smirk as she skipped up the stairs to tell her brother the news. She currently had her mother in the palm of her hand, and that was exactly where she wanted her.

Eddie Mitchell handed Vinny a drink. He'd calmed down a bit now, having flown off the handle earlier. He hadn't apologized to his business partner though. Eddie wasn't a man who used the word 'sorry' very often, he never had been. 'Did Oliver and Sammi have a good send-off, mate?'

Vinny shrugged. 'As well as could be expected. Gary Allen had a face like a smacked arse throughout, refused to speak to any of my family. But I suppose that was to be expected. Little Vinny held himself together well, so did Calum and Regan.'

'What about your mum and Michael?'

'They're OK. Us Butlers are professional fucking mourners now, the amount of deaths we've had to deal with. How about Stuart's?' Vinny asked. With both funerals within a day of one another, he and Eddie had decided to just attend their own family's rather than each other's.

Eddie sighed. 'It was sad, Stuart's mum was in bits. Nice woman, she is. I'll keep in touch with her, bung her a few quid 'ere and there. It's the least I can do, really.'

'Was Frankie OK?'

'She'd been boozing and fell arse over tit on top of some of the floral tributes, but apart from being tearful, she got through it better than I thought she would. The devil's spawn didn't come. I told Frankie I didn't want 'em there in case they upset Stu's mum. I sent a couple of the lads round Frankie's to watch over them. Brett wanted to be there though. Loved Stuart, he did. I feel sorry for that poor little sod. He's been living with us the past couple of weeks, don't wanna go home. He's great with my Aaron and Rosie, helps Gina out, so she's happy for him to stop there.'

'I hear your Frankie's going round my boy's tomorrow. Little Vinny belled her this morning.'

'Yeah, Joey said. Be good for them to chat. And for the kids to have a muck around together. Similar ages, the kids, eh?'

'Be even better if my boy and your girl start hitting it off. That would be some wedding, eh? A Butler and Mitchell one.'

Eddie looked at Vinny in amazement. 'I wouldn't order your suit just yet. My Frankie was well in love with Stuart, and he's only been dead five minutes.'

'So was Little Vinny with Sammi-Lou. But neither can be brought back from the dead, mate. Life goes on, so they say . . . '

CHAPTER TEN

'Please come with me, Joey. I don't think I can go on my own,' Frankie Mitchell begged. Apart from Stuart's funeral and a few sneaky trips to the local off-licence, she had not ventured outside the house since her fiancé's death. Now she was in her brother's car on her way to Little Vinny's, and the thought of being left alone there terrified her.

'You know I can't come with you, sis. Dom has taken the day off work for one reason: so he and I can spend it together. Little Vinny is a nice guy. He'll look after you.'

'Divvy dinlo whore,' Harry whispered in his sister's ear. Joey drove a red Mazda sports car and he and Georgie were all but crushed in the small space behind the seats.

Georgie pinched her brother as hard as she could. Harry could not see the wood for the trees at times, whereas she most certainly could. 'It'll be OK, Mum. I'll look after you too,' Georgie promised.

Frankie stared at her trembling hands while taking deep breaths to try and control the panic. She'd often gone out, once upon a time, but since Stuart's death leaving the house felt like a big deal. It scared her. Thankfully she'd had the foresight to sneak some vodka into her handbag. 'Can we stop at a garage or somewhere? I'm busting to do a wee,' she lied. As far as her brother was aware, she only drank wine of an evening now to help her sleep, and what he didn't know couldn't worry him.

Joey squeezed his sister's hand. ''Course we can.'

Queenie Butler was done up to the nines. Her bright red cashmere jacket was thin, flowing and to the knee, and her new black ankle boots with a three-inch heel were very modern and suited her. Vinny had told her that only yesterday. 'Mum, you look more like fifty-four than seventy-four in that get-up. Really suits you,' he'd said when she'd shown him the outfit she planned to wear today.

As per usual, Joyce was done up like a dog's dinner. She had a thing for animal prints and Queenie thought the long coat she had on today looked as common as muck. Her blonde bouffant hairstyle didn't do her any favours either. She stood out like a beacon in Lakeside.

'You know who you remind me of,' Joyce said. They were currently sitting outside a little coffee shop.

'No. Go on.'

'Barbara Windsor. Minus the big knockers, of course,' Joyce laughed.

'I don't look sod-all like Barbara Windsor. She wears wigs, for starters. I read that in *Bella* magazine the other day,' Queenie snapped. 'You remind me of someone too. It'll come to me in a minute.'

'Yootha Joyce?'

'You look a bit like Yootha, but it's not her I'm trying to think of. Me and Viv used to adore *George and Mildred*. Don't make 'em like that any more do they? Nor *Love Thy Neighbour*. The world's gone politically-correct-fucking-mad,' Queenie said bitterly. 'As for the music these days, don't even get me started. Ava had some shit blaring out in my house the other day. I said to her, "You can turn that bleedin' racket off." She said, "But it's Shaggy, Nan." Who's Shaggy when he's at home, eh? I couldn't even understand what the bastard was singing. I mean, what happened to the likes of Kay Starr and Johnnie Ray?'

Breaking into Johnnie Ray's 'Cry', Joyce spotted an awful sight and stopped singing. 'State of that over there. Has she not got a mirror indoors? Look at the fat hanging out over the top of those tracksuit bottoms. You think she'd wear a long baggy top, not a belly one, wouldn't you? It's enough to put you off your lunch.'

Queenie Butler felt melancholy as she nibbled at the scone and sipped her tea. Gone were the days when women would take pride in their appearance like they had on a Saturday down the Roman back in the day. Used to be like a contest, that did, to see who could get glammed up the most. This was her first trip to Lakeside shopping centre since Vivian had died, and she and her sister had spent many a happy day here.

'Nice of your Michael to give us a lift, wasn't it? Handsome sons you have, Queenie,' Joycie Smith said.

'Thanks, lovey. They're always well turned out. I drummed that in 'em as kids.'

'Eddie said you lost a daughter as well. What happened to her? I hope you don't mind me asking.'

'Nah, it's fine. Got stabbed, my Brenda did. Another one murdered in cold blood. To be honest, I doubt she'd be alive now anyway. She was an alcoholic – had her father's genes.'

'That's tragic. Did they catch her killer? Poor you, Queen.'

'No. Never caught him. Jake Jackson his name was and he fled abroad. Could be anywhere in the bleedin' world now.'

'Was it a random attack?' Joycie enquired.

'No. My boys had run-ins with Jake's father and grandfather many years ago. Still doesn't explain why the little shit targeted Brenda though. Too cowardly to have a pop at the men, I suppose.'

'You never get over it, do you? Not a single day goes past I don't miss and think about my Jessica.'

'I rarely think about Brenda any more, to be honest. She was her father's daughter all right.'

'Aww, was she close to Albie then?'

'No. Brenda hated him as much as I do. Now drink your tea, Joycie. It's getting cold. Nice scones these, aren't they?'

Little Vinny and Frankie Mitchell were sitting in the garden. The autumn weather was breezy, but the sun was shining and the birds could be heard tweeting away in the surrounding trees.

'Peaceful out here, isn't it? Sammi loved this garden. I was thinking of planting something and making some kind of shrine to her and Oliver down the bottom.'

'I think that's a lovely idea. It just doesn't seem possible that we are never going to see them again, does it? I keep expecting Stuart to walk through the door any minute, laughing and joking as he always did.'

Little Vinny nodded. 'I know where you're coming from, and even though people mean well, nobody really understands, do they? My mate Finn's been great. He pops round most days, but I find it difficult to open up to him, and my family. My dad's had too many deaths to deal with over the years, made him as hard as nails. And my nan's the same. They haven't got a sentimental bone left in their bodies.'

'I feel the same. The nights are the worst. I can't sleep unless I'm bladdered. My dad sent a private doctor round to me recently. I think he thought I was gonna top myself, so he gave me some pills. They haven't helped much though. Then he suggested I have counselling, but I can't be talking to strangers. Makes me feel uncomfortable. Have you been drinking or taking any pills?'

'Nah. I daren't. Got a bit of an addictive personality, me. I don't do anything by halves, and I made a promise to Sammi-Lou that I would be strong and take care of Calum and Regan for her.'

'Awww, that's lovely. Did you speak about stuff like this then when Sammi was alive? Me and Stuart didn't and I wish we had now.'

'No. I made Sammi the promise when she was dead. Excuse me a tick. Gotta pop to the loo, then I'll top your glass up. You're not in a hurry to get home, are you? I wasn't in a cooking mood, so thought we'd order a Chinese later. The shop opens at six and it's the boys' favourite.'

'We're not in no rush. I do hope Georgie and Harry don't run away again though. I always worry when they're out of my sight. How far away is the park?'

'It's only local. Stop worrying. They'll be fine.'

Georgie O'Hara was in fact more than fine. Regan Butler had a cocky confidence about him, a quality she had only ever seen amongst travelling lads, and she could not take her eyes off him. He looked much older than twelve, was as tall as Calum, and he reminded Georgie of a young Elvis Presley. Nanny Alice had always had the hots for Elvis, said she would have married him instead of Granddad Jimmy, given the chance.

Sporting a pair of Ray-Ban sunglasses, Regan Butler glanced out the corner of his eye. He was aware of Georgie O'Hara's interest in him, and the effect he had on girls. He'd sampled his first French kiss at the age of eight, and before he'd got banged up, had shoved his hand inside fourteen-year-old Sally Parker's knickers. 'What you looking at?' he asked.

Harry O'Hara burst out laughing. Regan was aloof and stroppy like himself and he preferred him to Calum already. He was also annoyed with his sister for her continuous flirting. She had a boyfriend, and he liked Ryan Maloney a lot. Georgie shouldn't be dressing like a slag, or acting like one. It was all wrong.

Calum Butler scowled at Regan. 'Don't talk to Georgie like that. She's a decent girl, bruv.'

'I never said she wasn't. I only asked her what she was looking at.'

Red-faced, Georgie marched her stupid brother out of earshot. 'Do you want to go back to Scotland and live with our real family again?'

'Yeah, you know I do.'

'Well shut the fuck up then. I know what I'm doing, Harry, you dinlo.'

Little Vinny poked his head around the lounge door. The kids had returned from the park as good as gold earlier, and were now playing games on the massive TV that was bracketed on the wall.

'I've never heard Georgie or Harry laugh like that before. What they up to?' Frankie asked.

'It's some dance game where you have to copy the moves. Regan won't play it, sees himself as too cool. They've asked to get the karaoke machine out now, so prepare to be deafened. Regan can sing really well. Calum ain't got a bad voice either. I sound like a cat being tortured, me, so they obviously have Sammi to thank for their musical talent.'

'I have no idea if Georgie or Harry can sing – I know so little about them still. I do remember Georgie loving country music as a little girl. She knew all the words to the songs. Her bastard of a father taught her them. Was

Sammi your actual first love, Vin? Or did you date beforehand?'

'Sammi was my first serious girlfriend. I just knew as soon as I met her that she was the one, but we had our ups and downs like any young couple. I worked in my dad's club in Whitechapel at the time, and I remember getting cold feet at one point 'cause she kept turning up there. How times change, eh? I'd give my right arm for her to walk in this kitchen right now. And Oliver.'

'I wonder if they're looking down on us? I'm sure Sammi and Stuart would want us to be friends, don't you think?'

'For sure. You're the only person I've been able to open up to since, and Sammi would be so pleased that the boys have brightened up today. They were sad and quiet leading up to the funeral. That's why I belled you yesterday morning. Was trying to think of ways to cheer them up.'

'My dad reminded me your little sister got murdered years ago too. Same happened to my granddad you know. It was Jed that killed him. Broke in my dad's—'

'Enough of deaths, eh, Frankie?' Little Vinny abruptly barked. No way did he want to discuss Molly. He then forced a smile. 'Let's join in with the kids' karaoke, shall we?'

Back in Lakeside, a few sheets to the wind, Queenie was opening up about Daniel and Roxanne's incestuous relationship. She'd dragged Joycie to the pub the other side of Brompton Walk by the lake.

'So Roxanne never had a clue that Daniel was her brother?' Joyce Smith asked again. Queenie was unsettled after bumping into a friend of Roxanne's outside Debenhams. Alex had been a bridesmaid at the ill-fated wedding and Queenie had believed her when she'd sworn blind she had not heard a word from Roxanne since.

'No. I've told you that three bloody times! Neither

Roxanne nor Daniel knew one another even existed. But you must never tell anyone, Joycie. When it all kicked off at the wedding, my family told everybody there was a mix-up. I mean, incest isn't something you can live down, is it? The police even visited us you know, to ask what had happened. Them nosy bastards would've had a ball if they'd had proof, so would the bloody press. Saw a programme on TV recently about another brother and sister who fell in love. It's called "Genetic Sexual Attraction".'

'I've never heard of it, Queen, but I know sod-all about sexual attraction of any kind. Only ever slept with Stanley and he weren't exactly Marlon Brando back in the day. We've slept in separate beds ever since the kids were born. I can't be waking up looking at that bald head and ugly face every morning. Turns my stomach, it does.'

The comment lightened Queenie's mood. 'Exactly the same as me and Albie. The only time I used to let him anywhere near me was when I wanted another child. Coming home pissed at all hours and snoring – made him kip on the sofa, I did.'

'What did Albie look like when you first met him? Bet he had more going for him than my Stanley.'

Queenie shrugged. 'Albie was a looker back in the day, I suppose. That's why I chose him, to be truthful. My old neighbour Doreen was a few years older than me. I used to look up to her as a kid, until she married Freddie Watts. Looked like he'd fallen out the ugly tree and hit every branch on the way down, he did. I'll never forget seeing her son for the first time. Ugliest baby I ever did see. Looked like an alien. It scared me.'

When Joycie started guffawing and banging her empty glass against the table, Queenie couldn't help but laugh too. She'd been racking her brain ever since she'd met Joyce as to whom she reminded her of, and it had just this minute occurred to her. Joyce was a ringer for that famous cook her and Vivian used to laugh at on TV back in the day: Fanny Cradock.

Frankie Mitchell clapped as Calum Butler finished his rendition of Eminem's 'My Name Is'. She would never have believed her children could mix so well with others, but Georgie and Harry had taken a real shine to Calum and Regan. It was a joy and relief to witness their happiness and laughter for once. They always seemed so miserable at home and had never enjoyed anything she and Stuart had organized for them.

Little Vinny was sitting on the opposite sofa, and when he playfully grabbed Regan in a headlock and threatened to sing again unless his son did, Frankie found herself joining in with her children's laughter. Sammi-Lou had described her husband as 'a brilliant father' who had 'a unique way with kids' and she'd been spot on. Little Vinny was a natural.

Eddie Mitchell wasn't having the best of days. His daughter Rosie had sicked up all over the back of his new Range Rover earlier. Then, minutes later, some dopey tart had pulled out of a side turning and pranged into him. Now, to crown it all, he'd been summoned to Lakeside to pick up an inebriated Joycie and Queenie, who had somehow managed to get themselves into a state only two teenage girls could dream of.

'Where's my Vinny?' Queenie asked again. She'd tried both her sons' numbers for at least an hour before Joyce suggested they ring Eddie to pick them up. Even Little Vinny wasn't answering his bloody phone.

'Queen, grab hold of the other side of Joycie, will ya? This is embarrassing, love,' Eddie spat as he saw yet another crowd of kids looking their way and laughing their heads off. He'd virtually had to drag the woman he would always refer to as his mother-in-law through the shopping centre like a rag doll, and he prayed no bastard recognized him. Everyone was looking and laughing, such was the state Joyce had got herself in. And Queenie was unsteady too.

'Put your arm around me shoulder, Joycie. We're giving all these old trollops down 'ere something to gawp at, that's for sure,' Queenie bellowed, much to Eddie's horror.

After what seemed like hours but was probably only in fact twenty minutes, Eddie finally had both women belted up in the back of his Range Rover.

'Sorry for being tipsy and having to ring you, but my Raymond's useless, you know that, Ed? You're a far better son to me than he is and we're not even blood-related, are we? It was the shock of finding out Queenie's granddaughter might be going to give birth to her grandson's baby what made us go to the pub in the first place, weren't it, Queen?'

'Yep! And where is my Vinny, by the way? Bet I can guess why Michael has his phone switched off. Fornicating with that Italian slapper, I dare say. More fool him, eh, Eddie? I bet you wouldn't go back with a woman who'd had your brother's dingle-dangle up her, would you? Makes me feel sick.'

'Dingle-dangle! I love that bloody word. Used to call my Stanley's a "tinky-winky",' Joycie shrieked.

Listening to his musical idol belt out a tune or two was far preferable to listening to two old-age pensioners discuss a man's anatomy, so Eddie cranked the volume up as loud as it would go.

Queenie and Joycie knew all the words to 'Maggie May' and sang along quite happily.

'Now Rod I could've quite easily fancied,' Joyce shouted in Queenie's ear.

Queenie ignored Joycie and instead tapped Eddie on the shoulder. Ed turned the music down and before Queenie could ask him the same question again, told her, 'Vinny's fine. I saw him earlier. But as I've already told you, I have no idea what his plans are for this evening.'

'Yes, you do. I might be knocking on a bit, but I haven't lost my marbles yet. My Vinny's got a bird on the firm, can tell by the shady way he's been acting recently. Nobody knows him better than his mother. So what's she like then? Come on, spill the beans, Mr Mitchell.'

Georgie O'Hara was most impressed. After much persuasion from his father, Regan had finally agreed to sing and he had a superb voice. Georgie had heard many a travelling lad croon an Elvis tune, including her own boyfriend, but Regan's version of 'Are You Lonesome Tonight' was truly captivating. That was Nanny Alice's favourite Elvis song too.

Harry leaned towards his sister. 'Put your tongue away. Flies might breed on it.'

Georgie punched her brother hard. Harry had been acting up today and was now grating on her immensely. 'You sure you're not a gay boy like Joey? Only you seem very obsessed with Regan yourself.'

Homosexuality was extremely frowned upon among travellers and when Harry lost his rag, like she knew he would, Georgie slapped him around the head before following her mother into the kitchen. 'What's a matter? You're crying.'

Fiercely wiping her eyes with her sleeve, Frankie smiled. 'Take no notice of me. Just having a weak moment. Been a nice day, hasn't it? I'm so pleased you and Harry have made friends.'

'We would've made friends ages ago if you hadn't locked us up. And we love music. We used to sing regularly back home. Travellers don't watch TV all the time like gorgers do. We sing and play music lots.'

Frankie knew the travelling way of life as well as anybody. Jed had loved to sing, and it was the norm that when families got together, everybody including the children would be urged to belt out a tune. 'How about I ask your granddad to buy you one of those karaoke machines? You and Harry can have it in your bedroom and play with it whenever you want.'

Exasperated, Georgie snatched her hands away. 'We're not five! We don't play with things. And how would you play with a karaoke machine anyway? You can't! You sing along with the music. We don't want one in our bedroom either. Other people need to join in to make it any fun and we live in the middle of nowhere with no friends.'

When her daughter stomped out the kitchen, Frankie topped up her wine glass. Then the tears came. Joey had told her last night that he needed to move back home next week and she had no idea how she would cope alone. Georgie was right: their house was in the middle of nowhere, but her dad had chosen it because its remoteness would make it more difficult for the children to escape. Now, however, it held far too many memories of Stuart and it was too big and cold. She realized she'd come to loathe the place with a passion.

'Hey, what's up?' Little Vinny asked.

'Everything. I can't do wrong from right when it comes to my children, and I do try my best. Joey's moving back home next week and I'm never gonna cope. Georgie and Harry hate it where we live and so do I. My youngest son doesn't even want to come home, he'd rather live at my dad's. And I keep expecting Stuart to walk in all the time. I even imagined I heard his footsteps the other day, coming up to bed.'

'Perhaps you should think about moving. You're only renting, aren't you?'

Frankie nodded. 'My dad's paying the rent and he's shelling out for those security blokes. I hate seeing them all the time too. They give me the heebies. But the lease isn't due to end until next year, and I can't stay there that long. Between me and you, once Joey goes home, I'm afraid I might get drunk one day and do something stupid. I don't think I would, 'cause I love my kids too much, but then I get these dark moods and I just don't want to be in this world any more. Life is shit, Vin, it really is. We must go to a better place when we die, surely?'

'Things will get better, Frankie. I've been through dark times in the past – and I mean really dark – but I've managed to pull through. If it wasn't for the boys, I could never cope with Sammi-Lou and Oliver dying. But I've got to be strong and so have you. We have children who rely on us.'

'You might have. I don't. I'm sure those two in there would celebrate if I died.'

Little Vinny sighed. He wasn't very good with awkward hugs or sympathetic words, but he was good with advice. 'That isn't going to do you any favours, for a start,' he said, pointing to the wine glass. 'Neither is locking your kids up in that prison you call home. Your dad isn't short of a few bob, Frankie, and I know he'd want you to be happy. If I were you, I'd try out the counselling thing, and move over this way. It's nice round 'ere, and central. I'll have a word with Finn if you like? His pal is a local estate agent and I'm sure he'd be able to help.'

'Really?'

'Yeah, 'course. Be nice for my kids to hang out with yours. I've also decided not to send Regan back to school, I'm gonna get someone in to teach him from home instead.

He's always got in trouble at school and I can't risk him being sent away again. Not many schools will want to take him anyway, after what happened. Perhaps they can teach Georgie and Harry as well.'

'Oh, Vin! That would be wonderful. Even if they could just learn to read and write, it would make me so bloody happy. And it will open up a whole new world to them. They'd love to live near Calum and Regan, I know they would. Shall I tell them the good news now?'

'Whoa! Hold your horses. Let me speak to Finn's pal first, and you can have a talk with your dad. Do ya want a coffee? I'm gonna make myself one.'

Frankie was about to reply when she felt the hair freeze on the back of her neck. Georgie not only had a voice like an angel, she was singing Tammy Wynette's 'Stand by Your Man'.

'Wow! Your daughter's got some voice on her. Let's go back in the lounge,' Little Vinny suggested.

Shaking her head, Frankie Mitchell held her face in her hands. 'I hate this song. It reminds me of Jed. I even lost my virginity to him while it was playing. My life is such a mess, and it's all my fault. Have you ever done something so wrong it eats away at you like a cancer? So much so, you can never forgive yourself. My mum would still be alive if I'd never met Jed.'

Overwhelmed by visions of himself strangling Molly, Little Vinny handed Frankie her bag. 'Look, it's been a long day and I think we should wrap it up now.'

'But I thought we were going to order a Chinese?'

Little Vinny pulled out his wallet, peeled off a fifty-pound note and handed it to her. 'I'm tired and need my bed. Get yourself a cab home and grab yourself something to eat on the way.'

Taken aback, Frankie stood speechless as Little Vinny

stomped upstairs. She knew she was tipsy and had probably repeated herself once or twice, but she hadn't said or done anything so wrong she deserved to be chucked out the house, had she?

CHAPTER ELEVEN

'Happy birthday, darlin',' Vinny Butler said.

Felicity Carter-Price excitedly put her hand inside the gift bag and pulled out a small Cartier box. Inside was a stunning pair of diamond drop earrings. 'Wow! They're amazing, Vinny. I love them. Thank you so much.'

'Only the best for my girl,' Vinny said, before urging her to try them on. This was all new to him, buying gifts for a girlfriend. It felt weird, but kind of cool at the same time. If somebody had told him a year ago that he'd be all loved up and buying Cartier earrings for his woman, he would've laughed in their face.

'How do they look?' Felicity asked.

'Gorgeous, just like you. Nah, don't take 'em off. I wanna look at 'em while I give you your other present.'

Felicity grinned as Vinny dragged what they referred to as 'Pandora's box' out of the walk-in wardrobe. He liked it rough and she aimed to please. That was why she trawled the internet regularly, looking for outrageous sex toys and props.

'Do you want me to answer that?' Felicity asked.

'Give us it,' Vinny said, snatching his phone out of her hands.

Felicity smiled as she thought of the evening ahead. All

Vinny's family would be at the opening of his new casino, and she couldn't wait to meet them at long last. Ava despised her, she already knew that. But she was hoping to make a good impression in front of the others, his mother especially. Vinny was a dark horse, and Felicity was eager to find out more about the man she virtually lived with now.

'That was me mother. Reckons she's got nothing to wear tonight. Three wardrobes she's got, full to the brim. Yous women will be the death of me,' Vinny joked, before ordering Felicity to turn over.

Handcuffing his girlfriend's wrists to the bedposts, Vinny stroked her long dark hair. She was a very beautiful girl and he was a lucky man.

Over in Essex, Georgie and Harry O'Hara were having a count up.

'How much we got now?' Harry asked his sister.

'Thirty pound, eighty pence. We need at least a hundred pound, perhaps even two.'

Harry tutted. Their mother wouldn't give them any pocket money as such because she was scared they'd try to run away again. They'd managed to nick a few quid. Harry had swiped a tenner out of Stuart's wallet when the police had given it to their mum, and they'd also nicked some coins out of her purse when she left it lying around, but other than that they had no way of getting or earning any cash. 'Why do we need more? That's enough for food and drinks, and Scotland ain't that far away. We can easy bunk the trains without a ticket.'

'We can't. They've got barriers and people watching ya. When Nan and Mary went shopping in Glasgow that time, they nearly got arrested. Nan was frit to death when she came home, don't you remember? She never got on a train again, said she'd rather walk and wear her shoes out.'

Having never been on a train or bus in his life, Harry knew very little about how public transport operated. Whenever he'd left the site back in Scotland, it had been in a car or van with his dad, uncle, or granddad behind the wheel. 'Why don't you ask Calum to help us? He well likes you, I can tell. I bet he'd give you money if you show him your titties.'

'I will ask him to help us, but not yet. We need to find out where we're going first, and how to get there. Our site weren't near any stations, and say nobody's there any more? If our dad and granddad are dead, Nanny Alice won't be there.'

'Ryan'll still be there. His dad owned the land,' Harry reminded his sister.

'We don't know that for sure. Ryan's dad probably came to rescue us with the others, and he might be dead too.'

'Cheerful, you are, ain't ya, Georgie?'

'I'm just stating facts.'

'Well now I'm stating facts. I hate Frankie and this shitty house, and if you won't come with me, I'll run away on my own.'

Vinny Butler shot his load up Felicity's backside, unlocked the handcuffs and then rolled on to his back.

'What time should I be ready for this evening? I'd rather not drive, if that's OK? Are we getting a cab?' she asked.

'I've booked a car to pick you and Anita up. It'll be here at seven.'

Felicity propped herself on her elbow. 'I thought we were going together? And you never said you'd invited Anita.' Anita was the bar manager at the Holborn club.

'I invited Anita so you'll have somebody to chat to. I'm gonna be working the room, babe, so I won't be able to stand with you. Look, I know I said I'd tell my family about us, and I will. But not tonight, eh? I don't want no dramas, so act a bit distant with me, if you know what I mean. My mum's suspicious I'm seeing someone as it is, and Ava's always thought something was going on between us.'

'I really don't see what the big deal is, Vinny. You're a grown man – so what if you have a love life? Hardly the crime of the century, is it?'

''Course not, but you are young enough to be my daughter. I promise I'll tell 'em soon, OK? I got to do it more gentle than just thrusting you upon them tonight though. My mother's a funny old bird at times.'

'Whatever! But I have no intention of being your dirty little secret forever.' When Felicity stomped into the shower, Vinny sighed deeply. That was the nearest they'd come to an argument since they'd been together. Unlike other birds he'd known, Felicity was very laid back and put no pressure on him, as a rule. That's why he had to man up soon. He was happy and didn't want to lose her, but his mother and Ava would go ballistic and he knew it.

Eddie Mitchell had an acute business brain and it had been his idea they divide the building in two, with separate entrances. The larger space was the actual casino, the smaller a plush piano bar where the finest wines, champagnes and spirits would be served to those who had paid the hefty private-membership fee.

The A13 wasn't exactly the King's Road Chelsea, but both Eddie and Vinny were confident they'd attract the type of clientele they wanted. Their notoriety alone should encourage many to travel from far and wide. The Circus Tavern was only a five-minute drive away, and back in the day that had been rammed most weekends.

Since the CCTV had been installed, there had been no

more unwanted deliveries, but Eddie wasn't taking any chances. He'd told his men to get there early and had hired some extra brawn just to be on the safe side.

'Bloody hell, Ed. They have less cameras surrounding prisons. Don't you think you've gone a bit over the top?' Gina asked, as she stepped out the vehicle.

Eddie hadn't told Gina about the dead rats, snake and weird bible quotes. It would worry her immensely and she'd only recently stopped fretting about his vendetta with the O'Haras earlier in the year. 'It's a dodgy old road, the A13, and we're aiming at the wealthy with this venture. They're gonna have top-of-the-range motors and loads of cash on 'em, Gina. We want our punters to feel safe and secure when visiting.'

'It looks lovely from the outside. Who came up with the names?' Gina asked, pointing at the two enormous glowing signs. 'Piano Bar' and 'The Casino' weren't exactly original, but looked good nevertheless.

'I chose the "Piano Bar" and Vinny the other. Keeps it simple, eh?' Eddie replied, before dragging his son away from a water fountain. Eddie crouched down. Aaron looked like butter wouldn't melt in his smart suit, but Eddie was aware it melted regularly. 'You be a good boy tonight. No touching things that don't concern you, OK? Else I'll chop them hands of yours off.'

Six-year-old Aaron shook his head. 'Nah you won't. I'll chop your hands off first.'

Eddie chuckled. The bar and casino had an over-twenty-five policy, but tonight was all about showing off their new project to family and close friends. Word of their venture had spread like wildfire this past fortnight and they'd already sold over a hundred memberships for the Piano Bar at five hundred quid per year. That allowed them to vet to an extent who was joining. The Casino had a walk-in policy, where you would pay a small fee on the door. But neither officially opened until next Saturday.

'Can I have a quick word, boss?' Terry Baldwin asked. Terry was one of Eddie's main men, part of what Ed liked to call 'The Firm'.

Clocking the serious expression on Terry's face, Eddie told Gina, 'Take the kids inside, babe. I'll be with you in a tick.' He turned back to Terry. 'What's up?'

'It's probably nothing serious, but there was a car loitering down by the entrance earlier. It kept pulling up, then disappearing again, so I told two of the lads to take a wander down there. It came back again, slowed down, and a lad shouted something out the window.'

'What?'

'Not sure, the boys couldn't understand the lad properly, but Jed O'Hara's name was mentioned.'

'Did they get the reg?'

'No. They got part of it, but the car was caked in mud and they couldn't see the rest.'

'Oh well, I doubt it would've been much use anyway. Bound to be pikeys if they're mentioning Jed, and those bastards don't even register their kids, let alone their motors. Just tell the boys to be extra vigilant, OK?'

Vinny Butler paid the cabbie, then turned to his mother and daughter. 'I don't want any more disagreements this evening about jobs, or anything else for that matter, understand?'

Ava looked like her father and also had his temper. Her bright green eyes blazed as she fumed. 'Nan started it. I'm not a child and I will not be told where I can and cannot work. This is an opportunity for me to make something of my life.' Ava had been gutted when her father told her it was too dangerous for her to be working at the club at present. She'd had a rubbish year, missed Daniel and Lee terribly, and would never get over seeing Oliver blasted to death right in front of her. She desperately needed something to focus on, a new beginning, so it had come as a huge relief when the Turks had been caught and her dad had told her she could start her new position as manageress of his club the following week.

'Make something of your life! What, in a knocking shop? Don't make me laugh!'

'It's a gentleman's club, Mum, and that's enough on the subject. So whaddya think of our statue? A friend found it online for me. Reminds me of one of the bedtime stories you used to tell me and Roy as kids. The one where we grew up from cubs and took over the world by becoming the fiercest, most feared lions of all. Awesome, ain't it? I could look at it all day.'

Queenie smiled. The statue was made of stone and it was the size of a real-life lion. Its mane was huge and it was lifting a paw and baring its teeth. 'I love it – and those fountains. Aren't they beautiful, all lit up like that? Truly stunning!'

Vinny put an arm around his mother's shoulders. No longer did she wear real fur. It had gone from being fashionable to frowned upon. She had a fake fur on this evening and looked marvellous in it. Bright red, it was. Her favourite colour and it matched her lipstick. 'I'll order you one tomorrow.'

'Order me what?'

'A fountain. You've got a big enough garden now.'

'Yeah, but that's too big.'

'They make 'em smaller. Do you want one?'

Queenie smiled broadly. 'I'd love one. I'll put it near Vivvy's shrine. You're a good son, you really are. Simply the best.'

When Ava threw her arms about wildly, while imitating

Tina Turner singing 'Simply the Best', Queenie couldn't help but find it humorous. She waved a forefinger at her granddaughter. 'And you are one headstrong little cow, young lady, who'll be the bleedin' death of me,' she chuckled.

'You sure I look OK? It's been ages since I've worn a dress and I feel so uncomfortable. Wish I'd put trousers on now,' Frankie said to her friend. Babs had stayed with her the past few days, and for the first time since Stuart's death, she'd felt a lot calmer. Her dad had stayed with her the previous week and he was enough to drive a deaf and dumb person doolally. She'd insisted he leave in the end, for the sake of the only bit of sanity she had left.

'Did you like wearing dresses when you were my age, Mum?' Georgie asked.

'No, love. I've always hated wearing them, even as a small child. Your Grandma Jessica used to despair with me. She said I was a tomboy and she'd hoped for a ballerina.'

'Nanny Alice says I'm a tomboy too, don't she, Harry?' Georgie said. Her brother rarely joined in with any conversation involving their mother and Georgie wished he'd lighten up a bit. Being rude and difficult wasn't getting them anywhere, and they'd never get any pocket money or be allowed out for long periods of time unless he started being nicer.

Harry glared at his sister before looking out the car window. Georgie had sat downstairs with Frankie and Babs last night and he'd been earwigging. Laughing and joking, she'd been, while asking lots of stupid questions about her childhood. His sister was a turncoat, that's what she was, and even though she denied it, he could tell she'd warmed towards the bitch who'd given birth to them. Well, he wouldn't. Not now, not ever.

*

The interior of the Piano Bar was spectacular. The walls and actual piano were white, the leather bar stools, armchairs and sofas all black. The flooring was white with a wooden effect, and the huge chandeliers that hung from the ceiling were dimmed. The bar area was black, lit up by white lights.

Queenie smiled as a member of staff took her coat and another handed her a glass of champagne. Both had called her 'madam' and she was pleased Vinny had employed pleasant staff with nice manners.

'You couldn't have chosen a better dress for tonight, Mum. It goes with the décor. So does your necklace and earrings.' Vinny winked.

Queenie beamed. When Vinny had urged her to treat herself to a new frock earlier, insisting he'd pay for it, Queenie had taken him up on his kind offer. She never usually wore black, it reminded her too much of all the family funerals she'd attended, but she'd fallen in love with her new dress on sight. It was long, sleeveless, with big diamantés around the neck. Queenie was no longer a fan of the gold herself and Vivian once draped themselves in. It looked ever so common and old-fashioned these days, so she'd been thrilled when Vinny had given her a spectacular diamond necklace for her last birthday and earrings to match at Christmas.

'They new shoes, Nan?' Ava asked.

Queenie lifted her frock slightly to show off her silver glittery stiletto sandals.

'I suppose they cost me a few bob an' all, Mother. I said buy a new dress, never did I mention any accessories to go with it,' Vinny joked.

'Queenie, Queenie! Over here.'

Spotting her new friend's bouffant before she spotted her, Queenie dashed over to the sofa Joycie was lounged across. She had an awful shocking-pink dress on, with lipstick to match.

'Got here early, I did. Best seat in the house this one. We can see everybody who walks in. I dunno about you, Queenie, but I'm a nosy one, me. He's got some handsome friends has Eddie, and although we're old enough to be most of 'em's mothers, we can still look, can't we?'

Laughing, Queenie kissed Joycie on the cheek before sitting down. She still missed Vivian terribly, but Joycie rang her every day now, at least once, and would always cheer her up. 'You look lovely, Joyce. That dress is beautiful,' Queenie lied.

'Old, it is. Bought it in Lakeside years ago, but rarely go anywhere posh enough to wear it. You look stunning too,' Joycie fibbed. In her opinion, black did not suit Queenie at all. It made her look hard as nails.

'Ta. My Vinny made me go out and buy this today. We got to go to that Bluewater next, Joycie. That's where I got this from. Little Vinny was going there to buy the boys a new suit for tonight, so I cadged a lift. Really posh, it is. Right up our street.'

'I've heard about Bluewater – opened a couple of years ago, I think. Isn't it hard to get to though? No way will Eddie give us a lift again after the last time,' Joyce guffawed. She couldn't remember much about the journey home from Lakeside when Eddie had come to their rescue. But after dropping Queenie off, Joyce could remember smelling sick in the vehicle which had unfortunately made her vomit herself, all over Eddie's back seat.

'Where's Stanley?' Queenie enquired.

'Playing with his cock in the shed, I should imagine. Talks to them bastard pigeons like they're children, he does. No way was I having him cramping our style tonight, Queen. Not with all these handsome men here. See him over there, in the pin-stripe suit?'

'Yeah.'

'That's James Fitzgerald Smythe. He was Eddie's QC at his trial and he also represented Frankie at hers. Speaks with a plum in his mouth, but I could listen to him all day – and night. Does it for me that posh accent, you know.'

Queenie chuckled. 'David's very handsome, the one chatting to Eddie and Vinny. He's Frankie Fraser's son, and that's his brother Patrick with him.'

'Mad Frankie Fraser?' Joycie enquired, craning her neck.

'Yeah. My Vinny knows him well an' all. Reckons he ain't mad, he's cute as a button. And see those two short old boys at the bar? That's the infamous Kelly brothers, Billy and Johnny. Been very loyal friends to my Vinny over the years, they have.'

Joyce nudged Queenie. 'You've not seen Gina yet, have you? You'll have to stand up and pretend you're looking for someone. She's sat on the sofa on the other side, in the left-hand corner. That's Eddie's two youngest kids with her, and the two women sat there are Ed's Auntie Joan and Sylvie. Sylvie was Harry Mitchell's lady friend.'

Queenie stood up and had a gander. Gina was extremely beautiful, but Queenie wasn't about to admit that. 'Known Joan for years I have, Joyce.'

'Do you want to go over and say hello to her? I'll save our seats.'

Queenie sat back down. 'Not really. Joanie's all right, but we've never been friends as such. I find her a bit of a cantankerous old cow, if you want the truth, but don't tell Eddie I said that.'

Joyce burst out laughing. 'Me too. She's never given me the time of day, the jumped-up old bat.'

Michael Butler wasn't in a partying mood. Katy had been spending his money like water again and issuing more threats. She'd now decided she wanted a brand-new

Mercedes and had told him that if he didn't buy her one, he could put the house up for sale, give her half the money and she would start afresh with their children in France.

'You all right, Michael? You look a bit glum stood there on your own,' Little Vinny said.

'Women trouble. Nothing new. How you doing, lad?'

'So-so. It's tough though, I miss Sammi and Oliver so bloody much. But I've been plodding on, taking Calum and Regan places to get our minds off things. We went go-karting yesterday. Loved it, the boys did. How's my granddad? Is he coming tonight?'

'Nah, he's not. Vinny didn't want him here and he didn't wanna come anyway. He's not been himself lately. Seems to have given up on life. Why don't you take the boys round to see him soon? I'm sure that would cheer him up. And, for the record, I think you're doing marvellously, Vin. Sammi-Lou is looking down with pride, I'm sure.'

'I'll give Granddad a ring tomorrow, sort something out. What do you think of Dad's new gaff then?'

Michael had been the first to jointly own a casino, and knew his brother had been peeved he wasn't included in the venture. 'I like this bar. Done it up nice, they have. As for the actual casino, I spend half my life in one. All look the same to me, they do, apart from that ropy one I visited up North once,' Michael chuckled. In fact, his brother's place did look top-drawer, but Michael wasn't about to admit that. Eddie and Vinny were both big-headed enough as it was, and if their heads swelled any more, they'd struggle to fit through the entrance.

Little Vinny looked over Michael's shoulder. Frankie had just walked in with the kids and a black girl. He had spoken to Frankie on the phone, but hadn't seen her since the night he'd all but slung her out of his home.

'Who's caught your attention?' Michael enquired.

'Only Frankie Mitchell. Me and her are good friends now. She wants to move over my way with her kids, and the guy I put some feelers out to rang me today.'

Michael glanced around, then turned back to his nephew. 'A word of warning – and don't jump down my throat. Make sure you keep it as just good friends. She's not only Eddie Mitchell's daughter, she's also damaged goods.'

Little Vinny looked at his uncle in disgust. 'As if I would look at her in any other way. Sammi-Lou was the love of my life. I couldn't even look at another woman. I can't believe you just said that, Michael.'

'I'm just watching your back for you. Frankie's a pretty girl and you're only human. You're also vulnerable, and I know how easy it is to fall into a relationship when the chips are down. I loved Bella, but moved straight in with Katy when we split up. And believe me, I've regretted that ever fucking since. Be careful, that's all I'm saying. Us Butler males are a good catch for any female.'

After arguing earlier with her nan, Ava Butler was now enjoying her company. Joycie was also hilarious, and Ava was thrilled her nan had made such a nice new friend. She'd been worried how her grandmother would cope after Auntie Viv's death, and it was as though Joycie had been sent to her as a kind of replacement. They even had the same humour, which was unusual, to say the least. 'Oh my God! What's that slapper doing here?' Ava exclaimed.

'Who?' Queenie asked, craning her neck.

'Oh, nobody. She's just some worthless tart who works at the club, but Anita's with her too. Dad must've invited them,' Ava replied, inwardly seething. Felicity Carter-Price had made it her mission to get those long nails of hers into her father from the second she arrived at the club, and Ava was annoyed her dad could not see that. Had he turned soft in his old age? Obviously not, by the way he was looking at the slapper, Ava thought crudely. She had never known him to have a proper girlfriend, and if he'd invited her here he must bloody like her, or worse still, something really was going on between them as she'd suspected all along.

Queenie craned her neck again. 'That young dark-haired one isn't your father's new girlfriend, is she, Ava?'

Ava shrugged. 'How should I know? Dad never tells me what he's up to these days. You should ask him yourself, Nan.'

'This is Babs, my best friend who I told you about,' Frankie Mitchell informed Little Vinny.

Little Vinny kissed Babs on the cheek, then turned to Frankie. 'I've got some good news for you. Finn's pal, the estate agent, rang me earlier. There's a property available to rent near me. Four bed, and he said it's decent inside. Modern, by all accounts. The owner is going abroad to work for a couple of years and you've got first shout on it.'

'That's amazing! Thanks so much. When can I view it?'

'Tomorrow, probably. Grant, the bloke's name is. I'll call him in the morning and give him your number. I dunno if I'll be able to view it with you, though. Meg and Millie Allen are popping over to see the boys.'

'That's not a problem. My dad is bound to want to view it with me, seeing as it'll be him paying for it. I'll text you once I've seen it, let you know the score. I can't wait to tell Georgie and Harry, they'll be thrilled. Thanks again, Vin. You're a true friend.'

Leaning against the bar surveying his domain, Vinny smiled as Billy Turner kicked off his set with Sinatra's 'Strangers in the Night'. Catching Felicity's eye, Vinny winked, then scowled as he clocked the drunken woman in the green dress walk up to Billy and dance idiotically right in front of him.

'Who's that woman, Dad?' Little Vinny asked.

'Not got a clue. But the fat cow won't be staying 'ere long.' Vinny loathed drunken women with a passion. They reminded him of his sister Brenda. Eddie had invited some blokes he didn't know and Vinny had a feeling the nuisance in the green dress must be with them. 'How's things with you? The boys doing OK?'

'Yeah. We're plodding along, as you do. I see you invited your new girlfriend. Are you and her common knowledge now then?'

'No. Only you and Michael know, so keep it schtum. What do you think of her?'

Little Vinny shrugged. 'Only said a few words to her at your place, but she seemed nice enough. Reminds me of Bella a bit, or shouldn't I say that?'

Vinny was over his fixation with Bella now, but that had been the attraction when he'd first seen Felicity. She looked very much like Bella had back in the eighties. 'Fliss is a better person than Bella. Very loyal, I feel. Trustworthy, like. Can't be having no wrong 'uns around me, boy.'

'I definitely recognize her, you know, but I can't think where from. Where does she live?'

'With me now, virtually. West London before that. The only place you would've seen her is in the Holborn club. Right, that's it. She's fucking going home, that pest,' Vinny spat. Billy was trying to sing Neil Diamond's 'Sweet Caroline' while the silly drunken tart was trying to grab the mike off him.

Vinny marched over to the woman and grabbed her roughly by the arm. 'Out you go, darlin'. A classy establishment this is. We don't entertain lushes, and this is also a private party.'

'Get off me. You're hurting me arm,' the woman yelled as Vinny dragged her towards the door.

'Oi! Leave my wife alone,' a stocky bald bloke roared.

'Crikey, Ed. There's trouble. No way would I have brought the children if I thought this would happen,' Gina said, trying to calm Rosie, who was now screaming.

Eddie leapt out of his seat and got in between Vinny and Tony Simmons. Tony had helped run his salvage yard for many years before he'd sold it.

'Bang out of order your mate is, Ed. My Lisa weren't doing sod-all wrong. It's a party and all she was doing was dancing and enjoying herself. Look what that bastard's done to her arm. It's bruised. You can see his finger marks, look,' Tony Simmons shouted.

Highly embarrassed as most of the guests were now looking their way, Eddie Mitchell hissed, 'Let's sort this out in the office.'

Once the office door was slammed, Vinny explained his version of events. 'Billy's trying to sing a song, Ed, and you got that lush trying to grab his mike, prancing around him like a fairy fucking elephant she was. It ain't on, mate. Family and friends we said we'd invite. Not drunken bastard nuisances.'

'Who you calling a fairy elephant, you cunt?' Lisa Simmons screamed.

Tony Simmons pointed at Vinny. He was a Dagenham lad through and through, wasn't scared of anyone. 'You better watch your mouth. That's my wife you're insulting. Ex-pro boxer me, ya know.'

Vinny Butler laughed out loud. 'This joker can't be a pal of yours, surely, Ed?'

'Just button it, Vin, for a minute.' Eddie turned back to his ex-employee. Tony was a good worker, but a notorious pisshead. He and his old woman were regulars in the Cross

Keys and Trades Hall and had definitely had a skinful before arriving. 'No hard feelings, Tone, but I think it's best if you and Lisa leave. There's little kids out there, mate, mine included. I don't want no grief. This is a quiet, social family gathering, so to speak.'

'But I haven't done anything wrong, neither has Lisa,' Tony Simmons argued.

'Yes, you have. You turned up pissed when I'd warned you on the phone to keep a lid on it tonight. Go on, off you go. I'll give you a bell in the week, OK?'

Tony Simmons respected Eddie Mitchell immensely, so did as he was asked. 'Come on, Lisa,' he urged, glaring at Vinny before shutting the door.

'What a pair of fucking numpties. Where did ya dig them up from?' Vinny asked cockily.

Eddie Mitchell's dark eyes clouded over. 'If you aren't careful, Vin, me and you are going to fall out before we've even had a chance to make a go of this business.'

'What you on about?'

Eddie was livid. Lisa's arm was badly marked and there was no need for that. 'Listen to me very carefully. You don't kick off in front of my wife and kids. Neither do you disrespect my friends or ex-employees. And I'm telling you now, if I ever see you manhandle a woman again, you'll have me to fucking answer to. Now, do we understand one another?'

Frankie Mitchell held her youngest son close to her chest. She'd barely seen Brett since Stuart had died as he'd opted to stay at her dad's. Gina had taken good care of him, and he loved spending time with Aaron and Rosie, yet she felt terribly guilty for neglecting him. But he seemed happier these days when he wasn't at home, and Frankie wanted him to be content.

'You're squashing me. Can I go now, Mum?' Brett Mitchell asked, squirming away from Frankie's tight grasp.

When her son ran back to the table where Gina was sitting, Frankie looked at Babs with tears in her eyes. 'We were always so close, me and Brett, until Georgie and Harry came home. I feel terrible for putting them first, but what else could I do?'

'You did the right thing, sweet child. Brett's doing just fine staying with Gina, and your Harry seems to be happier tonight too. He likes Little Vinny,' Babs replied.

Frankie looked up in amazement. Little Vinny had her son over his shoulder, and Harry was laughing like she'd never seen him laugh before. She walked over to them. 'What yous two up to?'

Little Vinny grinned. 'Your boy wants me to take him go-karting with Calum and Regan. I agreed, but only if he sings a song on our next karaoke night.'

'Put me down, you dinlo,' Harry giggled.

'Not until you promise to sing,' Little Vinny reiterated, much to Georgie, Calum and Regan's amusement, who were egging him on.

'OK. I'll sing, but only if you promise to take me go-karting soon,' Harry yelled as he was swung around in the air once again.

Frankie walked back over to the table where Babs was sitting. 'He's brilliant with the kids, you know. They seem to get him much more than they ever did Stuart – or me, to be truthful.'

Babs squeezed her pal's hand. 'It's great if you move home and have Little Vinny to help you with the kids. But do be careful, sweet child. You're vulnerable at present.'

Frankie Mitchell looked at her pal in horror. 'What do you mean, exactly? I don't fancy him, if that's what you think.'

'Of course I don't think that. I know how much you loved Stuart. But I was vulnerable once myself, and I know how easy it is to fall in love when you've suffered heartbreak. I just don't want you to make the same mistakes as me. And Little Vinny, babe, he has evil eyes. My mamma told me you see a man's soul through the eyes, and he has no soul, trust me.'

Queenie Butler had craned her neck so much during the course of the evening she now felt like an ostrich.

'Who you looking at now?' Joycie asked.

'That tart! It's definitely her he's knocking off, the dark-haired one. Ava, Ava!' Queenie yelled.

'Yes, Nan.'

'Those two women who work for your dad, what does the dark-haired one do?' Queenie was extremely astute and even though her son had spent very little time in either woman's company, she'd seen the knowing looks between them and Vinny's hand placed tenderly on her lower back.

'She was a dancer when she turned up earlier in the year. Not sure if she works there at all now. I haven't seen her recently.'

Queenie pursed her lips. 'So in other words, she's nothing more than a whore who flashes her lils for a living. No way will your father be getting involved with that. Over my dead body.'

Vinny Butler necked his Scotch in one, then asked for another refill. Eddie was standing next to him, talking to Flatnose Freddie, and Vinny glared at the back of his head. Eddie had spoken to him like a naughty schoolboy earlier and Vinny was none too impressed. Who the fuck did Mitchell think he was? The local headmaster?

'Eddie, can you come over here, please?' Joycie shouted

out. 'Can you call him, Queen? Your voice is louder than mine.'

'He's already acknowledged you. Said he'll be over in a bit. Give the man a chance, Joyce,' Queenie chuckled. 'And your voice is far bleedin' louder than mine. It's like a foghorn.'

'Most of those handsome friends of Eddie's and Vinny's have gone next door now. Don't want to be around little 'uns all night, do they?' Joyce said, stretching her neck. The children weren't allowed in the actual casino, so there were mainly women and kids left in the Piano Bar now. 'Your Michael's still in here though, and Little Vinny. Any of Michael's kids here tonight, Queen?'

'No. I don't see much of Michael's kids lately. Nor Michael, for that matter. Too busy with that Italian slapper to visit his poor old mum,' Queenie replied bitterly.

'What about Antonio? Is he here?'

'Goodness, no. Vinny wouldn't want him here. Kid looks like one of those poll-tax rioters. You know what I mean: all ripped jeans and long greasy hair – one of them tree-hugging types. Makes me shudder. My Vinny has worn a suit every day for as long as I can remember. How can his son turn out so bloody different?'

'That's the youth of today for you. Look at the way Georgie dresses. She's only bloody thirteen and looks like a tart. I've told Frankie what I think, but she's too worried about upsetting the child. Horrible kids, they are, Queen. Especially Harry. I cannot see one part of my Jessica in either. Brett's a little star, though, bless him. My Jess would've loved him.'

'Do you see a lot of Frankie and Joey? Apart from Ava and Little Vinny, none of my grandchildren bother ringing me now.'

'I hear from Joey every day – more than once, most days.

He's a good boy, Queen. Heart of gold, that lad's got. I know I shouldn't say it, but he's always been my favourite. Frankie's been a cowson over the years; put my Jess and Eddie through hell, she did. Let's be honest, Jessica would still be alive if it wasn't for that little madam taking up with Jed O'Hara. Shame Joey won't ever be able to have kids. He'd give me grandchildren to be proud of, and he'd make a fantastic father.'

'No reason he can't. Not long before my Vivvy died we watched a documentary together on one of them Sky channels. It was about two gay men and they'd both had a child with the same woman. "Surrogate mothers" they call themselves – and she weren't a lesbian either. Had a husband and kids of her own.'

'Really? That's wonderful! I'll have a word with—'

Eddie interrupted Joycie mid-sentence. 'What can I do for my two favourite ladies then?'

'Sack the pianist, for a start,' Joyce said bluntly. Billy had finished his set and his replacement was sod-all to shout home about. 'Very boring, listening to that crap for hours on end. Me and Queenie reckon you should hold a karaoke night once a week. That'll bring in the customers more than old miserable guts over there. Hardly Mrs Mills, is he?'

When Queenie put her two-penn'orth in, Eddie smiled and nodded in all the appropriate places. Joyce and Queenie weren't quite the clientele he and Vinny had in mind.

'Joey, there you are! Where you been? Come and say hello to Queenie.' Joyce stood up and grabbed her grandson's arm. 'Queenie, this is Joey, my gay grandson. And this is his homosexual boyfriend, Dominic.'

Seeing the looks of embarrassment on Joey and Dom's faces, Eddie managed to stifle his laughter until he'd walked away.

*

After getting some fresh air, Vinny Butler sauntered back into the Piano Bar like he owned it – which he did, of course. Eddie was trying to be nice to him now, but Vinny was still peeved and had been knocking the Scotch back like there was no tomorrow. 'Not now, sweetheart. My mum and Ava are giving me the evil eye,' he whispered in Felicity's ear.

'Oh, for goodness' sake, Vinny. This is getting slightly ridiculous. You've barely said a word to me all evening. Do your family have some kind of hold over you?'

Before Vinny had a chance to answer, his mother marched over with a face like thunder. 'So I take it you're the slapper he's been so cagey about? No wonder! An ex-stripper, how very classy. Spent a lot on you, has he? Do you hold your hand out while giving him a private dance?'

Outraged, Felicity knew she had to stand her ground. 'I beg your pardon. For your information, I am very much in love with your son, Mrs Butler. And I can assure you I do not ask Vinny to buy me anything. I am quite capable of supporting myself.'

'Yeah, by flashing your noonie to all and sundry. What a catch you are!'

Vinny wished the floor would open up and swallow him. His mother was bang out of order and he'd already lost face once this evening. Felicity was his woman, therefore he had to stick up for her. 'That's enough now, Mother. Go in the casino for a bit, eh, Fliss?' he urged his girlfriend.

'Fliss! What type of name is that? Oh, let me guess, a fake one – like her tits, nails and eyelashes.'

Felicity was livid. 'Who the hell do you think you are talking to?'

'You, ya slutbag.' Turning to her son, Queenie poked him hard in the chest. 'As for you, you truly disgust me. Did you not give a thought to your daughter or son when you started shoving your John Thomas up that thing? Or

Michael? She looks a bit like Bella – that the attraction in the first place was it, dear?'

Red-faced, Vinny yelled, 'That is below the belt, Mother. You owe Fliss an apology. Go on, fucking apologize.'

Lifting her glass, Queenie slung the contents in Felicity's face. 'That's the only apology she's getting off me. As for you, it's abnormal, being with a girl that young. She isn't much older than Ava. It's sick, and you're a pervert.'

The bar was now so silent a pin could be heard dropping. 'How dare you fucking speak to me like that?' Vinny bellowed and, doing the unthinkable, he slapped his beloved mother's face.

Michael grabbed hold of his brother, and with the help of Little Vinny dragged him away.

Eddie Mitchell emerged from the gents' in time to see the back end of the chaos. 'Whatever's going on?' he asked his son Gary.

'It's all kicking off between Queenie and Vinny. Gina's taken the kids outside. What a fucking palaver, eh?'

'That's me and you finished. You're no son of mine. Vivvy was right about you all along. What type of man hits the woman who gave birth to him? I never want to see you again,' Queenie screamed, holding the side of her face. To say she was shocked was putting it mildly. Never had any of her sons raised a hand to her in the past. They wouldn't dare.

'Get Queenie a brandy, Ed,' Joyce shouted out. 'Come on, love, let's sit you down,' she said, leading her friend back to the sofa.

Queenie was crying with rage. 'The things I've done for him, Joycie. Stuck by him through thick and thin and this is the thanks I get. I'm disowning him now. He can go to fucking hell for all I care. How dare he put that hussy's feelings before mine? Never will he darken my doorstep again, mate. Not on your nelly. I'll chop his bastard hands off if he has the cheek to ring my bell. My son, the cunt,' Queenie spat. Not only furious, she was also embarrassed. How dare Vinny treat her with such a lack of respect in front of the Mitchells and all their guests? People didn't just refer to her as 'Queen', she was treated as one too. How the hell was she ever meant to live this down? Her crown had well and truly slipped this evening.

As people started making excuses and leaving, Eddie Mitchell was thoroughly pissed off. Nobody wanted to be part of a Butler falling out. Even Gina had gone home with the kids.

Gary Mitchell walked up to the bar. 'I don't wanna say I told you so, but I did try and warn you, eh?' he reminded his father. Gary had never been a fan of Vinny Butler. He saw him as a loose cannon, and much preferred Michael. Yet his dad had chosen to ignore his concerns. 'You OK?'

'Nah, I'm not fucking OK, to be honest, son. Tonight's been a disaster. Butler better up his game, pronto. 'Cause I'm telling you now, he ever scares or upsets my wife and little 'uns again, I swear on my dear old mum's grave, he's a dead man walking.'

CHAPTER TWELVE

'Georgie, Harry, you're getting in the way down here. Go upstairs and unpack the boxes in your bedrooms, please. And you, Brett, there's a good boy.' Frankie Mitchell had loved the new house on sight, but had to endure a two-week wait before she could move in. It was detached, modern and, unlike the prison she'd just moved out of, had a good feel about it. It also held no memories of Stuart. Frankie only hoped she wouldn't think she heard his footsteps or his key opening the front door any more.

'Where do you want the sofa, Frankie?' Eddie Mitchell asked. He'd agreed to pay the lease up on her old gaff and fork out for the new one on one condition: that Brett live there too. It really wasn't fair on Gina for Brett to be living with them all the time, and a lad his age needed his mother.

Standing at the top of the stairs grinning like a buffoon was Harry O'Hara. 'There's a good boy,' he said, mimicking his mother's annoying voice.

Avoiding eye contact with his brother, Brett walked into his new bedroom and obeyed his mum's orders. Harry terrified him, so much so, he was shaking. Following Brett, Harry snatched a handful of his games out of the box. 'What's these then? They for your computer?'

'No. I play them on my TV.'

'Do you really? Don't you mean you *used* to play them on your TV?' Harry chuckled, dropping one of the games on the floor and stamping on it.

Determined not to let Harry see his lip tremble, Brett bit on it hard.

'Whoops,' Harry said, as he crushed another game.

Determined not to cry or respond, Brett said a silent prayer that his granddad and Gina would let him live with them again soon.

Harry waved another game in the air.

'Noooo! Not that one. That's my *Football Manager*. Don't smash it, Harry. Please.'

'My dad and granddad reckons football is a pansy's game. I'll be doing you a favour getting rid of it,' Harry taunted.

Georgie poked her head round the door. 'What you doing, Harry?'

'Whoops,' Harry said, crushing the *Football Manager* game under his right foot.

'Stop it. Leave him alone,' Georgie ordered.

'Make me. I'm only having a laugh.'

'He's only a little boy. If you wanna pick on someone, pick on someone your own age.'

'You've changed your tune. You used to find it funny,' Harry argued.

'No I never! Harry, I meant what I said,' Georgie replied sternly when her brother picked up another game. 'Put that back in the box, otherwise I swear I'll go downstairs and tell Mum and Granddad what you're doing.'

'You rat. Changing into a gorger, you are. Travellers don't grass,' Harry spat, pushing past his sister and storming out of the room.

The tears were streaming down Brett's face, so Georgie

sat next to him on the bed. Unlike Harry, Brett had the same colour hair as her, and his eyes were big and brown. 'Harry doesn't mean it, you know. He's just angry and he's missing our little sister. It's her birthday today.'

Brett's eyes widened. He didn't really know how to take Georgie. Sometimes she was nice to him, but not always. 'I didn't know you had a little sister. Is she my sister too?' he asked, genuinely interested.

'Yeah, she is. She's your half-sister too. You've got the same dad.'

'What's her name?'

'Shelby.'

'How old is she?'

'Two today.'

'What's my dad like, Georgie? My mum doesn't like me talking about him. Do you think he'd like me?'

Georgie stared into Brett's innocent eyes and for the first time since she'd met him, felt a sisterly connection towards the boy. ''Course he would. He'd love you just as much as me and Harry. Take no notice of what Mum says. Our dad's a good man. He's always singing and mucking about and stuff. I really miss him.'

'Do you think I will be able to meet him one day?'

'Hopefully. I don't know. I think he might be dead.'

When Brett's eyes filled with tears again, Georgie hugged him. 'I didn't mean that, our dad's not dead. But Harry will be if you tell your granddad what he did to your games. I'll do a deal with ya. You tell your mum them games got smashed in the move, and I'll watch your back from now on. If Harry does anything bad to you at all, you come find me in future, OK?'

Feeling relieved, Brett smiled. 'OK. Thank you, Georgie.'

*

Queenie Butler was rather bemused. 'Is it real? Do they actually all work in that office?'

'I thought that at first too. No, it's a piss-take, Queen. He's ever so funny, David Brent. The things he comes out with.' Joey and Dominic had been raving about a new TV programme called *The Office* and had lent Joycie a video tape of it.

'I don't think I understand it. Can we watch *Loose Women* instead?' Queenie asked. She saw Joyce most days now. They'd go shopping together once or twice a week; have a pub lunch on occasions, or just pop round one another's. Nobody could ever replace Vivian, but spending time with Joyce was certainly something Queenie looked forward to on a daily basis. Even if it was only for a few hours, it broke up the day.

Stanley poked his head around the lounge door. 'Don't mind if I pop out for a couple of pints with Jock, do you, love?'

'Depends whether you've put that new mirror up in the bathroom and mended that cupboard door, Stanley? Oh, and that dripping tap. Have you done all your jobs?'

'Cupboard and mirror are sorted, but I'm going to have to get Jock to have a look at that tap. I'm no plumber, Joycie.'

Joyce winked at Queenie. 'Bet you sorted that old tart Pat the Pigeon's pipes out though, didn't you? I haven't forgotten about your betrayal, Stanley, you still owe me an awful amount for allowing you to live under my roof again. Which is why I think you should pop to the pie-and-mash shop in Dagenham before you come home. I'll have my usual and you can get Queenie the same.'

'Hook-nosed old witch,' Stanley mumbled, shutting the door. He then grinned. Ever since Queenie had appeared on the scene he was allowed out far more than before.

Most lunchtimes he now spent in the Working Men's Club and the bookies. That suited him just fine.

'You and him do make me laugh.' Queenie chuckled.

'Men need to be kept in check, Queen. Whoever said it was a man's world never met me.'

'I wonder if that young prostitute keeps my Vinny in check?' Queenie said, her tone one of bitterness.

Knowing what a sore subject Vinny was at present, Joyce wouldn't mention him unless her friend did first. 'Any more news, love?'

Three days after he'd slapped her, Queenie had received a massive bouquet with a card.

Dearest Mum,

I am so sorry for lashing out at you as I did. I was drunk and out of order. But some of the things you said hurt me deeply. We need to both apologize for our actions and move on. Ring me if you want to sort this mess out. If not, I'll continue paying the rent on your new bungalow, but will leave you be in future. I love you dearly and always will. But I'm a grown man and will not be dictated to by you or anybody else over who I see or the way I live my life.

Hope to hear from you soon.
All my love,
Vinny xxx

Queenie had rung the florist up immediately and paid for the flowers to be returned to the sender. 'Nope. Not heard another word. He's obviously besotted with that silly young tart to have clumped me in the first place. Let him get on with it. Like they say, "There's no fool like an old fool", eh?'

'Christmas is only round the corner now. You're bound to hear from him before then. I take it you usually spend Christmas with Vinny?'

'Always. The only time we've ever been apart was when he was locked up. But even then, he'd ring me first thing Christmas morning. No way am I apologizing, Joycie. Not a cat in hell's chance. I mean, tell me the truth, do you think I said anything that bad?'

'Not really, but perhaps you should have left out the "pervert". I'm sure my Raymond would've flipped an' all if I'd said that in front of all his pals.'

'I was only saying what everybody else must be bloody thinking. It's ridiculous, a man of his age hooking up with her. And she's a stripper, don't forget. She's making him a laughing stock, Joycie.'

Joyce said no more.

Eddie Mitchell counted the previous evening's takings, then put them in the safe. The actual casino was doing OK, but the Piano Bar was empty most nights.

'All right, Ed? Got here as quick as I could. Traffic is chocka on the A13. Been an accident on the Barking flyover. Did Frankie's move go OK?' Vinny asked. He and Eddie had sat down and had a heart to heart after the fiasco of their grand opening. Both had been peeved over certain issues, so they'd said their piece and now moved on.

'Yeah. She was in there before lunchtime. Drove me up the wall though. "Dad, can you put this here? No, not there, it doesn't look right. Can we move it over there instead?" Daughters are a pain, mate. Hopefully I'll be on a Zimmer frame by the time Rosie moves out. Let some other bastard have the joy.'

Vinny had sworn to Eddie there'd be no more dramas. He'd been as good as gold since the opening night and there'd been no more nasty deliveries, so Eddie was willing to give his pal the benefit of the doubt, for now at least.

'What did the bar take last night?' Vinny asked.

'Sixty-eight poxy quid and thirty-eight crappy pence, to be exact. There was only two customers in all night. I reckon we're gonna have to look at waiving the membership fee until a later date, Vin. And I think Joycie and your mum might've been right about the pianist. Perhaps we should hire one of these Rat-Pack type singers? Bit of Sinatra, Dean Martin, stuff like that. Goes with our theme and what we're aiming for.'

'Yeah, I like that idea. Leave it with me. I think I might know just the geezer, looks the part an' all. As for the membership fee, why don't we allow five free visits and after that they have to pay the fee? Your Joey's a wizard with computers. He can list their names and he'll know when it's time for them to cough up.'

'Or, why don't we just allow it to be free entry until, say, March? The dudes who have already paid the fee, we'll tell them that now starts from March for one year. Everybody's happy then.'

Vinny smiled. He'd known Ed had the hump with him, and was pleased they'd settled their differences. 'Whatever you choose is fine by me, mate.'

Michael Butler handed his mother a small card. He'd had enough of being her chauffeur.

'What's that?' Queenie asked.

'It's the number of the cab firm I've set up an account for you with. They've promised to put you before all other customers if they're busy.'

'But I don't like using cabs, you know I don't.'

'And I have a business to run, Mum, and so does Little Vinny. We can't be at your beck and call for lifts on a daily basis. I've checked out the cab firm and the guvnor seems proper. Said he'll make sure he sends you a sensible driver, and I'll be settling the bill once a month.'

Queenie shook her head profusely. 'Thanks, but no thanks. No way am I getting in a car with a strange man and being taken down country lanes. Say he attacks me like Vivvy was attacked? And most drivers these days don't even speak a word of bleedin' English.'

Michael sighed. He wished Vinny and his mother would make up soon, because ever since they'd fallen out she'd been driving him up the bloody wall. His life wasn't great at the moment as it was. His relationship with Bella was rocky due to his inability to forget the past. As for Katy, she was the biggest bugbear he'd ever had the misfortune of meeting.

'Suppose I'll just have to stay indoors from now on if nobody is willing to pick me up. I always said if I became a nuisance in my old age I'd rather not be here.' Queenie was in her hard-done-by mode now.

'I give up, I really do,' Michael hissed.

'No need to be sharp with me, is there? I just want to feel safe, that's all. Can you blame me after what happened to your Auntie Viv? Isn't there a posh type of private hire firm that use nice cars like you and your brother drive? If it's a problem for you, money-wise, I'll be happy to help out via my pension.'

Spotting a clump of trees on his left, big oak ones, Michael imagined how good it would feel if he slammed his foot on the brake and rammed his mother straight into the lot of them.

'I'm starving, Mum. How long are they gonna be?' Georgie O'Hara asked.

Little Vinny had called Frankie earlier, said he would bring the boys round and a Chinese takeaway.

'They shouldn't be long now, love. I can do you a slice of toast, if you want?'

'Don't eat toast, Georgie. I once did, then I couldn't eat any of my dinner at all.'

Georgie laughed and ruffled Brett's hair. 'That's 'cause you're a dinlo and you scoffed too much.'

Watching her daughter and youngest son interact properly for the first time filled Frankie's heart with joy. It also gave her hope for the future. 'What's Harry doing upstairs?'

Harry was in fact sulking because she'd told him off earlier, but Georgie was no snitch. 'He's a bit sad today. It's our little sister's birthday and he misses her.'

'She's my sister too and her name's Shelby,' Brett added proudly.

'Go wash your hands and face, Brett. And change that sweatshirt too, there's a mark on the sleeve.'

Waiting until her son had left the room, Frankie turned to Georgie. 'I'd rather you not tell him too much, love. It's all very confusing for him. Unlike you and Harry, Brett's still young, and he's fragile.'

'That's only 'cause you made him that way. You treat him like he's about three. You're not doing him any favours, ya know. Brett has every right to know about his family, and that includes our dad.'

The doorbell saved Frankie from having to conjure up a polite reply. 'Answer that, Georgie.'

'Dad ordered half the shop,' Calum said, as he and Regan put four bags of food on the kitchen counter.

Little Vinny handed Frankie a huge potted plant. 'A moving-in present. My nan helped me choose it. She reckons it'll bring you good luck.'

'That'd make a nice change. Thanks, Vin. It's lovely.'

Having run down the stairs the second he heard the

doorbell, Harry's first question was: 'Have you booked to take us go-karting yet, Vinny?'

Little Vinny slung a casual arm around Harry's shoulders. The lad was a lost soul and his anger and attitude reminded Little Vinny of himself once upon a time. 'Nope. But providing you sing tonight like you promised, I'll book it first thing in the morning.'

'We ain't got nothing to sing on 'ere. So you're out of luck.'

'Oh yes we have. Karaoke equipment is in the car. A deal's a deal, lad.'

When Little Vinny grabbed him in a headlock, Harry tried to fight his way out of it like his dad had taught him. 'All right. Let me go. I'll sing,' he chuckled.

Frankie smiled as a full-on play-fight ensued between her son and Little Vinny. That smile was soon wiped off her face though when Harry said, 'You're OK, you are, Vin. You remind me a bit of my dad.'

Eddie Mitchell spotted Charlie Price immediately. A stocky, grey-haired man with a boxer's nose and one of the loudest voices Eddie had ever come across, he wasn't exactly hard to miss.

'Eddie, how you doing, lad?' Charlie asked, treating his pal to a handshake and slap on the back at the same time.

'Yeah, all good my end, mate. I wish I knew your secret though. Jesus wept! You don't look a day older than when I last saw you in the slammer.'

Charlie chuckled. He'd served an eighteen-year stretch for a gold bullion robbery and within months of his release had met and married a young lady from Thailand. 'My Mayura keeps me youthful. Got our third child on the way now, and we're still at it every night. Nothing wrong with my fiddle. It still plays a good tune.'

Eddie laughed. Charlie was in his seventies now, but seriously did not look a day over fifty-five. 'So what you doing back in England then? You once told me you'd never venture over 'ere again.' Charlie had been living on the Costa del Sol ever since the authorities had returned his passport.

'It's only a flying visit. I'm travelling back on Friday. Had a funeral to attend and a bit of business to sort out, you know how it is. I've heard lots about your new venture. The Casino and Piano Bar, very nice. How's it going? Not the usual type of establishment you'd spot along the A13.'

'It's early days. The Casino's doing fairly well, but the Piano Bar hasn't quite taken off like we'd hoped it would. We've decided to waive the membership fee for the time being. Got to get the balance right, ain't ya?'

'I take it "we" is you and Vinny Butler?'

'Yeah, who else?'

Charlie Price shook his head knowingly. 'I like you, Ed, you know I do, which is why I wanted to see you today. Hate to tell you this, but you've dropped a massive clanger going into business with Vinny. Hated, he is. Most people only give him the time of day because they fear him. Rumour has it Vinny Butler killed his ex so he could get custody of his daughter. Paid someone to force her off the road – she was in the car with her fiancé and his young son at the time. The boy was the only one survived – he's backwards now, by all accounts. Always pays somebody else to do his dirty work. The man has the scruples of an alley cat. Men like us don't toy with the lives of women and kiddies, Ed. We know right from wrong.'

'Yeah, yeah, yeah. Listen, Charlie, I've heard these rumours, but rumours is all they are. Vinny's no angel, he admits that himself, but he wouldn't kill a woman or harm a child. I went into this venture after a lot of deliberation, with my eyes open wide. I'm like you, old school, never intentionally would I harm a hair on any kiddie or female's head. If I thought for one minute that Vinny Butler was capable of what you're saying, I'd string him up by the bollocks myself.'

'You're turning a blind eye, Ed. Listen to me, back in the sixties, an old boy called Jack ran the café in the Whitechapel Road. His son weren't the full shilling and was found weighted down at the bottom of the Thames. And there was—'

Eddie held his hands up. If there was one thing he hated, it was people questioning his judgement. He was well aware Vinny wasn't Prince Charming. 'Enough's enough, Charlie. I'm not interested in forty-year-old fucking rumours. Look, I'm no mug, mate. Do you honestly think I'd have gone into business with Vinny if I'd thought he couldn't be trusted?'

'No. Which is why I decided to give you the heads-up. Vinny Butler is a twenty-four-carat-gold cunt, and no way is your Piano Bar gonna be a big success while you're in business with him. Do yourself a favour and cut your losses while you still can, Ed. If you don't, believe me, you'll live to regret it. Trouble follows Butler around like a puppy follows its mother.'

PART TWO

'Revenge may be wicked, but it's natural'

William Makepeace Thackeray

CHAPTER THIRTEEN

Hearing the enormous prison gates slam shut, Jamie Preston breathed deeply and took a moment to collect his thoughts. Twenty-one years was an awful long time to be incarcerated for, and there had been days when he'd thought this moment would never come.

It had been 1980 when Molly Butler's body was discovered in a shallow grave not far from Hackney Marshes. Jamie had never even visited that particular area, although he planned to now as it would hopefully bring him some form of closure. He had a lot of places to visit and people to see before he would reach that light at the end of a tunnel.

Jamie had been fourteen years old at the time. A wet-behind-the ears teenager who'd thought he was being clever, leading the police up the garden path, ringing them from random phone boxes pretending he had abducted Molly Butler. Every single day since he'd regretted his own stupidity. When witnesses came forward to say he'd been spotted ripping down the 'MISSING' posters and loitering outside the Butlers' club in Whitechapel on the day Molly had gone AWOL, it was the final nail in his coffin. The press had been all over the story like a rash and Jamie had cut the articles out and idiotically hidden them in his bedroom. At the time he'd proclaimed his innocence, but bar his nan, nobody had believed him. So he'd become the Old Bill's scapegoat whilst Molly's real killer roamed the streets, free as a bird.

Jamie sparked up a cigarette. When he was little he drove his mum mad, forever asking about the father he'd never seen. It was tough growing up without a dad, but the bitterest pill to swallow came when his mother finally told him, 'No, you bloody can't see your dad – because he never fucking wanted you, OK? Albie Butler is your father, and your so-called half-brothers Vinny and Roy turned up at my door with the money for your abortion. Vinny vowed that if I didn't get rid of you, he'd kick you out of my stomach himself. That's why we moved miles away. Happy now, are you? Because that's the truth.'

The truth had played havoc with Jamie's immature mind, even more so when he'd moved in with his nan, who lived in the East End back then. He'd hung around Whitechapel hoping to catch glimpses of the family who loathed him so much they'd wanted him dead – and found himself loathing them just as much. That's why he'd led the police up the garden path: a form of childish payback for Vinny wanting him dead.

'Over 'ere. Your carriage awaits,' a voice bellowed. Glen Harper was leaning against a white limousine.

Cursing under his breath, Jamie walked towards the vehicle. He'd told Glen he wanted no fuss. A decent meal and a visit to his nan's grave was all he'd hoped was on the agenda.

'Got some proper totty for you, lad. Have a butcher's,' Glen laughed, hugging his ex-cellmate. Because of the nature of the crime he'd been accused of, Jamie had gone through a torrid time in prison. He had a scar that ran in a straight line from his right ear to his mouth to prove it. But Glen had taken him under his wing when he'd arrived in Chelmsford, battered and bruised. Jamie was like the son Glen had never had and he'd never had any doubt the lad was innocent.

'For Christ's sake, Glen. I can't get in there.' Jamie was horrified. Not only was there music blaring out the limo, there were also four topless dolly birds sprawled across the back seats.

'Hop in and enjoy. You've missed out on life and you gotta lot of making up to do. Take your pick of the crumpet – I'm easy,' Glen chuckled.

Jamie could feel his hands shaking. Thanks to the way his life had turned out, he was still a bloody virgin.

'I spoke to that tutor, Frankie. She's agreed to teach Georgie and Harry too, for an extra one an' half a week. Will your dad pay that?'

'He'll have to. I had that woman round from social services again just before we moved, and she told me that the children must have some form of education. Will the tutor come here? Only I think Georgie and Harry would be better behaved at yours, especially if Regan's having lessons too.'

'Yeah, they can come to mine. Finn's happy to hold the fort for the time being and some of our work can be done from home anyway, which I'll tackle. If you're at a loose end and wanna come with Georgie and Harry, feel free. I've already bought a new computer for the study, which is where they'll be working. The tutor said she had the basic books that Georgie and Harry will need to start with.' Little Vinny liked spending time with Frankie. She was the only one who truly understood what he was going through. He could also tell she was struggling at the moment, which was why he was helping out. Keeping himself busy helped him sleep at night and he was rather enjoying the role of Good Samaritan. He couldn't change the past but being kind to others made him feel like a better person.

'Thanks. That sounds perfect. Harry hasn't stopped talking about go-karting, so Georgie reckons.'

'Well, the offer's still there if you want to come with us tomorrow. Let us know if you change your mind.'

'I won't come, but thanks anyway. Brett deserves to be spoiled and it's been ages since I spent a day with him alone.'

'No probs. Gotta go now. Landline's ringing.'

Frankie stared at the framed photo of Stuart. He'd loved her deeply, and Brett too, but even though he'd moved in with her, he hadn't had much patience with Georgie and Harry. Not like Little Vinny, who was marvellous with her children. Suddenly feeling awful for comparing her wonderful dead fiancé to a man she hadn't even known long, tears of guilt streamed down Frankie's face.

'How'd it go with your pal last night?' Vinny Butler asked Eddie Mitchell.

'Yeah, OK. I didn't stay out long, was knackered.'

Vinny wasn't silly. Ed had given him the cold shoulder this morning. 'Look, there's something I should've told you. We said no skeletons, didn't we? Well, me and your mate Pricey have history. I did a business deal with him donkey's years ago that went Pete Tong, and he blamed me 'cause he lost a few quid. He's never liked me since and, to be honest, I'm not a fan of his either. Charlie used to be partners in crime with Alfie Duggan when I first came on the scene. I had a tear up one night with Duggan in the London Hospital Tavern. Smashed seven bells out of him, and his face was never quite the same again. Spent a long while in hospital, he did. His jaw was operated on. So whatever bullshit Pricey has filled your head with, just take it with a pinch of salt, eh?'

Eddie was no grass. 'If you want the truth, your name didn't even crop up,' he lied. 'The world don't revolve around you, Vinny.'

An hour ago, Jamie Preston had never been laid, never tasted champagne or snorted cocaine. Now he'd done all three.

'Nah. Enough, love,' Jamie said, pushing the little blonde's hand away from his crotch.

Glen chucked a wrap Jamie's way. 'Shove some more of that up your bugle. Proper bit of gear, that is.'

Aware that two of the birds were now performing a lesbian act, Jamie chose to look out of the window. Instead of making him feel good, the drugs and alcohol had made him feel sick and dizzy. 'Can we turn that crap music down? I can't hear meself think.'

Glen put his todger away, moved next to Jamie and put an arm around his shoulders. 'Everything seems different to you, eh? Natural, that. Gonna take you a while to adjust.'

Jamie thought of Little Vinny. He knew without a doubt that he and Ben Bloggs were responsible for Molly's death. That's why Bloggs had hung himself on the day of Molly's funeral. There was no other explanation. 'Clearing my name is all I want, Glen. And revenge, served fucking cold.'

'Mum, Calum and Regan are going shopping in Romford. Can me and Harry go with them?' Georgie O'Hara asked hopefully.

Frankie knew Romford well. Her and Joey used to hang out there sometimes when they were teenagers and she knew it had a train station and many bus routes. 'No. You can't go there, love, but you can go over the park.' The security guys that had been paid to keep an eye on her kids were now redundant, and as always Frankie was concerned Georgie and Harry might try to do a runner.

'Please, Mum. Calum said Romford isn't far and his dad is going to drop us off and pick us up,' Georgie pleaded.

'Don't fucking beg her. She's a liar. She promised us when we moved we wouldn't be treated like prisoners no more, but she still won't let us do anything,' Harry yelled.

'I swear on my little sister Shelby's life, we won't run away,' Georgie added.

Frankie took the phone into another room to call Little Vinny, then returned to the kitchen with her purse in her hand. 'Give half of that to Harry and make sure you get yourselves something to eat while in Romford. It'll save me cooking tonight,' she told her daughter.

Grinning from ear to ear, Georgie snatched at the twenty-pound note, then ran upstairs to tart herself up for Regan. He still wasn't taking much notice of her, but she was determined he would, eventually.

It had been Vinny's idea to meet up town for a spot of lunch and Michael Butler was not in the best of moods. 'So what's this all about then? Making up with Mother, I hope, only she's driving me round the bastard twist.'

'Chill, Michael. Can't a man just treat his brother to lunch?'

'There is usually a reason with you though, Vin,' Michael hissed. Everything about their parents' welfare had been left to him lately and he was sick to the back teeth of it. Their father was drinking himself to death before his very eyes, and Michael had enough on his plate making regular trips to Barking to check on him without being at their mother's beck and call as well.

'Jesus! What's up with you? Get out the wrong side of the bed this morning?'

'No. I'm just sick of carrying the can.'

'Good afternoon, gentlemen. Soup of the day is grouse and the speciality of the day is roast goose,' the waiter said, handing Vinny and Michael a menu. 'Would you like to see the wine list? Or can I get you something else?'

Looking at his brother's miserable face, Vinny said, 'Some happy pills wouldn't go amiss, mate.'

After virtually being held captive for months, Georgie and Harry were thoroughly enjoying their new-found freedom. 'Look what I got,' Georgie crowed, showing off a big pair of hoop earrings, edged with diamantés.

'Where d'ya get 'em from?' Harry asked.

'I chored 'em from Miss Selfridge,' Georgie bragged, hoping to impress Regan.

'Don't be thieving around me. I'll be sent back inside if you get caught. I ain't allowed to get in any trouble,' Regan spat.

'Take no notice of him. He's the biggest thief going,' Calum whispered in Georgie's ear.

Georgie smiled. It was obvious Calum was totally besotted with her. 'You got any money on you?'

'Yeah, why?'

'Because me and Harry are potless. My mum's too scared to give us any in case we run off,' Georgie replied, smirking at Harry. Her brother had told her to save the twenty quid their mother had given them as they would need it when they escaped.

'What do you want? Something to eat?' Calum asked.

'Yeah, but some cash would be nice too. I don't want to get Regan into trouble by choring anything else.'

Calum handed Georgie a fiver. 'I'll give you some more later in the week.'

Georgie stood on tiptoes and planted a kiss on Calum's cheek. 'Thanks. You're cool, you are.'

'Look, Georgie. Over there,' Harry pointed. He'd spotted two travelling women selling lucky heather. 'Go speak to them. They might know Dad and Granddad,' he urged.

'I'm starving. Need to eat right now,' Regan complained.

Not wanting to upset the aloof lad she secretly fancied, Georgie grabbed Harry's arm. 'Let's ask them after we've eaten. You know what travelling women are like, they talk for England.'

Back at the restaurant, Michael Butler was pouring his heart out. 'Mum's definitely got worse since Auntie Viv died. Chas and Dave's "Ain't No Pleasin' You" could've been written for her. Her moaning is constant. She won't admit it, but I know she's missing you badly, Vin.'

'I miss her too, Michael, very much. But, I have to stick to my guns on this one. Can you imagine how embarrassing that was for me at the opening of my casino? There was no fucking need to mug me off like that. I've fallen over backwards my whole life for that woman, and that's the thanks I get.'

'I get what you're saying. Mum was out of order, but you know what she's like, Vin. No way is she going to apologize. The way I see it, Mum ain't getting no younger and God forbid something was to happen to her – you'd never forgive yourself if you two weren't talking. You're her golden boy, for Christ's sake.'

'Hang on, I've got to answer this,' Vinny excused himself.

'Who was it?' Michael enquired. His brother had only mumbled a couple of words before ending the call.

'Felicity. She's shopping up at Harrods with a pal and I said I'd meet up with her later.'

'It's serious then, you and her?'

'Yeah. I suppose so. Fliss don't give me GBH of the earhole like Joanna and that bitch Yvonne Summers, that's for sure. She's been hankering to move in with me – official, like – and I've resisted so far. She stays over mine most nights as it is, and you know what birds are like when they get their feet well and truly under the table. Give 'em an inch, they take a mile. I told her at the start I don't want no more kids and she reckons she don't want 'em either. You can never be too careful though, eh? Once bitten, twice shy.'

'You most certainly can't. Look at the shitty situation I'm in with Katy. I rue the day I ever let her talk her way into my underpants, believe me.'

'That reminds me, I saw Antonio the other day. Gave him a bit of a talking to. A pal of his is going travelling round the world and Antonio reckons he'd like to go with him. I've offered to pay for the trip – I thought it would give you and Bella some much-needed quality time together. Antonio asked me to break the news to his mother, but I thought that might be better coming from you.' Antonio was the outcome of Vinny's one-night stand with Bella and still a very sore subject between him and his brother.

'Fuck-all to do with me. Antonio isn't my son,' Michael snapped. 'Speaking of fathers, I think ours might not be with us for much longer. Don't you think it's time you buried the hatchet with him? Just swallow your pride for once, Vin, and make peace with him, and Mum.'

'No chance of that. You might see that old cunt as a father, but I don't.'

Eyes blazing, Michael slammed his drink on the table. 'Well, be it on your conscience when both our parents kick the bucket and you're speaking to neither of them. No wonder you get on so well with a bird not much older than your kids. You seriously are one immature prick.'

When Michael stood up, Vinny laughed. 'Erm, pot calling kettle springs to mind. If I remember rightly, Katy isn't that much older than Daniel and Lee, is she?'

Michael chucked a fifty-pound note on the table. 'You know what they say about people who bury their heads in the sand, don't you, clever bollocks?'

'No. Enlighten me.'

'One day they'll fucking suffocate to death.'

Georgie O'Hara marched into her brother's bedroom and slammed the door. Harry had spoiled a lovely afternoon by sulking all the way home and he was still acting up now. 'Whatever is wrong with you? Chances are those women had never heard of Dad or Granddad anyway.'

'Yes, they would have. Every traveller knows who our dad and granddad are,' Harry argued. He'd been upset when they'd left Burger King and the ladies selling the lucky heather were nowhere to be seen. It felt like a missed opportunity.

Knowing he needed a wake-up call, Georgie clumped her brother hard around the head with her fist.

'What was that for?' Harry shouted.

'To make you into a man. Our lot would be disgusted with your behaviour lately. All you do is whinge, play up, sulk and bully little Brett. You're twelve now, Harry. Start acting like a travelling man rather than some gorger dinlo child. Mum was so happy when we returned today, she said we could go to Romford again on Saturday. Plus, I got twenty-five quid to add to our running-away fund.

What are you doing to help our cause, eh? Nothing, that's what.'

'But I don't like Frankie, and I don't like living in a house. I miss waking up in the trailer and mucking about with Sonny.' Sonny Adams had been Harry's best friend in Scotland.

When tears appeared in her brother's eyes, Georgie held him close. She was eighteen months older than Harry and had certainly adapted to their new life better than he had. 'I'm sorry I hit you, but you need to be clever, like me. Calum said he'll give me more money later this week, and if you go downstairs and be nice to Mum, then she'll give us extra money to go to Romford on Saturday too. We got over a bullseye now, as soon as we have two hundred, we can leave here for good.'

Harry looked in Georgie's eyes. 'You promise?'

Georgie smiled. 'Cross my heart, hope to die. But do yourself a favour and enjoy the time we have left here. Have fun at the go-karting tomorrow, and at every opportunity you can. Also, chat to Mum and ask her anything you might want to know about the past. Because once we leave here, Harry, we ain't ever going to see her again.'

Glen Harper felt guilty. Jamie Preston had insisted on a quiet homecoming, yet it wasn't until the poor bastard had spewed all over his feet in the limo, that Glen realized he'd gone completely overboard.

'Proper enjoying this bit of munch. Tasted like cardboard those roast potatoes in prison,' Jamie said. It had been his idea to send the driver and girls packing. 'It's all too much too soon for me this, Glen. A nice carvery and chat is all I'm up for,' he'd informed his pal.

Unlike Jamie, Glen had barely touched his meal. A toot in the toilets was far preferable in his eyes to an overcooked roast. 'So what do you want to do tomorrow then? I know you're seeing your probation officer in the morning, but I can pick you up afterwards.' Even though Jamie was now technically a free man, in the eyes of the law he still wasn't. He was out on licence and wasn't allowed to move into Glen's flat yet.

'I wanna go to a library, dig out the archives surrounding Molly's murder. Then get a big bouquet to lay on my nan's grave. I'd like to see the area where Molly died as well. I also want to pay my disbelieving whore of a mother a visit and tell her her fucking fortune. And smash the granny out of Little Vinny until he admits the truth. But I suppose my last two requests will just have to wait until I'm no longer on licence, eh?' Jamie said angrily. He'd already been warned if he got himself into any kind of trouble his licence would be revoked and he'd be sent back to prison.

'Look, there's something I need to tell ya and don't be angry with me, 'cause the reason I never told you while you were inside is because I knew how pissed off you'd be. I didn't want you to get another lump added to your sentence, mate.'

Jamie put his knife and fork down. 'Go on.'

'Richie Woods was paid to give you grief. I got the truth out of his old woman a few months back.'

Jamie felt the hairs on the back of his neck stand up. He'd have been freed years ago if it wasn't for Richie Woods. Thankfully, the jury had believed he'd acted in self-defence. Because if they hadn't, he'd probably never have seen the light of day again. 'Vinny Butler?'

'Got it in one. But don't be worrying. I'm a man with a plan, me. Vinny's card is well and truly marked. Now, let me tell you the full story . . . '

CHAPTER FOURTEEN

As Christmas approached, Queenie Butler felt a loathing for the family she had once been so proud of. She'd been sure Vinny would have seen the error of his ways, dumped the young tart, and begged her for forgiveness. But Queenie hadn't seen hide nor hair of him. Michael still popped round to see her, but he never brought any of her grandchildren with him. As for Little Vinny, Queenie was absolutely fuming with him.

'What's up, Queen? You're not your usual jolly self today,' Joyce remarked. It had been her idea they have an early Christmas dinner in a local pub.

'I used to love Christmas. Even when Vinny and Roy were nippers and I had sod all, it was always my favourite time of year. Not any more though. My first one without my wonderful Vivvy. Dreading it, I am. Would've been Oliver's birthday on Christmas Day as well, God rest his soul.'

'Poor Oliver. I know how you feel. I've never enjoyed a Christmas since Jessica died. All about the grandchildren now, I suppose. But apart from Brett, I don't even like mine.'

'Don't talk to me about grandchildren, Joycie. I've forgotten what mine look like. Haven't got a clue what country Daniel and Lee are living in, and the ones in England never bother coming to see me. Well, Ava does, but only if she fancies a night out clubbing in Romford and wants somewhere local to stagger back to. Woke me up at four in the morning last weekend, the noisy little mare.'

'Aww, Little Vinny's been good to you though, hasn't he? Frankie thinks the world of him you know. Was singing his praises to me and Stanley the other day, saying how great he's been with her gypsy offspring.'

'Little Vinny's off me Christmas card list an' all. Short memory, he's got,' Queenie hissed.

'What's he done wrong?'

'Got that old bastard staying with him, Albie. Not sure if it's temporary or what, but he shouldn't be around Calum and Regan. He's a worthless old drunk. Makes my blood boil, it does. When Karen died, I raised that boy. My Vinny wasn't exactly father of the year, and I had to do everything for him. He reckons he was worried his granddad was wasting away. Load of old bollocks. Albie's an attention-seeker – would you believe, he once pretended he had cancer. Puts on that doleful-eyed look, the old goat does, and bar me and Vinny, the whole family seem to fall for it. Even my Vivvy warmed to the lying old git. He'll outlive me, I'm telling ya.'

'Don't say that, Queen. So what you doing on Christmas Day?'

'I'll be sitting indoors on my own, I should imagine, Joycie. Michael will be flitting from one tart to the other, and Vinny has broken my heart.'

Leaning across the table, Joyce squeezed her friend's hand. Since Queenie had come on the scene, life was no longer boring, it was fun. 'There'll be no sitting indoors on your own, dear. I insist you come to mine for the day. As for your Vinny, I'd put my life on it he'll be in touch before Christmas.'

Unusually for Queenie, her eyes filled with tears. 'No, he won't. I went too far, now I've lost him for good.'

Parked up close to Little Vinny's home, Jamie Preston was watching with interest. 'That's my so-called father,' he spat. Jamie's mother had informed him years ago Albie had known she was pregnant, and Jamie had despised him ever since. What type of man didn't bother to track his own son down?

Glen Harper folded his newspaper. The man in question was old, tall, thin and was walking with the aid of a stick. 'You sure?'

'Positive. I saw him coming out the Blind Beggar once, and thought it might be him. Then the press printed his photo.'

'You wanna follow him?' Glen asked.

Jamie was convinced that Little Vinny and Ben Bloggs had something to do with Molly's murder. Little Vinny was looking after Molly when she went missing and his story about falling asleep just didn't ring true. How could a three-year-old child open the door of that club and wander alone through Whitechapel to near Hackney Marshes without anyone seeing her? It just didn't make sense. Little Vinny was a ringer for Jon Venables, one of the monsters that'd murdered that poor little mite Jamie Bulger. He had the same wicked-shaped eyes as Venables and an evil look about him.

'Nah. I wanna see the other shitbag's movements,' Jamie replied. 'There must be somewhere he goes regularly by himself, surely?'

Jamie was itching to abduct, then torture the truth out of Little Vinny. Three days they had watched his house for now and had only seen him leave the property twice, with his sons in tow both times. It was too risky to involve his kids. Jamie would be sent straight back to prison if he was caught, but Jamie's gut feeling told him Little Vinny wouldn't grass him up. How could he go to the police without opening up a can of worms?

Frankie Mitchell shook her head. 'No. It doesn't look right there. Can you put it back in the other corner?'

Sighing, Joey Mitchell dragged the enormous Christmas tree across the room once more. Frankie had always been indecisive, even as a child. 'This is the last time I'm moving it, Sis. Doing my brain in today, you are.'

'That'll do,' Frankie exclaimed.

'Thank Christ for that. Queen Frankie is satisfied.'

When her brother bowed, Frankie laughed. 'How's it going, working with Dad?'

'OK. I'm not doing too many hours and a lot of the admin stuff I can do from home. How's the kids' tutoring coming along? Have they learned the words "please" and "thank you" yet?'

'Not quite, but they can both write their names now. Rome wasn't built in a day, Joey, but they seem much happier living here. I still worry they aren't going to come back every time they go out, but hopefully my fears will ease in time. Georgie is great with Brett now and he also seems settled, so that's a relief too.'

'Good. I'm pleased. Nan called me last night, invited me and Dom over for Christmas. Has she rung you yet? She said she was going to.'

'No, and I've already made plans. The kids and I are going to spend Christmas Day at Little Vinny's house. We're both going to feel miserable without Stuart, Sammi-Lou and Oliver, so we can be depressed together.'

'I wonder what homophobic gift Nan will buy me this year?' Joey laughed. 'Perhaps she's had another "GAY AND

PROUD" T-shirt printed?' It was a standing joke since Joey had come out his grandmother over-embraced his sexuality and always bought him some dodgy present aimed at him being homosexual.

Frankie was deep in thought. 'Would've been Oliver's birthday Christmas Day, you know. Going to be tough for Little Vinny, isn't it?'

Bored, Joey puffed out his cheeks. 'You're spending an awful lot of time with Little Vinny, Sis. Don't get me wrong, I like him and I'm glad you two are there for each other, but don't become too reliant on him, will you?'

Frankie banged the kettle on the worktop. 'And what is that supposed to mean? Are you accusing me of sleeping with him?'

'No. I know you're not like that. But you are a bit needy when it comes to men. You should go out with Babs more to pubs and clubs. You missed out on all that when you were younger.'

'How am I needy?' Frankie shrieked.

'Look, I haven't come round to argue with you. You're my sister and I love you. I also know you have feelings for Little Vinny. He's the main topic of conversation whenever we speak, and I just don't want to see you get hurt. You need to grieve for Stuart properly before you even think about getting involved with another man. It's way too soon.'

'For your information, I haven't got the hots for Little Vinny. We're just good friends. You really are fucking patronizing at times, Joey. And you're too fond of sticking your nose into other people's business. Wasted, working for Dad you are, should've been an agony aunt instead. Dear Deidre has nothing on you.'

Joey held his hands in the air. 'Touched a nerve have I, dear?' he asked, laden with sarcasm. 'I wonder why?'

*

Jamie Preston refused the line of cocaine, then enjoyed the sound of silence while he could. Glen was no man's fool, but he was a party animal. Most days he would snort gear and drink sporadically throughout. He'd then chew Jamie's ear off about one subject or another.

'Want the opinion of a wise old man, lad?' Glen asked.

'Go on,' Jamie replied, knowing he had no choice.

'I think you need to plan all this a bit better. The Butlers have eyes everywhere. You have no proof those boys had anything to do with Molly's disappearance. And what do you expect to happen once you've given Little Vinny a good going over? Only I very much doubt he'll march into the police station the following day screaming it was him and Ben Bloggs.'

'I thought perhaps a written confession. Then I can take it to the Old Bill. Might be a good idea to scare the shit out of him in the woods. Threaten to bury him alive. That should get him spilling his guts.'

'You march into a cop shop with his written confession, you'll be shoved straight back in a cell,' Glen warned. 'Little Vinny's bound to say he was forced to write it under duress, and he'll have the broken bones and bruises to prove it. As I said, you really haven't thought this through properly. Slowly, slowly catchy monkey, lad.'

'What do you suggest then?'

The tap on the window accompanied by the words, 'Excuse me, young man,' nigh on made Jamie jump out of his skin. Composing himself, he wound down the window. 'What's up, love?' he asked the old dear.

'I have a leak in my bathroom. There's a wet patch on the ceiling. Would you be kind enough to take a look at it for me, please?'

It had been Glen's idea to buy an old van and get some signwriting on it. BARRETT & SONS PLUMBING

& HEATING was proudly displayed, alongside a mobile number of a pay-as-you-go phone that was registered in a false name. 'At least we'll know if Little Vinny or any other nosy bastard is on to us. Bound to ring the number if they're suspicious and I'll answer it,' Glen had told Jamie.

'I'm sorry, but we're currently busy with another job around the corner,' Jamie lied. 'Have a look in the Yellow Pages. There's loads of plumbers in there.'

'See the way she was looking at our clothes. Told you we should dress like plumbers, didn't I? Navy sweatshirt and tracksuit bottoms is what we should be wearing. We'll get navy baseball caps an' all. Start the engine,' Glen urged.

'She didn't clock our clothes, Glen, and we're wearing tracksuits anyway,' Jamie reminded his pal.

'Nope. I ain't taking no chances. I saw her looking at me funny. We're going shopping,' Glen argued.

Jamie sighed as he pulled away from the kerb. That was the trouble with cocaine: it caused paranoia. And Glen, unfortunately, was more paranoid than most.

Eddie Mitchell was no fan of shopping, especially as the festive season drew close. However, once a year he would accompany Gina to Harrods. Aaron and Rosie had expensive tastes when it came to visiting Father Christmas. They only liked the one in Knightsbridge.

'If another Arab barges into me, man or woman, I swear I'll knock 'em out,' Eddie moaned.

'Dad, Mum, I want this,' Rosie demanded, pointing to a doll that looked almost lifelike.

'No point telling me and your father. You need to tell Father Christmas what you want. He's the one who delivers the presents – and don't forget to say please, otherwise he won't bring you any,' Gina replied.

Bottom lip protruding, Rosie put her hands obstinately on her hips. 'He bloody better.'

Chuckling, Eddie scooped his daughter into his arms.

'Hello, Ed. You being dragged around this bastard shop an' all? Women, eh? We should've stayed single,' Flatnose Freddie joked, squeezing his wife's hand.

'Tell me about it, Fred. How you been, mate? Not seen you since The Casino opening, have I?'

'You know me, plodding on as always. How's your new venture doing?'

'Yeah, all right. Word's started to get around now. Last week was our best so far.'

'Glad to hear it. 'Ere, I meant to ask you something. Vinny's young bit of fluff – what's her name?'

Flatnose Freddie's wife smiled at Gina. 'I hate to think what he refers to me as,' she joked.

Gina laughed. 'I think I'm known as "Her Indoors".'

'Her name's Felicity, Fred. Why do you ask?'

'Because I recognize her from somewhere and I can't place where. Been racking my bleedin' brain ever since, I have. What's her surname? Did she ever live south of the water?'

Eddie shrugged. 'I don't know much about her to be honest, mate. But I'll ask Vinny and get back to you on it.'

Frankie had that feeling of dread in the pit of her stomach as she dashed around to Little Vinny's. 'What's happened? Where is he?' she gabbled. All Little Vinny had said on the phone was that there'd been an incident with Harry and the tutor.

'Calm down. Harry's fine. He's gone round the chippy with the others.'

'What was the incident?'

'He lost his rag and threw all his books at the tutor. I think he got frustrated because she was urging him to read some words out loud and he couldn't understand them.'

'Oh, I'm sorry, Vin. Is she OK?'

'No need to apologize. It isn't your fault. And, no, she was thoroughly pissed off, which is why we've come to a mutual agreement that her coming here wasn't working. It's not just Harry; Regan's been playing her up as well. He called her a "four-eyed cunt" yesterday and I had to clump him one.'

'So what will happen now? I can't send Georgie and Harry to school. They'll cause mayhem, and probably run away.'

Little Vinny squeezed Frankie's trembling hands. 'Stop panicking. Everything's going to be fine. No point in employing somebody else this side of Christmas, but that doesn't stop us interviewing someone who's willing to start in the New Year. That woman was too weak. Perhaps we should hire a geezer next time? An ex-army type who won't take no crap. Discipline is what all three need.'

Frankie stared into Little Vinny's eyes. Jed's eyes had been a brightish green too, but nowhere near as striking as Little Vinny's. Joey had been right earlier, she had developed feelings for Little Vinny, that's why she'd flown off the handle. Did he have feelings for her too? He must do, otherwise he wouldn't be holding her hands.

'You OK, Frankie? You look a bit bemused.'

It was only the kids arriving back from the chip shop that stopped Frankie from making a total fool out of herself.

Originally from Basildon, Glen Harper had earned his wealth and reputation through being a big-time drug dealer and taking out any cheeky bastard who upset him. But after that cost him his liberty, Glen chose not to get his hands dirty any more. He still ran what he referred to as 'a little empire', but there was no need to dirty his own hands when he had decent trustworthy men working for him who were willing to do anything for the right price.

'My old stomping ground this, lad. Could do with a bit of a makeover, don't ya think?' Glen laughed, introducing Jamie to a big-built bloke with a shaved head. The boozer was called the Bull's Eye and Jamie had to agree it wasn't the most well-decorated establishment he'd ever seen. He liked it though as it reminded him of how pubs used to look before he'd got banged up.

Slipping the bloke he referred to as 'Dusty' an envelope, Glen said, 'Two K in there, plus a personal message. You'll get the rest of the dosh as soon as the job's done. I gave you the address, didn't I?'

'You sure did and I've already checked it out. He'll be easy to get at.'

'Good man, but whatever yous do, don't fucking kill him. Jamie hasn't been out five minutes and we don't want the Old Bill sniffing round.'

'I take it you want this done ASAP?'

'Yeah. And make sure it's a hospital job. I want him to have the worst Christmas of his fucking life.'

Vinny Butler drove towards his mother's house with his brother's words still ringing in his ears. Michael might be a patronizing cock at times but had been spot on when he'd said, 'If anything happens to Mum and yous two aren't talking, you'll never forgive yourself.' Which is why Vinny had decided to bite the bullet and bow down to her. Christmas just wouldn't be Christmas if he didn't spend it with his mother, and even if that pissed Felicity off, Vinny didn't care. His mum had always been the most important woman in his life and she always would be, faults an' all.

Pulling up outside Queenie's bungalow, Vinny felt nervous. He'd rung his mum and left numerous messages on both her phones this afternoon, but she hadn't replied. So he'd popped uptown to buy her the diamond bracelet to match her earrings and necklace. He hoped that might act as a sweetener.

Queenie opened the door with a look of hatred on her face. She missed Vinny more than words could express, but still could not get over the fact he'd hit her. 'What do you want?' she spat.

'Mum, I'm so sorry. Please can we sort things out? I miss you so bloody much. Life just ain't the same without you. Can I come in, please?'

'No, you fucking can't. I want nothing to do with you. Hitting me over some young whore! I have never felt so humiliated in all my life. I've been a bloody good mother to you. Stuck by you through thick and thin, even when you killed Lenny. And Old Jack's son. As for the alibis I've given you over the years, I've lost count. You need to take a long, hard look at yourself, boy, because Vivvy was right all along. You're a wrong 'un.'

'It's over between me and Fliss. She meant nothing to me,' Vinny lied. 'Look what I've bought you,' he added, waving the gift bag in the air. 'It's the diamond bracelet to match your earrings and necklace. Please let me in. I know I'm not perfect, but I love you so fucking much. You know I do.'

Queenie snatched the gift bag out of her son's hand and lobbed it up the pathway. 'That's your trouble, Vinny. You think you can buy your way out of any situation. Well, you need to remember the old song, "Money Can't Buy Me Love" – the Beatles had it fucking right. You've lost my love forever, and my respect. Give the bracelet to your whore for Christmas. I want nothing off you. Dead in my eyes you are – dead,' Queenie screamed.

Tears streaming down his face, Vinny picked the gift bag up and walked away, shoulders slumped.

Queenie slammed the door, then leaned against the hallway wall. Hearing the diesel engine of her son's Range Rover pull away, she put her head in her hands, slid down the wall and bawled her eyes out. She loved Vinny too much, always had done from the very first moment she'd held him in her arms. And that was the reason she could not forgive him.

CHAPTER FIFTEEN

'Vinny, stop it! For goodness' sake, put the knife down. Whatever's happened? Talk to me,' Felicity Carter-Price pleaded. She'd been on a rare night out with the girls, and couldn't believe what she'd returned to. Vinny had no shirt on, was clearly high, drunk, or both, and was kneeling on the beautiful leather sofa he'd only recently purchased, hacking it to pieces with a meat knife.

'Materialistic, me! I'll show her how fucking materialistic I am when I dump this on her driveway tomorrow. Or should I say my driveway? Only I'm the muggy cunt paying for the gaff.'

'Who you talking about? Vinny, no! Not the TV!' Felicity screamed, when her lover picked up an ornament and aimed it at the flat-screen, narrowly missing.

'New year, new start. Michael can bastard well support her from now on, I'm telling ya, babe. Done with her, I am. A lonely, sad, miserable old woman, that's how she'll end up.' Vinny picked up the bottle of Jack Daniel's and greedily slurped from it.

Felicity crouched in front of her man. He'd opened up to her more recently, but had been cagey when she'd asked where he was going earlier. Now it was obvious why. 'Don't bottle it up. Tell me what happened. Your mum's obviously upset you greatly.'

After leaving his mother's, Vinny had headed to his club in Holborn and dragged Carl out on a pub crawl. It had depressed him rather than cheered him up though. Back in the day, the East End had some brilliant boozers, but lots had now shut down and the rest were virtually unrecognizable. So he'd ended back at his own club, much to Ava's dismay. 'You're drunk, Dad, and showing yourself up. Go home, before you lose us any more customers,' Ava insisted, after he got into an argument with a group of men.

Driving home after the amount he'd drunk wasn't as easy as Vinny had anticipated. He'd hit some stationary shit-heap of a motor, and damaged the passenger side of his Range Rover. That had pissed him off as well.

'Talk to me, Vin,' Felicity said gently, squeezing his hands. She could tell Vinny had taken something by the look in his eyes, but wasn't about to interrogate him. She'd learned her lessons with her ex-boyfriend never to ask too much.

'Even brought up the past, she did. Old Jack's son deserved everything he got. Somebody had to fucking stop him kiddy-fiddling, didn't they? And she patted me on the back at the time, saying I'd done the area proud. As for Champ, she knew that was an accident. I loved that lad. How dare she fucking accuse me of killing him?'

'I don't want to pry, Vinny, but if you ever need to talk about things, I am here for you.'

Judgement clouded by alcohol and the first illegal substance he'd taken in years, Vinny clamped his hands around the top of Felicity's arms. 'I can trust you, can't I? You must never repeat anything I tell ya,' he said, shaking her rather violently.

'I would never betray you, Vinny, but neither do I want you to blurt things out you might regret. You've had an awful lot to drink this evening, so why don't we chat tomorrow? This is the happiest relationship I've ever been part of, and I would hate anything to spoil what we've got.'

Unusually for Vinny, he locked lips with Felicity. He didn't do kissing as a rule, found it far too intimate for his liking. That slut Yvonne Summers had a lot to answer for, she really did. If she hadn't mugged him off and ripped his heart to shreds, he was sure he'd have found love in the past. A young teenager he'd been when Yvonne had run off with not-so-clever Trevor, and apart from his nearest and dearest, Vinny had despised anything with a vagina ever since. Trevor had paid the price, of course. Vinny had set fire to him while he was still alive.

'You OK, Vinny? You're looking at me strangely.'

Vinny moved Felicity's dark hair away from her face while staring into her eyes. 'Move in properly with me. We can make this work, I know we can. I like you a lot, Fliss. And I really mean that.'

Aware that Vinny was now amorous; Felicity unzipped his trousers and put his above-average-sized penis in her mouth. Knowing how her man liked it, she got him excited, then lay on her front.

'No. Turn over. I wanna make love to you properly.'

And for the first time in his life, Vinny actually meant it.

'I want to open that one,' Rosie Mitchell insisted.

'No. It's unlucky to open it early,' Gina told her daughter, snatching the Harrods advent calendar out of Rosie's hands. The cheeky little blighter had already found some of her presents that had been hidden and opened them.

Eddie burst out laughing when Rosie called Gina 'wicked' and marched out of the kitchen, hands on hips. 'I don't know where she gets it from, seriously.'

'I do. You!' Gina exclaimed, pretending to be angry.

Eddie put his arms around his stunning wife and pressed his groin against her. 'You love me really. Bet you couldn't believe your luck when I gave you the time of day,' he goaded.

Gina playfully punched her husband. 'Get over yourself,' she chuckled. Eddie still looked as bloody handsome as the day she'd first met him. He had the most beautiful dark come-to-bed eyes, and instead of being turned off by the enormous scar that ran down his face, Gina found it a turn-on. 'You're not going to be late home tonight, are you? The kids are bound to wake us up before dawn.'

'Vinny's offered to lock up, so I won't be too late. I doubt there'll be many in The Casino, but we've sold eighty-odd tickets for the Piano Bar. Got a Sinatra-type singer performing, so I'll see Christmas in there, then come straight home. One at the latest, I reckon.'

'Dad, your phone's ringing. Can I answer it?' Aaron asked.

'Yeah. Then bring it straight in 'ere.'

Aaron mumbled a few words then handed his father the phone. 'It's a man called Flatnose Freddie.'

Eddie put the phone to his ear. 'All right, pal? What's up?'

Gina realized very quickly as the colour drained from Eddie's face that whatever news Freddie had wasn't the best.

'Oh, for fuck's sake. Vinny's gonna go apeshit. I'm positive he has no idea.'

'What's wrong?' Gina asked, when the call ended.

Grabbing his bunch of keys off the table, Eddie puffed his cheeks out. 'Don't ask, babe. I'm gonna have to shoot out. I'll fill you in with all the gory details later. Wish me luck.'

*

Georgie and Harry O'Hara were in Romford town centre doing some last-minute Christmas shopping. Calum and Regan were spending the day with Sammi-Lou's parents and Georgie had managed to wangle thirty quid out of her mother, on the pretence of buying gifts. Little Vinny had also given her fifty pounds and told her, 'Make sure you get your mum something nice from you and Harry. It will make her day.'

'Well?' Harry said, when his sister walked out of Debenhams. Georgie always made him wait outside when she was shoplifting. She reckoned he looked too much like a traveller and travellers in pairs always got followed.

'I chored some perfume for Mum, but then some woman started looking at me funny, so I couldn't get anything for Calum and Regan. Perhaps you can go in one of the sports shops, see if you can chore 'em something in there.'

'With the money you've got today, we must have two hundred now?' Harry asked eagerly. He missed his dad dreadfully, and his grandparents and little sister. This would be the first Christmas they'd spent apart.

'We'll have a count up when we get home. We don't want to run away in the winter though. If Nan ain't on that site, we'll probably have to sleep rough until we find her. We should keep saving up until spring.'

'No way, Georgie. You promised we would leave as soon as we had the money. You don't wanna leave, do you? Half that wonga is mine and I'll go on my own if I have to.'

'Look! Over there,' Georgie said, grabbing Harry's arm and pointing. They'd not seen the travelling women since their very first trip to Romford.

'Ask 'em if they know Dad. Tell 'em where we're living,' Harry urged.

The two women looked to be in their sixties and when Georgie marched over, one offered her some lucky heather and the other asked if she wanted her fortune read. 'No, thanks. Me and my brother are travellers. What site do you live on?' Georgie enquired.

'Rush Green. What about you?' the shorter lady asked. Even though Georgie and Harry had lived in Scotland, unlike gorgers, who tended to pick up on accents, all English travellers sounded pretty much the same.

'We were on a site not far from Glasgow, but now we're living in a house. We can't get used to it, can we, Harry?'

'No. We hate it. Our mum's a gorger and we hate her too. You probably know our dad and granddad. Jed and Jimmy O'Hara?'

The two women shared a shocked, awkward glance. Everybody knew everybody in their world. Gossip would spread like wildfire at horse fairs, especially Appleby. And Derby Day at Epsom. They were two of the biggest traveller events of the year, where the whole family were allowed to attend instead of just the males. So both women were well aware that Alice O'Hara's grandchildren had been snatched and Jimmy and Jed O'Hara were presumed dead.

Harry could tell the women were startled and knew his family. 'They ain't dead, my dad and granddad, are they?' he asked, panicked.

'I don't know where they are, love. But I do know of them. Why don't we sit on a bench and have a proper chat? You must never tell your mother you've spoken with me and Mary though. Us travellers stick together, don't we?'

'You better sit down, Vin,' Eddie Mitchell suggested. He'd be amazed if his partner already knew; gobsmacked, in fact.

'What's up? More dead creatures and bible quotes?' Vinny had known something was wrong when Ed had rung him and told him to head straight to The Casino.

Eddie poured a large Scotch and slid it along the desk. 'Drink that, I think you're gonna need it.'

After his exploits the previous evening, Vinny had a seriously bad hangover and wasn't in the mood to play games. 'Whatever it is, just spit it out, Ed.'

'Do you know Dave Newton?'

'Not personally, but the name rings a bell. Is he out of South London?'

'Yeah, originally. But he lived on the Costa del Sol for years. He's banged up now for a road-rage murder. They extradited him back from Spain and sentenced him to eighteen years.'

'What's this got to do with me?'

'Dave's young girlfriend dobbed him in, then turned Queen's Evidence during the trial. She was with him on the night the murder happened, and rumour has it the Old Bill gave her a fat juicy pay-off to turn QE.' Eddie pushed a white envelope towards Vinny. 'Look inside.'

Vinny did so, and for a minute was dumbstruck. Inside the envelope was a photocopied article from page seven of the *Daily Mirror*. The photograph wasn't particularly clear, but there was no doubt the nineteen-year-old girlfriend of Dave Newton, named as Amanda Carter, was in fact his girlfriend, Felicity Carter-Price.

'You OK, mate?' Eddie asked, rather stupidly.

Vinny's lip curled angrily. 'No way. This has to be some kind of a joke. Who gave this to you?'

'It's kosher, Vin. I'm so sorry, pal.'

Seeing red, Vinny leapt out of his chair, grabbed hold of the office desk and threw it across the room. 'Cunt.'

Frankie Mitchell eyed her eldest two suspiciously. Since arriving home from Romford they'd been acting oddly and kept whispering to one another.

'What time do you think Father Christmas will come, Mum? Will he know we've moved?' Brett Mitchell asked innocently.

'There ain't no Father Christmas, you dinlo. As if some silly fat old bastard with a white beard is really gonna climb down a chimney with a sack full of presents for you,' Harry goaded. Apart from the odd verbal dig, he had stopped physically picking on Brett now. But that's only because Georgie had threatened him. He still didn't like his younger brother, thought he was a stupid wet-behind-the-ears gorger.

'Take no notice of Harry, Brett. He's winding you up,' Frankie said, glaring at her eldest son. 'Santa will arrive in the middle of the night when you're fast asleep. So why don't you go and get ready for bed. Wash your hands and face. Clean your teeth and put your jim-jams on, then I'll make you a hot chocolate.'

'Jim-jams,' Harry sniggered.

When their mother and Brett left the room, Georgie punched her brother in the arm. She felt sorry for her youngest brother. He wasn't clued up like her and Harry, but that wasn't his fault. Her mother was the one treating him like a baby and if Harry bothered to give Brett the time of day, he'd grow fond of him like she had. 'We're gonna be gone soon. Can't you be nice for just one day?'

Harry's eyes shone with excitement while quietly discussing the travelling ladies. They'd said they didn't know his dad and grandparents personally, but their husbands did and would be able to get a message to their nan. 'I still say you should have told 'em our address, Georgie. Then we know they'd definitely come for us.'

Georgie shook her head. The women had asked where they lived, but she'd kicked Harry as he'd been about to open his big mouth, then replied, 'We're not sure. But it's near Hornchurch.' Georgie didn't want anything bad happening to her mum or Brett. They didn't deserve that.

'When can we go to Romford again? They might speak to Dad really soon.'

Georgie put an arm around her troublesome brother. She'd clocked the look between the women when their dad and grandfather were mentioned, and was now sure they were both dead. She didn't want to ruin Harry's Christmas though, neither did she want him kicking off any more than usual. 'We'll go to Romford again soon. But in the meantime, be nice. Someone will come and take us home soon, Harry. I promise.'

'Nan's bound to tell Ryan and he'll definitely come to get you back. You still gonna marry him?'

Feeling guilty because the only lad she'd thought about lately was Regan, Georgie shrugged. 'Probably. But I'll decide for definite when I'm sixteen.'

Vinny Butler was in shock. He'd trusted Felicity.

Seeing her name flash up on his phone again, Vinny switched the poxy thing off. How could he have been so stupid? It made him feel sick to the stomach that he'd let the bitch drive a wedge between himself and his beloved mother. Whatever had he been thinking?

Knowing his loser of a father was currently staying at his son's, it had been Vinny's idea that he meet Michael in Barking.

'What's wrong now?' Michael asked, as he stepped out of his BMW X5.

'Inside,' Vinny hissed, turning his nose up as the front door was opened. The gaff smelt of his father. Had a nasty, musty whiff about it.

'Do you want a cup of tea?' Michael asked.

'I need something stronger. Has the old bastard got any alcohol here?'

Michael poured his brother a brandy. 'Fire away then.'

When Vinny explained what had happened with Eddie

Mitchell, Michael sat in silence until his brother had finished ranting. 'Felicity was only a kid back then, so perhaps she had her reasons? You ain't got nothing to worry about, you're legal now. I very much doubt she's got her claws into you for a reason.'

'Have you not listened to a word I've said, Michael? The tart got paid to turn fucking QE by the Old Bill. She's a definite wrong 'un and she knows too much.'

'You're now the proud owner of an extremely above-board business. What can she know? It'd be different if you were still importing, then supplying half the country with illegal substances, but you aren't, are ya? I think you're panicking over nothing, Vin. I've heard of Dave Newton, and by all accounts he's a wanker.'

'You can bet he's the one behind those dead creatures. Obviously heard I'm with Fliss and wants revenge. What she did was fucking wrong, bruv. The geezer's doing eighteen years, thanks to her. She has to go, Michael. She knows stuff about the family.'

'Don't talk such rubbish. What can she know about us?'

'What me and Roy did to Old Jack's son, and what you and I did to Trevor Thomas. She also knows it was me who was driving the night Champ died.' Vinny and Michael had never referred to their cousin as Lenny. Auntie Viv's son had been born with special needs and in their eyes he was a 'Champ'.

Michael was fuming. 'You're a fucking liability, an absolute prick,' he bellowed. 'What made you tell her family business? I thought you were meant to be clued up, you tool.'

'I'm sorry, OK? I was pissed and let my guard down. I thought I could trust her and made a mistake. Never again, I'm telling ya. For all we know, she could be chatting to one of her copper mates as we speak. We need to stick together on this one. I can't involve Eddie. You're the only one that can help me, bruv, and it's in both our best interests that you do.'

Queenie Butler lit the candle and placed it in front of her sister's photo. Somebody once told her that it was a way of connecting with the deceased. 'Hello, Vivvy. Hope you're happy up there and looking after Mum. Not gonna be the same without ya this Christmas. But I know you wouldn't want me to be sad, so I'm going to try and make the most of it round at Joycie's. You'd have liked Joyce too, Viv. She's a case, a bit like us in many ways. Nowhere near as modern and smart, mind. Wears some bastard clothes. Leopard and zebra print. Looks like she's escaped from a zoo. Have you seen Roy, Molly and Adam? Please tell 'em I love and miss them if so. And Oliver. Oh, and also Brenda. I keep hoping you'll send me a sign of some kind, Vivvy, to let me know you're OK. I've had a couple of white feathers, but I need something more. If you can see and hear me, please send me something distinct. We always promised we'd contact one another if we still could, didn't we?'

Minutes later, an astonished Queenie put her hand over her mouth. She hadn't imagined it. It was still doing it. The DVD player was opening and shutting the compartment she put the DVDs in, on its own.

When it finally stopped, Queenie had tears of joy running down her cheeks. She picked up her sister's photo and smiled. 'You're still with me, my angel. Thank you so much for letting me know. You've made my Christmas. Best present I could've wished for.'

Michael Butler's brain didn't know if it was coming or going. He was trying to think rationally, but was far too angry to do so. For all Vinny's faults, he had never been a blabbermouth and must have been seriously shitfaced to tell Felicity such guarded family secrets. 'I'm gonna ask you this once, Vin, and don't you dare lie to me. Had you been on the gear?'

'Yeah. But it was the first time in years, I swear on Little Vinny's life it was. I was so upset over Mum's harsh words; I went on a pub crawl and bought some off Scottish John. I ended up back at my Holborn club where, according to Ava, I made a right tit of meself. I must've been out of my nut to smash the motor up on the way home. I really am sorry, Michael. You will help me clear this mess up, won't you? Despise the bitch now, I do. Cannot believe I argued with Mum over her. Never again will I be involved with a bird, I can promise you that much.'

'You sure she weren't wired up when you told her?'

'Positive. She was naked. I told her after we'd had sex.'

'Switch your phone on now,' Michael ordered.

'Why?'

'Because you're going to ring Felicity and behave completely normal. Tell her your battery died or something. Then you're gonna go home later, and act like you haven't got a care in the world. Do not drink at work, and as for snorting that other shit, grow up, you dickhead. Who d'you think you are, Peter Fucking Pan? What are your plans for tomorrow, by the way?'

'I've booked a restaurant for just the two of us. I suggested we visit her parents, but she said they were in the South of France. Fucking liar. No wonder she has never wanted to introduce me to them. Was probably scared they'd blow her cover.'

'Look, we don't know for sure she has any contact with the Old Bill now. But you need to get her out your gaff at some point soon, so you can check your bedroom thoroughly and make sure it isn't bugged. I can't believe you told her what you did, Vin. You of all people. Unfuckingbelieveable.'

'I know. You don't hate me any more right now than I hate myself. I'm losing the plot, not having Mum in my life. She's always been there for me.'

'Well, you're just gonna have to man up now and do as I say. If Felicity gets an inkling you know what you know, we could both be in big trouble.'

Vinny locked eyes with his brother. 'Which is exactly why we need to shut her up.'

It was two in the morning when Vinny Butler finally got to lock up the Piano Bar. He'd taken his brother's advice; stayed sober, and had told Eddie, 'I can't hate Felicity. She's a sweet girl and I'm sure her intentions are genuine towards me. However, the age gap is way too wide and dating a grass is no good for my image or that of our business. I've decided to get New Year out the way and let her down gently.'

Vinny's favourite band was Roxy Music and as he whacked up the volume of their CD, he couldn't help but feel mugged off yet again. 'Angel Eyes' had been his and Felicity's special song. He'd even danced with her to it. Apart from his mother and Auntie Viv, he'd never danced with a woman before Fliss.

Cursing his bad luck, Vinny put his foot on the accelerator. As hard as it was going to be, he'd digested Michael's advice and knew his brother was right. Acting like nothing had happened was the only way forward, for now at least. Michael had promised he would put his thinking cap on, and Vinny knew deep down this meant his brother would be there for him. Apart from when Bella had come between them, they'd always stood by one another.

As a rule, Vinny was extremely alert. Being who he was, he'd never have survived so many years had he not been.

But as he stepped out of the Range Rover in his safe underground car park, an attack was the last thing on his mind.

'What the fuck!' Vinny exclaimed as three men wearing balaclavas jumped out on him. Something was sprayed in his eyes and instinct made him fall to the floor and cover his head with his hands. He was temporarily blinded and could smell the distinct vapour of CS gas. The men said nothing as they kicked their victim repeatedly in the head. Within a minute, Vinny Butler was out for the count.

CHAPTER SIXTEEN

'Damn. We've forgotten Lucy's watch,' Robert Holmes informed his wife Juliet. 'You get in the car, love, and I'll nip back. Put the gifts in the boot. Make sure they're upright.'

Juliet took the two big bags off her husband and walked towards their Mercedes. She then let out a deafening scream.

'Juliet, what's wrong?' Robert yelled, hot-footing it back towards her.

Shaking like a leaf, Juliet pointed towards the beaten and bloodied body of a man wearing a suit. Next to him was a box with a dead headless feathered chicken inside. 'He's not moving. I think he's dead. Do something, Robert, quickly.'

Unaware she'd been sitting on her DVD remote, which was why the DVD drawer had repeatedly opened the previous day, Queenie Butler woke up with a smile on her face. Knowing Vivvy could hear and was watching over her was an enormous comfort, it really was.

Thinking of Vinny, Queenie chose to banish him from her mind. Every time he popped into her thoughts lately, she literally forced herself to think of something else. It was the only way she could deal with what had happened. To think that Vinny had clumped her over some worthless tart filled Queenie with a feeling of rejection, the like of which she'd never experienced.

Making herself a cup of tea, Queenie shuffled into the lounge. She was annoyed with her eldest grandson for inviting Albie to stay at his, but at the same time her heart went out to the poor lad. Today was bound to be an extremely difficult one for Little Vinny and, deciding to be the bigger person, Queenie picked up the phone. 'Hello, boy. You OK? I lit a candle for Oliver last night. Put it next to his photo.'

Surprisingly, Little Vinny sounded very upbeat. 'I've been up since six preparing the food. Good job Sammi-Lou taught me how to cook, Nan. I've got Frankie and her kids coming over for dinner. Granddad's here too, and Finn's probably going to pop over later. Why don't you and Joycie pop round later this evening too? I'm preparing supper as well.' Keeping busy was the only way Little Vinny could cope with the loss of Sammi-Lou and Oliver. Especially today on what would have been Oliver's seventeenth birthday.

'Pretty girl, Frankie, isn't she?' Queenie blurted out. She was prying, but didn't want Little Vinny to know.

'I suppose so. Never looked at her in that way, if I'm honest.'

'Well, perhaps you should. Comes from good stock, and you could do a lot worse than being with Eddie Mitchell's daughter. I know you're still grieving, but Sammi-Lou wouldn't want you to be lonely.'

Shocked by his nan's unfeeling suggestion, Little Vinny hissed, 'Sammi-Lou is barely cold. And forget coming around later, I can do without the match-making. You're not welcome.'

*

Michael Butler hated Christmas Day. He'd liked it up until he had kids dotted about all over the place, but now it was no more than a pain in the arse to him. It was impossible to please everybody, and this year Bella had the hump because he'd decided to spend the day with Nathan and Ellie. As far as Bella was aware, he and Katy were history. Well, Katy was to an extent, but Michael still slept with her here and there just to shut her up. Anything was better than the bitch's continuous nagging, and after the lies Bella had told him, why should he feel guilty?

In his heart, Michael would always love Bella, but he was struggling to forgive and forget. The thought of her and Vinny together made his skin crawl and Antonio was a constant reminder of their fling. Bella had finally agreed to Antonio going off travelling with a pal, and Michael couldn't wait for him to leave. Only then would he truly know if he and Bella had a future together.

Michael picked his phone up. 'You all right, Mum? What time you going round Joycie's?'

'I've booked me car for twelve. Did you hear from Daniel and Lee at all?'

'Nothing. I really thought they'd have sent us a card or something. I get it that Daniel wants to forget what happened, but it seems as though he and Lee have just washed their hands of the lot of us. I even rang Beth yesterday to see if Lee had been in touch with her, but she hasn't heard a dickie either. It's hurtful. I was a bloody good dad to those two.'

'I know you was, boy. But I'm sure they'll get in contact when they're good and ready. Probably too busy enjoying themselves to be sending cards. Did you ring Nancy like I told you to?'

'Yeah. She still hasn't heard from Roxanne. It's gonna

cost a fortune, but I've told Nancy I'm hiring a private detective to help find her.'

'When? You promised that weeks ago.'

'I'll definitely sort it early January. Don't worry, we'll find her.'

'She should have been found ages ago. Nancy could've done more, seeing as it was her lies that caused all this. That baby must be due soon. Please God she had the abortion. Bound to be something wrong with the child if not.'

Michael felt queasy as he ended the call. The whole situation was so sickening. If Roxanne did keep the child, nobody could ever find out Daniel was the father. Never would his family be able to live that one down. It was disgusting.

Nearing Tunbridge Wells, Michael decided to turn his phone off. He would ring Vinny later; make sure he was holding it together. Some Christmas this was going to be. Knowing Vinny's track record, he'd want to dispose of Felicity as soon as Big Ben chimed in the New Year. His brother was a fucking nuisance, always had been and always would be.

Queenie Butler was sitting in Joyce's lounge sipping her first Baileys of the day. Joyce had really gone to town with the decorations and her taste was a bit too in your face for Queenie's liking. 'Looks beautiful the way you've done it up, Joycie,' she lied.

'Thank you. I do try to make an effort. Joey, Dom, sit down, will you. I want us to open the presents now.' Joyce already had her main present. She'd recently caught the internet bug and would spend hours looking things up. Anything was better than talking to Stanley, and Eddie had sent a man round yesterday to set up her new posh laptop.

'There you go, Granddad. From me and Dom,' Joey said,

handing over three gifts. He then gave two each to his nan and Queenie.

'You shouldn't have bought me anything else, you daft sods. Your dad said the laptop was from all of yous,' Joycie said, clapping her hands with glee when she saw the book giving tips on how to research a family tree. She was desperate to find out about her ancestors, had been going on about doing so for ages.

'That is the right perfume isn't it, Nan?' Joey asked.

'Yes. Love my Rive Gauche. Oh, bless 'em, Queen. They've bought you the same perfume. I told them you always said mine smelt nice, didn't I, boys?'

Suddenly wishing she didn't lie so often, Queenie thanked the lads and faked a smile as Joycie sprayed the perfume on her. It smelled awful. She loathed it.

Stanley was thrilled with his jumper, book on pigeons and waterproof jacket. Joey and Dominic always put a lot of thought into what they were buying, and thankfully had good taste.

'Wow! These are lovely, Queenie. Thank you,' Joey said. Queenie had bought him and Dom a matching set of Calvin Klein boxer shorts.

'You've got Little Vinny to thank for choosing them. I didn't know what to get, so I asked him to pick something for me. Always been into fashion, he has. Wears posh pants himself,' Queenie said.

'They're lovely,' Joyce gushed. 'Do gay men wear those?' she asked her grandson.

Joey raised his eyebrows. 'How would I know? I've only ever been with Dom.'

Dominic smiled. Joey's nan couldn't help the way she was, and he found her funny rather than offensive. 'As far as I know, Calvin Klein is popular with both gay and straight men,' he explained.

'Be wasted on your granddad,' Joyce cackled, handing the boys their presents. 'Open the big ones first,' she ordered.

The Fred Perry jumpers were nice, but both were pale blue and Joey wished his nan wouldn't buy them stuff in matching colours. He and Dom were partners, not four-year-old twins. Opening the second, Joey stared at his nan quizzically. 'What's this?'

'Read it. It's a new gay club in Brighton. I found it on the internet. Those tickets are for the actual opening night. Be nice for you both to meet other gay men. Not many where you live in South Woodham Ferrers, is there?'

'You'll never change the busybody in her,' Stanley mumbled, embarrassed.

'Who asked for your opinion, you old goat?' Joyce retaliated.

When Dominic burst out laughing, so did Queenie. Joyce was funny without even realizing it.

Opening the final present, which was in a small white envelope and addressed to him and Dom, Joey stared at the photo. It was of a woman with dark hair and he didn't recognize her from Adam. 'Who's she then?'

'Her name's Maria and she's a lovely lady. I've checked her out thoroughly, so please don't worry. She produces wonderful kids. Her two sons are so bleedin' handsome and the daughter is stunning. Reminded me of a young Ava.'

Joey was confused. 'But who is she?'

'The surrogate mother I've found so you boys can become fathers,' Joyce beamed, rubbing her hands together excitedly.

Joey and Dom looked at one another with incredulous expressions. 'You are joking, Nan?' Joey asked.

'No. 'Course I'm not joking. This is a serious subject. Didn't like the first one I met – fat and ugly she was. Maria's perfect though.'

'But Dom and I haven't discussed having children. We're happy as we are, thanks.'

'You can't leave these things for ever, you know. You need to decide while you're still able. Your grandfather's tinky-winky stopped functioning properly years ago.'

Stanley Smith was old school. He hated filthy talk and got embarrassed extremely easily. Red-faced, he stood up. 'You should be bloody ashamed of yourself, you silly interfering old cow. Every Christmas you try to show these boys up, and you've excelled yourself yet again. I've had enough. I'm off to feed my pigeons.'

'Too late. I've cooked the bastards for dinner,' Joyce shouted out.

Queenie could not stop laughing. Joyce had told her she had a 'big surprise' for Joey and Dominic, but she hadn't told her it was a middle-aged surrogate mother. The woman in the photo looked at least thirty-five.

'Welcome to Christmas at the nut-house, Queen. I actually got admitted to one of those once,' Joyce admitted.

Queenie did not disbelieve that. Christmas at the Smiths was destined to make her own brood seem half normal.

Little Vinny jovially ordered the kids to sit at the table. He'd not cried since Sammi and Oliver's funeral, but had been unable to stop himself shedding a few tears this morning. His handsome, strapping lad would have been seventeen today. Oliver had adored Christmas, and so had Sammi-Lou. Little Vinny could remember last year like it was yesterday. Such a wonderful Christmas they'd had, and he would never have believed just a year later his beautiful family would've been ripped apart at the core.

'Who wants breast and who wants leg meat?' Little Vinny asked, waving his electric carving knife in the air. Keeping himself busy was the only way he got through the day and he was glad Frankie and her kids were here. It would have been awful to spend the day alone with Calum and Regan.

'I'll cut it if you want, Dad?' Calum offered.

'No. Let me do it,' Harry said. He'd never seen an electric carving knife before and thought it was an amazing creation.

Not realizing Georgie and Harry had stolen the bottle of aftershave they'd given him, Little Vinny had been extremely touched by the gesture. Frankie had also been thrilled with the perfume and top the kids had given her, but had panicked over where they'd got the money from. So he'd had to admit he'd given it to them.

'Only a little dinner for me, boy. I can't digest food like I used to,' Albie said. He hadn't wanted to stay with Little Vinny at first, but watching the boys open their presents this morning had cheered him up a bit. He was still pining for Viv though. Probably always would.

'Who the bloody hell's that? Answer the door, Calum,' Little Vinny ordered.

Returning seconds later, Calum announced, 'It's the Old Bill, Dad. They want to talk to you.'

Little Vinny dropped the carving knife on the floor. The last time the police had turned up at his home on Christmas Day they'd carted him off for questioning over Molly's murder.

'You OK, Vin? Do you want a glass of water?' Frankie asked worriedly. Little Vinny's complexion had turned white.

Feeling a full-blown panic attack arising, Little Vinny picked up his grandfather's brandy and downed it in one. Surely after all this time the police hadn't unearthed more evidence?

'You look weird, Dad. Like a ghost,' Regan said.

Little Vinny knew he had to pull himself together. 'I'm

OK. Stay here,' he ordered. How his trembling legs managed to get him to the front door, he did not know. But when he was informed, 'There's been an incident involving your father. We don't know the exact extent of his injuries, but he's been taken to the Royal London Hospital,' Little Vinny literally breathed a huge sigh of relief.

Jamie Preston turned the radio off. He'd found it difficult to adjust to life on the outside, didn't recognize the country any more. So much had changed, especially the fashion and music. He'd been a Mod before his arrest, had dressed and worn his hair like his idol Paul Weller. The pop charts had been great back then, and like most teenagers, Jamie had religiously listened to the Top Forty on the radio every Sunday. The Specials, Madness and The Jam used to be worth listening to, not like the crap that was now played.

Watching with interest as the police left Little Vinny's house, Jamie wondered what had happened. He'd been thrilled to hear via Glen that Vinny had been got at, and wondered if Little Vinny had just found out. With no family to speak of, Jamie had fancied having a little spy today, alone. He'd seen Frankie Mitchell arrive with her kids earlier, but he'd yet to see his old man again. In spite of everything, part of him wanted to meet Albie. There were so many questions he had and that old bastard was probably the only person who could answer them.

When Little Vinny leapt into his flashy BMW and sped past him, Jamie debated whether to follow, but decided he probably couldn't keep up. Having only recently passed his test, he was no Ayrton Senna.

Talking to himself had become second nature to Jamie in prison, especially after Glen had been released, so as he headed home instead, he spoke his thoughts aloud. 'Watch that skinny fucking back of yours. I've got big plans for you.

Won't be long now. I'm coming for you. You'll be in a far worse state than your father is, trust me, you lying cunt.'

Michael Butler glared at his youngest daughter. Ellie had opened at least a grand's worth of presents, yet was still complaining because she hadn't got the saddle she'd wanted for her horse. 'You gonna send her to her room, or shall I, Katy? Ungrateful spoilt brat don't know how bastard-well lucky she is.'

'Don't talk to her like that. I told you weeks ago that's what Ellie wanted and if you wasn't too busy gallivanting all the time, you would have bought it for her. I bet Princess Camila got what she wanted, didn't she?' Katy argued. She knew Michael was extremely close to the daughter he'd had with Bella and that grated on her immensely.

Michael stood up. 'Like mother, like daughter,' he spat.

'Where you going, Dad?' Nathan asked. Unlike his sister, he had a great relationship with their father, adored the ground he walked on.

'Outside, to make some phone calls. I haven't spoken to Vinny yet today.'

'Liar! You're ringing her, I bet,' Katy screamed, referring to Bella.

Michael switched on his mobile and was alerted he had answerphone messages. 'Shit,' he cursed, listening to Little Vinny's.

'Where do you think you're going?' Katy yelled when Michael grabbed his jacket and keys.

'Hospital. Vinny's been done over. He's in a bad way.'

Back at Joyce's, a game of Charades was being played.

'Hair?' Joyce shouted.

Stanley shook his head.

'Bald?' Joey guessed.

Stanley nodded.

Joyce clapped her hands. '*Ironside*?'

'No, you daft old bat. Ironside was a cripple, in a wheelchair. It's *Kojak*,' Stanley blurted out.

'Bleedin' useless, you are. Sit your arse down, it's my turn now,' Joyce ordered.

Stanley was fuming when his wife began simulating what he imagined to be a blow-job. Not only did it bring back awful memories of the time Pat the Pigeon had tried to put his John Thomas in her mouth, he found it highly embarrassing in front of Queenie and the boys.

Joey grabbed his boyfriend's arm. 'Oh my God! What is she like?'

Dominic laughed.

Joyce tilted her hand backwards and forwards, before bending over and simulating something being shoved up her backside. When she'd first been told Joey was gay, she'd been shocked. But she'd soon embraced his sexuality, and was now very proud her grandson was a gay man. Which was why she'd become addicted to the TV drama *Queer as Folk*. It had aired last year and she'd recorded it and watched it numerous times since. Some of the things the lads got up to on that were eye-watering and she wondered if Joey and Dom did similar.

'I've had enough of this. The woman's off her head,' Stanley snapped, marching out the room.

Queenie thought she might wet herself she was laughing that much. She'd been dreading today without Vivvy, and Joyce was just the tonic she'd needed.

'I'm so sorry about this, Dom. I really am,' Joey said, tongue in cheek. His boyfriend had tears of laughter running down his face. Joyce was now thrusting her hips in and out, like she was shagging thin air.

'Queer, the first syllable was. *Queer as Folk*! I thought

yous two would have got that,' an exhausted Joyce said, plonking herself on the sofa. 'Thick as pigshit, my family, Queen,' she added, winking at Joey.

'We expecting anyone?' Joey asked. His grandmother did nothing by halves. Even the doorbell chimed 'Ding Dong Merrily on High'.

'Perhaps it's your granddad's fancy piece, Pat the Pigeon. Stick a bow and gift label on him and shove him out the front door. He's all hers,' Joycie guffawed.

Even though he was in the kitchen, Joyce's voice carried like a foghorn and Stanley cringed at the mention of Pat. She was dead now, but he'd never told Joyce that. She'd make his life even more of a misery if she thought he had nowhere to run off to. 'I'll get the door, dear,' he said sarcastically.

Queenie was scoffing a Thorntons' chocolate when Michael walked in the lounge. 'What you doing here? What's the matter?'

'Vinny's been badly beaten up, Mum. He's got hypothermia an' all. I'm going to the hospital now and thought you might wanna come with me?'

Queenie's face crumpled. 'No! Not my Vinny.'

Felicity Carter-Price wept as she lay on the bed and took in the scent of her man from the pillow. She had no idea of the extent of Vinny's injuries. The doctors had refused to tell her anything because she wasn't family.

Shutting her eyes, Felicity willed the phone to ring. She hadn't slept at all last night waiting for him to arrive home. So many theories had run through her mind as to where he was. Had he got drunk and ended up in another woman's bed? Had he had an accident on the way home? Or had somebody told him about her past?

Vinny was registered as living at his apartment alone, so

when it had got to nine o'clock in the morning with still no sign of him, Felicity had decided to ring around some local hospitals. She'd once found her ex by doing the same. She'd then sat in the hospital corridor alone for hours, until Little Vinny had arrived and advised her to go home. 'My nan and uncle are on their way here, so it's best you're not. Give us your number and I'll call you later with an update,' he'd said bluntly.

Rubbing her stomach, Felicity felt in limbo. The baby certainly wasn't planned – she'd been shocked herself, and had no idea how Vinny was going to react. But she would do whatever he wanted. She loved him that much.

'I'm cream-crackered, boy. Don't mind if I slip off to bed, do you? Obviously, wake me if you need me,' Albie Butler said.

'That's fine, Granddad. I'll let you know if there's any more news.'

Frankie Mitchell sat on the sofa next to Little Vinny. Brett was staying with her dad and Gina tonight, Georgie and Harry had gone round to one of Calum's friends with him and Regan. 'So will he be OK, your dad?'

Little Vinny shrugged. He'd left the hospital as soon as his nan and uncle had arrived. The Old Bill turning up on his doorstep earlier had put the fear of God into him, and he still felt panicky, which was why he was now having a couple of beers. Alcohol seemed to calm his nerves. It always had done.

'I didn't understand what you were telling your granddad. What did the doctor say was wrong with your dad?'

'They're not sure of all his injuries yet. He lost consciousness and was laying in the cold all night they reckon. They need to treat him for the hypothermia first, before they can X-ray him for broken bones and other stuff. The doctor said they're going to do a "cardiopulmonary bypass". I don't know what that means exactly, but he said something about withdrawing blood from Dad's body, then they warm it up and insert it back. I know I should've stayed there, but I couldn't face it, Frankie. Say I lose him an' all?'

'You won't. Your dad's a fighter, like mine. That's why they're best pals.'

Since Sammi-Lou and Oliver had been so cruelly taken from him, Frankie had become an important part of Little Vinny's life. Sammi had been fond of Frankie in the short time she'd known her, so he knew she would totally have approved of their friendship. Besides, their kids did stuff together, so it was as though he still had some kind of a family unit. That was something Little Vinny needed. It helped keep him sane.

'What you thinking?' Frankie asked, hopefully. He was staring at her with a wistful expression. She knew it was probably too soon in most people's eyes, but she couldn't stop thinking about Little Vinny just lately, and was sure he felt the same about her. The way he was with her children was enough to make her fall for him. Plus she missed having a physical relationship with a man. After spending years stuck in prison, there'd been no better feeling than making love and waking up with Stuart.

'Just thinking what a great support you've been to me. Dunno if I'd have coped anywhere near as well without you and the kids being around. It's helped Calum and Regan deal with things too, having Georgie and Harry in their lives. It's great they all get on so well, isn't it?'

'I bet Sammi-Lou, Oliver and Stuart are looking down now and smiling. No way would they want us to be lonely, Vin,' Frankie said. She'd taken Little Vinny's kind words out of context, thinking he was trying to tell her something.

'I bet they are too. It's fate we all met when we did and hit it off immediately, don't you think?'

Taking that as a come on, Frankie leaned in for the full-blown kiss and was mortified when Little Vinny pushed her away, then leapt off the sofa. 'What the hell do you think you're playing at?'

Frankie was crushed. 'I'm sorry. I thought you liked me.'

'Of course I like you, but not in that way. Jesus, Frankie, our partners are barely cold! What the fuck is wrong with you?'

When Frankie started to cry, Little Vinny crouched next to her. 'Look, I'm sorry, I shouldn't have said that. I'm just a bit shocked and worried about my dad, that's all. You've had a lot to drink, which is why this has happened. Let's forget about it and get some supper ready for when the kids get back, eh?'

Feeling stupid and totally belittled, Frankie stood up. 'Where's my coat and bag? I'm going home.'

'Don't go. The kids'll be upset and wonder what's happened. It was nothing, so let's just forget about it.'

Searching around, a frantic Frankie found her belongings. She opened the front door and turned to Little Vinny, the look of hurt in her eyes clear to see. 'Please don't follow me or ring me any more. The kids can still be friends, obviously, but I think it's best we go our own ways from now on. I hope your dad pulls through, I really do. And please don't tell any of your family what happened between us. I feel humiliated enough as it is.' Having supped wine all day, Frankie could not help being overly dramatic.

'Don't be daft, Frankie. This is silly. Let's sort it out. You're taking it to heart and it's not that I don't fancy you – you're a very beautiful girl – but I'm still grieving for Sammi-Lou.'

Instead of replying, Frankie sprinted down the driveway like an Olympic gold medallist.

CHAPTER SEVENTEEN

Queenie Butler chewed furiously at what was left of her fingernails. They'd been long and polished red up until yesterday, now there was little left of them.

The hospital staff had been kind. They'd allowed her and Michael to wait for news in a small room. There were only a couple of chairs in there, but it was better than waiting in a corridor with strangers gawping at them. A nurse had even brought them tea and biscuits, but no way could Queenie eat. Not until she was reassured Vinny was out of the woods. As far as she and Michael knew, her first-born was still in intensive care, fighting for his life.

'Michael,' Queenie hissed, prodding her son.

'Sorry. I must've dozed off without realizing.'

'Go and find someone. I know no news is good news, but they must be able to tell us more by now. It's torture sitting here in limbo. Enough to make anybody lose their bleedin' marbles. Tell 'em we want to see Vinny. If he's still out for the count, I'm sure our voices might wake him up, mine especially.'

When Michael left the room, Queenie shut her eyes. She hated this bloody hospital. It was where Vivvy had died and she'd spent weeks here keeping vigil beside Roy's bed when he'd lain in that coma. Picturing Vinny and Roy as small boys, a tear slid down Queenie's face. She'd had lots of nicknames for her sons over the years. But Vinny, she'd called 'Baby Blue' from the first moment she'd held him in her arms. As he got older, started walking and talking, she shortened it to just 'Blue'. Roy's was 'Sunshine', then when Michael came on the scene, being the youngest, he was fondly referred to as 'Half-Pint'. Being the eldest, Vinny had always ruled the roost. Mischievous little toe-rags from a young age, Vinny and Roy were. Queenie could see them now, dressed in their shorts, socks crumpled around their ankles, swinging on her old wooden gate. They'd chat to every passer-by in the hope of earning a bob or two, and their natural charm had been visible even back then. Persuasive go-getting little sods, an early sign of what was to come in the future, she supposed.

Saying a silent prayer, Queenie thought about what the doctor had said earlier. She didn't know many medical words and had found his accent hard to understand, but Michael had got the gist of it. Queenie hadn't a clue what a cardiopulmonary bypass was, but was now aware that it was often used in heart surgery as it helped maintain the circulation of the blood and oxygen's content to the body. In Vinny's case, it had been used to warm his blood. Her son's body had taken a serious battering, although he hadn't quite said it in those words, and Vinny would need to have scans to see if he had any internal damage.

Queenie sighed and chewed on her nails once more. Vinny was as strong as an ox and had taken a few beatings over the years, so she was sure he'd recover physically. The doctor saying her son was confused was what worried Queenie the most though. Apparently it was a common side-effect of severe hypothermia, but Queenie was concerned her son might have been kicked in the head and have some kind of brain damage. Roy had never been the same person again.

'Well? What did they say?' Queenie asked on Michael's return.

'He's still a bit confused and will be having a scan shortly. The other procedure worked though, by all accounts. They said his temperature is rising.'

'Don't like the sound of that confusion one little bit, boy. If he ain't right in the head, your brother wouldn't want to be here.'

About to joke that Vinny had never been right in the head, Michael decided it wasn't the time or place.

The nice young blonde nurse poked her head around the door. 'The police are here and want to speak to you, Mr Butler. I can't put them off again.'

Breathing a sigh of annoyance, Michael stood up. 'Here's the season to be fucking jolly,' he mumbled.

Having recently treated himself to a top-of-the-range coffee machine, Little Vinny made his favourite, an espresso, and sat at the kitchen table. He'd called the hospital first thing and been told his dad's condition was 'serious, but stable'. He'd have to pop up there again later. He despised hospitals now. They reminded him of his final goodbye to Sammi-Lou.

'Calum and Georgie have both been sick again, Dad, and me and Harry are starving. Can you make us some breakfast?' Regan asked.

Little Vinny eyeballed his brazen son. He'd had no option but to force Georgie to ring her mother last night and tell Frankie that she and Harry were having a sleepover. All four kids had arrived home slightly worse for wear and after Calum had admitted they'd stolen some drink out of the garage, Little Vinny had felt responsible. 'If you're old enough to go out and get bladdered, then you're most certainly old enough to make your own breakfast. Same goes for your partners in crime. Did I ever tell you about that lad I went to school with, Billy Watts? He got drunk at your age and his body couldn't cope. Died of alcohol poisoning, Billy did; we had a special assembly for him,' Little Vinny lied. He was a calm-headed modern-day parent who preferred to use the odd shock-factor fib rather than hand out punishments to his children. Calum and Regan had been through enough this year without being grounded, and he couldn't be too angry with them as he and Ben Bloggs had got up to similar mischief at their ages. Worse, in fact. They'd sniffed glue and got stoned as well.

Wearing nothing but a pair of grey baggy tracksuit bottoms, Regan shoved his hands down the front and frowned. 'So was Billy Watts sick before he died, Dad?'

'Dunno. I'd imagine so. Which is why you should warn the others. Your liver doesn't develop until a certain age, so it can't break down the alcohol properly. I'd lay off it if I were you and Calum. By all accounts, Billy Watts was in terrible pain before he croaked it an' all.'

When his shocked-looking son darted upstairs, Little Vinny rubbed the stubble on his chin. He'd already tried to ring Frankie twice this morning, but she'd blanked both calls. He definitely had feelings for her, would hate her to not be in his life now. Truth be known, he needed her just as much as she now relied on him. She made him feel useful, appreciated and wanted. No way could he look at her in the same way he had Sammi-Lou though. True love only happened once in a lifetime.

Felicity Carter-Price was shocked when Michael Butler turned up at the apartment, unannounced. 'What's wrong? Vinny's alive, isn't he?' she asked, her lip quivering.

'He's still in a serious way, but the hypothermia seems to be under control. He's got to have scans and stuff to see if there's any other damage.'

'Who would beat him up like that?'

Eyeing Felicity suspiciously, Michael shrugged. Chances are, Vinny's beating was something to do with her ex, but Michael hadn't told the police that, neither had he mentioned the bible quotes and dead creatures that had been sent to the casino. Vinny was a closed book when it came to the Old Bill and would hate them to know anything of importance.

'Can I go and see him now?' Felicity asked, hopefully.

'No. My mum's still up the hospital and I don't want her any more upset than she currently is. As soon as she leaves, I'll call you and then you can see him.'

'Will that be today?'

'I don't know. Doubt it, to be honest, as my mum's insisting on hanging around until she knows Vinny's OK. Look, between me and you, Vinny's always asked me to keep an eye on his place if anything like this were to happen. His businesses are totally legal, but he's paranoid the Old Bill might start snooping around and try to fit him up somehow. You've had a dreadful Christmas already, so why don't you go and stay with family or friends? I'll call you as soon as I have more news.'

'I'd much rather stay here as it's near the hospital. My family live miles away,' Felicity explained.

The whole idea of Michael turning up unexpectedly was to search the apartment thoroughly in case Felicity had it bugged. He still could not believe Vinny had been stupid enough to tell her so much, especially seeing as it implicated him too. 'You can't stay here, love. I'm sorry, but I have to be here and I need to be alone.'

'Do I have to go today?'

'Yeah, pack some bits now and make a move. It's only temporary. You can move back in once Vinny is better.'

'But say he doesn't get better?'

Michael shrugged. The deceitful cow was obviously hiding her past from Vinny for a reason. 'Best you keep your fingers crossed, eh?'

Frankie Mitchell felt stupid, and had already made a New Year resolution never to drink again. She'd honestly thought Little Vinny liked her in the same way she liked him and could not believe how thick she was. Frankie was also feeling terribly guilty. She had genuinely adored Stuart and would never have even looked at another man if he were still alive.

It was loneliness that had made her do what she did, that and too much alcohol. Well, from now on she was going to get her act together, as she never wanted to show herself up in such a way again. It was an insult to Stuart's memory, and her dad would go apeshit if he found out she'd made herself look like a complete desperado.

The doorbell made Frankie jump and as she glanced at the CCTV her dad had insisted on installing, Frankie's heart sank as she spotted Little Vinny on her doorstep.

'Frankie, it's me. I know you're in there, so answer the door, please.'

Hoping he would go away, Frankie stood rooted to the kitchen floor. She couldn't face him, felt too ashamed.

'Frankie, don't be silly. I miss you, and we need to talk. My dad's still in intensive care and I could really do with a friendly shoulder to cry on. Please, just open the door.'

Reluctantly doing as she was told, Frankie held the door open. 'I'll put the kettle on. Does my dad know about yours yet? I haven't spoken to him since yesterday morning.'

'I think Michael told your dad. If not, I'll ring him later.

I'm gonna shoot up the hospital in a bit and was hoping you'd come with me. I could do with some moral support.'

'Where are Georgie and Harry?'

'They're watching films with my two. My granddad's keeping an eye on them, and I've told him they're not to go out until I get back. Will you come with me, please? I don't think I can face it alone. Just the smell of hospitals reminds me of Sammi-Lou lying dead in that bed.'

'Yeah. But about last night. I just want to—'

Little Vinny silenced Frankie with an awkward hug. 'You've no need to say anything. It was what it was and who knows what the future holds. I need you in my life, Frankie, and I truly mean that. You're the only one I can really talk to lately. You're my rock.'

Having had a good root around Vinny's apartment and satisfied himself it wasn't bugged, Michael arrived back at the hospital early Boxing Day afternoon. 'Any more news?' he asked. Eddie Mitchell had arrived just before Michael had left earlier and had promised to stay with Queenie until he returned.

'He's having some scans now. The nurse said he seems far less confused than he was. I need to see him with my own eyes though, boy. I'll know instantly, like I did with Roy, if something terrible is wrong. Was she at the apartment, the tart?' Queenie asked.

'No. I'm not sure if they're still an item,' Michael lied. Felicity had become very upset when he'd taken her keys off her, insisting that he needed to use them himself. Michael didn't want her to suspect anything was amiss, so had called her on the way back to the hospital and acted much friendlier. 'I'll give you another ring later today with an update, darlin',' he'd promised.

'I'm gonna have to make a move in a bit. Got the family

coming to mine this afternoon and I promised Gina I wouldn't be long. Ring me as soon as you hear anything. I'll pop back tomorrow when things are a little less frantic. Hopefully he'll be able to have visitors then.'

Michael followed Eddie outside. 'I didn't want to say sod-all on the phone or in front of my mum, but the Old Bill told me there was a box left beside Vinny's body. It was a headless chicken and another bible quote.'

Eddie felt the colour drain from his face. Whoever was behind all this meant serious business.

Glen Harper and Jamie Preston looked around the warehouse. It belonged to a pal of Glen's who used it sporadically throughout the year.

'There's all bits of Christmas decorations. Did your pal hold a party here?' Jamie asked. The warehouse was situated just off the A127 and there were no other buildings in sight.

Glen chuckled. 'Mark is Wickford's answer to Del Boy Trotter, trust me. Rammed with decorations up until Christmas Eve, this gaff would've been. Near Easter, you can't move for poxy eggs, but his biggest earner is the fireworks. Fucking full of 'em from September onwards. He'll know all about it if someone was ever to strike a match 'ere, put it that way.'

'You told Mark what we're using it for?'

'Sort of. Not mentioned no names though. Don't worry about Mark. He's sound as a pound. Good setting, eh? Little Vinny will be blindfolded all the way here, so he won't have a clue where we're taking him. I know a bloke who'll clear up after us. Bound to be splashes of blood and gore.'

Jamie Preston grinned. He'd been thrilled when Glen had finally agreed to help him abduct Little Vinny. With his father in hospital, it was too good an opportunity not to snatch him. 'I reckon we'll strike gold tomorrow. He's bound to visit his shitbag of an old man again, and if yesterday and today were anything to go by, he'll visit alone. All we have to do is park near his motor, stick our balaclavas on, and Bob's your uncle. I can't wait to torture the truth out of him, Glen. Poor little Molly. I never knew her, but she was still my niece. Deserves to rest in peace, doesn't she?'

Glen put his arm around his young pal's shoulders. It had become clear in recent weeks that Jamie was not going to enjoy life on the outside until Little Vinny was dealt with. So deal with him they would. Jamie had waited a long time to get the truth from the horse's mouth, and he deserved peace almost as much as Molly Butler did.

'Vinny's awake now, but still feeling a bit fragile. You can see him, but only two at a time. No more than ten minutes each visit, either. He needs to rest,' the nurse said.

When Michael and Little Vinny stood up, Queenie ordered them to sit back down. 'I want to see him first, on my own.'

Queenie was led into the intensive care unit and as she laid eyes on her usually so-well-turned-out son, she gasped. Vinny's face was black and blue and he seemed to have more tubes sprouting from him than Roy had ever had.

'Mum, you OK?' Vinny croaked.

Having already been told Vinny's left arm was broken, Queenie clung to her son's right. Unable to stop the tears streaming down her cheeks, she said, 'I'm so sorry, boy. You're my world, you know that. My Baby Blue.'

Vinny could barely open his swollen mouth, but when he mumbled the words, 'You're my world too, Mum,' Queenie's tears turned to ones of joy. There was sod-all wrong with Vinny's brain. Queenie had always had that acute motherly instinct, and knew immediately her beloved son was over the worst. Perhaps there was a God after all?

Little Vinny ended the call and smiled at Frankie. 'They're fine and behaving themselves. Georgie's just made a buffet for everyone – us included, so my granddad reckons. Wonders will never cease, eh?'

Frankie grinned. Little Vinny had been so nice towards her today, the awkwardness she'd felt earlier was already forgotten. 'I'm going to sort myself out in the New Year, Vin. I know I've been drinking too much since Stuart died and I'm knocking it on the head. I might even see if I can get a little part-time job that fits in with the kids. I get bored at home alone, that's my problem.'

'There's nothing wrong with you, Frankie. I'm the oddball, not you. I'm a bad drinker, have done some stupid things in the past. That's the only reason I steer clear of the stuff.'

'Where we going?' Frankie asked, when Little Vinny turned off the A13.

'Out on our own for once. There's a pub not far from here. And instead of being a boring bastard, I am going to join you in sipping a glass of champagne. Not only is it Christmas, and so far ours had been crap, but I'm proper chuffed my dad seems to be out of the woods and we can toast his recovery.'

Frankie smiled. 'Sounds the perfect reason to celebrate.'

Having barely slept a wink the previous night, Queenie Butler kicked off her high heels and slumped on to the sofa with her precious photo albums by her side. Joyce had phoned, asking if she wanted some company, but Queenie was shattered, could barely speak on the way home and she was glad she'd taken Michael's advice. He'd told her, 'You'll make yourself ill, Mum, if you stay up this hospital another night. Vinny wouldn't want that and neither do I. He's gonna be just fine; I could see it in his eyes and the doctor told us he was on the mend too.'

When she'd moved to Hornchurch, Vinny and Michael had joked that they needed a separate lorry just to carry all the photo albums. Flicking through in hope of finding snaps of Vinny and Roy as young boys, Queenie felt terribly sad as she instead stumbled across pictures of Molly. She'd been such a clever, angelic, beautiful blonde child who was surely destined for great things in life.

Studying one particular photo where Vinny had Molly held above his head and Little Vinny was standing next to them looking as miserable as sin, Queenie slammed the album shut. That little girl's final moments on this earth had always played on her mind. She must've been so terrified, God rest her soul. No way could Queenie think about that today. It had been a bad enough Christmas as it was.

Alice O'Hara hugged her son close to her chest. He was the only one she had left now. Those bastards the Mitchells had seen to that. 'Make sure you ring me as soon as you get there and don't worry about this little chavvie, he'll be fine with me.'

'I'll ring you every evening as well. They'll be home soon, I'd bet my finest trotting filly on that, Mum.'

Following her son out of the trailer, Alice poked her head in the window of Mickey Maloney's Shogun. 'I bet you can't wait to see her, Ryan. Make sure you spoil her all the way home. She is your wife-to-be, after all.'

Fifteen-year-old Ryan grinned. 'I'll look after her good and proper, don't you worry about that, Alice. Missed her so much. I loves her, I do.'

'Bye, Alice. Keep my Linda company for me,' Mickey Maloney winked.

When the Shogun zoomed off into the cold December night, Alice O'Hara felt a mixture of nerves and excitement. It had been the best Christmas present ever when she'd received that phone call. She'd been singing along to Loretta Lynn's 'Coal Miner's Daughter' and would never forget the moment her son bellowed: 'They've been found!'

'Where's me dad gone, Nan?'

Much to his annoyance, Alice picked up her nine-year-old grandson and smothered him in kisses. 'He's gone to find Georgie and Harry, bring 'em home where they belong, boy. Not long now and we'll be a big happy family again.'

CHAPTER EIGHTEEN

Three days after the attack, Vinny Butler was out of intensive care and had been moved to a plush hospital in central London.

On strong painkillers that seemed to make him constantly sleepy, Vinny was trying his best to buck his ideas up and sound in good spirits. His mother was visiting and he didn't want her worrying about him any more than she usually did. 'Nice gaff, ain't it? Beats listening to every Tom, Dick and Harry crapping and farting while you're trying to sleep.'

'Or watching 'em scratch their cobblers like your father used to. I'm very impressed with it, Vin. Never been in a private hospital before. It's ever so posh and you've got Sky TV. You should watch a film later,' Queenie suggested.

'Yeah. I probably will,' Vinny lied. His mind was all over the place, and concentrating on a movie was a non-starter. He kept trying to work out who had done this to him and why. Could think of little else.

Queenie unpacked the bag of goodies she'd picked up on the way, 'I got you a couple of books from WH Smith in case you fancy a read. They're crime ones. I also popped in Marks and Spencer's and got some nice yoghurts and trifles for ya. There's a tasty soup in there I made especially an' all. Get the nurses to warm that up for your supper. Worrying me, you can't eat any solids. You look like you've lost weight already. Don't want you slipping down a drain, do we now?'

As well as a fractured arm and ribs, Vinny had been kicked repeatedly in the left-hand side of his face which was why he couldn't eat properly. Two of his teeth had been dislodged at the back and he'd bitten straight through his tongue. The pain was unbearable as soon as the tablets started to wear off, and Vinny was aware he'd need a few visits to the dentist soon. He was just thankful the teeth weren't at the front where you could see the damage. 'Thanks, Mum. Do you mind giving me and Eddie five minutes alone? We've got some business we need to discuss.'

Queenie stood up. Michael was spending the day with Camila, so Eddie Mitchell had given her a lift. 'You take as long as you need. I can't be doing with man talk. I'm gonna have a wander round the rest of the hospital; see if all the wards are as nice as yours. If I'm ever seriously ill, this is where I'd like to suffer, boy.'

Knowing his mother's words were a hint, Vinny promised to take her out a private health-care policy, then told her to shut the door behind her.

'Well? You remembered anything else about them yet? There must be something you can think of that'll give us a clue,' Eddie Mitchell said. He was a worried man right now, didn't need this crap at his time of life, and was determined to get some answers out of Vinny today.

'They sprayed poxy CS gas in my eyes, mate, but I do remember a couple of their voices. They weren't pikeys, neither were they Turks. Sounded like London or Essex boys to me. I know what you must be thinking, Ed, but I swear to God I haven't upset anybody for a long, long time. Like yourself, I've calmed down over the years and just want a quiet life now. I've been racking my brains since the moment I woke up, and the only conclusion I can come up with is Felicity's ex is behind all this.'

'I can't believe you were stupid enough to fall for a fucking bird that randomly wandered into your club to ask for a job. You're no man's fool as a rule. Didn't you smell a rat? Whyever didn't you get her checked out before you started banging her?'

'I dunno. She seemed all right, I suppose. Look, I'm sorry for being such a mug. Not a lot else I can say really, is there? But at least you now know it ain't you who's being targeted. It's only gonna be my blood Dave Newton's after.'

Eddie rubbed the stubble on his chin. 'We don't know anything for sure. It might be sod-all to do with Dave Newton and I might be next on whoever's it is hit list. What about Jamie Preston? He's swanning around with Essex's answer to Peter Pan, that prick Harper. How d'ya know it isn't them?'

'Jamie killed my daughter, Ed. I'm meant to have it in for him, which I do. Not the other way round. Jamie will get his just desserts. Just biding me time until I find the right man for the job. I'll be the prime suspect, so it has to be right. I couldn't face another long stretch behind bars, not even for Molly. Anyway, Preston was still in prison when all that crap started to get delivered to us.'

'Dave Newton is still in prison now. Look, mate, I don't want to sound harsh, but I'm telling you loud and clear: if trouble comes to my door and upsets or affects my wife and kids in any way, I am going to be seriously pissed off. Maybe we should part company sooner rather than later? I've got the dosh to buy you out.'

Vinny sneered. 'Stick your dosh where the sun don't shine, Ed. I'm going nowhere, pal.'

*

'What you doing? Leave it out,' Glen Harper hissed, grabbing his pal by the arm. 'We can't make our move while those people are stood there rabbiting. If they were to clock the sign on the van, chances are we'll be nicked before we're even halfway to our destination. Be much better if we can nab him in the dark, trust me. You need to calm down, Jamie lad. Patience is a virtue.'

Cursing the three middle-aged chatterboxes who'd decided to put the world to rights directly on the pavement outside Vinny's driveway, Jamie Preston smashed his fist against the van door in annoyance. He'd lived for this day for a very long time, and the thought of it happening had got him through his darkest days in prison. Even though he had no proof that Little Vinny or Ben Bloggs were behind Molly's murder, he knew in his heart either one or both were. He certainly hadn't throttled that little girl to death and all arrows were pointing their way. Since Bloggs wasn't around to tell the truth any more, Little Vinny would have to do the honours. Which was why Jamie was salivating at the prospect of getting his hands on the bastard. If his time in prison had taught him anything, it was how to put the frighteners on shitbags like him.

Glen put his hand on the back of Jamie's neck. 'Don't worry, pal. He'll be back later and, fingers crossed, we can strike then. Better to be safe than sorry.'

'Are you and Little Vinny having sex, Mum?' Georgie O'Hara asked out of nowhere.

Dropping the TV remote, Frankie picked it up and quickly pulled herself together. 'No. Of course not. Why would you ask such a thing?'

'Because Harry's positive you fancy Little Vinny and Calum reckons he fancies you too. We were talking about it yesterday.'

'Well, you shouldn't have been, and I do hope it wasn't in front of Albie.'

'Albie wasn't in the room. You can tell me things, you know, Mum. I won't tell the boys, I promise.'

'There's nothing to tell, Georgie. Little Vinny and I are good friends, that's all.'

Georgie smiled knowingly. She had seen the way her mother looked at Little Vinny and could tell she felt the same way about him as Georgie herself felt about Regan. Not one to be palmed off, Georgie squeezed her mum's hand. 'It's OK, you know. Even Harry likes him. Little Vinny's a nice man, like our dad.'

Frankie snatched her hand away. If she thought for one minute that Little Vinny was anything like bloody Jed O'Hara, she would run a mile.

'I take it that's a hint I'm to make myself scarce again, is it?' Queenie Butler asked, her tone one of angry pretence. Eddie Mitchell had left the hospital earlier, then Michael had arrived. Queenie wasn't daft, could always tell when her son wanted to talk business.

'Just give us ten minutes, Mum. Me and Michael need to get our stories straight in case the Old Bill start poking their trunks in again.'

Queenie's smile slipped as soon as she closed the door. Much as she was relieved Vinny was on the mend and elated that the two of them had sorted their differences, she still wasn't sleeping well. It was awful knowing somebody wanted her son dead, but even worse was the fact they didn't have a clue who it was. The worry of it was eating away at her insides like maggots.

Feeling older than ever, Queenie sat down on the first chair she saw. Vinny recuperating at her bungalow was the only answer for now, at least. She wasn't scared of no bastard, neither was she frightened of death. She'd brought that boy, her 'Baby Blue', into the world, so protect and care for him she would.

It wasn't often she found herself alone with Regan, and Georgie O'Hara was determined to make the most of it.

'Got any New Year resolutions?' she asked, flopping next to him on his bed.

'Not sure yet. Might not drink alcohol any more after my dad telling me about that Billy Watts.'

Georgie started to laugh.

'What's so funny?'

'You. Bet your dad only made that story up to scare ya. Nanny Alice used to make stuff up to me and Harry when she didn't want us to do something. Bet Billy Watts didn't even exist.'

Regan glared at the girl he'd recently started thinking about whilst masturbating. 'Calling my dad a liar, are ya?' he asked angrily.

'No. There's a difference between lying and having a wind-up.' Georgie leaned closer, held her stomach in and pushed her breasts outwards. 'So is that your only one? Me and Harry had never heard of resolutions before. We don't know of any travellers who made them at New Year. We didn't even know what the word meant until my mum told us. Do you have to make a wish?'

Regan shrugged. 'Dunno. I think you just give something up. Why you so interested in crap like that anyway?'

'If I tell you, you can't tell Calum or your dad. And you mustn't let Harry know I've told you either.'

'All right.'

Georgie and Harry had made a pact not to tell a soul about their conversation with the travellers in Romford. Calum and Regan were trustable, but if they slipped up and it got back to their mum, Georgie knew she and her brother would be grounded again. Or worse still, moved away.

Regan listened with interest while Georgie told him the story. 'So do you wanna leave?' he asked, his expression one of shock. He and Calum had got used to having Georgie and Harry around since his mum and Oliver had been killed and he couldn't quite imagine life without them now. He even saw Harry as a sort of brother rather than just a friend.

Georgie shrugged. She was pleased that her words had startled Regan and he looked a bit upset. 'I don't really know what I want, but Harry definitely wants to leave. We miss our dad, grandparents and little sister, but I don't really miss anybody else,' she said truthfully. Ryan, she barely thought about any more. She much preferred Regan to him now.

Regan grasped Georgie's arm. 'Don't go. Stay round 'ere.'

Thrilled with the reaction she'd got, Georgie took the bull by the horns and leaned towards Regan. The kiss that followed was absolutely wonderful.

Michael Butler handed Little Vinny an orange juice. It had been his nephew's idea to pop in a pub after leaving the hospital and Michael had guessed the lad had something on his mind.

'So apart from Dad being done over, how was your Christmas?' Little Vinny asked.

'Crap. Yours?'

'Felt really weird, Sammi-Lou and Oliver not being with us. I really missed them.'

'For the record, I think you're doing marvellously. I was a complete wreck after Adam got killed. If it weren't for Bella, I'd have probably gone down a slippery slope. It was her helped me get through that.'

'Frankie's helped me. Actually, that's why I wanted to go for a drink: to talk about her.'

'Spill the beans.'

'What would you do if you were me?' Little Vinny asked after explaining the situation. His father was a joke when it came to relationships, which was why he always turned to Michael for advice in that field.

'I don't know. It's a tough one to call, Vin. But what you need to remember is, if you go there, there ain't no going back. She's Eddie Mitchell's daughter, for fuck's sake.'

Remembering his brother's lecture, Vinny Butler greeted Felicity Carter-Price with a false gush of warmth. 'I've missed you so much,' he lied through gritted teeth.

'Not as much as I've missed you.'

'Wipe your eyes – you look like a panda, babe.'

When Felicity turned to pick up her handbag, Vinny visualized stabbing the deceitful slut right in the back.

Felicity turned around and stared the man she loved in the eyes. She was incredibly nervous and Vinny noticed.

'Why you shaking sweetheart?'

Felicity's eyes welled up. 'Please don't be angry with me, Vinny. I swear this isn't my fault. I would never deceive you on purpose.'

'What isn't your fault?' Vinny asked gently. He deserved an Oscar for his performance, and knew he would have to keep it up until he was well enough and had a proper plan in place to get rid of her. 'Something's on your mind, come on babe, tell me.'

Fully expecting Felicity to come clean about Dave Newton, Vinny Butler could not have been more astounded when she instead mumbled the words, 'I'm pregnant.'

*

Frankie Mitchell was astute when it came to young love. She'd only just turned sixteen when she'd fallen head over heels for Jed, and even though Georgie was younger than she'd been, she looked and acted a damn sight older for her years, and so did Regan.

Aware of another intimate glance shared between the two, Frankie called her daughter out into the kitchen.

'What's up?' Georgie asked.

'Nothing. Little Vinny's going to pick up an Indian takeaway for us on the way home, so I thought you could help me choose what we all want.'

'Harry only eats chicken tikka and chips. Calum likes chicken tikka too, but with rice. And Regan likes prawn dhansak. But we all like them onion bhajis, so get us lots.'

'And you like Regan too, don't you?' Frankie stated, with a twinkle in her eyes. 'Something's happened between you and him, hasn't it? Have you kissed?'

'Shhh,' Georgie urged, shutting the kitchen door.

'Well?' Frankie asked.

'I'll only tell you if you tell me the truth about Little Vinny. But you mustn't say anything to anyone,' Georgie said. Unlike other children her age who might be embarrassed to have such a conversation with their mother, because she hadn't grown up with Frankie, Georgie could talk to her as a friend too.

'OK. But it's between me and you. Don't you dare tell the boys.'

'I promise I won't, Mum.'

'I do think fondly of Little Vinny, but nothing has happened between us yet. Hopefully, in time, it might. We'll have to wait and see. It's a difficult situation and we're both still grieving precious loved ones.'

'Have you kissed him yet?' Georgie enquired.

'No. Not properly. What about you and Regan?'

Georgie's eyes lit up. 'We kissed properly for the first time today. He's so nice. I really like him. I think I might marry him when I'm older, instead of Ryan.'

'Regan's very handsome. He's the type of boy I would have gone for at your age too. But you don't want to be married too young. Enjoy your life first.' Frankie knew it was the norm in the world Georgie had grown up in to get married at a very young age. She also knew it was forbidden for girls to have sex before marriage, so was glad she wouldn't have to worry about that. Jed and Alice would've drummed those values into her daughter, if nothing else.

When Georgie threw her arms around her mother's waist, Frankie stroked her hair. 'I'm honoured. What's that for?'

'I don't know. I just felt like doing it.'

'I'm going to order the food now. Run upstairs and ask Albie what he wants from the fish-and-chip shop. He doesn't eat Indian.'

'OK. And I enjoyed our chat.'

Frankie Mitchell could not wipe the smile off her face. When her kids had first been rescued, she'd felt like giving up many a day. They had been truly unbearable at times. Dark days, when she would never have envisaged things getting any better, but finally a corner had been turned. Harry was currently laughing his head off about something in the front room, and she and Georgie had shared their best mother-and-daughter moment to date. It was onwards and upwards from now on, surely?

Little Vinny was still in deep thought as he picked up the food then made the short journey home. Chatting to Michael had helped, but hadn't really given him an answer. His uncle had been spot on about one thing though: Frankie was Eddie's daughter, so he couldn't mess her around. Not unless he had some kind of death wish.

Deciding not to drive himself mad any more unless Frankie tried it on again, Little Vinny got out of his motor to open his gates. They'd never worked electronically since a tree surgeon had reversed his lorry into them.

Hearing heavy footsteps behind him, Little Vinny looked around, and was startled to see two blokes wearing balaclavas. 'What the hell! Whaddya want? I ain't got no money or jewellery indoors, I swear. Who are you? Fuck off,' he panicked.

Glen Harper punched Little Vinny hard in the side of the head. 'Shut it,' he hissed.

'Frankie, Fran—' Little Vinny started to scream, before a large hand wearing gloves was clamped over his mouth.

'All clear. Come on, let's go,' Glen barked.

Eyes bulging like organ stops, Little Vinny had never felt so terrified in his life as he was dragged towards a van, bundled in the back, then blindfolded.

CHAPTER NINETEEN

'Frankie, our neighbour Maggie just buzzed, asking if Dad was here. I said he weren't, but she reckons his car's outside with the engine running and door open,' Regan explained.

Perplexed, Frankie said, 'Perhaps one of the other neighbours called your dad. He wouldn't have left the engine running and gone far.'

'We're starving. Me and Georgie will see if we can find him,' Calum said, grabbing his object of affection by the arm.

Frankie followed her daughter and Calum down the driveway. A man and a woman were standing either side of Little Vinny's vehicle. 'Hello. My husband and I didn't want to leave the car unattended but we've been here for a while.' Frankie began to feel the first stirrings of unrest. She looked up and down the road. There was no sign of Little Vinny, or anybody else for that matter. She turned to her daughter. 'Go get me my phone. It's in the kitchen. Run.'

Eddie Mitchell put his arms around Gina and playfully shunted his groin up against her. 'Stop it!' Gina exclaimed. 'The kids might walk out here.'

'So? If you want to go to that five-star resort in Puerto

Banús you ain't stopped banging on about, best you up your game, Mrs Mitchell.'

When Eddie handed her the confirmation of the holiday he'd booked for next June, Gina squealed with delight. She'd read about it in a magazine. It was popular with footballers and celebrities and looked incredible. There was also a wonderful kids' club that provided all sorts of activities and entertainment to keep her two happy. 'I can't believe you went and booked it. You know you've got to definitely come now, don't you? No last-minute excuses,' Gina said, hugging the man she adored. Trying to drag Eddie on holiday was like trying to drag an elephant around Lakeside shopping centre. Because he hated leaving others in charge, he never wanted to go far, or book anything in advance as a rule.

Eddie kissed his wife. 'Told you I was a changed man, didn't I? All legal and above board now, so I can swan off without worrying. You're a lucky woman, Gina,' he joked.

'Granddad, Mum's on the phone,' Brett shouted out. 'She says it's urgent.'

Eddie darted out of the kitchen and snatched at the phone. 'What's up?'

Gina's heart sank when she heard Eddie say, 'Don't panic, I'll be straight over.' Gina wasn't daft. She knew what she'd signed up for when she'd married him. But would the drama ever stop? Only Gina was finding it a bit tedious now, especially when it involved Frankie.

Little Vinny could barely breathe, such was the terror he felt inside. The only anxiety he could even compare it to was when the police had turned up on his doorstep to haul him in over Molly's murder. Somehow, he'd managed to dig himself out of that hole, but being blindfolded was incredibly scary. He had no idea where he was being driven to and why. The only thing he could assume was he'd been taken hostage by the same men who'd beaten up his father.

Jamie Preston was staring at the quivering scumbag that was unfortunately related to him. He'd wanted to tell Little Vinny who he was, but Glen had ordered him not to. 'For all we know, he might go squealing to the pigs. If that were to happen, you're straight back inside. Not worth the risk, plus it'll be far scarier for him to be confronted over his sister's murder by two strapping strangers in balaclavas. He won't know if he's coming or going,' Glen had told Jamie.

Taking deep breaths, Little Vinny thought of his sons. They needed him, especially now they had no mum. 'Who are you? Where we going?'

'Well, I'm certainly not Father Christmas, so we're not going to Lapland,' Glen Harper chuckled.

Jamie Preston stood over the shitbag who he was 99 per cent sure had something to do with ruining his life. He was gagging to mention Molly by name, but needed to see the look in Little Vinny's eyes as he did so. Only then could he be 100 per cent certain. 'Not nice, going on a journey when you have no idea where you're being taken, is it?' Jamie taunted.

Desperate not to antagonize his captors by ignoring them or saying the wrong thing, Little Vinny mumbled, 'No.'

The brutal kick that landed in his stomach was confirmation that he'd said the wrong thing anyway.

Frankie Mitchell was by now in an inconsolable state. Something terrible had happened to Little Vinny, there was no other explanation, and the thought of losing him so soon after Stuart was terrifying. He was the only true friend she really had these days, the only one she could rely on to be there for her and her children at the drop of a hat.

'What we gonna do, Frankie?' Regan asked, desperately trying not to cry. He didn't want to show himself up in front of Georgie.

Calum couldn't help but cry. His dad meant the world to him. 'We got to call the police. They'll help us.'

'No gavvers,' Georgie and Harry said in unison. Gavvers was a traveller word for police, and Nanny Alice had been petrified of them. She said they were evil and not to be trusted.

The conversation was interrupted by Queenie Butler's arrival. Michael had told her the awful news and picked her up on the way over. 'Nobody has said anything to my Vinny yet, have they?' Vinny was still recovering in the private hospital in central London.

Frankie shook her head.

'Well, let's keep it that way, for now at least. Poor bastard. If he finds out about this he'll discharge himself. That can't happen, I won't allow it. That boy needs to get himself better.'

As petrified as he was, Little Vinny was trying to take in everything. His father had always drummed into him how important it was to remember details if a situation such as this were ever to occur, and Little Vinny was sure he'd been driven along the A127, as they'd definitely turned on to a road then driven at speed not far from his home. They hadn't stopped at any traffic lights either, which was another clue.

Suddenly the van swerved off the road and came to a standstill. Little Vinny was then grabbed by the arm and dragged along roughly on what felt like gravel beneath his feet.

Losing his footing, he tumbled to the ground and was treated to a sharp kick in the face accompanied by the words, 'Get up, wrong 'un.' He then heard some padlocks being undone and was led inside a freezing cold building with a stone floor. 'What you doing? I won't run off, I promise,' he pleaded as he was forced down on to some kind of wooden chair and his hands were tied to the back of it. 'Stop! That hurts,' he gasped.

'You'll know all about pain soon,' Glen Harper laughed, ripping the blindfold off his prey.

Little Vinny took his first proper look at his captors and immediately feared the worst. Both men still had their balaclavas on and they were dressed in navy tracksuits and black trainers. The pair of them were built like brick shithouses. He'd never seen a more menacing sight.

'What's this about? Has my dad upset you?' he gabbled, trying desperately to hold it together. At least his hands being tied up had stopped them from shaking, but he could do nothing to control his trembling legs.

Both men were of similar height, but one was more broad-shouldered than the other and it was he who spoke: 'This ain't got nothing to do with your dad. You're the one who's been a naughty boy, haven't you?'

'I haven't done anything wrong, I swear. If this is to do with Frankie, we're not together, we're only friends,' Little Vinny pleaded.

Glen Harper got off on violence and intimidation. It gave him a buzz. Determined to torture Little Vinny both mentally and physically, he grinned manically behind his balaclava. 'Nope. Nothing to do with Frankie Mitchell. If I were you, I'd cast my mind back further,' he taunted, opening the bag of goodies. He pulled out some pliers and waved them at Jamie. 'Do you think if we remove a couple of teeth it might help jog his memory?'

The sight of the pliers was enough to make Little Vinny's bladder do him an injustice. He was scared out of his wits.

Jamie Preston took the machete out of the sports bag

and placed the tip against the wet patch that had appeared around the crotch of Little Vinny's faded jeans. He turned to Glen. 'Seems he has problems in this department. Do you reckon his memory will improve if we slice the tip of his cock off?'

Reduced to a sobbing, quivering wreck, Little Vinny begged for his life. 'I've got two sons. They haven't got a mum. Please don't do this to me. I've done nothing wrong. I don't know what I'm meant to have done, honest I don't,' he pleaded.

Grabbing Little Vinny by the neck, Glen Harper smashed him and the chair on to the concrete floor. He squeezed his throat as he kneeled down next to him. 'Think back, scumbag. 'Cause me and my pal know exactly what you did and we're determined to get justice.'

Alison Bloggs fleetingly popped into Little Vinny's thoughts. Surely one of these men wasn't Ben's younger brother who had got wind he'd done his mother in? But how could he get wind of that? Alison had been a junkie and the police hadn't batted an eyelid when she'd been found dead. They'd just presumed she'd overdosed on heroin. And bar Michael and his father, nobody knew that Little Vinny had knocked her out with temazepam and vodka, then injected her with a lethal dose. The woman had deserved to die. She'd been a terrible mother who'd led Ben a dog's life. The disgusting blow-job she'd given Little Vinny when he was only fourteen affected him so terribly, he'd never let a woman give him a blow-job since, not even Sammi-Lou. 'I can't think of anything, honest I can't,' Little Vinny choked. The man was holding a massive hand against his windpipe and he could barely breathe, let alone talk.

Loosening his grasp, Glen grabbed the machete from Jamie and placed the blade against Little Vinny's neck. 'I'll jog your memory, shall I? Think back to the summer of 1980.'

The realization that the man was referring to Molly knocked Little Vinny for six. The colour drained from his face, and his silence, accompanied by a stunned expression, told Jamie Preston everything he needed to know.

Stanley Smith hated drama of any kind, especially when it involved Eddie Mitchell or his gangster cronies, but he now found himself sitting in Little Vinny's front room, thanks to Joycie insisting he should be there to support their granddaughter.

'Say something then, Stanley. Sitting there like silly boy lemon isn't going to solve this. Answer my question,' Joyce ordered.

Aware that Michael Butler was also looking his way, Stanley shuffled nervously in the armchair. Whatever he said was bound to be wrong, it always was with Joycie. 'If it was our Raymond, gone missing like that, I'd definitely involve the police.'

'No, you would not. Raymond works for Eddie, and Eddie isn't a fan of the police. Can't you think of anything more constructive to say other than the obvious?'

'No, love. And that's probably because I spent my working life driving buses. Not many of us down at the depot had the misfortune of being abducted.'

Clocking Michael wink at her stupid husband, Joyce was far from amused. 'Now isn't the time for sarcasm, Stanley. Your granddaughter is very upset over this, and so is my dear friend, Queenie. You should be ashamed of yourself.'

Eddie Mitchell entering the room saved Stanley from replying. 'You all right to stay here, Joycie, and look after Frankie while I shoot out? I'm gonna make some enquiries. I won't be long.'

'Of course,' Joyce replied, smiling fondly at the man who was responsible for the death of her daughter.

Queenie chased Eddie down the hallway. 'My Vinny must not find out about this, Ed. Not yet anyway.'

'I understand that, Queen,' Eddie lied. He didn't want to break the news to Vinny over the phone, which was why he was heading up to the hospital. Ever since those dead creatures had been sent, apart from briefly wondering if the gypsies were involved, he was damn sure they were sod-all to do with him. So if Vinny was hiding something, he would look him in the eyes, tell him his son had gone missing and find out the truth once and for all.

Little Vinny was a bit of a poser. He and Sammi-Lou had loved nothing more than going shopping for clothes together, and he was even more obsessive about his hair. Marcus, who owned a top salon up town, had been his hairdresser for many years, and Little Vinny loved his current style, which he spent ages gelling every morning. 'Not my hair. Noooo. Leave it alone. Please,' he shrieked, as one of the men took a razor to it.

'Talk then, cunt. We know full well you know who killed Molly, so be a man and admit it. If you do as we say, you can see them lads of yours again. Calum and Regan – nice names. Handsome-looking lads an' all. We've been watching 'em,' Glen Harper taunted.

'Nah. He's the silent type. You shave his head, while I do some dentistry,' Jamie Preston added. He was enjoying every second of Little Vinny's anguish, and why shouldn't he? Being locked up for a crime you did not commit wasn't much fun. Especially when you got labelled as a child killer.

Now sobbing like a baby, Little Vinny watched his precious hair fall to the floor. These men obviously knew something and he needed to get out of this terrible situation alive for the sake of his sons. 'I never killed Molly. It wasn't me, honest,' he lied. 'You have to believe me. She was my sister. I loved her.'

Remembering the broken bones, beatings, scars and burns Jamie'd had the pleasure of receiving in prison, he picked up a hammer and ordered Little Vinny to open his mouth wide. 'Best if I loosen 'em first. Easier to take them out then.'

As the hammer connected with his mouth, Little Vinny squealed like a pig. These men meant business and he was desperate to see his sons again. 'Stop,' he pleaded. 'I didn't kill Molly. It was Ben Bloggs. He was my mate. Ben Bloggs killed my little sister, OK?'

After a taxing day of having to put on an act and be nice to Felicity, Vinny Butler was fast asleep and did not hear the door open. 'For fuck's sake! You scared the shit out of me then,' he spat, when he was woken up by Eddie Mitchell prodding a finger in his arm. 'What you doing here? What's the time?'

Eddie pulled a chair up next to Vinny's bed and plonked himself on it. 'It's time to tell the truth if you're hiding anything whatsoever, mate.'

'What you on about?'

'You know exactly what I'm on about.'

'Don't do this to me, Ed. I'm your pal. I've had that lying slag up here today declaring her undying love, and guess what? She's up the bastard spout. I really ain't in the mood for playing games. I've already told you, I know nothing about what's been happening. I might be a lot of things, but a liar I am not.'

Eddie Mitchell stared intently into his pal's eyes. 'I'm not accusing you of anything, mate. But Little Vinny's gone missing. Got snatched outside his gaff late afternoon. Your mum forbade me to tell you. But in my eyes, you've got every right to know. I'd want to be told if it was one of my sons.'

'You fucking what!' Vinny exclaimed. 'How do you know he was taken? Did somebody see? What happened?'

Explaining everything he'd managed to piece together, while watching and listening to Vinny's reaction, Eddie Mitchell finally knew his pal was telling the truth. Vinny Butler was just as much in the dark over this madness as he was.

Frankie Mitchell was in pieces and all she could think about was how scared Little Vinny must be – assuming he was still alive. 'I'm not sitting here doing nothing. He's been gone over two hours now. Where's my phone? I'm ringing the police.'

Joey grabbed hold of his twin. He'd driven to Emerson Park as soon as he'd heard the news. 'You will do nothing of the sort, Frankie. Hold your horses until Dad gets back. He'll know what to do for the best. You start involving the Old Bill, you'll only make matters worse.'

'How could they possibly be any worse?' Frankie screamed, pummelling her fists against her brother's chest. Joey had changed of late, was far steelier and less compassionate than he'd once been. He wasn't even that camp now, and Frankie could always remember him being camp, even as a small child. 'I don't recognize you these days. You're not my twin any more. You're a stranger to me.' Upset and angry, Frankie wanted to take her hurt out on anyone and everyone.

'Acting like a drama queen isn't going to bring Little Vinny back. Get a grip, Frankie, you're upsetting the kids. And don't drink no more bloody wine. If the police do get involved, they're bound to want to question you, and how is it going to look if you're pissed?'

When her brother finally softened and held her in his arms, Frankie sobbed on his shoulder, taking in the comforting smell of the Lacoste cologne she'd bought him for Christmas. Little Vinny wore the same and the smell reminded her of him. 'I just want him back, Joey. I think I'm in love with him.'

For once Little Vinny didn't care what he looked like. His hair had been completely shaved and the hammer had dislodged some of his teeth. A top front tooth seemed to be hanging by a thread and his pale blue Ralph Lauren jumper was soaked in blood. But all he could think about was Calum and Regan and seeing them again.

'So what happened next, pretty boy?' Jamie Preston asked, prodding the tip of the machete against Little Vinny's right shoulder. The deceitful, no good piece of shit had sounded convincing enough as he'd given his account of falling out with his father and going along with Ben's idea of pretending to abduct Molly, just to scare his dad.

'I weren't a nice lad back then and Ben was even worse. He used to lead me astray and make me do stuff I didn't wanna do,' Little Vinny lied. The truth was, it had been the other way around. Ben had always danced to his tune. 'We were sniffing glue that day and we were stoned. I went for a piss, came back and Molly was lifeless in Ben's arms. He said he was playing with her and he hadn't meant to hurt her. I panicked. I was only young and was worried we'd both get put away,' Little Vinny wept.

'So you buried your sister in a fucking hole and left her there to rot?' Glen Harper bellowed.

Remembering the startled expression on poor Molly's face as he'd put his hands around her neck and throttled the life out of her, Little Vinny could barely be understood due to his racking sobs. 'Yeah. And I'm sorry. So very sorry.

I should have spoken out at the time, told the police the truth. But I was a fucking idiot of a kid back then.'

When Jamie Preston suddenly went ballistic, threw Little Vinny and the chair on to the floor and began kicking at his head like a football, it took a massive amount of strength for Glen to pull his pal away. 'No. Don't be so fucking daft. We've got a plan. Stick to it.'

'Oh my gawd! What you doing here? I told you not to tell him, didn't I?' Queenie hissed, punching Eddie Mitchell in the arm. 'Look at the state of him. He's too ill to be here,' she added, when Eddie ignored her and steered Vinny's wheelchair inside the house.

Albie Butler decided to make a swift exit upstairs. He was so upset, adored his grandson and had already guessed his abduction had something to do with the lad's horror of a father. Therefore he couldn't be in the same room as him, nor Queenie for that matter. That old crow seemed more concerned over Golden Boy's welfare than that of Little Vinny. 'Let me know if there's any news, please. I'll be upstairs,' Albie mumbled.

Stanley had thought he would hate Albie Butler on sight, but he hadn't. They'd had a man-to-man chat outside and Stanley could tell Albie had been just as downtrodden throughout his married life as he had. Albie had also spoken openly about how he and Vinny didn't see eye to eye and Stanley admired the man's morals. There was something evil about Vinny Butler's eyes and Stanley didn't care for him one bit. 'I'll sit upstairs with you, Albie.'

Watching her husband having the cheek to stand up, Joyce pushed him in the chest and he fell back on the sofa. 'No, you will not. You sound like our Joey, wanting to go upstairs with another man. You'll stay there and support me and your granddaughter.'

'What do you mean, sounds like me?' Joey asked, glaring at his grandmother. Usually he ignored her silly homophobic references, but he seriously wasn't in the mood for them today.

'Nothing, dear.'

Running into the lounge, Calum and Regan all but pounced on their grandfather. 'Do you know where Dad is? Is he coming home?' Regan asked Vinny.

'Has someone contacted you and asked for money in exchange for Dad? Harry said they would,' Calum gabbled.

'Get away from your granddad. He's got broken bones and you're hurting him,' Queenie ordered. She turned to her son, who looked so unlike his normally strapping handsome self in that bloody awful wheelchair. 'You didn't discharge yourself, did you? I take it you told the doctors you were leaving?'

'Can everybody shut up, please,' Eddie Mitchell bellowed. When the room fell silent, he said, 'Vinny and I haven't got a clue who's taken Little Vinny or why, so we're gonna give it another couple of hours and if we've not heard a dickie by then, we'll have to involve the Old Bill. We've got no other choice. For once in our lives, we're baffled. Not even we can sort what we know fuck-all about.'

'Now repeat to me exactly what you are going to do next,' Jamie Preston ordered, his face only inches away from the relation he'd never met until tonight.

Little Vinny shivered as he stared at the bright green eyes that peered out of the black balaclava. At one point earlier he'd wondered if that bastard DS Terry had set this up. He'd once threatened to get justice for Molly. But after spotting the piercing eyes, Little Vinny was sure his broad-shouldered captor was none other than Jamie Preston. He remembered his father saying during the trial that Preston had inherited Albie's green eyes, like the rest of the males in the Butler clan. But no way was he going to ask him; it would be safer to act dumb. 'I'm gonna go to the police and tell 'em Ben killed Molly.'

'And what else you gonna tell 'em?' Jamie hissed.

'That I helped him bury her, and was too scared to tell anybody what had happened in case I got put away too.'

'He's got to get them teeth sorted first, mate. Mustn't have a mark on him when he signs his statement, or his brief is bound to go down the "he was forced to confess under duress" road. We don't want that happening,' Glen Harper insisted.

Lifting Little Vinny's chin with the head of the hammer, Jamie Preston asked, 'Did you hear what the man said? You lowlife fucking degenerate.'

'Yeah, I heard,' Little Vinny stammered. If he didn't get out of this freezing warehouse soon, he would end up with worse hypothermia than his father and die from that alone. 'Can I please go home now? I promise I'll do everything you've told me. I just wanna see my boys. I'm a good father, and I swear to you I won't mess you about.'

Little Vinny screamed in agony as the hammer smashed across his left kneecap. The pain was excruciating.

'Enough,' Glen barked. He could fully understand Jamie's ferocity, but they needed Butler to be able to walk into that police station, not crawl.

Unable to control himself, Little Vinny began to cry again. Apart from Sammi-Lou and Oliver dying, this was by far the worst day of his life and he knew deep down it was all his own doing. If only he could turn back time, if only Molly was still alive. Reliving her death so vividly had been just as bad as the pain he'd endured. Whatever had possessed him to do such a terrible thing? He was a good person now – he loved children, even Frankie's.

'He ain't looking too healthy. Let's get out of 'ere now, mate,' Glen said to Jamie. Little Vinny looked close to passing out.

'OK. But let me just get rid of that wobbly front tooth. It's gonna have to come out anyway. Save him a dentist bill,' Jamie smirked.

Little Vinny's head flopped forward like a rag doll as his chin was let go. He'd been traumatized enough, and if they were going to kill him, he wished they'd just get on with it. His Uncle Michael would hopefully take care of his boys. He was a better father than his own, far more understanding. And would death be that bad? At least he would get to see Sammi-Lou and Oliver again. Unless the rumours of hell were true. God would look him in the eyes and slam the pearly gates shut for what he'd done to Molly.

Glen Harper untied Little Vinny's hands and clamped one of his arms around his shoulder. 'Put the blindfold back on and grab his other arm,' he ordered Jamie.

Jamie obeyed Glen's orders and couldn't resist one sly last kick in the ankle. 'That one's for Molly,' he spat.

Approximately half an hour later, Little Vinny's blindfold was taken off and he was turfed out of the van a few streets from where he lived. 'You know what you've gotta do – and if you haven't done it as soon as those injuries are healed, we'll be back to get your fucking kids,' were the last words he heard before the van screeched away.

Totally exhausted from his terrifying ordeal, Little Vinny tried to stand up, but tumbled back on the pavement. He couldn't think straight, but somehow knew at that very moment his life would never be the same again. His past had finally caught up with him.

PART THREE

Thus I will punish the world for its evil.
And the wicked for their iniquity. I will also
put an end to the arrogance of the proud.
And abuse the haughtiness of the ruthless.

Isaiah 13:11

CHAPTER TWENTY

2002

'Don't go out. Stay with me. Please,' Little Vinny urged, grabbing Frankie by the hand.

'I've got to go out. I promised Joey and I can't let him down at such short notice. The offer's still there if you want to come with us. You can't stay indoors forever,' Frankie replied. It had been over four weeks since Little Vinny's horrendous ordeal and he'd refused to leave the house since. She'd temporarily moved in with him, but had started to go a bit stir crazy this past week or so.

Clutching his head, Little Vinny rocked to and fro. 'Where's my tablets?'

Frankie handed them to him. Little Vinny had been in a terrible state when a man had found him crawling along the pavement and dropped him home that day. Everybody had begged him to get checked out at a hospital, but he'd refused. Instead his dad had called out a private doctor. He still hadn't been for the scans on his head and knee the doctor had recommended; neither had he visited a dentist. Drinking alcohol like water and popping painkillers like Smarties was the way he'd coped ever since, and Frankie was concerned for his long-term health. His once chirpy personality had all but disappeared and he was gaunt and depressed. He was also acting oddly, which concerned Frankie, but he'd made her promise not to tell anybody about his nightmares and bed-wetting as he didn't want his family on his case.

Little Vinny stared out the window while frantically scratching at his arms. 'I'll have a look on the internet while you're out. Lincolnshire's nice. Finn's parents live there. The kids'll love it.'

Frankie sighed. All he kept on about since his ordeal was moving away, and she was reluctant to uproot the kids again. They had a new tutor now, were learning to read and write properly. Even Brett seemed to have settled in since the move to Emerson Park. He loved his new school. 'Jump in the shower and put some of your nice clothes on if your dad's coming round. He's worried about you, Vin, we all are.'

'So, later we'll tell the kids then, yeah?'

'Tell 'em what?'

'About us. I feel safer when I'm with you and I'm sure I'd sleep better if you were lying in bed next to me. I want us to be a proper couple now, tell everyone we're an item.'

Frankie chewed on her fingernails. They'd only had sex twice, and an awkward drunken fumble was the best way to describe both occasions. 'I don't think Calum and Regan will be too happy, Vin. This was their mum's bedroom, remember. I don't think we should say anything yet. It's very early days.'

'What's that supposed to mean? You told me you loved me.'

'I do, but the kids don't need any more shocks at the moment. It isn't fair on them.'

Little Vinny stared at Frankie with a steely glint in his eyes.

'I'm telling 'em and that's that. Their mother's dead, you're alive, and they're just gonna have to like it or lump it.'

Vinny Butler had been waiting in the pub car park for over forty minutes by the time his brother finally arrived. 'What time d'ya call this? You having a laugh or what?'

'Sorry, Vin. Traffic was murder heading out of town. Everything OK? Was a bit worried when I heard your message.' Vinny had stayed at their mother's bungalow while he was recuperating, and had only moved back to his apartment a couple of days ago.

'Not really. I want to slit that lying snitch's throat every time I look at her. And knowing she has my child inside her makes it even fucking worse. We need to get rid of her.' Vinny still felt incredibly stupid for having feelings for Fliss, but his hurt had now turned to hate. He should have known better than to trust anything with a vagina between its legs – and to think he'd fallen out with his mother over her. Never again would he get close to a bird. That was it for him now. A bachelor he would remain for the rest of his days.

Michael had been dreading having this conversation. 'We can't kill her, bruv. But we can scare the living daylights out of her and get rid of her that way.'

Vinny shook his head. 'You know the rules, bruv: gotta put the safety of the family first. Dave Newton obviously has some serious back-up and I can't get to him in Frankland.' Vinny had a lot of contacts in the local Category A prisons, but Frankland was in County Durham and he didn't know a soul currently serving there. 'Little Vinny said them geezers who kidnapped him were only interested in me and no way am I putting my boy through that again. Anyway, fuck Newton; Fliss knows too much, end of. She's a police informer, she has to go.'

Michael sighed. He was too old for dirty deeds such as this, and no matter what she might have done, he could not kill a woman. It wasn't in his nature. 'Can't Eddie help you?'

'Eddie's gone all saintly on me, so I'm gonna ask the Kelly brothers for help. The sooner she's out the fucking equation, the better.'

'What has Eddie said?'

'That I should just end things with her, and send her on her merry way.'

'The Old Bill are bound to start sniffing around, Vin. People must know you're a couple,' Michael warned.

'So what! I'll just say we split up and she left. I've never met her family or any of her friends. The Old Bill'll have a job on their hands to prove otherwise, won't they? The slag'll be nothing more than a pile of ashes by the time I've finished with her.'

Michael winced. Vinny had always had the capability of turning his feelings off, like he was turning off a tap. He was a cold, brutal bastard at times, he really was.

Little Vinny tossed and turned, his soul tortured by the visions in his head. She was smiling at him again.

'Where we going, Vinny?' she asked, so trusting. Pink tracksuit and white trainers she was wearing. She had a cute voice, everybody said so.

Vinny grinned back at her. 'On an adventure.'

'Is Daddy coming too?' she giggled excitedly.

'No. Daddy's busy mopping up the flood in the cellar,' Little Vinny replied.

'Molly, Molly,' Little Vinny mumbled in his sleep. He turned over, then found himself at the police station being interviewed by that bastard, DS Terry.

'I know you killed your sister, so why don't you just be

a man and admit it? Ben Bloggs helped you, didn't he? That's why Ben killed himself.'

'I didn't do it. I loved Molly,' Little Vinny muttered. Then he saw her. He knew he'd seen her somewhere before. Felicity Carter-Price was at the police station. She was in uniform talking to Terry.

Sweat pouring off him, Little Vinny woke and sat bolt upright. He swung his legs over the edge of the bed, put his head in his hands and cried. 'I'm so fucking sorry, Molly, but you got to stop torturing me like this. Don't visit me when I'm sleeping any more. You're driving me insane.'

Joey Mitchell was determined to get to the bottom of what was going on. He knew his twin better than anybody and, from the stilted phone conversations they'd had recently, knew something was amiss. That's why he'd insisted on taking her out for lunch today.

'How's it going at The Casino, Joey? Dad been driving you up the wall, has he?'

'I've been working from home quite a lot. I've set up a website to advertise the business. Considering it's January and everybody should be skint, The Casino's been relatively busy. Not so much the Piano Bar, but I've come up with some ideas for that and we'll give them a whirl in spring. So how's things your end? Is Little Vinny on the mend?'

'Yeah, sort of. Everything's good.'

Topping his sister's glass up, Joey said, 'OK, now tell me the truth.' He was close to his father, clashed far less with him these days than Frankie did, but if he ever had a problem he would rather discuss it with his sister, and vice versa. They'd been the same growing up, would always confide in one another. It was what twins did.

Tears immediately sprung to Frankie's eyes. 'I do think the world of him, Joey, but he isn't the same man as before he was attacked. I'm just praying he will get better soon. He keeps talking about moving miles away, and I don't want to move again. Do you think I should consider it, for his sake?'

'No, I bloody well don't. Are you sleeping with him?'

'Not really. We've had sex a couple of times. It happened when we were drunk and the kids were in bed. I couldn't stop thinking about Stuart though. It didn't feel right and I felt guilty the next day. Whereas Little Vinny seems to have forgotten all about Sammi-Lou since he was attacked. He tells me he loves me at least ten times a day now.'

Joey raised his eyebrows. This sounded like a case of too much too soon, like Jed O'Hara all over again. 'What do you mean, he isn't the same man? I know he got badly beaten up but, aside from that, what else has changed?'

'Everything. He was so bubbly before he was attacked, but all I see now is this forgetful, forlorn image of his former self. I think he might have taken a bad blow to the head, but he refuses to go for a scan. And he used to take such pride in himself, but now it's an effort to get him to take a shower. He never dresses up any more; it's as though he's given up on himself. He manages to act normally in front of the kids or any visitors, but I see a different side to him when we're alone. He keeps having nightmares about his little sister's death. I heard him shouting Molly's name the other night and had to calm him down. He was drenched in sweat and thrashing his arms about, didn't know where he was.'

'Has his dad not been helping you out?'

'Big Vinny's popping round today, but we haven't seen that much of him, to be honest. He's been ill himself, hasn't he? Finn's always asking if he can help. But for some strange reason, Little Vinny doesn't want him round the house. I think he's embarrassed because his head was shaved and he's lost a tooth, I know how much pride he used to take in his appearance. But oh, Joey, he's wet the bed a few times in the night too, and once while he was sat on the sofa.'

Joey held his sister's hands. 'I don't want to sound unfeeling, Frankie, but you have to put this relationship on hold, at least until he gets better. Little Vinny isn't your problem. Dad would go mad if he knew all this. Have you spoken to him about what's been going on?'

'No. And I don't intend to. What I have told you is between the two of us. You're not going to say anything, are you? If I can't trust you, who can I trust?'

'I would never betray you, Frankie, but you're making a rod for your own back, yet again. You have your own house that Dad is paying good money for. You're not a bloody nurse, neither do you owe Little Vinny anything. You're grieving and, even though you've been through a lot together, you've only known him five minutes. I can't force you to do anything, but my advice would be to run for the fucking hills – seriously.'

'How you doing?' Vinny Butler asked, giving his son an awkward hug. Little Vinny had never been a touchy-feely lad. Not even as a small child.

'Not bad. Getting there slowly but surely.' Little Vinny told his family very little about how he was really feeling as he didn't want them visiting. It was an effort for him to try to act normal let alone jovial, when he knew one day soon those bastards who'd terrorized him would be back.

'Where's Frankie and the kids?'

'Frankie's having lunch with Joey. Brett's at Eddie's gaff, and the other four are in Romford. They hang around down there a lot since that new shopping centre's opened – the Brewery.'

'Frankie being a good nursemaid, is she?'

'Yeah. We're a proper couple now. Can't live in the past, can you? Getting a good hiding made me realize some important things. Life's too short and Sammi-Lou and Oliver are gone for good.'

Vinny Butler was surprised, to say the least. He knew his son and Frankie were close, but last time he'd hinted at them being more than friends, Little Vinny had been furious and insisted it would be years before he could consider moving on from Sammi-Lou. 'So when you say a proper couple, you mean—'

Interrupting his father, Little Vinny blurted out, 'We're shagging. I take it that's what you were gonna ask?'

Under normal circumstances, Vinny would have been overjoyed that his son and Eddie Mitchell's daughter were an item. But if anything, he was a bit startled. His son's hair had begun to grow back, but there was a vacant expression in his eyes and an oddness about the lad's choice of words. Unlike himself, his son respected women and had never bragged about shagging any bird in the past.

'What you looking at me like that for? I thought you'd be pleased me and Frankie have got it on.'

''Course I'm pleased. Frankie's a lovely girl. Listen, tomorrow I'm gonna pick you up about half nine. We'll go and get your scans done, then I'll take you to the dentist to sort those gnashers out. Gotta look your best for your new woman, eh?'

Little Vinny put his hands on top of his head, then shook it vehemently. 'I don't need no scans, I'm fine. And sod my teeth. Frankie ain't bothered about 'em, so why should you be?'

'I'm not. But I am worried about you and so is your nan. You took a hell of a battering, lad, and unlike me, you never got checked out properly. It's time you did. You're still limping badly. Nothing to be scared of, I'll be with ya.'

'Who said I was scared? You a fucking doctor now, are ya?' Little Vinny chucked his glass of Coke at the wall. 'Leave me alone. I'm not a kid, I'm a man, and I make my own decisions. Sick of people interfering in my life, I am, which is why I'm moving away. Bollocks to the lot of ya.'

When his son stomped out of the room, Vinny began clearing the glass up off the floor. He'd thought Little Vinny had been doing OK, until today. But now he knew different, and he hadn't a clue how to help him, unless the lad was willing to help himself. Could hardly put a gun to his head and force him to get his brain X-rayed, could he?

Harry O'Hara had the hump. He wasn't daft; he'd been observing the smouldering glances between his tart of a sister and Regan for a while now, but today they'd been flirting even more than usual. Not only was Harry worried about losing his best mate to his sister, he was concerned Georgie would change her mind about leaving Essex. She once used to look at Ryan in the same way she now did Regan.

'Let's go see if Emily and Mary are there,' Harry said, grabbing his sister's arm. He was bored with wasting time walking around the shops when they could be looking for the lucky-heather sellers they'd met back in December. The travellers had promised to get word to their family and he was anxious for news.

'We've already looked twice today, Harry. They ain't gonna turn up now, are they? And we've looked for 'em at least twenty times since Christmas. Perhaps one of 'em's died, or something.'

Harry leaned towards his sister's ear. 'If you don't come

with me, I'm gonna tell Calum you're getting hold of his brother's cory,' he hissed.

Georgie leapt up. 'Harry wants to look for someone. We won't be long.'

'Don't you wanna look for 'em as well? I wonder whyever not,' Harry taunted, as they walked briskly from the Brewery to the spot in South Street where they'd first seen the women.

'There ain't nothing going on with me and Regan, you dinlo. You don't like it because me and him are friends. Want him all to yourself, don't ya? I swear you're gonna turn out gay like Joey. Nanny Alice will disown you, I'm telling ya,' Georgie mocked. She'd learned off her father that attack was the best form of defence.

Furious over what Harry considered to be a terrible insult, he was still arguing with his sister as they turned the corner. 'They're there, Harry. Look!' Georgie exclaimed.

Harry ran excitedly towards the two women. 'Do you remember us? You said you could get a message to our family. We're Jed O'Hara's chavvies.'

Mary and Emily shared a triumphant glance. Neither they nor their husbands were now in good health and when word had got back to the O'Haras, they'd been promised a thousand pounds for reuniting those children with their family. In a lot of travellers' eyes, a thousand pounds was peanuts, but to Mary and Emily it was a small fortune.

It was Mary who did the talking. 'We got the message to your family. Can you meet us here tomorrow?'

'Why?' Georgie asked suspiciously.

'What did my dad say? Did you talk to him?' Harry asked. Georgie had said a couple of times that their father might be dead, but he didn't believe that. His dad was his hero and heroes didn't die.

'Just say a time and we'll meet you here tomorrow.

Come alone though,' Mary urged. She'd spoken personally on the phone to Mickey Maloney the other day, and he'd warned her: 'If and when they do turn up, do not tell them we're in the area in case word gets back to the Mitchells. All you got to do is arrange a time for the following day and tell 'em you have some news. Don't mess this up, Mary. My Ryan has not been the same since Georgie went away. Wants to marry her on her sixteenth birthday, he do.'

'What's the big secret? Is my dad and granddad dead? Is that why you won't tell us nothing?' Georgie spat.

Harry punched his sister on the arm. ''Course they're not dead, and stop being nasty. These ladies are helping us. Show some respect.'

Desperate for the thousand pounds, Emily trod on Mary's toes to shut her up. 'We have messages from your family, but we didn't know if you would be here, so left them hidden in the trailer. We got phone numbers for you to call them. Can you meet us here at nine in the morning tomorrow?'

'Yeah,' Harry said. He was absolutely elated.

'No,' Georgie replied. 'Our mum, she got us this tutor to teach us to read and write. If we run off before he arrives, Mum'll know we're up to something. But if we do our lesson first, then meet you ladies here at, say, three, our mum won't suspect anything.'

Mary and Emily nodded at one another before smiling at the children. 'OK,' Emily said. 'Three o'clock it is.'

After being spoken to as if she were no more than some idiotic loved-up teenager, it was no wonder Frankie Mitchell arrived home in a temper.

Having missed the only rock he felt he now had, Little Vinny held Frankie close to his chest. 'What's wrong?'

'Just Joey being Joey. Sick of my family poking their noses in my life. It's been the same for as long as I can remember. I never seem to do anything right.'

'Same 'ere. I told my old man where to go earlier. Please let's move, Frankie. We can buy a nice gaff in the country, start afresh.'

'It's not as easy as that, Vin. What about your job?'

'I've given it up.'

'What!'

'I rang Finn earlier. After everything that's happened recently, I need a new beginning. I've got plenty of dosh and we can set up a business together when we move. It'll be a laugh and the kids'll love the fresh air of the countryside. We can even buy 'em a dog and keep chickens. Nothing tastes better than a newly laid egg.'

Frankie was cautious. 'I don't know, Vin. It's a big decision, but I will think about it.'

'Best you think about it quickly then. Only I rang an estate agent earlier and put a bid in for a property in Lincolnshire.'

'You did what!'

'Can I stay here with Aaron and Rosie tonight please, Granddad? I'll be a really good boy, I promise,' said Brett Mitchell.

'No. You got to go to school tomorrow. Get your stuff together and I'll drop you off home on the way to The Casino.'

Eddie hated cry-babies and when Brett started to blub, he tore him off a strip.

Gina sent Rosie and Aaron into the lounge before she hugged the distraught child. 'Tell your granddad what you told me earlier, darling. He won't be angry with you, once you tell him why you want to stay here.'

Brett stared at his shoes. 'No. Don't want to.'

'Tell me what?' Eddie hissed. He hated being kept in the dark about anything.

'Tell him, Brett. Explain to Granddad why you're upset, love.'

Brett's lip wobbled. 'Mummy was making funny noises when I came downstairs to get some orange juice the other night, so I looked in the lounge to see if she was OK. She had no clothes on and Little Vinny was on top of her. I think he was doing something bad to her. I don't like him no more, Granddad. I miss Stuart.'

'Go in the front room with Rosie and Aaron, boy. You can have the day off school tomorrow.'

Red-faced with temper, Eddie waited until his grandson was out of sight, then booted the kitchen door shut. 'Didn't take her long to move on, did it? She's got a bed in her bedroom, hasn't she? Why didn't she use that? I'll fucking swing for her and Little Vinny. Are they retarded, or what? Oh hang on; I think he might be doollally since he got his head caved in. Another great choice my daughter has made. I'm going round there to tell the pair of 'em exactly what I think.'

Gina put her arms around Eddie's neck. 'No, you're not. You're overreacting, it was obvious with Frankie and Little Vinny spending so much time together, something like this was bound to happen. He seems a nice enough lad and he's been great with Georgie and Harry, hasn't he? Frankie's had it tough, Eddie. She deserves to be happy.'

'Well, she ain't going to be happy with him, is she? He's Vinny Butler's son, and even I've come to the conclusion that the Butlers are more agg than they're worth.'

Harry O'Hara's lip curled. He hated seeing his mother constantly topping her wine glass up. It made him despise her even more than he already did. 'You're disgusting, Frankie. You make me want to vomit.'

'What have I done now?' Frankie asked, perplexed.

'Shut up, Harry,' Georgie ordered.

'Nah. Why should I? Women ain't meant to get drunk. That's what the men do.' In the travelling community, the men regularly rolled home inebriated from pubs or horse fairs, but it was very much frowned upon for their women to drink. On a special occasion, a travelling woman might be allowed one or two, like at Christmas or at a wedding. But getting drunk like his mother did on a regular basis was unheard of for a woman.

Georgie glared at her brother. 'Go upstairs, Harry. You're getting on my nerves.'

'Nanny Alice says only old gorger slags get drunk,' Harry spat, before stomping out the kitchen. Calum and Regan had gone out for a meal with Sammi-Lou's mum and sister, and he was peeved that he hadn't been invited. He had wanted to spend as much time as possible with his mates before he left Essex.

Frankie sat at the kitchen table, her eyes brimming with tears. 'I used to drink with your dad. He never took me out much after you were born, mind, but before I fell pregnant he did. Having said that, he stopped taking me out pretty much the minute I moved in with him. He'd leave me at home with Alice while he went out with Jimmy.'

'Dad doesn't let Lola drink. Lola's the woman he's with now – that's if Dad's still alive. She's a traveller, though, so that's probably why. She's also got my little sister Shelby to take care of. I'm never gonna let a man dictate to me, not even if I marry 'em. If I want a glass of wine when I'm older, then I will,' Georgie said adamantly. She knew Harry got annoyed when she sipped alcohol now, which was why she was probably better off marrying a non-travelling lad like Regan. It was certainly a man's world in the travelling community. The life of Riley her granddad had while her nan was at home cooking and cleaning. And most travelling men cheated on their women. She knew that because Ryan told her what the men on the site got up to when they were out in pubs. 'What the eye don't see, the heart don't grieve over, Georgie. But I'm loyal, me. I will never cheat on you,' he'd sworn.

'Tell me about Lola. What's she like?' Frankie enquired.

Georgie was about to reply when Little Vinny burst into the kitchen. 'I forgot to tell you, I know where I remember my dad's girlfriend from now. Dreamed about her and that's when it came to me. She was in the police station with DS Terry when they arrested me,' Little Vinny proclaimed, a manic expression in his eyes.

Not having a clue what Little Vinny was on about, Frankie told Georgie to pop upstairs and check on Harry. 'What you rambling on about? You're not making any sense.'

'Felicity Carter-Price, my dad's bit of skirt. She's undercover Old Bill.'

'Don't be daft. She can't be. Whatever makes you think that?'

His mind playing tricks with him, Little Vinny genuinely believed that it was Felicity Carter-Price he had seen when arrested all those years ago. 'It was definitely her, I'm telling ya. She gave me a cup of tea and chatted to me a bit. Then she brought me a sandwich in the cell. I remember her clearly because she chatted to me again.'

Frankie put her hand over her mouth. 'Have you told your dad this? Are you sure you haven't got it wrong?'

'No. I just dreamt about her again, and remember her as clear as day. Ring my dad now. You tell him. I don't wanna talk to him, not after earlier.'

Vinny answered on the third ring.

'Hi. It's Frankie. Little Vinny has just remembered something important.'

'Go on,' Vinny replied, his tone bored.

'Felicity Carter-Price. He thinks she's undercover Old Bill.'

'You fucking what?'

Michael Butler met his brother at ten o'clock in the car park at Palms Hotel. 'This better be important,' he grumbled. He'd been at a restaurant with Bella and Camila when Vinny had called him saying they needed to meet urgently.

'Little Vinny reckons Felicity is undercover Old Bill,' Vinny explained bluntly.

'What! Never! She can't be. That has to be bollocks,' Michael insisted. The Old Bill might go to extreme lengths to nail a potential target, but no way was a female officer going to pose as a stripper, then move in with and fall pregnant by his lunatic of a brother. That was laughable, bordering on insanity.

When Frankie had called him earlier, Vinny had driven straight over to his son's house. Repeating Little Vinny's version of events in full, he told Michael, 'I can't quite believe it either, but no way can we take any chances. Little Vinny would never make something like this up. He remembers chatting with Fliss, said she took him a sandwich in the cell.'

'And what was in it? Cheese and pickle? Or ham and mustard?' Michael asked sarcastically. 'Listen, I don't care what Little Vinny reckons, no way is Felicity Old Bill. A police informer, perhaps, but come on. It was years ago when Little Vinny got hauled in. Felicity would have been too young back then.'

'Not necessarily. For all we know, she could've lied about

her age. She's lied about everything else, the treacherous bitch. Anyway, it wasn't that many years ago Calum and Regan were both born and they weren't exactly babies. I remember them greeting him when I drove him home. It was Boxing Day, if I remember rightly.'

'I think you're being paranoid.'

'I don't think you understand how serious this is, Michael. You and me are looking at going down for life if she blurts anything I've said out. We need to sort this mess out once and for all.'

Fuming that he'd been dragged into such a situation, Michael Butler grabbed his brother round the throat. 'A fucking liability, that's what you are. The bane of my bastard life.'

CHAPTER TWENTY-ONE

'Harry, why haven't you written anything down?' the tutor asked.

'I got a headache,' Harry O'Hara lied. He hadn't been able to sleep at all last night, was so excited at the prospect of seeing his real family again. Just the thought of talking to them later today filled his whole body with joy.

Georgie kicked her little brother in the shin. 'Just do your work, Harry; else Mum might not let us go into Romford later.'

When the tutor told them to take a short break, a clued-up Regan followed Georgie into the kitchen. 'What's going on?' he asked.

'Nothing,' Georgie fibbed. As much as she adored Regan, instinct told her not to say anything until she had spoken to her family. Not knowing if her dad and granddad Jimmy were alive was torture, and Georgie was determined to spend time with her gypsy family again, no matter what the future held.

'You're lying.'

The doorbell saved Georgie from replying. 'Where's your mother?' asked her none-too-happy-looking grandfather.

'Upstairs. What's wrong?'

'Nothing that concerns you,' Eddie replied coldly.

Harry looked at his sister fearfully. Surely she hadn't opened her big gob to her new love interest and word had got back to the granddad he loathed? 'I'm gonna have a lie down to get rid of this headache.'

Knowing full well Harry would be earwigging, Georgie showed her approval via a wink.

Little Vinny and Frankie were sitting on the bed watching a film when Eddie barged in, uninvited. 'Nice to see you've got your clothes on for once.'

Frankie leapt off the bed. 'We're only watching a film. We often sit up here while the children are having their lessons,' she panicked. Joey had promised her he wouldn't say anything to their father until she had, and if he'd betrayed her trust, she'd bloody disown him.

Kicking the door shut, Eddie glared at Little Vinny and Frankie in turn. He'd promised Gina he wouldn't lose his rag completely, so took a deep breath before wagging his right forefinger wildly. 'What yous two get up to is your business, unless it upsets my grandkids, then it becomes my fucking business. So I'll say this once and best you listen carefully. Next time you want to get jiggy-jiggy with each other, do so in private behind a locked bastard door where the kids can't walk in on you humping.'

Feeling embarrassed, Frankie felt her face go all hot. 'I don't know what you're talking about.'

'Don't come that innocent old flannel with me, Frankie. Brett came downstairs to get a drink and saw ya. Pissed, was we? Unable to perform such a meagre task as walking up the stairs?'

Without thinking, Little Vinny leapt off the bed and pushed Eddie in the chest. 'Don't talk to Frankie like that. She's my girl now and I won't allow it.'

'Vin, stop it, no!' Frankie screamed.

Had it been anybody else, Eddie would have clumped him, but as he looked into the glazed eyes of the once-not-bad-looking lad, Eddie shook his head in despair. 'Great choice, Frankie, yet again. I hope you'll both be very happy together.'

Felicity Carter-Price arched her naked body around Vinny's. It was great to finally be back together in his apartment and wake up with him every morning again. 'Have you thought of any names you like yet? I love Donte for a boy, but I doubt you do,' Felicity chuckled. Vinny was old school and she couldn't imagine him agreeing to name their child anything remotely unusual.

Knowing he had to play along, Vinny turned over and forced a smile. 'You're right. I hate it. How about Sid? Sid Butler has a ring to it.'

Felicity turned her nose up. 'That sounds like an old man's name. What about Rio, if it's a girl? Or even Rhianna? I'll tell you what, how about if it's a boy you get to choose, and if it's a girl I pick the name? That's fair, don't you think?'

Bored with chatting about a child that was destined to be burned before it could be properly formed, along with the bitch who was carrying it, Vinny turned Felicity over and rammed his cock as forcefully as he possibly could up her backside. Just imagining her shock and cries for mercy when she realized she was about to meet her maker made him as hard as a rock. When it involved a slag who had wronged him, death was most definitely a turn-on.

Queenie Butler knocked on Joycie Smith's front door. 'Morning, lovey. You ready? Not the best transport today, I'm afraid. Seats have seen far better days. I shall be putting in a complaint later.'

'Won't be a tick. Driven me mad this morning has Stanley, I'll be glad to get out. One of his pigeons isn't well and the way he's acting anybody would think it was our Raymond at death's door.'

'State of these seats and carpet, look. Meant to be a VIP company, Joyce. Pays big bucks, does my Michael, for this account. Not on, is it?' Queenie said in her extra-loud voice.

The driver sighed, then apologized. The majority of his colleagues hated ferrying Queenie and Joyce anywhere. It was a standing joke in the office who had drawn the short straw. They were a nightmare, especially when half-pissed. Never had a good word to say about anything or anyone.

'I won't be wanting this car again. Lakeside please, and turn your music up so we can talk in private,' Queenie ordered, lips pursed. She turned to Joyce. 'How was your night out with the daughter-in-law and granddaughter from hell? I was thinking of you last night.'

'Awful, as ever. They took us to a restaurant in Loughton with her parents. I'm sure they're swingers, those two. He's a letch and she's an alkie. The brat of a child had one of its tantrums and as for Polly, he spends a fortune on that jumped-up madam, does my Raymond. Got it made, with her designer this and designer that, she has. Lazy cow doesn't lift a finger, has never done a day's work in her bleedin' life. He could have done so much better, my boy.'

'I know that feeling well. Christ knows what's happening with Michael and the Italian slapper. I'm sure he's still reefing round her. I mean, how could he, knowing my Vinny's had his Hampton up her?'

'These women get their claws in 'em, Queen. That's the problem. Any news on Vinny's young tart?'

'He reckons he's not with her. I believe him; can always tell when he's lying. Still no news on Roxanne, and that's worrying me terribly. I told my Michael to find another private detective, a better one. The dopey bastard he hired has been searching for weeks now and we still don't have a lead. She's only just turned fifteen, Joycie. How can she be so hard to track down? Hardly Ma Barker, is she?'

'I'm sure she'll turn up soon, Queen. Excuse me – giving me a headache, that racket. Can you turn it down please, now?' Joycie asked, poking the man's shoulder.

'Don't talk about nothing else of importance then. You know how nosy they are,' Queenie remarked.

The driver sighed loudly. No way was he picking these two witches up again later. They were bound to have a few sherbets while out, and be even more unbearable on the way home. Let some other poor bastard have the pleasure.

Vinny Butler grinned as he finished counting the takings. 'Just over twelve and a half grand, Ed. Not bad for this time of year, eh? And very pleasing that we took a grand in the Piano Bar, alone. Picking up nicely, don't you think?'

Eddie Mitchell was looking over some paperwork. 'Yeah, great,' he said in a disinterested tone.

'What's wrong now?' Vinny asked abruptly. Eddie had turned up an hour ago with a definite cob on and Vinny wasn't in the mood for guessing games.

Eddie threw the paperwork on the desk. 'Did you know your son was fucking my daughter?'

Vinny held his hands up. 'Yes. But before you kick off, I only found out yesterday. Thought I'd give Frankie a chance to tell you herself before I stuck my oar in. I take it you're not thrilled by the news then? Not being funny, Ed, but what did you expect? They've been inseparable since Sammi-Lou and Stuart got bumped off. It was hardly the shock of the century to me.'

'I get where you're coming from, and yeah, I could see it happening an' all. But what worries me is, since he got a clump, your son don't seem quite right, pal. There's something missing in there, if you know what I mean,' Eddie said, tapping his forefinger on the side of his forehead.

Fiercely loyal when it came to family, Vinny wasn't about to share his own concerns. 'What you on about? He took a bad beating, that's all. You can hardly expect him to be jumping through hoops right now, but he'll be OK – in time. Made of strong stuff is my lad.'

'Well, let's hope you're right. Only Frankie has been through a lot in her life and she certainly doesn't deserve any more misery. Now, what's going on with you and the rat? You told her to get rid of the baby yet?'

'Nah. But I'm meeting up with her tomorrow, so I'll tell her then. I think she's got an idea what's coming,' Vinny lied. He'd promised Eddie he would make sure his baby was flushed from her system before ending the relationship verbally.

Eddie eyed his partner suspiciously. 'No funny business, Vin. If she goes AWOL, we'll have the filth swarming all over this gaff and that really ain't no good for trade.'

'Don't worry. There'll be no funny business. You have my word.'

'No, Calum. Me and Harry need to speak to them alone. I swear on my baby sister Shelby's life we aren't running away. They've got messages for us from our family, that's all,' Georgie reiterated. Calum and Regan had insisted on accompanying her and Harry to Romford and even though it was nice they cared, Georgie wished they would shut up. She couldn't think straight.

'We'll just hang around nearby. Don't sound right to me

that they left the messages in their trailer. They might snatch you or something,' Regan said.

'You can't come with us,' Harry snapped. 'Travellers ain't like gorgers – if Mary and Emily clock you they'll be frit to death. You wait at the Brewery and me and Georgie'll meet you there. No way will they snatch us. They're old ladies.'

Georgie looked pleadingly at the two lads who fancied the pants off her. 'Please don't follow us. We'll only be about ten minutes.'

'OK. But if you're longer than fifteen, me and Cal are coming to find yous,' Regan threatened.

'Come on,' Georgie urged, grabbing Harry's arm. They'd be late at this rate.

Harry's heart beat wildly as he spotted Emily and Mary. 'Told you they'd turn up, didn't I?' he said, breaking into a run.

Georgie grinned as she approached the two women.

'This way,' Mary said, walking inside an arcade.

'Where we going? You got our messages?' Harry asked.

'Yes. Follow us,' Emily gestured.

'Why can't we have them now? Where you taking us?' Georgie enquired, her tone one of suspicion.

'You'll soon see,' Mary said.

Harry's eyes lit up as he spotted a familiar face. 'Uncle Billy! Is me dad and granddad with you?'

Georgie was gobsmacked when Ryan suddenly appeared out of a shop doorway. 'What you doing here?' she asked, rather stupidly.

Billy O'Hara handed Mary and Emily an envelope each. 'Thanks.' He grabbed Harry's arm. 'Come on, let's get out of 'ere. Motor's not far.'

'I've missed you so much, Georgie,' Ryan said, squeezing his wife-to-be tightly. 'You pleased to see me?'

'Yeah, 'course. Where's me dad? And Granddad? Is Nanny Alice with you?'

'We gotta go, come on. We'll chat in the motor,' Ryan said.

Georgie stopped dead in her tracks. 'We can't just leave here. Our friends are in the Brewery.'

Harry grabbed his sister's arm. 'We can ring them, Georgie. Come on, I wanna see me dad.'

Rather reluctantly, a shocked Georgie found herself being steered by Ryan's arm around her shoulders to a stationary Mitsubishi Shogun. Mickey Maloney leapt out and opened the back door.

'Where's our dad?' Georgie asked, fearfully.

'Just get in, will ya?' Harry told his sister.

'But what about Regan and Calum? And Mum?' Georgie asked, backing away from the vehicle.

Realizing his niece wasn't quite as keen to see them as he'd hoped, Billy O'Hara had no option but to lie. His mum would be devastated were Georgie not returned to her rightful family. 'Dad and Granddad are stopping on a local site. We'll be there in about ten minutes, so get in the motor. There's a good girl.'

Doing as she was told, Georgie was stunned when the vehicle pulled away and Billy ordered her and Harry to hand over their mobile phones. 'But why? We need them,' she insisted.

Ryan snatched at Georgie's shoulder bag, delved inside and handed the phone to Billy. She'd seemed more shocked to see him than thrilled.

'Give me that back. It's mine!' Georgie shrieked.

'Not any more. And why ain't you that pleased to see me, eh? Met some other mush, have ya? You'd better not have done,' Ryan hissed.

'Leave it, boyo,' Mickey Maloney ordered. It was he

who'd forked out the thousand-pound reward money. The O'Haras were skint and his son had pined badly for Georgie.

Billy O'Hara took the SIM cards out of both Georgie and Harry's phones and crunched them between his teeth.

Had Georgie not been sitting in the back of the vehicle with Ryan one side of her and Billy the other, she'd have opened the door and thrown herself out.

Harry said nothing when his uncle threw both their phones out of the window, but Georgie screamed blue murder. Billy pleaded with her to stop. 'I'll buy you a new phone tomorrow. You can choose whatever one you want, OK?'

Mickey Maloney glanced in the interior mirror. Unless Georgie calmed down a bit, this was going to be a horrid journey back to Lancashire, for sure.

'Don't drink any more, Vin,' Frankie Mitchell urged. 'Not if you're still adamant about telling the kids tonight. I still think we should wait, but if you're not going to then you need to break it to them gently. Those boys loved their mum.'

'So did I, but now she's gone. And you're a fine one to preach about alcohol. I had to carry you up to bed the other night,' Little Vinny chuckled, rocking to and fro on the chair.

Frankie sighed. So much for her New Year's resolution, but she had cut alcohol out in the daytime now. It was difficult not to drink in the evening though, with Little Vinny pouring it down his throat like water. A case of if you can't beat 'em, join 'em.

'Are Georgie and Harry here?' Calum yelled, bursting into the kitchen alongside Regan.

'No. I thought they'd gone to Romford with you?' Frankie replied.

Regan punched his brother. 'Told you they weren't playing a game, didn't I? You div.' Regan had wanted to keep looking for Georgie and Harry, but his stupid brother had got it into his thick skull that Georgie and Harry were teaching them a lesson for being over-protective.

Panic rising inside, Frankie asked, 'What's going on?'

Calum's eyes welled up. 'They promised they wouldn't run away, and we believed 'em.'

Little Vinny leapt up, eyes blazing. 'Where did you see them last?'

'In Romford. They went off to meet the gypsy women who sell the lucky heather, but they never came back.'

'Nooooo,' Frankie Mitchell cried, banging the palms of her hands against the kitchen counter. Her voice trembling, she shrieked, 'Not again. I can't lose 'em. Not now. We turned a corner. Georgie loves me, she wouldn't leave me. Not like this. They must have been snatched.'

Queenie Butler and Joycie Smith were in a buoyant mood. Their shopping trip had been a successful one and they'd bagged a few bargains. But the news they'd heard on the phone via Vinny was the reason they were now sitting in the Italian restaurant having a celebratory drink before their meal.

'Always on the cards, wasn't it? I mean, they've been inseparable since they lost their loved ones,' Joyce said.

'Oh yes. It's wonderful news after all the heartache they've been through, don't you think? And the kids all get on so well. I've no doubt we won't have to wait that long for a wedding. He's a homely settling-down type is Little Vinny now. Was a horror growing up, but I'm so proud of the way he turned out. He'll most certainly treat your Frankie like a princess. He's not a womanizer either. Very respectful towards women, that boy is.'

'Glad to hear it. It's about time Frankie had a bit of luck with men. 'Ere, I wonder if they'll have a kiddie of their own? Still young enough, aren't they? Frankie's not even thirty until later this year.'

Queenie grinned. 'Wouldn't that be grand? We could do joint great-granny days out with the baby. And we'll sort of be related when they get married, won't we?'

'We sure will. They might even have twins, you know. My Frankie's a twin, it's in the genes. I wonder if a boy would turn out to be gay like Joey? That might be in the genes as well.'

Queenie pursed her lips. 'I don't think so. Butler sperm doesn't create gays, Joycie.'

Joycie held her glass aloft. 'To us, the wedding and the babies that follow.'

Queenie clinked glasses. 'And a special toast to you, Joycie Smith. Never thought I would smile again after my Vivvy died, but I am and that's all thanks to you. Not usually such a soppy old bird, me, but you're the best friend I could've wished for.'

Joycie's eyes filled with tears. 'Likewise, Queenie.'

Eddie Mitchell ordered Calum and Regan Butler to sit at the kitchen table. He already had the lads out searching frantically for Georgie and Harry, even though he guessed it was a fruitless task.

Frankie was beside herself. 'See, I told you they'd been snatched. No way would Georgie swear on Shelby's life if she was planning to bolt. Nobody knows my daughter better than me these days,' she sobbed.

Eddie turned to the inebriated mess he hoped would not become his future son-in-law. 'Take Frankie in the other room, Vin. I wanna talk to the boys in private.'

Eddie ordered the boys to tell him everything they

remembered while jotting down notes on a pad. 'I need you to be totally honest with me now. No bullshit, OK?'

Calum and Regan nodded. They already missed Georgie and Harry, and just wanted them back.

'Yous two were closer to my grandkids than anyone else. Did they ever tell you they wanted to leave or were planning on running away?'

'Yeah, but that was ages ago. Georgie told me that as soon as they had enough money, she and Harry were going to leave. But they weren't happy here back then. They are now though, honest. We all have a right laugh together, don't we, Regan?' Calum said in earnest.

Regan nodded and stared into Eddie's angry eyes. Part of him wanted to tell the truth as he was desperate to see Georgie again. But having done time, he knew grassing was the worst thing ever. 'Calum's right. They were well happy here now.'

Eddie eyed the boy sceptically. He hadn't been born yesterday, could always tell when a person was holding something back. 'You totally sure about that, Regan? Have another little think, eh?'

Visualizing Georgie speaking about her New Year resolution and threatening to leave only weeks ago, Regan tantalizingly held Eddie's gaze. 'I'm perfectly sure. Why would I lie?'

Georgie O'Hara was her father's daughter all right. She'd been clued up and streetwise from a very early age, so when Ryan kissed her again, she responded. Instinct told her acting normal was the only way out of this situation.

'How long till we get there now? Will everybody be waiting for us?' Harry asked. He was making buttons to see his dad and granddad again.

'Two minutes, we'll be there,' Billy O'Hara replied, feeling guilty. He'd had to pretend his father and Jed were alive throughout the journey as his mother had insisted on breaking the bad news to the kids herself.

As the motor swung into a concrete yard with no more than a handful of trailers, Harry was disappointed. 'Ain't we got no land and horses now? And where's me dad's motor?'

Alice O'Hara darted from her trailer to greet her beloved grandchildren. 'Me chavvies. Come 'ere you two,' she cried, hugging both close to her large bosoms.

Harry was the first inside the trailer. 'Where's me dad and granddad?'

'Ryan, go with your dad and Billy to your trailer. I want to speak to Georgie and Harry alone.'

'Just fucking tell me where they are,' Harry yelled.

Georgie held her little brother close to her chest. Unlike him, she'd already prepared herself for this moment. She didn't even feel tearful.

'Sit down, please,' Alice pleaded. It was so good to have the kids home again, but such a pity their reunion couldn't be a joyous one.

'Tell us then,' Harry shrieked.

'Your dad and granddad have gone, my darlin', for good. I'm so sorry, but you still got me, Shelby, Billy and Ryan. We'll take good care of you, you know that.'

'Gone where?' Harry spat.

'They're dead, you dinlo. Told you that ages ago, didn't I? It was obvious. They'd have come and got us if they weren't dead, I told you that too,' Georgie reminded her brother.

Tears streaming down his cheeks, Harry asked, 'How did they die?'

'We don't know. We never saw them again after you got taken. They never returned home,' Alice wept. 'Miss 'em so much, I do. Life ain't the same without 'em.'

'Where are their bodies then?' Georgie asked.

Their nan's face twisted with anger. 'You should've asked your gorger family that question.'

Frankie Mitchell lay on her back staring at the ceiling. Sleep wouldn't come, but how could she expect it to when she had no idea what part of the country her children were in? The only thing she could be sure of was that they weren't abroad. Even though her one-time in-laws called themselves travellers, foreign shores were all but alien to the O'Haras.

It had been an awful evening as well as day. Ava had arrived at the house with her father and he and Little Vinny had had the screaming match of all screaming matches.

'Do you know who you remind me of? Ben bloody Bloggs, the way you're slumped there, teeth missing, can of cider in hand. That's how that retard would've turned out, ya know. Pull yourself together before it's too late,' Vinny had yelled.

Little Vinny had gone ballistic and started smashing the house up, and Frankie was extremely glad her dad had already left. She could tell he wasn't a fan of Little Vinny at present.

Frankie pictured her children's faces. She could see Jed in Georgie; she had the same dark brooding looks but was so beautiful with it. Harry was a funny-looking boy, but in a good way. His strawberry blond hair always looked messy and unkempt – as did the rest of him, come to that. Harry had the look of a young rock star about him. Even when he'd just got out the bath he still looked like he needed a good wash.

Feeling a tear drip on to the pillow, Frankie fiercely wiped her eyes. She was determined not to fall to pieces like the last time her kids had been taken. It was different now;

they'd got to know her and they were too old and headstrong to be kept against their will. No way would the O'Haras be able to keep them prisoners like she had. They didn't have the resources or lifestyle to do such a thing.

Convincing herself that Georgie and Harry would return home of their own accord, Frankie turned on her side and shut her eyes. A minute or so later, she sat up. Little Vinny was having another of his terrible nightmares.

'It's an adventure. Don't cry, Molly. I can't stop the rain. You'll be dry soon. No, Molly. You can't have anything to eat. Just stop fucking whinging, will ya?'

Not wanting to wake the boys, Frankie crept into Little Vinny's room. Usually when this happened she would just wake him, give him a glass of water and comfort him until he calmed down, but as she heard him say the name 'Ben' she decided to listen to his ramblings instead. That's when he'd lost it completely earlier, when his father had mentioned Ben Bloggs, and Frankie wanted to know why. Ben's name had cropped up in previous conversations between Little Vinny and his dad and nan, and each time Frankie had noticed he'd start acting really odd – and that was before he'd got beaten up.

'Put your hood up, Ben. People might see us. Push Molly faster. Molly – no, Molly. Don't look at me like that. I didn't mean it. I love you. I'm sorry. You're my sister.'

Frankie edged nearer to the bed. Little Vinny was sweating and tossing and turning as though he was having some kind of a fit. Scared, she tapped his arm. 'Wake up, Vin. It's OK. I'm here.'

Little Vinny was still half asleep as he sat bolt upright and burst into tears. 'It's not OK. It will never be OK. I killed her. My own little sister. I throttled her – to death.'

CHAPTER TWENTY-TWO

Little Vinny held his throbbing head in his hands. 'Stop hurting me head. Please don't do this to me,' he mumbled, rocking to and fro, his legs dangled over the edge of the bed.

He could remember the details of that day so clearly. He could even recall what he was wearing when he'd popped round to Ben Bloggs in the morning, asking for a special favour. 'I'll pay you fifty quid,' he'd told his pal. Poor Ben, being skint, had jumped at the opportunity, just like Little Vinny had known he would.

He'd made Ben steal the pushchair, of course. Little Vinny wasn't one to get his own hands dirty when he had a gofer to do the necessary. Then he'd ordered Ben to hide in the disused garage near the club until he arrived with Molly.

It was Ben who'd pushed his little sister through Victoria Park in the torrential rain. Little Vinny had ordered his pal to take Molly to what they referred to as their 'special place': a little den they'd created in a secluded spot amongst the trees, not far from the River Lea in Hackney.

When Little Vinny finally arrived at the spot, Molly was confused and hysterical. She'd lost her beloved doll on the journey and just would not shut up. 'Where's Molly Dolly?

I want my doll and Mummy and Daddy,' she'd screamed, inconsolable.

'Stop it. Go away. Noooo,' Little Vinny pleaded. He started to cry. He didn't want to think about what happened next, but there were voices in his head urging him to . . .

Frankie Mitchell ended the call to her father. There was no news yet regarding Georgie and Harry, which did not surprise Frankie in the slightest. They'd get word soon though, she was certain; Georgie would find a way to make contact. A mother and daughter bond is an unbreakable one, she'd convinced herself.

'Morning. I had another of those nightmares, didn't I?' Little Vinny asked sheepishly. Wetting himself on the bed covers seemed to have stopped the voices in his head, and he'd managed to pull himself together, for now.

Brett was at her dad's place and Frankie had insisted under no circumstances was he to be allowed out of Gina's sight, not even to go to school. For all she knew, the O'Haras could still be lurking, waiting to snatch him too.

'Take your cereal in the other room, boys. I need to talk to your dad,' Frankie said, feeling anxious. What Little Vinny had said about Molly had chilled her to the bone. He'd seemed in some kind of a trance, but she had to be sure it was just his subconscious playing tricks with him. The alternative didn't bear thinking about.

Ordering his sons to do as they'd been told, Little Vinny turned to Frankie. 'Any news yet?'

'No. Listen, about last night, Vin: you said some really weird stuff when I came into your room.'

Little Vinny knew roughly what he'd said, but was determined to bluff it out. 'Like what?'

'About Molly. You were rambling on about her death, then you sat bolt upright and said it was you who'd killed her.'

'I was having a nightmare. I've always blamed myself 'cause I was meant to be looking after her. If I hadn't fallen asleep, she'd still be alive.'

'But you said you throttled her, Vin. Then you started crying.'

Little Vinny slammed his fist against the wooden table. 'So, I talk a load of old rubbish in my sleep. Big fucking deal.'

Approximately fifty yards from Little Vinny's house was a black six-seater vehicle with heavily tinted windows.

'This is bollocks. He ain't gonna go out, I'm telling you. I think we should just knock on the door and drag the bastard out by his neck,' Jamie Preston said. The desperation to clear his name was eating away at his insides and if Little Vinny was going to admit all to the Old Bill as he'd promised, surely he'd have done so by now?

'We don't want to piss off Eddie Mitchell too much, mate. We can't be involving his daughter,' Glen Harper said.

'But she don't go out either. We can't sit here day after day, Glen. We're already getting funny looks off the neighbours. Told you we should have kept the van, didn't I?'

'Never use the same vehicle twice, Jamie. Tempting fate, doing that.'

'Fuck Eddie Mitchell. I ain't scared of him. Hardly a spring chicken, is he?'

'No. But he's no mug either, and he has plenty of backup. Listen, by the time this is all over, Mitchell will be thanking us. Better than going to war with the geezer, Jamie, trust me. I know it's difficult, but you need to calm down and try to be patient. Good things come to those who wait.'

*

Georgie O'Hara pushed Ryan Maloney away and stood up. He was suffocating her with his need for endless kisses and cuddles, and she felt nothing for him any longer. Her heart definitely belonged to Regan now.

'Something ain't right, Georgie. You gone off me, ain't ya? I bet you have met another mush. Kill him I will, I swear. You're my woman.'

Georgie picked up her little sister. Shelby had grown so much and hadn't recognized her or Harry at first. She'd kept crying when they held her. 'The world don't revolve around you, Ryan. There's other people I've missed too.'

When Ryan started to argue, it was Alice and Lola who shut him up. Lola was Shelby's mum, and still lived in hope that one day her beloved Jed would walk through the door again. 'Leave her alone, Ryan. You're out of order,' she demanded.

'You're not giving Georgie time to breathe. She's had a terrible ordeal, being forced to live with that gorger whore of a mother of hers. Go to your own trailer for a while and come back later,' Alice bellowed.

Ryan stormed out of the trailer, followed by Harry. Harry had the hump because his one-time best pal Sonny Adams was still living in Scotland somewhere. Also, he was struggling to come to terms with the news about his father and grandfather. He kept expecting them to shout his name, as they'd done thousands of times before.

'Is there any shopping centres nearby, Lola?' Georgie asked.

'There's one I been to in Blackburn. That ain't far from here, about four miles,' Lola explained.

'Can you give me some money, Nan? I'll go there and get some new clothes. I'll need a phone as well. Billy chucked mine out the window.'

'I don't have no spare money now your dad and granddad

aren't around. But what do you need a phone for? Who ya gonna ring?' Alice asked suspiciously.

'Nobody in particular. Got no numbers, have I? Just got used to having one back home, that's all.'

Alice grabbed Georgie by the arm. Her granddaughter was not the same girl she remembered. 'Home! This is your home, I brought you up. You're a traveller, not a gorger, and don't you ever fucking forget that.'

'What's up?' Vinny Butler asked his brother. Michael had rung him earlier and asked if they could meet, urgently.

'I can't go through with it. Something's gonna go wrong, I can sense it,' Michael gabbled.

'Whoa, whoa, whoa. What you on about?' Vinny enquired, even though he'd already guessed.

'Felicity. Silencing her is one thing, us doing it another. Can't you just hire someone to stick a bullet in her nut, Vin? Make sure she'll be at a certain place at a certain time and we'll have a watertight alibi elsewhere? I've got enough on my plate at the mo, without worrying about this an' all.'

'You sound as though you've lost the plot, Michael. Calm down, for Christ's sake. No way am I trusting anyone else to top a bird again, not after what happened the last time. We have to do it ourselves. It's the only way.'

'Burning her and the motor is a fucking ridiculous idea.'

'Can you think of a better one?'

Remembering the stench and squeals of Trevor Thomas, the last person to suffer the same fate at the hands of his brother, Michael shook his head furiously. 'It's too much, Vin. Fliss is a woman, she don't deserve that. And I genuinely think she loves you.'

Vinny shrugged. 'Shame she never told me about her ex in the first place then. A sinner's a sinner, Michael. She has to go, end of. And we can't have blood dripping all over the fucking breakers yard, can we? Not only will it look suspicious, it'll ruin their concrete.'

As his brother started to chuckle at his own sick joke, Michael wished – not for the first time – that Roy was still alive and Vinny had taken the bullet in the head that was meant for him in the first place.

'Why we stopped here? This ain't no shopping centre,' Georgie O'Hara tutted. Ryan Maloney switched the engine off. He wasn't old enough to hold a driving licence yet, but his father allowed him to have his own truck and drive it around anyway. He'd never been pulled up, was a far better driver than most he had witnessed on the roads. And even if he did get a tug, he could always produce his older cousin's licence, or a fake. Travellers were experts at conning the law and authorities. 'I want a bit of us time, Georgie. Missed you so much, girl, and the feeling just don't seem mutual,' Ryan said, shoving his tongue down his young girlfriend's throat while fondling her ample breasts.

Knowing that playing along was the only way out of this, Georgie responded and even tantalizingly brushed her hand against Ryan's groin. 'I have missed you, and I still want to marry you when I'm old enough. But first I need to buy some clothes, Ryan. I've got none, the ones Nan kept are all too small for me now. I'm going to surprise you, buy something proper sexy, then we can stop the truck again on the way home. That sound good?'

Ryan groaned, then grinned. 'You bet it do.'

'Go to Romford then. Do whatever you want,' Little Vinny screamed at Calum and Regan. He didn't care that his sons were pining for Georgie and Harry, could not deal with anybody else's problems at the moment bar his own.

'You've changed, you have. You used to be a great dad

to us, but ever since you got beaten up, you're a horrible bastard,' Calum shrieked.

Regan grabbed his brother by the arm. 'Leave it, Cal. He can't help it; he ain't well at the mo.'

'There's sod-all wrong with me, OK? I'm absolutely fine,' Little Vinny bellowed, before darting into the bathroom and slamming the door.

'You go out, lads. Don't worry about your dad. I'll look after him,' Frankie said in a hushed tone.

Frankie tapped gently on the bathroom door. Something was amiss and she was determined to get to the bottom of it. Surely the man she was living with wasn't capable of strangling his own little sister to death, was he?

'Go away, Frankie. Can't I have a shit in peace now? I'm fine, honest. Just want to read the paper,' Little Vinny lied, staring in the mirror and scratching at his arms until they bled.

Once again, he couldn't silence the voices in his head as that day returned to his thoughts so vividly. Ben had been cradling Molly, singing nursery rhymes, when he'd arrived. 'Molly's upset. I don't ever want to do anything like this again, Vin. We need to take her home now,' Ben had insisted.

Little Vinny hadn't been thinking straight as he'd put on those yellow Marigold gloves. He was sick of the spoiled brat – and why wouldn't he have been? From the moment his little sister had been born she'd been the apple of every single member of his family's eye. The superstar wonder had arrived on the planet and he'd been totally fucking ignored, especially by his father. That was the reason he had done what he did. It wasn't Molly's fault, nor was it his. It was all his dad's fault. His father was a cunt of the highest order.

The voices in Little Vinny's head switched off as Frankie shouted, 'Your dad's on the phone, Vin.'

Taking a deep breath, Little Vinny did his best to sound

normal. 'Tell him I'm busy, babe, and make us a coffee. I'll be out in a bit.'

'There's his sons. Let's grab 'em,' Jamie Preston hissed. He was absolutely fuming that Little Vinny hadn't yet gone to the police. The urge to clear his name was now keeping him awake at night.

Impatience finally getting the better of him, Jamie leapt out of the vehicle. 'Your dad indoors, lads?' he shouted.

'Get back in the motor,' Glen urged.

Jamie ignored his pal and walked towards Calum and Regan. He didn't care about his face being seen. Why should he? He'd spent years inside, an innocent victim of Little Vinny's deceit. No way was that scumbag going to grass him up after what he'd done. How could you help a friend bury your little sister in a shallow grave, then say sod-all as her disappearance hit the national news and the police searched high and low?

'Yeah. Why?' Calum Butler asked.

Regan kicked his brother in the shin. He shouldn't be telling complete strangers their father was at home, seeing as their dad had recently been beaten up. 'Who are you then?' he asked, suspiciously.

'An old pal. Can you give your dad a message for me, please?'

'Depends what it is,' Regan replied.

'Just tell him his old mucker popped round to remind him to visit the police. He'll know what it's about.'

'What's your name?' Regan asked.

Jamie smirked. 'Mr Bloggs.'

'I'm cooking us salmon fillets for dinner. Hope that's OK with you?' Felicity Carter-Price asked, draping her slender arms around Vinny Butler's neck.

Responding to her hug, Vinny smiled. 'I thought of a name I like for a boy. Fred. My Ava once had a dog called Fred. Proper little character he was. My mum used to pretend she loathed him, but she loved him really. Used to drive my Auntie Viv mad, he did. So much so, she renamed him the "Ratpig". Fred Butler. Got a good ring to it, don't you think?'

Felicity looked at Vinny adoringly. She hated the name, but if it pleased him then Fred Butler it was. 'It wouldn't be my first choice of name, so let's just hope it's a girl,' she chuckled.

Vinny felt rather sad. If Felicity hadn't been a deceitful, grassing bitch, she truly could have been the one.

Little Vinny crouched next to the bath. He could see the look of bewilderment and horror in Molly's eyes as he'd laid her on the ground and put his hands around her neck. 'I'm so sorry, Molly. I really am,' he whispered.

Molly was grinning at him now. 'Tell the truth. Tell the truth. Tell the truth,' she cackled.

'No. Go away. Leave me alone,' Little Vinny ordered, clutching his head in his hands.

'Calum's on the phone, says it's urgent. Open the bloody door, will you?' Frankie Mitchell shouted. Little Vinny had been in the bathroom for over half an hour now and she was beginning to get seriously annoyed with him. No way had she signed up for this shit. She needed a man to look after her, not the other way round.

Little Vinny opened the door and snatched the phone out of Frankie's hands. 'What's up?'

'Some bloke asked me and Regan to give you a message,' Calum explained.

Little Vinny immediately felt the hairs on the back of his neck stand on end. 'What bloke? Where are you?'

'We're on a bus going to Romford. The bloke was outside

the house – well, a bit down the road. He said his name was Mr Bloggs and we was to remind you to visit the police.'

Stunned, Little Vinny dropped the phone.

Georgie O'Hara had her thinking cap on. The plan had been to pocket some of Ryan's money and use that to get back to Essex, but Ryan was stuck to her like glue. He was even insisting on queuing up and paying for her clothes in the typical traveller fashion of pulling out a massive wad of notes at the till.

Plan B was to find a payphone, but they seemed to be a thing of the past. Georgie had been having secretive glances all around the shopping centre and had yet to spot one. 'Will you buy me a mobile phone, Ryan?' she asked hopefully.

'Not today. I'll get you one another time. Pal of mine gets hold of hooky ones. Half the price of the shops. Shall we get something to eat now? My stomach feels as though me throat's been cut.'

When Ryan pulled her towards him and stuck his tongue down her throat yet again, Georgie wanted to gag. It was incredible to think she'd been in love with him not so long ago. She must have been blind, as he now made her skin crawl. Spending time with Regan and Calum had shown her just how chauvinistic and needy Ryan was. 'I'm not that hungry, but I'll eat something small.'

Arm around his beautiful girlfriend, Ryan said, 'You'll get used to that new site in time, ya know. And I promise when we get married I'll find us somewhere better to live that has a bit of land. We'll organize our wedding for your sixteenth birthday, eh? Be a double celebration.'

Thinking of Regan, Georgie nodded dumbly.

*

'Calm down, for Christ's sake, Vin. What did Calum say to you?' Frankie Mitchell asked. Her boyfriend was pulling out drawers and rummaging through them like a madman.

'Just pack some clothes will ya, and anything else you might need. We gotta get away from here today, Frankie. It's not safe to stay.'

Frankie grabbed Little Vinny's arm. He was shaking like a leaf. 'You need to tell me what is going on. No way am I putting Brett in any danger, and my dad is bringing him home later.'

'I can't tell you. If I could, I would. Let's go to Lincolnshire. We can stay in a hotel tonight, then tomorrow we'll rent somewhere until the property I've put a bid in for goes through.'

'If you think I'm leaving this area while my children are on the missing list, you've got another think coming. This is all getting a bit silly now, Vin, and unless I know what's going on I really can't help you. Perhaps you should go away with the boys and I'll move back in my house?'

Little Vinny held his head, tears streaming down his face. 'Please don't leave me, Frankie. I need you more than ever right now. So do the boys. They think the world of you.'

'There's little point being in a relationship if we can't trust one another, is there? Jed was a compulsive liar and I'm not going through that again. Once bitten, twice shy.'

'But I'm not fucking lying, am I? If I told you the truth, you'd hate me. But it wasn't my fault. It was meant to be a joke, a little adventure.'

Frankie held Little Vinny in her arms. 'Look, we've all done things in the past we're ashamed of, me especially. I'm the last person to judge anyone, so whatever it is I'm sure it'll be fine.'

'It won't. It can never be fine again. I did something really bad when I was young and now some men have found out about it and if I don't confess all to the police, they're gonna kill me.'

'What did you do, Vin? I won't tell a soul, I promise.'

'No. I can't.' Little Vinny could visualize Molly again. She was laughing at him. '*Tell her, tell her, tell her, tell her,*' his little sister was chanting in that cute sing-song voice of hers.

'Vin, look at me,' Frankie urged.

His head pounding, Little Vinny collapsed to his knees. Molly was torturing him and he wanted her to go away. Tears streaming down his face, he grabbed Frankie's hand. He was sure he could trust her. Perhaps if he opened up somewhat the voices in his head would go away? 'If I tell ya, you gotta swear on your kids' lives you'll never repeat it. It's really bad, but it wasn't my fault. My little sister, Molly. Loved her so much, I did. But my mate Ben strangled her, and I helped him cover it up.'

Frankie wanted to speak, but couldn't. She was dumbstruck.

Dreading the journey back to the trailer as she knew Ryan was expecting a lengthy groping session, Georgie O'Hara had barely touched her food.

'Not pining for another mush, are you, Georgie? 'Cause I will find out if you've been lying to me,' Ryan threatened. The change in her personality since being taken by her gorger family was immense. She'd once been such fun, always laughing and joking with him. Now it seemed an effort for her to even bloody talk.

'Just shut it, Ryan. You're doing my head in. Promised to marry you, didn't I? If you must know the truth, I miss my mum. She weren't too bad in the end.'

Ryan looked at Georgie in horror. 'How can you say that when the slag's responsible for the death of your dad and granddad? And your uncle, don't forget him. That's bang out of order, Georgie. Talk about stab your family in the back.'

Realizing she'd said the wrong thing, Georgie tried to retract her words. 'I don't miss my mum that much, but I do miss the house. It was like a mansion, Ryan, like something you only see in films. It had stuff me and Harry had never seen before, like computers and dishwashers. As for the oven, it was enormous. I think it was called Aga or something. I learned to cook better on that, so I'll be a good wife to you now,' Georgie lied.

'But you're not a gorger, you're a travelling girl. Forget all that shit you've seen, because you won't be seeing it again. Gorgers live their way and we live ours.'

Georgie was on the verge of reminding Ryan she was actually half traveller and half gorger, but didn't bother. It would only rile him up. 'I need to use them toilets over there. Busting to go again.'

'But you've only just been to the toilet.'

'Well, I'm very sorry, but I need to go again,' Georgie replied, voice laden with sarcasm. She was truly tempted to punch Ryan, or kick him in the nuts. He was such an irritating arsehole.

'Go on then. I'll wait 'ere.'

Georgie darted inside the ladies and was relieved to see five women inside. Two were applying make-up in the mirror, the other three queuing. 'I know this is a cheek, but I need to make an urgent call and I haven't got a phone. Please can I borrow one of yours?'

'Not got a phone,' one woman replied.

'Don't lend her yours. She's a gypsy, she'll run off with it,' another whispered to her pal. A traveller's accent stood out like a sore thumb.

Guessing what the woman had whispered, Georgie

pleaded. 'I'm not gonna nick it, I swear. I'm a decent travelling girl and I need to ring my mum, she doesn't know where I am.'

'Pull the other one, it's got bells on,' one of the women joked.

Eyes brimming with angry tears, Georgie was about to slap the trappy bitch when an elderly lady came out of the cubicle holding a phone in her hand. 'There you go, pet. You can borrow this.'

'Thanks so much. Is it OK if I take it inside a cubicle? Only I'm afraid my boyfriend might walk in, he's waiting outside.'

The woman nodded and as a cubicle became free, Georgie jumped the queue and darted inside. It was a godsend she'd memorized her mother's number in case anything untoward should ever happen. 'Please answer, Mum. Please,' she mumbled.

When the phone rang for what seemed like ages before connecting to the answerphone, a deflated Georgie wanted to cry. 'Mum, it's me. Me and Harry didn't run away. We wouldn't do that to you. We're up north somewhere with the O'Haras. They turned up in Romford. We're OK, so please don't worry. Just wanted you to know that I'll be back home soon. Tell Regan I miss him, but do it on the quiet. I gotta go now as some kind lady borrowed me her phone. Love you, Mum.'

Unaware that her beloved daughter had been in touch because Little Vinny had switched all phones on silent mode, Frankie Mitchell was sitting at the kitchen table in a stunned silence.

Little Vinny was in bits as he explained his version of events. He was sticking to the same story he'd told his captors, while trying to convince himself of this new story.

'So when I saw Molly weren't breathing, I tried to revive her at first. I remember pumping her heart and giving her the kiss of life like I'd seen on the TV. Ben didn't mean to kill her, I know he didn't. He loved kids, looked after his brothers and sisters. His mother was an old whore and a junkie, she couldn't even look after herself,' he spat bitterly. The fact that Ben's mother had once given him a blow-job when he'd been out of his nut as a young teenager was a secret Little Vinny would take to his grave with him. He'd despised her for doing that, and truth be known that was the main reason he'd drugged her up with temazepam before shoving a lethal dose of heroin into her skinny, wrinkled arm. Alison Bloggs had blackmailed him afterwards, threatened to tell his dad, and would've continued to do so had he not killed her. 'Say something, Frankie, please,' Little Vinny urged.

'Nobody accidentally throttles a little girl to death. That's unheard of, you fucking idiot. Your mate was obviously a psycho child killer. Why didn't you tell your dad instead of burying her in a shallow grave? That's sick, that is. My dad told me it was a while before Molly was found, that all the police were out searching for her for days on end. And you knew where she was the whole time. Why the hell didn't you say something?'

Tears of guilt brimming his eyes, Little Vinny tried to dig himself out of a bigger hole than he'd buried Molly in. 'Because I was scared. I wasn't the person I am now. Back then, I used to sniff glue and smoke weed. I'm not proud of what I did, it's haunted me every day of my life since. But Ben wasn't a psycho, honest. Molly's death was an accident and that's why I never said anything. We'd have both been banged up for years and neither of us deserved that. I panicked, but wish now I hadn't. I was only a bloody kid and kids do stupid things. Look at my Regan, stabbing his school teacher.'

'Stabbing a school teacher in the arm with a screwdriver is so not on a par with strangling a poor defenceless three-year-old child, Vin. Feel sick to the stomach, I do. Your mate Ben must've been pure evil. A monster.'

'Ben wasn't like that. On Calum and Regan's lives, Ben wouldn't hurt a fly. That's why I never dobbed him in it. His brothers and sisters would've never survived without Ben living at home, and I felt so sorry for them too. I did what I thought was right at the time, Frankie. What more can I say?'

'So how did these blokes find out what Ben did? Who are they?'

Little Vinny stood up and punched the door. 'How the fuck should I know? But they know everything. That's why we need to get away, go somewhere they'll never find us. I had to admit the truth to them when they were torturing me. I swear they'd have killed me otherwise. I know I said they didn't do much to me, but I didn't want to worry anybody, especially you. They tortured me badly, Frankie. Never felt such pain in my life. That's why I haven't been myself lately, but I'll be fine once we move.'

'No way are we moving. I'm not living the rest of my life looking over my shoulder.'

'You don't fucking get it, do you? I'm a dead man walking if I stay round here,' Little Vinny shrieked. 'We need to get away, change our names. Only then will we be safe.'

'Fat lot of good changing our names will do. People will still be able to track us down if they really want to.'

'What we gonna do then?' Little Vinny asked dejectedly.

Frankie stared at him sternly. 'There is only one thing to do. You have to go to the police, Vin. You need to tell them the truth, the whole truth and nothing but the bastard truth.'

CHAPTER TWENTY-THREE

'Don't lie to me, Frankie. I know you better than you know yourself at times. Just tell me what's wrong. I won't tell Dad, or Dom, I promise,' Joey Mitchell said.

'There's nothing wrong,' Frankie replied, playing Georgie's answerphone message again. It was almost a week now since Little Vinny had spilled his guts to her and she'd been in a quandary over what to do about his dreadful revelation ever since. He wouldn't go to the police even though she'd begged him to, and his alcohol consumption was on the increase. He'd get up, have some breakfast, then drink steadily until bedtime. He was also popping strong painkillers like sweets, and kept complaining about voices in his head.

'I know it's not Georgie and Harry, because every time I mention them you sound positive that they'll be home soon. So that leaves Brett and Little Vinny, and seeing as Brett is as good as gold, that narrows it down to your new boyfriend. Are you not happy with him? Is he hitting you or something?'

Frankie sighed. She'd kind of guessed when Joey had insisted on cooking her lunch at his that he'd be asking plenty of questions. The trouble was she had no answers to the latest pickle she'd got herself into. The option of moving back to the home her father had rented for her was no more. Sick of paying extortionate rent for an empty property, her dad had let it out to another couple earlier this week. 'I can't tell you Joey, I swore on the kids' lives I wouldn't tell anybody.'

'God's hardly going to strike all three down because you made some silly schoolgirl vow, is he? Just spit it out, for goodness' sake. Twins are meant to be able to trust one another.'

Desperate to share the awful burden she'd been carrying around this past week, Frankie gabbled wildly.

'Slow down. I can't understand you. Start again,' Joey ordered.

'I said it wasn't Jamie Preston who killed Molly Butler. It was a boy called Ben Bloggs. He was Little Vinny's mate and between them they buried Molly's body and covered up the murder.'

Joey was open-mouthed. 'You what!'

'What are you grinning at?' Felicity Carter-Price asked Vinny.

'Not a crime to smile at a woman I love, is it?'

'Of course not. I was thinking, I must register with a local doctor sooner rather than later. I rang one yesterday, but they aren't taking on any more patients.'

Vinny's face clouded over. 'What did ya do that for? I told you I would sort you with a private doctor. You know how superstitious I am. It's unlucky to be involving doctors just yet. What did you say to them?'

'Oh, I never told them about the baby.'

'What did you tell 'em then?'

'Only that I was new to the area and was looking to register with a new doctor.'

'Didn't they ask your name or address?' Vinny asked. Here in Canary Wharf, people tended to keep themselves to themselves. He hadn't a clue who most of his neighbours were and hoped they hadn't seen too much of Felicity coming and going. The less people who knew she was living at his, the better, and that included any nosy bastard GP sticking their oar in.

'No. The receptionist was quite abrupt actually. Just said the doctor wasn't taking on any more patients.'

'Come and sit 'ere,' Vinny said. 'I've got a bit of a confession to make.'

'What?'

Vinny put an arm around her shoulders. 'Got a bit excited last night and blurted out about our sprog to the lads at work. Just sort of slipped out, you know how it is. Not pissed off with me, are ya?'

'Of course not. I still haven't told a soul, but seeing as you've told your friends, I will ring mine on Monday after I've told my parents.'

Pinning Felicity to the bed, Vinny held her wrists together with one hand and tickled her with the other. 'Don't lie. I bet you've told loads of people already. Tell me the truth, go on,' he chuckled falsely. He hadn't told anyone bar Michael and Eddie and needed to make sure she hadn't spilled her guts.

'I haven't told a soul, honestly,' Felicity squealed. She despised being tickled.

'It's gonna be a boy, I know it is. Swear on our Fred's life you haven't told anybody.'

'On Fred's life, I haven't. I don't see anybody to bloody tell.'

Vinny stopped tickling her. 'I'm feeling too horny to go to work today. Go get Pandora's box.'

When Felicity happily did as asked, Vinny sighed. He

might as well sow his oats while he could. From tomorrow the bitch would be unable to breathe, let alone fuck.

Over at Joycie's, Queenie was desperately trying not to laugh as she was caught up in a heated marital dispute.

'You're a wicked, hooked-nose old witch, that's what you are. Not got an ounce of compassion in your body, you,' Stanley Smith bellowed.

'And you were born a dwarf and should think yourself lucky any woman married you, let alone me. What that old slapper Pat the Pigeon ever saw in you I will never know, but she's welcome to you now. Go on, pack your case and ask her if you can move in with her. And you can take them stinking bastard pigeons with you, otherwise I'll cook 'em in a pie,' Joyce cackled.

'I'm going out for a pint with Jock. And I swear, if you lay one hand on those pigeons, I will call the police and have you arrested,' Stanley threatened.

As her husband slammed the front door, Joyce yelled, 'I'm cooking your cock first.'

With Stanley gone, Queenie finally allowed herself to burst out laughing. 'I thought Albie and me were bad, but yous two are far bleedin' worse. Do you ever regret marrying Stanley? I do and I don't with Albie. Don't get me wrong: I despise the old bastard. But, he was a good-looking man and I always knew he'd give me handsome kids, which he did. Well, except for my Brenda, God rest her soul. Runt of the litter, she was. I think I was always meant to only give birth to boys.'

Joyce sighed wistfully. 'For all Stanley's faults, he did give me two wonderful children. Raymond's away with the fairies now, thanks to that money-grabbing tart he married. But my Jessica – one in a million that girl was. Such a stunner, and with a beautiful heart. Had a look of

Marilyn Monroe about her around the time she met Eddie, you know. Do you mind if I ask you a personal question, Queenie?'

'Go ahead.'

'Did you ever enjoy sex with your Albie?'

'Goodness, no. Never really knew what to do, if I'm honest. My dear old mum told me and Vivian that sex was evil but necessary. We were never taught about the birds and the bees at school like kids are today. On the morning of my wedding I remember my mum saying, "Queenie, Albie's a looker, a character, and he has a kind face. He will never beat you like your father has me."'

'Your dad knock her around then?' Joycie enquired.

Queenie's eyes welled up. 'Terribly. Me and Vivvy would huddle on the stairs as kids, while he was beating Mum black and blue. Horrible bastard, he was. One minute he'd be nice as pie, the next he'd turn into the devil. He hated women, was a proper man's man,' Queenie admitted, not realizing the description also applied to her eldest son.

Not wanting to upset Queenie, Joyce lightened the subject. 'Did you ever have one of them thingummy-bobs with your Albie?'

'What do you mean?'

'You know, an organism. I've seen women talk about 'em on TV. Never had one, me. Just laid there and made my shopping list in me head while Stanley did what he had to do.'

'An organism!' Queenie burst out laughing. 'I think you mean an orgasm, Joycie. No, love, never had one of those. My Albie couldn't organize a piss-up in a brewery, let alone work magic with his dingle-dangle.'

'My Stanley's dingle-dangle was that small it looked like a button mushroom,' Joyce said seriously.

Queenie very nearly wet herself laughing. 'You're a case, you are, Joycie Smith. My Vivvy would've loved ya.'

In the Bluebell restaurant in Chigwell, Eddie Mitchell was having lunch with his eldest son. Both were dressed in expensive black suits and crisp white shirts accompanied by black ties, as they'd earlier been to a funeral of an old Jewish pal of Eddie's father.

'You've pulled, Dad. The blonde two tables away to your right can't take her eyes off you,' Gary informed his father.

Eddie smirked. 'Can't help being a handsome bastard, can I? I took Gina and the kids out for a bite to eat last Friday and some little dolly bird followed me to the toilet and waited outside to hand me her phone number. She was only about twenty, with false tits – the works,' Eddie chuckled. 'I didn't tell Gina until we got home in case she lumped her one.'

'What did Gina say?' Gary asked. He was tall and dark-haired like his father, but didn't quite have his old man's pulling power. His dad seemed to mesmerize women of all ages and Gary had always found that funny.

'You know Gina, doesn't take a blind bit of notice, she just laughed and said if I didn't get someone in to decorate the front room soon, the dolly bird was welcome to me.'

'Don't think my Nicole would be so easy going if that were me. She'd probably drive back to the restaurant and scratch the bird's eyes out,' Gary laughed.

Eddie smiled. Considering the close bond they'd shared, Gary had dealt surprisingly well with his brother Ricky's death last year. Ricky was a casualty of his feud with the O'Haras, had met his maker on the evening they'd snatched Georgie and Harry. Truth be known, that was another reason Eddie couldn't take to his gypsy grandchildren. He'd lost a son because of them and they weren't even grateful to be rescued. Many a time Eddie now wished he hadn't intervened. Ricky was worth a thousand of Georgie and Harry.

'That's the woman who's got the hots for you. Walking past us now,' Gary said.

Eddie looked up. The woman was reasonably attractive, in her late thirties he'd guess, but Pamela Anderson could try and cop off with him and he'd still knock her back. He loved the arse of his Gina. 'How's the debt-collecting going?' Eddie asked Gary. He had now stepped away from his loan-shark business, but Gary and Raymond had wanted to continue it even though they both worked for him at The Casino.

'OK. Had to give a couple of geezers a dig last week, but I was gentle with 'em. They've since coughed up, so all's well that ends well.'

'Anyone I know?'

'Don't think so. The Singhs. Brothers, they are. Car dealers from Manor Park.'

'Watch your back, son. You got a lot to look forward to now,' Eddie warned. Nicole, Gary's thick bimbo of a wife, grated on Eddie immensely, but he was thoroughly chuffed she and his lad had their first nipper on the way. 'So, you got a due date yet?'

'Beginning of June, they reckon. If it's a boy, I'm calling him Ricky.'

Eddie put his knife and fork down. 'That's a lovely touch, son. And Nicole's in agreement, is she?'

'Yeah, she gets it. She's chosen the name if we have a girl – India.'

'How very patriotic,' Eddie mumbled.

Gary chuckled. 'She's a good girl, Nicole. Whatever makes her happy, eh?'

Eddie said no more. Rather than upset his boy, he tended to keep his thoughts about Nicole to himself. They'd had a tough life growing up had Gary and Ricky. Their mother – his first wife – had been a beauty when he'd married her, but had later become a raging alcoholic. She was dead now. Gary and Ricky had broken into her house and discovered her rotting corpse, the poor bastards.

'How you getting on with Vinny now? It's hard to chat properly at The Casino. Any more unwanted gifts turned up?'

'Nope. All quiet on that front. Vinny's been pulling his weight, so all's OK for now. I'm not happy about his son and Frankie though. Not the full shilling, that lad, since he got a clump, and I bet poor Stuart's turning in his poxy grave.'

'What you on about?'

'Little Vinny and Frankie are now an item. Let her get on with it. Fallen over backwards to help her, I have. Well, no more. Little Vinny can look after her now. Rented her gaff out to another couple the other day. Talk about taking the piss. Twelve hundred a month that was costing me and she weren't even living there. Not shelling out on any more properties for her. She's made her own bed, so let her lie in it.'

Gary shook his head in dismay. Stuart had been a good guy. 'Does Vinny know they're an item?'

'Yeah. Happy as Larry about it, he seems. Oh well, what will be will be. I'll always love her, but Frankie's a law unto herself. I'm done with her and those poxy kids.'

Joey Mitchell was astounded by what Frankie had told him – and he wasn't easily shocked. The search for Molly Butler, and her subsequent death, had been splashed all over the newspapers in 1980. She'd been an angel-ic-looking little girl, and it was one of those murders you did not forget. 'Remind me again who Jamie Preston is?

How must he feel, being locked up for a crime he didn't commit? It's awful, Frankie, I can't quite get my head around it.'

'Jamie is Albie's son by a woman called Judy Preston. Albie had an affair with her while he was still with Queenie. What am I going to do, Joey? I have Brett to think of. Plus Georgie and Harry. They're bound to be home soon.'

'I think you're on the rebound from losing Stuart. Nobody moves on as quickly as you have. God forbid anything terrible ever happens to Dom, but if it did, it would be years before I could move on.'

'Oh, don't get all sanctimonious on me. I didn't plan any of this, it just happened. You have no idea how it feels to lose somebody you were planning on spending the rest of your life with. Neither do you know if you would jump into bed with the first man you met afterwards. Until you've been in that situation, you shouldn't judge.'

'OK. I'm sorry. But, Frankie, you cannot be with this bloke. He buried his own little sister, for Christ's sake, then stood by as the world searched for her. That's pretty fucked up, even by our family's standards. You need to tell Dad.'

'No way! Dad will go apeshit and tell Big Vinny. It'll cause mayhem. I am going to convince Little Vinny to go to the police himself. I will even go with him, if need be.'

'Are you in love with him?'

Frankie Mitchell shrugged. 'I thought I was, but now I'm not so sure. He's changed beyond recognition since he got beaten up. And this Molly thing has put me off. I mean, you and I would never have done such a thing as teenagers, would we?'

'No, we wouldn't. Hate to be the one to break the news to you, but I told you so.'

*

Finn O'Marney was shocked by his pal's gaunt appearance. Little Vinny had always been a follower of fashion, would spend fortunes on clothes, but today, in a dirty Adidas tracksuit that was far too big for him, he looked dreadful.

'Come in,' Little Vinny urged, furtively glancing around to make sure his captors weren't lurking nearby. He was now positive one was in fact Jamie Preston.

'How you doing, mate?' Finn asked jovially.

'I want some Charlie. Get us half ounce and I'll give you the dosh. Don't mention it to Frankie though. Or anybody else, for that matter. The painkillers aren't working and I need something to take the edge off.'

Finn was a bit taken aback. In all the years he'd known Little Vinny his pal had never taken drugs to his knowledge – if anything, he'd always been anti-drugs. 'Snorting coke isn't the answer to your problems, Vin. You're a brilliant dad; don't spoil it by taking that shit around those boys of yours. They've lost their mum and brother, they rely on you now.'

'Forget it. I'll ask somebody else.'

Finn sighed. 'Why don't you come back to work next week? We were a great team, weren't we?'

Little Vinny leapt up, pointed repeatedly at his face, and walked over to the mirror on the lounge wall. 'Look at the fucking state of me. How can I go anywhere? Let alone deal with clients. Are you blind?' he shrieked. 'One favour I ask you. One poxy favour. And you can't even do that for me. Some mate you turned out to be. Ben Bloggs would've done anything for me, and I mean anything,' he ranted.

'Vin, calm down, mate,' Finn urged. His pal had turned red in the face.

Little Vinny grabbed the mirror off the wall, threw it on

the carpet and jumped up and down on it. 'Get out my house. Go on, fuck off.'

Vinny Butler watched intently as Felicity prepared dinner. She was a crap cook, so he wouldn't miss her culinary skills.

'You're putting me off. Why do you keep staring at me?' Felicity laughed. Vinny had told her earlier he had a surprise planned for her tomorrow and she was hoping he was going to propose. He was dead excited about their baby just lately, so it would make perfect sense to get wed. She didn't even care if she waddled up the aisle ready to drop, as long as he was waiting at the altar for her.

'I'm just excited about tomorrow. Got a blinding day out planned and I cannot wait to see the look on that beautiful face of yours.'

'Ooh, give me a clue,' Felicity urged. He must be going to pop the question. What else could it be?

'Won't be a surprise then,' Vinny grinned. He'd checked out his alibi earlier and all was in place. The Kelly brothers were sound, and Carl was going to drive his car over to them, then drive it back the following morning, hitting a speed camera both ways in Kent. The Kellys had friends in high places. A bent ex-cop and judge would swear blind he'd been participating in an all-day poker session with them, if need be. Not that they knew what he was up to. All he'd said was he needed an alibi and even if the shit hit the fan – which it wouldn't – there'd be no questions asked. That was the way it worked in the circles he mixed in. See no evil, hear no evil, speak no evil. Like the three wise monkeys.

'You're smirking now. What are you thinking?' Felicity asked excitedly. Vinny was a man of style and she could not wait to lay eyes on the engagement ring. It was sure to be the rock of all rocks, and that would be guaranteed to shut her condescending parents up when she visited them for the first time in ages on Sunday. If it wasn't for Vinny insisting she should build bridges with them, she would not have even arranged the date.

'Just thinking. I don't know much about you. You told me about Craig, your first love at school. But you must have had a serious relationship since then, Fliss?'

Felicity thought carefully before replying. She had been debating whether to come clean with Vinny about her ex for a while now, but had decided against the idea. Unlike Vinny, Dave Newton was a small-time gangster as well as an evil bastard. There was also the issue of her collaborating with the police to send the monster down. He'd been involved in a heinous crime which he thoroughly deserved to be banged up for, but Felicity was not sure Vinny would understand her way of thinking.

'Well? Come on, spill the beans,' Vinny chuckled. 'I swear I won't be jealous.'

It was on the tip of Felicity's tongue to blurt out everything. Unbeknown to Vinny, she wasn't a grass, or a police informer. Dave Newton was a monster who had threatened to kill her on numerous occasions. He'd beaten her senseless throughout their relationship and, appalled when in an act of road rage he laid into a defenceless young man so ferociously that he killed him, Felicity had done what any decent human being would have. She'd told the truth.

'Speak up then. I can't hear you,' Vinny urged.

Unfortunately for Felicity, she chose to keep schtum. Had she come clean, the truth might just have saved her life.

CHAPTER TWENTY-FOUR

Michael Butler hoisted his legs over the edge of the bed and put his weary head in his hands. Had he slept at all? Five minutes, ten at most. He didn't feel like he had.

Bella D'Angelo switched the light on and got out of bed. Things weren't great between herself and Michael. 'You've kept me awake all night, tossing and turning. Is there something on your mind? I have never known you to be so restless as of late.'

Michael stared at Bella's nakedness. She still had a good body for her age, but he didn't want to look at it in the cold light of day any more. Ever since he'd learned about her fling with Vinny, he'd always insisted on sex with the lights switched off. The thought of his brother groping Bella's perfect tits and arse made him feel sick to the stomach. 'Turn the light off and go back to sleep,' he hissed.

'No. Not until you tell me what's bothering you. You barely said a word through dinner last night. Even Camila asked me what was wrong with you.'

Michael made up some cock-and-ball story about Roxanne playing on his mind. He could hardly tell Bella the truth, could he? That he wasn't sleeping because later today he'd be helping to murder somebody.

Suddenly feeling nauseous, Michael ran into the bathroom. He wasn't cut from the same cloth as Vinny, he could not go through with killing that poor girl. It just wasn't right.

Ryan Maloney felt himself harden as he squeezed Georgie O'Hara's buttocks and nestled his groin against her lithe body. 'Come with me and my dad. We can stop for lunch somewhere on the way back,' Ryan urged.

'No. Driving miles in a stinking horsebox is not my idea of fun, Ryan. Can you give me some money, please? I need some more clothes.'

'You ain't going shopping on your own. I'll take you tomorrow.'

Georgie sighed. She truly despised him now, loathed his domineering ways. 'Lola is coming with me. We are leaving Shelby with my nan. Please, Ryan. I only want to look nice for you.'

Rather reluctantly, Ryan pulled a wad of money out of his pocket and handed Georgie three fifty-pound notes. 'Make sure you're back 'ere when I get home. Probably be about four-ish.'

Georgie grinned. 'I will.' She actually had no intention of returning to this shithole of a site ever again.

Vinny Butler handed his Range Rover keys to his employee, Carl. 'Right, I've had a change of heart. Only get flashed by one camera, two looks too false. You hit the camera on the way down, then any time between say three and five I want you to get a parking ticket not far from where the Kellys live. Don't care how you do it, whether it's double yellows or you go in a car park and don't put a ticket in the window. But make sure you somehow do it, and there are no CCTV cameras that can capture your face nearby.'

'The motor might get towed away if I park on a double yellow,' Carl warned.

'Just use your loaf and make sure the motor gets noticed. And don't stop at any petrol stations on the way down or back – they're all CCTV'd up these days. I've left you with a full tank of juice. And keep to the speed limit for the rest of the journey. The last thing we need is the Old Bill stopping you.'

'No worries. You want me to give you a bell later?'

'Nah. I'll ring you. And don't say nothing on the phone apart from yes or no. You know the score.'

Carl stared at his reflection in the mirror. He'd put one of those wash-in/wash-out black dyes on his hair and had slicked it back with Brylcreem like Vinny did. Putting his dark shades on, Carl turned to his boss and grinned. *Stars in Their Eyes* was his dear old mum's favourite TV programme. 'And today, Matthew, I'm going to be Vinny Butler.'

'Bye then. We're off now,' Georgie said casually. She'd been debating whether to take her brother to one side and convince him to run away with her, but it was too risky. Harry had perked up a bit since he'd started working with their uncle and if he grassed her up, she might never escape.

'Give Shelby her lunch around noon, Alice,' Lola said.

'Will do. You enjoy yourself, girls,' Alice replied. Georgie had seemed so miserable when she'd first arrived back, but had been much more like her old self these past few days.

Georgie ruffled her brother's hair. She was really going to miss him. 'Be good for Nan. See you soon.'

Harry was too busy scoffing his full English to bother looking up or replying.

'The taxi's waiting. Come on,' Lola urged.

Georgie had wanted to go shopping alone, but her nan

was having none of that, so she'd had no choice but to have Lola tagging along. It shouldn't be too hard to give her the slip though. Lola wasn't as bright as herself. Not many people were.

Vinny Butler could not believe his ears. 'You having a laugh, or what? Please tell me this is some kind of a sick wind-up, Michael.'

'Look, I'm sorry. But I just can't go through with it. My conscience has been playing havoc with me. I've hardly slept for a poxy week. Something don't feel right about it, Vin. It's gonna land us in trouble, I know it is.'

'Oh, don't talk bollocks. You can't back out on me now. If the boot was on the other foot, I'd do it for you,' Vinny proclaimed.

'I think the bird genuinely loves you, Vin. I'm sure she ain't gonna blab about anything. Can't you tell her you was testing her out and made up those stories, or something? She's carrying your baby, for fuck's sake. We murder her, we murder your kid an' all.'

'That thing ain't even formed properly yet, and I don't want no more kids at my age anyway. Have you forgotten me and my son got beaten to fuck recently? Well, that's all down to her. That's why me and Little Vin got targeted – and don't forget he saw her down the station. I gave her a chance to spill the beans last night, and the bitch blatantly fucking lied to me. She has to go before she grasses us up too. Fancy a life sentence, do you?'

Michael shook his head.

'Well then, man up. I'll do all the dirty work, all you gotta do is drive the other motor then keep lookout. Not too much to bastard well ask, is it?' Vinny bellowed.

Michael held his hands up. 'OK, I'll do it. But I'm telling you now, Vinny, don't you ever ask me for another favour again. Because after today I'm done with cleaning up any messes you create – for fucking good.'

Desperate to keep himself occupied, Little Vinny was pacing up and down the living room carpet while counting his footsteps. He'd been woken up earlier by the voices in his head again. Molly had been taunting him. 'Liar, liar, bum's on fire. Ben never killed me, it was you,' she'd cackled.

'The boys OK? Was there anyone outside? Nobody followed you, did they?' Little Vinny gabbled, when Frankie returned. He peered through the blinds. Since he'd got done over, he'd had the electric gates repaired, but was paranoid Jamie Preston's next move might be to snatch his boys.

'There was nobody out there to follow us. But we can't go on like this, Vin. Something has to change. It's not fair on the boys if they aren't able to go out to play. It's bad enough they're missing Georgie and Harry, they need to be allowed to lead normal lives and see their old friends,' Frankie said.

'No,' Little Vinny shouted. 'It's too dangerous. Once we get to Lincolnshire they can do what they like, but not until then. I don't mind them hanging about that Brewery with their pals, but not round 'ere. Did you tell 'em to ring when they want a lift home?'

'Yes. But you can go and pick them up. I'm not a taxi service,' Frankie complained.

'I can't drive. I've been drinking. Everything will be all right when we move, I promise,' Little Vinny said, trying to give Frankie a cuddle.

Frankie pushed him away. 'I am not moving. How many times I got to tell you that? You have to go to the police, Vin. Sort this mess out once and for all. I don't want Brett living here in case he's in danger, and it's not fair on my dad and

Gina for him to be staying there. My dad's dropping him back tomorrow and says I need to start looking after my own son more. Something has to change, else I will have to move in with Joey or my nan. I can't go on living like this.'

Little Vinny grabbed hold of Frankie's shoulders and shook her violently. 'Stop fucking pushing me away. I love you.'

'Get your hands off me, Vin. I mean it. Don't ever shake me like that again because I'm unshakeable. My father is Eddie Mitchell, remember? And if you really loved me, you would go to the police. Once you tell them the truth, those blokes will leave you alone and we can all get on with our lives.'

'Sorry for shaking you.' Little Vinny crouched and held his head in his hands. 'But say they lock me up? They can't prosecute Ben, can they?'

'You are not a murderer, Vin. Your lunatic of a mate was. What you did was bad, very bad. But you were young at the time and the police will understand that. No way can I carry on living like this. If our relationship is to stand a chance, you need to come clean.'

'OK. But let's get the weekend out the way first. I'll make a statement on Monday. My dad will never speak to me again, Frankie. He's gonna kill me.'

'No, he won't. My dad will talk to him. Time is a healer and your dad knows what a good father and person you are now. If me and Joey can forgive my dad for killing our mum, yours will forgive you for covering up for Ben Bloggs. Just tell him you were scared.'

Hearing Molly's voice in his head taunting him again, tears streamed down Little Vinny's face. This was God's way of paying him back. It had to be.

*

Felicity Carter-Price was beside herself with excitement. Vinny had been extra nice to her today. He'd cooked her her favourite breakfast – smoked salmon and scrambled eggs – which she'd eaten in bed, and then he'd tied her up and quite brutally fucked her. Felicity didn't mind that. She had always been a man-pleaser, especially when it came to Vinny. He was her world, the man she had been waiting to meet all of her life. 'Beautiful area, this is. I bet it's gorgeous in the summer. Where exactly are we?'

'High Beach. Not far from Epping Forest. You heard of that?' Vinny asked.

'No. I don't think so. Are we staying at a country manor?'

Vinny had totally got off on this morning's charade and had come like a steam train after tying up and nearly strangling the lying slag. Any bird who was capable of her deceit and getting himself and his son so badly done over was in his eyes a total liability and deserved all that was coming their way. However, he was now feeling a bit sad. It was a damn shame she had turned out to be such a wrong 'un as their relationship had been perfect. Or so he'd thought.

'We'll be there soon. Don't wanna spoil your surprise, do I, babe?' He could not wait to see the look of shock on her face as she realized her fate. Shame he couldn't video the whole thing really. Be something to remember her by.

'Well, it can't be a picnic you're taking me to. It's far too cold for that,' Felicity chuckled. It had thrown her a bit when Vinny had told her to wear something casual. He had a tracksuit on, which was a rarity in itself. She had only ever seen him wear such clothes on the odd occasion they were lounging about indoors.

Vinny drove towards the destination. Barry Gold was a heavy gambler and punter at his casino. He also owned a clothing wholesaler down the Commercial Road, and Vinny had known him over thirty years. Barry had been a regular at his old club in Whitechapel too, and ever since Vinny had known him he spent what he described as the 'Kipper Season' abroad. Barry wasn't a question-asker, neither was he a loudmouth. So when Vinny had asked him if he could use his barn for a bit of payback to somebody who'd wronged him, Barry had happily given him the go ahead in exchange for fifteen grand. Vinny would send one of his men back tomorrow to torch the barn so there'd be no trace left of the lying slag, and reimburse Barry for the cost of the rebuilding. Years ago, before all this DNA palaver came in, it had been relatively easy to get away with murder, but not any more. You had to be extra clever to get away with sod-all in this day and age.

Felicity glanced at the pocket of Vinny's tracksuit bottoms to see if she could spot the ring box. She truly could not wait to become Mrs Butler. Vinny was everything she had ever wanted in a man, and more.

Georgie O'Hara was flustered and scared. She had never travelled on a train before, had never been on any form of public transport alone. 'I need to get to Essex. How do I get there?' she asked one of the station staff.

'You need to travel to London first. Then you can ask there. Whereabouts do you have to go to in Essex?'

'I don't know the nearest station, but it's not far from Romford. I know how to get home from there. Can I go straight to Romford from here?'

'No. You need to travel to London first. Then get on the underground.'

'What's the underground?' Georgie asked, startled. She'd always been a bit claustrophobic. Liked being in open spaces.

When the man explained what it was, Georgie's eyes brimmed with tears. She wasn't cut out for the gorger way of travelling and wished Harry was with her to hold her hand. Now she had a big decision to make. Should she go back to Nanny Alice's and pretend she'd got lost in the shopping centre? Or should she conquer her fears and go where her heart told her she should be?

Michael Butler froze as Felicity's Porsche drove past him. Vinny was at the wheel as planned, and Michael could swear he'd seen his brother smirking.

Felicity stepped out of the passenger seat. 'Michael! What are you doing here?' she exclaimed. Perhaps Vinny had got all the family together and was planning to propose in front of them? If that was the case, she hoped his mother would be kinder towards her than the last time they'd met. 'Why are you driving a hired van? You haven't had an accident in your car, have you?'

Michael stared at his feet and said nothing. He was a good judge of character, was sure Felicity was genuine even if she had made mistakes in the past. No way was she undercover Old Bill like Little Vinny reckoned. He must've lost his marbles to even suggest such a thing.

Still not aware anything was amiss, Felicity turned to Vinny. 'This property reminds me of one my parents own in the South of France. Have you got the keys?'

Vinny's eyes bore into the woman he once thought he might be in love with. He grabbed her by the neck and lifted her feet off the floor. 'You ain't going inside no property, sweetheart. You're going to hell and back.'

Since Jimmy and Jed had been gone, money had been tight for Alice O'Hara. Her Billy would give her a few quid here and there, but he wasn't as bright as her husband and youngest son had been. Jed and Jimmy were wonderful providers, could have sold snow to the Eskimos.

'Waste of time eh, Alice? Four pound is all I earned. We should look for another patch,' Brenda Jackson moaned.

Alice trudged along dejectedly. Her arthritis was playing her up awfully today and the lucky heather had only earned her a measly three pounds fifty pence. She and Brenda usually had at least one or two touches telling fortunes for a fiver a time, but not today. The weather had not helped either. It had been teeming down with rain all day.

'Nan. Nan! Hurry up.'

Alice felt the fear of God as she spotted Harry running towards her. She'd had one of those funny feelings in her stomach ever since she'd spotted a lone magpie staring inside the trailer this morning. Alice was a big believer in the 'One for sorrow, two for joy' tale that surrounded those evil-looking birds. 'What's wrong?' she yelled.

Harry waited until he'd caught up with his nan before explaining. 'It's Georgie – Lola lost her at the shopping centre. Nobody knows where she is. Billy has gone to look for her.'

Felicity Carter-Price was in a state of shock. When Vinny had first dragged her into the barn she had honestly thought it was some kind of a sick joke and he was going to start laughing and propose. Now as he tied her hands to the back of a wooden chair, she wasn't quite so sure.

Feeling as sick as a dog, Michael Butler mumbled, 'I'll leave you to it,' before walking out of the barn. He couldn't watch. Trevor Thomas's still played on his mind and he'd had balls and a dick.

'Is this some kind of silly game, Vinny? Only you're scaring me now, so please, untie me.' Michael's behaviour had unnerved Felicity too. Usually so amiable, Vinny's brother had not been able to look her in the eye.

Vinny paced up and down the barn. He was hurt and extremely angry.

'Did you think I wouldn't find out?' he spat.

'Find out what? Please, Vinny, untie me. My wrists are hurting,' Felicity pleaded. The man of her dreams suddenly looked like a madman to her. There was evilness about those penetrating green eyes of his that she'd never noticed in the past.

Instead of getting off on Felicity's realization as he thought he would, Vinny suddenly felt upset. He truly had started to love her, might have even raised this kid with her had she not been a deceitful, lying cow.

'Vinny, please. This chair is giving me splinters.'

'Trusted you, I did. Allowed you into my life, my home – and this is how you repay me.'

Felicity started to cry and the penny started to drop. 'I don't know what I'm meant to have done. Is this about Dave, my ex? Only I was going to tell you about him, but I didn't know how you'd react. Please untie me, Vinny. My wrists feel like they are breaking.'

'I'll break more than your fucking wrists,' Vinny yelled. He walked over to the chair, grabbed Felicity by her long dark hair and smashed the back of her head and the chair against the concrete floor. Clasping his big hand around her chin, Vinny stared at her. 'So disappointed I am in you, Fliss. I genuinely thought you loved me.'

'I do love you. You're the best thing that's ever happened to me.'

Vinny spat in her face. 'Don't fucking lie to me, cunt. You're undercover Old Bill, ain't ya? Come on, admit it.'

Felicity was terrified. Dave Newton had always been an evil bastard. He'd knocked her about from the first day she'd moved in with him. But not Vinny. He was her soulmate, or so she'd thought. 'Of course I'm not undercover police. Whatever would make you think such a thing? I love you, Vinny, and I'm genuine. You have to believe that. It's the truth.'

'Truth! You wouldn't know the meaning of the word. You're an informant then, aren't ya? You work for the Old Bill, tip 'em off about things. Planning on putting me away for years, was ya? Only you've come unstuck now, eh?'

'No. I don't work for the police. I don't even like them. They were horrible to me after Dave—'

Finally getting off on her terror, Vinny laughed out loud. 'Oh, I know all about Dave Newton an' all. Caught you out on all your lies, you twisted bitch. Tell me more about your ex then. Go on, I'm all ears. Have a bigger cock than me, did he?'

Felicity was sobbing now. 'I was only young when I met him, Vin. He was a horrible person, used to beat me up regularly. I was going to tell you about him, but I thought you might get jealous, or not understand what happened. It wasn't like what we've got, I swear to that.'

'Liar.'

'I'm not lying. I promise you.'

Vinny put his right hand around Felicity's throat. She looked petrified now, and so she bloody well should. Never again would he allow a woman into his life. The ones he attracted could not be trusted. Two-faced slags, every single one of them. Backstabbbers of the highest order. 'How much did the Old Bill pay you for snitching on your ex?'

'Nothing. I'm not like that. Dave had a terrible temper. He killed a young lad because he cut us up in the car. Stabbed him to death right in front of me. I was scared for my own life as Dave kept threatening to kill me afterwards too. I had to tell the police the truth. I remember seeing that young lad's parents on TV appealing for witnesses. Gavin, his name was. He didn't deserve to die. I only did what any decent human being with an ounce of compassion would have done. Gavin's mother was heart-broken.'

'Well, aren't you the good little Samaritan,' Vinny hissed.

'Please untie me, Vinny. We can talk properly then. Sort this misunderstanding out. I'm not one to hold grudges. I love you and we're having a baby together.'

Vinny leapt up and unzipped the bag he'd brought with him. He pulled out a big knife and waved it in the air. 'You mean we *were* having a baby together. I don't believe a word you say any more.'

'But I'm telling the truth,' Felicity cried.

Knife in hand, Vinny walked towards Felicity with a manic expression on his face. 'Too little, too late, treacle.'

Little Vinny sniffed and cleared his throat as the line of cocaine hit the back of it. Finn had rather reluctantly come up trumps. He'd turned up earlier and virtually slung what he'd requested at him. 'Sort yourself out, Vin. This is a one-off,' he'd vowed, before stomping away.

'The boys are in the cab on their way home, Vin. I told them to buzz the gate so the cabbie can drive up to the house. What do you want me to order food-wise? They want a pizza,' Frankie shouted out.

'Not bothered. I'm not overly hungry, to be honest. Order whatever and I'll eat something later.' Little Vinny stared at his reflection. His hair seemed to be growing at an alarming rate now, and as soon as he moved he would get his broken teeth sorted. No way was he staying around here much longer. He would give Frankie an ultimatum. She either moved to Lincolnshire, or it was over between them.

*

Jamie Preston smashed his fist against the steering wheel in annoyance. He'd hung about all afternoon to snatch either one or both of Little Vinny's sons and now he wouldn't be able to as the cab had driven inside the property.

Seeing Glen's name flash up on his phone again, Jamie blanked it. His pal had told him under no circumstances should he involve Little Vinny's kids, but Jamie didn't care any more. He had visited his nan's grave again yesterday, and had sworn to her he'd clear his name. That had been her dying wish. She'd been a diamond had his nan.

Cursing his luck, Jamie turned the ignition on. There was no way Little Vinny was going to go to the police now, so if he had to take one of the boys to force the issue, he would. Bollocks to what Glen or anybody else thought. He deserved justice, and so did his nan and poor little Molly Butler.

Michael Butler crouched and put his hands over his ears. It was sickening to hear Felicity's screams and cries for help, but he couldn't stop what was happening now. It had gone too far.

Yards away, Vinny picked up the knife and put the tip on Felicity's midriff. 'Admit it, you bitch. You're a grass.' He'd only managed to rip out one of her front teeth. The silly tart had nearly passed out after that, so he'd stopped.

Blood pouring from her mouth, Felicity's eyes resembled a rabbit's caught in glaring headlights. Dave Newton might have knocked her about a bit, but he'd never attacked her anywhere near as viciously as this. The man she'd thought she had loved was obviously mentally ill, but she had to fight for the life of her unborn child. 'I don't work for the police. On our baby's life, I don't. Stop this madness, please. Michael, help. Please help me,' she screamed.

Vinny dug the knife in deeper, drawing blood. He was

turned on now, feeling exceptionally horny. He undid Felicity's jeans and with difficulty tried to rip them off.

Felicity was frantically screaming Michael's name. She knew she was going to die unless Vinny's brother stepped in.

'Please, Vinny, don't do this. It's insane. I only ever loved and was faithful to you,' Felicity pleaded. She had never felt so scared and bewildered in her lifetime. Apart from being rough in the bedroom department, Vinny had always acted as the perfect gentleman, until now.

'Shut it, whore,' Vinny spat, ramming his penis inside her. He'd watched a couple of snuff films where women were strangled as they were being fucked and had always found it the ultimate turn-on.

Michael stood up. Were his ears deceiving him or had he just heard Felicity cry rape? Surely even Vinny would not stoop that low?

Felicity was hysterical. 'Get off me, you animal,' she screamed.

Michael looked inside the barn and could not believe his eyes. Vinny had his tracksuit bottoms around his ankles and had Felicity's legs over his shoulders as he pumped away, grunting and groaning. To say Michael was appalled was putting it mildly. 'Whaddya think you're fucking doing?' he bellowed.

'Giving her one for the road. I won't be a minute.'

Seeing red, Michael lunged at his brother and grabbed the hood of his tracksuit. 'Get off her, you sick cunt. You disgust me,' he spat, punching Vinny hard in the side of the head.

'Chill, will ya. Ain't like I've never tied her up and shagged her before, is it?'

'I'm done with you after this. Don't you ever fucking try to contact me again, and I truly mean that.'

'The baby. The poor baby. Untie me, Michael. Please help

me,' Felicity begged. Vinny could go to hell now for all she cared. But she was still desperate to save her baby. She'd move over to the South of France, bring it up there alone. Start afresh.

Vinny pulled his tracksuit bottoms up, then held the palms of his hands in the air. 'Look, I'm sorry, OK? I didn't plan that. A spur of the moment thing. Let's finish the job and get out of 'ere, eh?'

'Let her go,' Michael hissed.

'Don't be daft. We can't let her go now.'

Ignoring Vinny, Michael walked over to Felicity and began untying her hands. 'Thank you. Thank you so much,' she whispered.

Panicking, Vinny picked up the fire extinguisher. 'Watch out,' Felicity shrieked. Unfortunately for her, the warning was too late. As the metal connected with the back of Michael's head, he hit the ground like a sack of potatoes.

'Now look what you've made me do,' Vinny roared. 'Baby! I'll give you fucking baby, you cunt.'

One hand untied, Felicity desperately tried to untie the other, but she couldn't.

A glazed expression on his face, Vinny picked up the butcher's knife. He was infuriated. Not only had this lowlife slut made him slap his mother, driving a wedge between him and Queenie, she'd now forced him to clump his own brother. She was evil, manipulative trash, that's what she was. 'Let's see if I was right about the sex of the baby, shall we? Wanna see little Fred, do ya?'

Felicity screamed blue murder when Vinny kneeled down beside her, knife in hand. He was laughing like a hyena, spit flying out of his mouth and she knew at that point she and her baby had no chance of survival.

As the knife made contact with her stomach, the sobbing Felicity made one last plea to save the life of herself and her unborn child. 'Please, Vinny, don't do this. Think of the blood. You'll get caught, go to prison. Just let me go and I promise you'll never see or hear from me again. I'll move abroad, get out of your life for good. Our baby doesn't deserve to die like this. It's innocent.'

'But you're not. You're a wrong 'un. A snitch,' Vinny snarled.

Felicity's last living memory was of her stomach being sliced open. Luckily for her, she was unconscious before Vinny's hand delved inside.

Frankie Mitchell studied Little Vinny carefully. He was different today, talking a lot and upbeat. But he also looked high, his pupils were big. 'Did that doctor give you different medication this time?' she enquired.

Guessing she was on to him, Little Vinny nodded. 'Yeah. Gave me some stronger pills. They seem to be working better. Best I have felt in ages. What about a bit of karaoke, lads? Fancy that, do ya?' Little Vinny laughed, slapping his sons on the back.

'I don't,' Regan mumbled. The karaoke machine reminded him of all the fun he'd once had with his mother and Oliver when his dad was normal. And more recently with Georgie and Harry. Nothing was the same any more. Even Frankie seemed stressed and miserable all the time, which was why himself and Calum talked about their mum a lot more. They missed her so much, and Oliver.

'I'll answer it,' Calum said, when the buzzer rang.

Having felt bullish all day thanks to the cocaine, Little Vinny suddenly turned paranoid. 'No. Don't answer it. We're not expecting anyone. Leave it.'

'But it might be important,' Frankie said. Her father had the right hump with her lately and she wondered if he was dropping Brett off earlier than expected.

'This is stupid. I'll answer it,' Regan scowled, pushing past his father. His old man seemed to be acting odder today than ever before. And whoever was at the door wasn't taking their finger off the buzzer. 'Who is it?' Regan asked.

'Don't let anybody in,' Little Vinny pleaded. 'Not even family.'

Regan's grin lit up the hallway. 'It's Georgie,' he squealed. 'She's back! She's come home.'

Hands and tracksuit covered in blood, Vinny Butler ripped the last of Felicity's teeth out, then removed the sock that he'd rammed towards the back of her throat. She didn't flinch, obviously. Hadn't since he'd put his hands inside her stomach and pulled out the foetus. She'd lied about that too. No way was she only two months pregnant. Vinny was no doctor, but the foetus was formed in the shape of a baby, and it had tiny fingers and toes. 'You messed with the wrong man, didn't ya, sweetheart?' he muttered.

Michael was still lying on the floor. The back of his head looked a bloodied mess, but Vinny had regularly checked on his breathing and pulse. What choice had he had but to knock him spark out? He was protecting his family. Felicity could have got them both locked up for life, had she been allowed to live.

Vinny glanced at his watch. He wasn't sure whether he was coming or going, to be honest, but he knew the Kelly brothers had arranged for Felicity's car to be discreetly picked up from here as soon as it was dark. High Beach was the perfect area to commit such a crime.

Hearing a grunting noise coming from Michael's direction, Vinny quickly picked up Felicity's lifeless body and carted it over to her motor. The boot was already open, so he shoved her in it. Michael was bound to freak out when he came round properly, and Vinny was desperate to check he'd left no clues behind.

'Where is she?' Michael mumbled, as he tried to stand up, but failed.

'I'm sorry for clumping you one, bruv. But I did it for us. You know she was up the Old Bill's arses. What else could I do? You was going all sanctimonious on me, and no way could we have let her walk away. We'd have been looking over our shoulders the rest of our lives. It's over now. We can breathe easy again.'

Michael sat up and put his hands around the back of his aching head. They were immediately covered in blood and so was the patch of floor where he'd last seen that poor defenceless woman lying. 'Where is she?' he asked again. His head was throbbing; felt like a herd of elephants had trampled all over it.

'In the boot. It was quick in the end, and I got all her teeth out afterwards. She didn't suffer too much.'

The scene in front of Michael resembled something out of a horror movie and as he crawled towards what looked like a lump of bloodied meat, he put his hand over his mouth and recoiled in horror. It was no bigger than a new-born kitten, but he could clearly see it was human. It had a head, arms and legs, tiny fingers and toes.

For the first time ever, Michael felt scared of his own brother. He'd known from an early age that Vinny was different. Not the full shilling, so to speak. But this was taking Vinny's madness to a whole new level.

Vinny crouched on his haunches and stroked Michael's face. 'I'll make this up to you, I promise. You wait 'ere while I tidy up a bit. I'll siphon the petrol out first so her car don't go up in too many flames. You rest, bruv, and I'll give you a shout when I'm done, OK?'

Michael nodded dumbly. He was in a trance, could not

think of a word to say. After today, he no longer had a brother. But he still had kids and was determined to get out of this dreadful situation alive. If his brother was capable of ripping that poor girl's baby out of her stomach, then he was capable of anything.

Michael shut his eyes. He didn't open them again until the putrid smell of burning flesh hit his nostrils. It was only then the full realization of what had happened hit him like a ton of bricks. Unable to control his emotions, Michael Butler started to weep.

CHAPTER TWENTY-FIVE

'Morning, darling. How did you sleep?' Frankie beamed. She was so thrilled her daughter was back home, where she belonged.

'I slept OK, but I'm missing Harry already. We've never been apart before, not even for a night. Do you think he'll come home too, Mum?'

'I don't know, love,' Frankie replied honestly. Her daughter had explained she felt it too much of a risk to include Harry in her plans to leave, and Frankie fully understood that. It didn't stop her worrying about and missing her eldest son though, and if Harry did unexpectedly knock on her door one day, it would be the icing on the cake.

'I know you don't like her, but is it OK if I ring Nanny Alice later? She's been good to me and Harry over the years and even though I don't want to live with her, I don't want to lose contact either.'

'I don't know if that's wise, love. Let me speak to Granddad first. The O'Haras might trick you and abduct you again.'

'No they won't. I'm not a dinlo. And Eddie ain't my granddad no more. He's a murderer who killed my other granddad and dad. I hate him.'

'Don't be daft. Granddad Eddie is no murderer.'

'Yes, he is. Nanny Alice said so.'

Regan sauntering into the kitchen spelled an end to the awkward conversation. 'All right?' he asked, grinning at Georgie. Two days she'd been home now, and they'd been inseparable apart from sleeping in different bedrooms at night. Calum wasn't happy, had the right hump. But Regan could not help the way Georgie made him feel. She made his tummy all fluttery and his brother needed to move on. There were loads of other girls out there.

'What do you want for breakfast? Ask your dad and Calum too,' Frankie said.

Squeezing Georgie's hand under the kitchen table, Regan informed Frankie: 'My dad's acting weirder than ever and Calum ain't talking to me. So best you ask 'em yourself.'

Queenie Butler was more clued up than most women her age, especially when it came to her sons. Today was an extremely important day. The fabulous stand-out headstone that had been imported from Italy was due to be placed on Vivian's grave. Bright blue it was. Vinny had found it on the internet for her. Her Vivvy was a legend and Queenie had insisted her headstone must go down in history too. Something that stood out from the rest. Her sister's wish had been to be buried in the same plot as her beloved son, so Lenny had a new heartfelt inscription too. Queenie loved the photo she'd chosen to be placed at the top of the headstone. Lenny was a toddler and Vivian looked so pretty and happy holding her pride and joy in her arms. So did Lenny; he had a smile on his face that would light up the cemetery even on the rainiest of days.

Vinny Butler opened the passenger door. 'You OK, Mum?' he asked, holding her arm. The Range Rover had a steep step for a woman of his mother's age.

'No. I am not OK. So stop bastard well lying to me. When Michael asked me for an alibi for Saturday, I knew you two were up to something. Now he's not coming 'ere today and I demand to know why?'

Vinny being Vinny, he held his composure. His brother had refused to speak to him since the Felicity saga. Michael's parting words had been, 'You are one fucked-up, evil cunt. If I ever have to lay eyes on you again, even if you're lying in your coffin, it will be too soon. We're finished, for good.'

'You know what Michael's like, Mum. He'll always be jealous of my fling with Bella. I don't think things are going too well between them, if you want the truth. Neither of 'em are attending the leaving party I've arranged for Antonio. Oh well, shit happens.'

'Why did Michael ask me for that alibi at the weekend?' Queenie enquired. Michael had told her a week or so beforehand that he needed to pull up outside her bungalow in his motor, and make sure he spoke to at least a couple of neighbours before he hopped over the train tracks the other side of her back garden fence. He hadn't picked his motor up until the following day and Queenie knew her boys well enough to tell when something serious was occurring.

Vinny shrugged. 'I dunno. Sod-all to do with me. Knowing Michael, he's probably got another bird on the firm.'

Albie Butler placed a single red rose on top of Vivian's grave. 'How are you today, my sweetheart?' he mumbled sadly.

Speaking to Vivian as though she could actually hear him was a great comfort to Albie. Michael had insisted he get his act together and Albie had, to an extent. Whatever the weather, he would visit Vivian's grave of a morning, then he'd pop to his local pub and bookies for a few hours before heading home with a takeaway and a few cans. The nights were the worst. That's when the unfairness of it all would hit him and loneliness would creep in.

Singing Vivian her special song before he left the cemetery had become a ritual to Albie, but what he did not realize as he hit the chorus of 'Spanish Eyes' was that the ex-wife and son he wished he'd never laid eyes on were only yards away.

'Get away! What are you doing singing that goddamn awful song? Killed her, that did. She was alive before you sung that to her, you wicked old bastard,' Queenie shrieked.

Avoiding eye contact with Vinny, Albie turned to Queenie. 'I often come here to visit all the family now. It reminds me of the good old days.'

'You can't even remember the good old days. You spent most of your time in a drunken stupor,' Vinny sneered. 'And Mum's right. Don't you dare sing that song over 'ere. Auntie Viv'll be turning in her grave, God rest her soul.'

Albie stared at his freshly polished shoes. Like his sons, he always dressed as real men should. His suits were made of cheap material compared to Vinny's, but he would religiously wear one and polish his shoes every Sunday morning. 'I'll be getting off now,' he mumbled.

Hands on hips, Queenie spat, 'Good riddance. And next time you come here, don't you be going near Vivvy's plot at all. Hated you, she did.'

Trundling away, Albie allowed himself a wry smile. If only that old witch knew the truth. He hoped his Vivian was looking down watching this; she'd be laughing her bloody head off.

Once upon a time, cocaine had made Little Vinny paranoid. Now it seemed to have the opposite effect. Mixed with a regular top-up of alcohol, he felt as though he could conquer the world, alone. 'I've decided to leave it six months before

I put this gaff on the market, Frankie. That'll give you enough time to sort yourself out, won't it?'

'What do you mean by sort myself out?'

'Well, you don't want to move away with me, do you? So, you're gonna need somewhere else to live. I won't pull the carpet from under your feet – think too much of you to do that. Shame you don't think as much of me.'

Frankie stared at the man she had once thought she'd loved. He didn't just look and dress like a different person, he acted like one too. Jed had been bolshie, and the way Little Vinny had acted last night reminded her of him. After they'd argued, they'd had sex and Frankie regretted that now. Little Vinny was by far the worst lover she'd ever had. He was cold, distant, and the sex was boring, almost robotic. 'I do think a lot of you, but Harry will be home soon and I need to be here when he arrives. How about I wait for him to come home, then I follow you to Lincolnshire?' she lied. She had no intention of following him anywhere.

'Whatever. Where's Regan? He needs to pack. Finn's picking us up first thing in the morning. He's driving us up there in a van.'

'Regan's gone to the shop with Georgie. They aren't going to want to be parted, Vin. You know that, don't you? Love's young dream, bless 'em.'

Little Vinny slurped the rest of his cider and banged the can down on the kitchen table. Sammi-Lou would never have turned her back on him like Frankie had. Sammi would've moved to the end of the earth to be with him, had he asked her to. 'Tough shit. I'm leaving first thing in the morning and my boys are coming with me. Unlike you, they're loyal.'

*

Eddie Mitchell wasn't in the best of moods. The London Hospital had just rung and informed him his dear old Auntie Joan had a suspected broken hip and ankle after a bad fall. Ed adored his aunt. She'd helped raise him and his brothers after his mum had died so young.

Eddie picked up the phone. He, Gina and the kids were meant to be flying to Ireland tomorrow to spend a bit of time with her family. 'Babe, it's me. I'm really sorry, but you're gonna have to go away with the kids on your own. My Auntie Joan's had a bad fall and the hospital are keeping her in. I can't sod off and leave her. I'm all she's got.'

Before Gina had a chance to respond, Ed was disturbed by a knock on the office door. 'The Old Bill are here, Ed. They asked for Vinny first, but have now asked to speak to you. What shall I tell 'em?' Terry Baldwin asked.

Telling Gina he'd call her back, Eddie flung open the door. 'Make us a coffee while I see what they want. Where are they?'

'I left 'em on the doorstep. Didn't know if you wanted to speak to them or not.'

Eddie opened the main door. 'Hello. What can I help you with?'

The female officer waved a photograph under Eddie's nose. 'Felicity Carter-Price. Her parents have reported her as a missing person, and we have reason to believe she was in a relationship with your business partner, Vinny Butler. May we come inside, please?'

Eddie could sense the colour drain from his face as he nodded dumbly. Surely Vinny had not been stupid enough to defy his orders? Because if he had, enough was fucking enough.

*

Regan Butler looked at his father as though he'd completely lost his marbles. 'No thanks. You and Calum can go away if you want, but I'm staying here.'

'You can't and you're not,' Little Vinny snapped. Regan had always been a defiant, difficult child. Even as a toddler he'd always been full of backchat.

'You can't make me go anywhere. Off your head, you are lately. Look at the state of you – like a bleedin' tramp. Even pissed yourself again – you got a wet patch.'

Little Vinny had never hit his sons, not hard. But unable to control his temper, he punched Regan in the side of the head. 'Get up them fucking stairs and get your stuff packed.'

'Leave him alone,' Georgie yelled, pushing Little Vinny in the chest.

'Go upstairs yous two. I'll sort this out,' Frankie urged. She could not wait for Little Vinny to leave now. It would be so nice to spend some time with Georgie without having him around.

Regan was livid as he stomped up the stairs. 'I ain't going anywhere with that loony. I wish my mum was still alive and he'd died instead,' he told his girlfriend.

'We could run away together, but where? I don't really want to leave me mum again,' Georgie admitted.

Regan sat on the bed and urged Georgie to do the same. 'Running away ain't the answer. What we'll do is get up early in the morning and sod off out for the day. By the time we come home, me dad and Calum will be gone.'

'But say they haven't? Say they wait for you?'

'Then I'll ring my granddad and tell him everything that's been going on. That'll put the cat amongst the pigeons.'

Michael Butler parked up a short distance from his mother's bungalow, turned off the engine and let out a huge sigh. He wasn't sleeping well; felt drained both emotionally and physically.

Felicity Carter-Price's murder was at the forefront of Michael's mind. He could not stop thinking about that poor woman and her baby, and what trauma she'd gone through while he was knocked out cold. As for her cries for help when he was conscious, they haunted him on a daily basis. He'd known in his heart that he should never have got involved, but yet again he'd let Vinny talk him into a dreadful situation. The worst to date. Well, never again. He and his brother truly were history after this latest turnout.

When Michael's phone rang, he stared at it before switching the bloody thing off. That was another thing playing on his mind: Charley Rideout. Nobody knew about his fling with Charley. She was only in her late twenties and Michael loathed himself for being attracted to one so young. But he'd slept with her half a dozen or so times over the past few months, and yesterday she'd informed him she was pregnant. As if he didn't have enough on his plate with Bella, Katy and the kids he already had. No way did he want or need any more complications. But it was all his own doing. He'd come to the conclusion he must have some form of super sperm, and once again, he'd thought via his cock rather than his brain.

Feeling as though he had the weight of the world on his broad shoulders, Michael reluctantly stepped out of his motor. He had no idea why his mother had summoned him to her house, but guessed whatever she had to say wouldn't be good news. It never was, if she couldn't say it on the phone. He just hoped the Old Bill hadn't turned up to check out his alibi. There'd been no mention of Felicity on the news or radio as far as he was aware, and

Vinny would most certainly have got word to him if there were any hiccups regarding the cleaning-up process.

Trudging dejectedly up his mother's path, Michael truly wished Daniel and Lee were still around. His sons had been his rock. And it broke his heart he had not heard a word from either since they'd scarpered. He knocked on the door.

'You look dreadful. Terrible bags around your eyes and you've lost weight, like you haven't been eating or sleeping. You'll lose your looks, if you aren't careful. Don't wanna end up like your father, do you?' Queenie asked. Tactfulness had never been her strong point.

'Had a lot on me plate, Mum. Katy reckons she's off to the South of France next month so I've had to get a solicitor involved because of the kids. She can't just take 'em away from me. I've got rights too.'

'Why don't you cut her a deal? Tell the gold-digging cow Nathan stays in England with you and she can take the spoiled brat with her. That's fair, isn't it? You should never have got involved with that one in the first place. But you can't help being like your father, I suppose. Look at the trouble his wandering todger caused. Molly would still be alive if it wasn't for that old bastard.'

'Leave Dad out of this. That poor old sod has done fuck-all wrong for years. Look, I'm tired and really not in the mood to listen to your ranting and raving.'

'That's a nice way to talk to your mother! I've barely seen you for bloody weeks. Turned out to be a terrible son, you have. Bet you visit that Italian slapper regularly, though, don't you?'

Realizing his mother did have a point, and not wanting to get into a full-scale argument with her, Michael said, 'I'm sorry. I've been so busy I just haven't had time to visit you nowhere near as much as I should. I will rectify that from now on, and that's a promise. Real life just seems to pass me by at times.'

'Hurt me terribly that you didn't bother to come with us to see Vivvy's new gravestone put in place. She was a damn good aunt to you. Should be ashamed of yourself.'

Michael puffed his cheeks out. 'Something cropped up that I couldn't get out of. I'll pop over to see the headstone after I leave here, take some flowers with me.'

Queenie poured her son a large Scotch. 'Get that down your 'atch, then you can tell me what's going on with you and Vinny. I know you've fallen out again, and I want to know why.'

'We haven't fallen out.'

'Yes, you bloody well have. I wasn't born yesterday, boy. He reckons it's Bella, says you can't get over what happened between him and her. If that's the case, why don't you just move on? You can't let a trollop like her come between you and your brother. It's ridiculous and she's not worth it.'

Finally snapping, Michael slammed his glass down on the coffee table. 'Got a lot to say for himself has Vinny. Fills your head with lies and because you look at him through rose-tinted specs, you believe what you wanna believe. Well, I'll let you into a little secret, shall I? Your number one son isn't the golden boy you think he is. He's a twisted, evil, fucking psychopath!'

Vinny Butler had just stepped out of the shower when the buzzer in his apartment sprang into life. He rarely had visitors; very few people had the slightest clue where he lived.

Guessing it might be the Old Bill, Vinny put a towel round his waist and pressed the intercom button. One look at the screen told him his intuition had been correct. Plain clothes, a bird and a bloke. 'Hello, how can I help you?'

It was the woman who spoke. 'I am DI Sharp and I have my colleague with me, DS Lawrence. We need to have a quick chat with Vinny Butler. It's regarding a person who has been reported missing to us.'

'Well, I'm Vinny Butler, so best you come on up.'

Vinny was still wearing only a towel around his waist when the officers knocked on the door. He had a good body, was proud of it and he hoped his partial nakedness would make the bird feel uncomfortable. Opening the door, he grinned. 'I would offer you tea or coffee, but I'm afraid I've run out of milk.'

'We're fine. But thanks anyway,' DS Lawrence replied.

'So, what can I help you with? You said someone is missing.'

DI Sharp showed Vinny the photo of Felicity. 'We believe you were in a relationship with Felicity Carter-Price, Mr Butler. Is that correct?' Bar Michael having one of his hissy fits, everything else surrounding Felicity's murder had gone to plan. The car had been crushed successfully with the remains of her burned body and their baby in the boot. The barn had been torched, so there was no evidence or DNA left at the scene, and he'd personally got rid of her teeth by lobbing them one by one out of the car window on the way home whilst making jokes to try and cheer his miserable brother up. Carl had gone through a red light on the journey to Kent, got a ticket on Vinny's car while up there, then had been driven home while lying on the back seat of a vehicle belonging to a pal of the Kelly brothers. And Vinny had driven his own car home the following morning, after making a show of pretending there was an issue with his brakes to ensure he was noticed by the Kellys' neighbours.

Vinny smiled at the officers. 'I wouldn't call it a relationship, but yeah, Felicity and I have a casual thing going on. She used to work for me at the club I own in Holborn.

Nice girl, but too young for me to get serious about. Can't remember her exact age, but I'm sure she's only in her twenties. How come you reckon she's gone missing? I saw her on Friday. She stayed 'ere the night, left early on Saturday morning.' Vinny had made sure Felicity had left the apartment before him. He'd told her he had a couple of geezers coming round to talk business and she needed to make herself scarce. He'd given her some money and insisted she fill her motor up with petrol locally, knowing full well she'd be caught on camera. Then he'd arranged to meet her down the bottom of a quiet road not far from where Molly was found dead. He'd said one of the lads would drop him off there, which they had. Then he'd pretended to have a migraine and needed to lie down in the back of Felicity's car until they'd reached a quiet part of Essex. So no way had anybody spotted him and her together, of that he was confident.

'Felicity was due to visit her parents on Sunday. She never arrived and was reported as missing yesterday. Have you heard from her since she left here on Saturday morning?' Lawrence asked.

'No. Not a dickie-bird. But as I said, we're not together as in joined at the hip. Casual sort of suits us both, if you know what I mean. I know she was going to visit her parents on Sunday, though, remember her telling me that,' Vinny replied.

'Did Felicity say if she was going anywhere on Saturday? Meeting friends? Or going shopping perhaps?' Sharp asked Vinny.

'Nah. Not that I remember. The only thing I remember her telling me on Saturday was that her car hardly had any juice and she needed to fill up. I told her where the nearest garage was and gave her some dosh as she didn't have much on her. You don't think anything bad has happened to her, do you? Perhaps she's just gone on a bender or something, eh? She was into clubbing and stuff. Garage nights, that type of thing. Chances are she's gone out Saturday night, got bladdered and is still recovering.'

'Do you know what friends she hung out with?' Sharp asked.

'No. We never spoke that much about general stuff, to be truthful. As I said, she was a lot younger than me. Her pals were of little interest to me, and I doubt my pals and The Casino were her idea of fun. A purely sexual relationship, that's what me and Fliss have. That's what I call her for short: Fliss. We get a takeaway, have a few bevvies, then fuck all night. There's never much chit-chat,' Vinny said, holding DI Sharp's gaze. He could tell she was unnerved by him. Then again, what woman wouldn't be? He had the body, looks and the charm.

'OK. Well, if Felicity does make contact with you, could you call me on this number please?' Sharp said, handing Vinny her card.

'Or if you remember anything else that might help us trace her whereabouts,' DS Lawrence added.

Vinny took the card and smiled. 'Of course. She's a top lass. I do hope you find her soon, for my sake as much as yours. She's one of the best fucks I've ever had.'

When the blushing DI Sharp grabbed her colleague by the arm and said an awkward 'goodbye', Vinny waited until he'd closed the front door and they were out of earshot before laughing out loud.

CHAPTER TWENTY-SIX

Having dropped Gina and the kids off at the airport, Eddie Mitchell put his foot down on the M11. After visiting his Auntie Joan yesterday, he'd decided not to go into work last night. He'd been livid, would have wanted to have it out with Vinny, and for all he knew the filth might have bugged The Casino or the Piano Bar. He had never trusted those bastards as far as he could throw them. Neither had his father.

Eddie had yet to speak to Vinny about the Old Bill turning up. He was seething, but would rather confront his business partner in person. They were meeting outside a café along the A13, and Eddie could not wait to hear what cock-and-bull story Vinny would come out with. It was far too much of a coincidence that Felicity had just disappeared into thin air and if Vinny dared to insult his intelligence, Eddie would not hesitate in cutting all ties. Even if he had to do so violently.

Unlike Vinny Butler, Eddie Mitchell was the perfect gentleman. Until he was extremely upset, of course. Then he turned into the devil.

Outside the café, Vinny awaited his pal's arrival. He wasn't an idiot, had guessed the Old Bill had paid a visit to The

Casino also, which was why Eddie had insisted on meeting him here.

Munching on an egg-and-bacon sandwich, Vinny thought over his story once more. Ed was no man's fool, wasn't going to be easy to convince, but unless Eddie could prove otherwise, what option did he have other than to believe him?

When Ed's new Range Rover skidded to a halt next to his own, Vinny rammed the rest of his sandwich into his mouth, got out of his vehicle and into the passenger seat of Eddie's. 'All right, mate. The Old Bill turned up round mine yesterday. Seems as though Fliss has done a disappearing act since aborting the kid. My own fault for getting involved with one so young and immature, I suppose. She'll turn up soon, tail between her legs, you mark my words. I'm having sod-all else to do with her though, Ed, I can promise you that much.'

Eddie stared into his pal's eyes. They looked innocent enough, but Vinny was a sly fox. 'The filth turned up at The Casino too. Now I'm only gonna ask you this once, but you need to be fucking truthful with me. I'm not gonna judge you, but did you do away with her?'

'What the hell do you take me for?' Vinny bellowed. 'I've told you in the past, I would never harm a woman or child. I'm no angel, Ed; I'm the first to admit that. But Felicity's disappearance has sod-all to do with me. The Old Bill told me she was meant to visit her parents on Sunday and never showed up. I wasn't even about at the poxy weekend. Was down at the Kellys' in Kent, playing cards. Eight of us, there was. Ask 'em if you don't believe me, go on,' Vinny said, waving his phone in the air.

Eddie pushed the phone away. 'I've no desire to ask the Kellys anything. It's you I'm asking.'

'And I'm telling you the truth: Fliss got rid of the kid, so I decided to end things with her gently on Friday night. She left my gaff early on Saturday morning. I gave her some dosh for petrol, a peck on the cheek and wished her well for the future. She was a bit upset, sheepish, but seemed all right other than that. I bet she couldn't face her parents – they weren't that close, by all accounts – so she's gone to stay with a friend or something without letting anybody know. Put money on it, she'll turn up like a bad penny soon, you mark my words.'

'She'd better,' Eddie hissed.

Frank Sinatra was an idol of Eddie Mitchell's, and as he drove towards home singing along with Ol' Blue Eyes to 'That's Life' he wasn't convinced by Vinny's explanation. Neither had he forgotten about the dead reptiles and rodents that'd been delivered to The Casino. Vinny Butler was becoming a liability and that didn't bode well. Eddie wasn't happy. Not happy at all.

Jamie Preston peeked in between the driver and passenger seat as he heard a commotion. He was parked up at least half a dozen houses away from Little Vinny's, in a van a pal had purchased with a false name out of the *Exchange and Mart*.

Jamie ducked as he spotted Little Vinny chasing his youngest son and Georgie down the road. Little Vinny had no shoes or top on, just a pair of grey tracksuit bottoms. 'Get back 'ere now, Regan. I mean it. Don't mess me about or you'll regret it.'

'Bollocks. I ain't leaving here and you can't make me. I'm staying with Georgie,' Regan yelled.

When Little Vinny broke into a sprint, Frankie Mitchell chased after him. 'Leave them alone. Don't you dare lay a finger on them,' she ordered.

The windows in the back of the van were tinted, so you could see out but not in, and Jamie could not help but chuckle as Little Vinny roughly grabbed hold of his son's arm and Georgie O'Hara kicked him hard in the goolies. Little Vinny collapsed to the pavement, and as he did so the two teenagers got away.

Jamie clambered into the driver's seat and started the engine. This was the best opportunity he'd had so far to abduct one of the boys and he was determined not to waste it.

Vinny Butler was getting the Piano Bar ready for Antonio's leaving party. He had never been close to the lad, did not really understand him, but had nevertheless decided to throw his son a bash to wish him well on his travels. It would look bad if he didn't.

'How many people we expecting tonight, roughly?' Eddie Mitchell asked. He'd decided to act normal and hold fire with any more accusations in case Felicity turned up as Vinny had predicted. Gut instinct told him she wouldn't though.

'About seventy or eighty, I should imagine. Antonio's invited some pals and the rest are friends and family. Invite whoever you want as well. I'm footing the bar bill. The Kellys are coming and the Frasers. Ask the Kellys about the card game at the weekend, if you like. Went on most the night. Me mum's coming too, and Ava. I was with them all day Sunday, we went out for a meal in the afternoon. You can check that out if you want an' all.'

'Nah. I believe you,' Eddie lied. 'Michael coming?' he asked.

'No. He and Antonio have never seen eye to eye. Michael's been acting weird lately. Got the hump over all the Bella crap. I don't think he and her are getting on, so obviously that's my fault. Sick of it, I am. Needs to sort his life out once and for all, does Michael.'

Wondering if Michael was also in on Felicity's disappearance, Eddie decided to pay him a visit soon. Vinny might be an outstanding liar, but he doubted Michael was as devious. He could prove to be the source of vital information Eddie needed to sever ties with Vinny for good.

'Get off him! Run, Regan, run,' Georgie shrieked, kicking the man in the shin. A blue van with darkened windows had just pulled up out of nowhere and a man had leapt out and grabbed hold of her boyfriend.

Seeing the man hit Regan over the head with an object then bundle him in the back of the vehicle, Georgie screamed blue murder. 'Help, somebody. Please help us,' she yelled. Apart from an elderly man on the other side of the road, there didn't seem to be anybody else about.

When the van screeched off, Georgie burst into tears. The elderly man crossed over the road. 'What's the matter, dear?'

'A man, he hurt my boyfriend. He hit him and took him away. His dad must've sent the man. He's trying to make my boyfriend go away with him,' said a breathless Georgie.

'Did you get the number plate?' the man asked.

'No. It all happened so quick. Please help me. But no gavvers. Don't ring them.'

'Gavvers? Who's that?' the man asked, bemused.

'The police.'

'Where do you live?'

'Only a couple of streets away. Can you come home with me? I need to tell my mum what's happened. He's a nutter, Regan's dad. How can he do that to his own son? The man hit him hard – with a piece of wood, I think. I saw him do it.'

'OK. I'll help you. Let's get you home.'

*

Eddie was just about to pop up to Whitechapel to see his aunt in hospital when the police turned up again. 'Vinny, you got visitors,' he shouted out.

Vinny was as cool as a cucumber as he sauntered towards the same two officers who'd visited him at his apartment the previous day. 'Turned up, has she?' he enquired.

'No. But we've found some footage of Felicity at a petrol station on Saturday morning. That seems to be the last clue we have as to her disappearance at present. Is there anywhere we can speak in private, Mr Butler?' DS Lawrence asked. He was well aware of who Vinny Butler was, but what he had not realized before doing some digging around yesterday was that two of Vinny's former girlfriends had died in unfortunate accidents. The mother of his eldest son had overdosed on heroin, and the mother of his daughter had been rammed off the road and into a ditch by an unidentified red truck. Her killer had never been caught and Vinny had had a watertight alibi.

'Listen, I've got nothing to hide. Eddie is my business partner. You can say whatever you've got to say here,' Vinny told the officers.

'Where were you on Saturday and Sunday, Vinny?' Sharp asked abruptly. 'Obviously, we aren't accusing you of anything. But you were the last person to see or speak to Felicity.'

'Well, technically I wasn't. Not if you have footage of Felicity after she left mine,' Vinny said, before accounting for his whereabouts, then giving the names of the Kelly brothers and his mum and Ava. 'There was eight of us in total playing cards. Not sure of all the others' full names. They're friends of the Kellys. As for Sunday, the restaurant I took my mother and daughter to was packed to the rafters, so I'm sure somebody will vouch for me there. I've got the receipt for the grub and drinks, if you would like to see it?'

'That won't be necessary at the moment, Mr Butler. But for obvious reasons we will need to check out your alibis. In the meantime, if you can think of anything Felicity might have told you that could hold a clue to her whereabouts, it would be greatly appreciated if you could let us know,' Lawrence said.

'OK. I'll put my thinking cap on. But as I've already explained, there wasn't much in-depth conversation between me and Fliss. It was all about the sex.'

Spotting the GOOD LUCK ON YOUR TRAVELS banner, Lawrence asked, 'Are you having a party?'

'Yeah. My son's going away for a year, travelling the world. Why do you ask? No law against that, is there?'

'No. Of course not,' Lawrence replied, before gesturing to his colleague it was time to leave.

Once outside, Lawrence turned to Sharp. 'What's your instinct?'

'That he's a cold, calculating, evil bastard who knows exactly what has happened to Felicity Carter-Price. Yours?'

'The same. But proving it is going to be difficult, I fear. Unless we can find a body.'

Frankie Mitchell invited Finn inside the house. 'Follow me,' she whispered, shutting the kitchen door behind them.

'What's up? Where is he?' Finn asked.

'Upstairs, having a meltdown. Regan ran off. My Georgie's with him. They don't want to be parted. Please try and make him see sense, Finn. He might listen to you. He's been smashing all of Regan's things up. I can't tell you how odd he's been acting lately. He's like a different person to the Little Vinny I once knew. He's never been the same since he got beaten up, you know.'

Finn felt a tad guilty. Little Vinny had rung him yesterday, begging him to score more cocaine. Finn hadn't wanted to, but had done so to appease his pal. They went back a long way and Finn just hoped, once in Lincolnshire, Little Vinny would get his head together and sort himself out. 'Has he still been knocking back the booze?'

'Yeah. And those tablets he's on don't seem to be agreeing with him either. He looks and is acting out of his nut all the time. It's not fair on the kids – no wonder Regan ran off. You don't think he's taking anything else, do you? He's not been out to buy anything and he was so anti-drink and drugs when we first met.'

'Nah. I think that good hiding knocked the stuffing out of him, literally,' Finn lied.

Hearing loud bangs and crashes, Finn darted up the stairs. 'Calm down, mate. What you doing?' he asked worriedly. The window was wide open and his pal was throwing stuff outside.

'He's throwing all Regan's stuff away, but he's chucked some of my things away too,' Calum explained, near to tears.

Ordering Calum to leave the room, Finn grabbed hold of Little Vinny. 'This has to stop. You're not thinking straight. Sit on the bed a minute. Talk to me.'

'Did you get the thingy? We can't leave yet. Gotta wait for Regan to come back first. I'll tie him up to get him to Lincolnshire if I have to. He's only a kid. No way is he gonna dictate to me what he can and can't do,' Little Vinny gabbled.

About to reply, Finn was stopped from doing so by an ashen-faced Frankie bursting into the bedroom. 'Did you get a pal to snatch Regan and bundle him into a van?'

Little Vinny was startled. 'What? No! 'Course not.'

Georgie barged past her mother. 'Yes, you did. And you told 'em to hit Regan over the head. You're an animal,' she yelled.

Hands and legs trembling, Little Vinny shook his head repeatedly. 'What did the man look like? Where did this happen?'

'As we were walking to the bus stop. The man had a balaclava on. I saw him hit Regan, shove him in the van and drive off,' Georgie cried. The old man who'd witnessed the event had walked at a snail's pace, so she'd taken his address, then run home alone.

Hyperventilating, Little Vinny put his head in his hands and paced the room. 'It's him – the bastard who abducted me. We mustn't tell anybody. Not the police, or our dads. It's me he's got it in for. As long as I do what he says, Regan will be safe. It's definitely him, I know it is.'

Vinny Butler awkwardly shook hands with Antonio. They'd never had a proper father–son relationship, and probably never would. With his long hair, scruffy dress and layabout attitude, Antonio was an embarrassment to Vinny. He was nothing like a Butler – the complete opposite, in fact – and Vinny just hoped this travelling lark would help the boy figure out what he wanted to do in life and he'd return home a different person. 'The drinks are all free, lads. Just go up the bar and help yourselves,' Vinny urged. As far as he was aware, Antonio only had one friend, so he guessed these lads were pals of his travelling companion, who was also present.

'Evening, Vin. Everything OK?' the Kelly brothers asked in unison.

Glancing around surreptitiously to check Eddie wasn't lurking nearby, Vinny gave both men the sort of slap on the back that the Mafia tended to greet each other with. 'Don't say nothing in here,' he whispered. 'We'll chat later, outside.'

*

Regan Butler stared at his captor with a look of defiance. He'd been knocked out cold, had a sore head and was now in what seemed to be a bedsit. He wasn't scared though. The man had apologized for what he'd done, and had made him some Marmite on toast and tea. He'd also said he could watch any programme on TV that he wanted until he was allowed home again.

'Want another cuppa?' Jamie Preston asked. The coolness of this lad had impressed him massively. He was nothing like his father.

'No. I just wanna know what I am doing 'ere and why. You got the same colour hair and eyes as my family – well, apart from Oliver, he was blond. You look a bit like my granddad's brother too. Are you related to my dad?'

Jamie Preston sighed. Taking to this lad was something he had not banked on. 'You've done nothing wrong and I swear I am not gonna hurt you again, OK? It's your dad that has done something wrong and you're gonna stay here with me until he realizes the error of his ways. I'm sorry about all this. You're a good kid, you are, deserve better.'

'I'm not a kid. So what has my dad done to you that's so bad?' Regan asked, genuinely interested.

Jamie felt terrible as he spotted blood on the boy's hair. He hadn't meant to hit him that hard, but had needed to stun him to get him here. 'It's a long story. One that I'm sure your dad would rather tell you himself. You'll find out soon enough.'

Regan Butler was clued up, had a brain on him far beyond his years. Instinct told him he could trust this man. Something about his eyes and general persona convinced Regan he was in safe hands. 'You haven't answered my question. You're either related to the Butlers, or you are a Butler, ain't ya?'

Jamie Preston handed Regan a bag of salt-and-vinegar crisps. 'You really don't want to know all the ins and outs, lad. But if your dad don't see sense when we ring him in a bit, I'll tell you everything – and that's a promise.'

Done up to the nines, Queenie and Joycie were seated at their usual table. Whenever they came to the Piano Bar, Vinny or Eddie would reserve them their seats.

'Look, your fancy man's over there,' Queenie nudged Joyce.

'Who? Where?'

'David Fraser. He's with his brother Patrick, look by the door. You were gushing over how handsome David was last time they were here.'

Joyce chuckled. 'If you had to look at my Stanley all day every day, so would you be. Both handsome men, those two. I wonder if they're taken? We could go out in a foursome,' she joked.

Queenie laughed. 'Bit old for all that dating lark, me. My Vinny would have a cardiac if he thought I had a man. So protective of me, he is.'

'I'm only bloody joking, Queen. That old goat I married has put me off men for life.'

'State of Antonio. Looks like a bundle of shit tied up ugly, doesn't he? Needs a good barber, and a decent scrub.'

Joyce looked towards the group of youngsters. Most had their hair long. 'Which one is he? They all look the same to me.'

'Scruffy jeans, black T-shirt, white trainers. Not even said hello to me, the ignorant little tramp.'

'Your Ava's just walked in. Got a bloke with her,' Joyce commented.

Queenie stood up, craning her neck like a giraffe. Apart

from one meal in a restaurant, she had seen little of her granddaughter lately and neither had Vinny. She still helped run the Holborn club for her father, but Queenie knew little else about what she got up to these days. 'Ava! Ava!' Queenie waved.

Ava smiled as she approached the table. 'Hi, Nan. Hello, Joycie. This is Tommy, a friend of mine.'

'Hello, Tommy,' Queenie said rather coldly before turning back to her granddaughter and asking, 'What sort of a friend is he, dear?'

'A friend friend. What do you mean?' Ava giggled awkwardly. She and Tommy had been dating for a couple of months now, but she had yet to tell her family because she knew how interfering they could be. That's why she'd decided to bring him with her tonight, introduce him as a pal and hope and pray they liked him.

Tommy smiled. He had a kind, baby face and only looked about nineteen. 'Can I get you a drink, ladies, while I'm at the bar? What would you like, Ava?'

Queenie pursed her lips. 'We're fine, thanks. You sort yourselves out.'

Grabbing Tommy by the arm, Ava led him away from her rude grandmother.

'Seems nice enough, doesn't he?' Joyce said.

'My Vinny's gonna go apeshit. Look, he's got his hand on her lower back. He's more than a friend, I'm telling you.'

'So. Hardly a kid, is she? Hasn't she had boyfriends before?'

'No. Not really. And Tommy isn't English.'

'Sounded English enough to me,' Joyce commented.

'But his skin doesn't look English, does it? He's tarbrush. Vinny ain't gonna be happy, I'm sure of that.'

'We're not in the sixties now, Queen. And Tommy

seems pleasant enough. Never had your Vinny down as a racist.'

'My son is not a racist and neither am I. Michael's best friend Kevin was always round my house when they were young and he's black. Not being funny, but nobody blinks an eyelid when the Asians arrange marriages. They stick to their own. Same goes for the Jewish, and good luck to them. Nothing wrong with wanting your kids or grandkids to marry one of their own.'

Joycie chuckled. 'You are an old-fashioned one, Queenie Butler. Don't know how you'd have coped if your grandson was a gay man like my Joey.'

'No. Neither do I. Shhh, they're coming back.'

Joyce smiled at Tommy. 'Sit here if you want, next to me.'

Queenie leaned across the table. 'So, where are you from, Tommy?'

'Peckham. Born and bred.'

Unable to talk openly in front of Finn, Frankie insisted he leave. 'As soon as there's any news, we'll call you. Please don't tell anybody what's happened though. Not until we've decided what to do.'

'You need to call the police. Regan could be any bloody where,' Finn argued.

When Little Vinny started shouting the odds again, Frankie led Finn out of the kitchen and into the hallway. 'There's stuff you don't know about that Vin and I need to discuss. Can you take Calum with you? I don't want him to see his dad in this state.'

'How about I take Calum and Georgie for something to eat? Then hopefully by the time we get back you might've heard something.'

'I'm not going anywhere until Regan gets home,' yelled a tearful Georgie, who'd been earwigging.

'Just go, Finn. The kids'll be fine here,' Frankie said, nigh on pushing the man out the front door.

'Say they kill him, Mum? I love him,' Georgie wept.

Frankie hugged her daughter close to her chest. 'Regan's going to be fine. That's my gut feeling. Now I need you to be brave and go upstairs with Calum while I talk to Little Vinny, OK?'

Marching into the kitchen, Frankie slammed the door. 'Drinking litres of strong cider isn't the answer, Vin. You're going to have to go to the police like you promised those men you would in the first place. Running away is not the answer either. They'll hunt you down in the end.'

'I can't go to the police, not today. We need to be here in case they ring us. My world, my boys are. They better not have hurt Regan like they hurt me. Say they've shaved his head and stuff? They tortured me big time. Can't stand the thought of him being scared like I was. Makes me feel physically sick.'

'Then you need to man up and tell the police that Ben Bloggs murdered Molly. You're hardly dobbing him in it. Ben's dead. Regan is still alive. He has to be your priority right now.'

Tears streaming down his face, Little Vinny mumbled, 'Yeah. You're right. First thing tomorrow, I'll go to the police.'

Jamie Preston watched Regan out the corner of his eye. The lad was staring at the TV while munching his pizza. The many years he'd spent in prison had stopped him from becoming a father, but Jamie hoped that one day, once his name was cleared, he'd be able to settle down to a normal life and have a kiddie with a nice girl. A son like Regan would be magical.

'What you looking at? I ain't gonna run away, if that's

what you're thinking. Would've alerted the pizza delivery bloke if I were gonna do that,' Regan said.

'How's your headache now? Those tablets helped?'

'Yeah. Me head feels better. When we gonna ring my dad?'

'Now, if you like. I'm gonna talk to him first, then I'll pass the phone over to you so you can tell him you're OK, that you're being looked after. Don't tell him nothing else. And anything I say to him, take with a pinch of salt. I gotta pretend there's a chance you won't be going home, just to get him to admit the truth, if you get my drift?'

'The truth about what?'

'Something that happened a very long time ago, before you were born. What's your landline number?'

'Don't know it offhand. It's on my phone that you took away from me. Won't the police be able to trace you here if you ring from your phone? My dad's bound to have called 'em and they'll be out looking for me.'

Jamie handed Regan his phone. 'Your dad has too many skeletons in the closet to be telling the Old Bill anything, that's the problem. You ring home, let them know you're OK, then pass me the phone.'

'OK. Can I finish my pizza first, though?'

Jamie gently ruffled the lad's hair. ''Course you can.'

There was nothing more off-putting to Frankie Mitchell than a blubbering wreck of a man. Her dad she'd rarely seen cry, only when he'd killed her mum. Neither had Jed or Stuart been cry-babies. 'Stop with the tears, Vin, and let's get your story straight.'

When the landline rang, Frankie was the first to it. 'Regan! Where are you? Are you OK?'

'Yeah, I'm being looked after well. Tell Georgie I miss her. Put Dad on the phone. A man wants to speak to him.'

'Mr Bloggs here, Mr Butler. How's it hanging?' Jamie asked, winking at Regan.

'I'm sorry I never went to the police. I'm going first thing in the morning. Don't hurt my boy though. Promise me you won't. You haven't shaved his hair, have you?' Little Vinny gabbled.

'Not yet. But I got the clippers at the ready. Nice lad, your Regan. Deserves more than a snivelling self-pitying wrong 'un of a father like you. Tell the truth and you'll get your son back unharmed. Fuck with me again, and you'll regret it.'

'I won't fuck with you again. On Regan's life, I won't.'

'Strange comment to come out with when I got your son. But then again, you've always been a strange one, haven't you, Vin? Not many lads would bury their own little sister in a shallow grave and allow an innocent person to take the blame for it, is there?'

It was at that point Regan Butler's eyes opened wide. 'Molly,' he mumbled.

Vinny Butler led the Kelly brothers away from the cars and offered them both a cigar. 'Didn't wanna chat inside because the Old Bill have paid me a couple of visits since the card game. You heard from 'em yet?'

'Not a dickie,' replied Billy Kelly. He and his brother were from the East End originally, and had known Vinny since he was a rising star in the underworld. They were knocking on now, had retired so to speak. They'd been faces back in the day, mind. Had given Vinny and Roy a leg up when they'd first started out, and were always happy to be used as an alibi these days. Vinny was an extremely generous man. Paid them more for a single alibi than their pension paid out in a year.

'Meet me tomorrow. I'm gonna give you another twenty K

to share out between yourselves and the card lads. Got a feeling the Old Bill will sniff around for a while on this one, so just make sure everybody sticks to my alibi. If it gets messy, which I doubt, there'll be more money to follow.'

'No worries, Vinny. Our circle is thoroughly trustable, as you well know. Not a soul will ever blab, I can assure you of that,' Johnny Kelly vowed.

'Cushty. That's what I like to hear.'

'There you are! Been looking all over for you,' Queenie Butler exclaimed.

Dismissing the Kelly brothers, Vinny turned to his mother. 'What's up? You seem a bit stressed.'

'I've been worried about you, that's why. Ava's brought a friend with her, hasn't she? Blackish boy.'

Vinny smirked. 'You mean Tommy.'

'Yes. You met him yet?'

'Not in person, until this evening, but I knew Ava was dating him, so between me and you I had him checked out. He's OK and treats Ava well. He's also a professional footballer – tipped to play for England one day. Plays for the under-twenties or one of those younger categories at the moment.'

'Really! Oh, that's wonderful, Vin. They earn so much money, footballers these days. I must tell Joycie. Seems a lovely lad, knew that the moment I laid eyes on him. Was only worried about your reaction. You know, with him being on the dark side.'

As his mother scuttled away, Vinny could not help but chuckle. She was as old school as old school could be. But he wouldn't swap her for all the tea in China.

'Are you Jamie Preston?' Regan Butler asked bluntly. He'd heard lots of family stories and had never forgotten them, even though some were slightly cloudy.

'Yes, I am. Which makes us related, me and you. I got the same dad as your granddad and Uncle Michael. Never met Albie though. Not to talk to.'

'He stayed with us last Christmas. I call Albie "Granddad" even though he's actually my great-granddad. He would like you, I think.'

Jamie was sitting on the sofa next to Regan and as his phone rang yet again, he put a finger to his lips to warn the boy not to say anything before answering. 'All right, Glen? Sorry I ain't been answering, mate. Got myself a little bird on the firm. She's just popped out the room, but'll be back in a sec. I'll call you when I finally leave here, OK?'

'Tell me about Molly,' Regan demanded.

'I'll do you a deal. You tell me about Albie, then I'll tell you about Molly.'

'Albie's all right. A bit old, and drinks too much, but he has a good heart. My dad used to live with him when my granddad went to prison. Albie was kind to him and he's always been kind to me and my brothers. Life ain't really been the same since my mum and Oliver died, but I do like Frankie. Her and my dad drink too much as well though, and then they chat shit. I ain't never gonna drink no more. Georgie won't either. She's cool, Georgie is. My brother isn't talking to me 'cause he fancied her first, but that's life, eh?'

'Sorry about your mum and bro, Regan. Must've been so tough for you. I haven't spoken to my mum for years. The whole family disowned me over a crime I did not commit. Except my nan – she always stuck by me until the day she dropped down dead. That's the main reason I want to clear my name. That was my nan's dying wish. Why do you think Albie would like me?'

'Dunno really. He hates my granddad, Vinny. They've

never got on. But Albie gets on well with Michael, and you remind me a bit of Michael. Tell me about Molly now.'

With a heavy heart, Jamie Preston explained his hunch in prison. 'I'm sorry I had to beat your father up. But it was the only way to get the truth out of him. Promised me he would go to the police and tell them everything as soon as his injuries healed, but he never did. That's why I've had to bring you here today. To force your dad's arm, so to speak.'

'If my dad knew Ben killed Molly, why wouldn't he tell the police?' Regan asked. He did sort of believe Jamie's version of events, but was very confused.

Jamie shrugged. 'No idea, pal. Your guess is as good as mine. But in defence of your father, he was only young back then. Perhaps he thought at the time he was doing the right thing, eh?'

'That's bollocks. I'm virtually the same age now as my dad was then. Don't get me wrong, I'm a bastard when I want to be, even stabbed my school teacher with a screwdriver and did time for it. But how could you do that to your own little sister? Molly was only young. It's terrible.'

Jamie put a comforting arm around the lad's shoulders. 'I don't know the answer to that one. But I feel you and me are cut from the same cloth, boy. I really do.'

Michael Butler pulled up at the arranged meeting place and switched off the headlights and ignition. He looked at his watch. He was early.

Desperate to take his mind off what he was doing here, Michael studied the interior of his new vehicle. Years ago, it was mainly people who lived in the sticks that drove four-by-fours, but lately they were all the rage in his world. Anybody who was a somebody was driving a

Range Rover now, so he'd treated himself to a black Vogue yesterday.

The smell of leather overpowering him, Michael opened the window and closed his eyes. This hadn't been an easy decision to make, but after what had happened recently he'd felt he had little choice. His mother would be beside herself, obviously, but she'd get over it in time. So would Ava and Little Vinny.

Hearing the sound of a vehicle approaching, Michael felt edgy. What he was doing was very wrong, but he was doing it for all the right reasons.

A small white van pulled up and a guy with dreadlocks peered out the window. 'Yo, you Kev's mate?'

'Yeah. Green onions,' Michael replied. His pal Black Kev had arranged this deal and told him he needed a password. 'Green Onions' had been one of his and Kev's favourite songs when they were Mods, which was the reason Michael had chosen it.

When a motorbike suddenly zoomed towards him, Michael felt extremely wary. He wasn't used to dealing with Rastafarians. Kev didn't know these guys personally either. They were friends of a friend of his.

'It's OK. He got your goods,' the Rasta in the car said, sensing Michael's apprehension. He held out his hand, 'Money.'

'I need to see the goods first,' Michael insisted.

The Rasta sucked his teeth, making a kissing sound. 'You do business our way or not at all.'

Rather reluctantly, Michael handed over the envelope. The guy looked inside, seemed satisfied, and gesticulated to the guy on the bike with his hand.

An Asda carrier bag was thrown through the window, landing on Michael's lap, and as the blokes sped off into the night, he wondered if he'd been ripped off. He hadn't.

Inside the carrier bag, wrapped in a cloth, was the Glock 17 he'd requested.

Hiding the gun under the seat, Michael felt incredibly sad. Killing Vinny was not going to be easy, but he was determined to go through with it. His brother was a danger to the family. Enough was enough . . .

CHAPTER TWENTY-SEVEN

Frankie Mitchell opened her eyes. She could hear music that sounded old-fashioned, like something her nan would play.

Frankie looked at the clock. It was just gone five a.m. Had Little Vinny not gone to bed yet? She'd sat up drinking wine until the early hours because it was the only way she could endure him. She really could not wait to see the back of him now. He had dragged her down, and as soon as he left she planned to eat healthy, join a gym and hopefully make some new friends in the area.

Worried that Little Vinny was now too drunk to go to the police station, Frankie put on her dressing gown and crept downstairs. As she poked her head around the lounge door, her worst fears were confirmed. The front room looked like a party had been held in it, there were that many empty bottles and cans. And Little Vinny was crouched over the coffee table, snorting a white powder. 'What the hell do you think you're doing?' she hissed, closing the door so the kids wouldn't wake up.

Little Vinny stood up, startled. 'It's not what you think. I couldn't swallow my tablets so I crushed 'em up,' he lied, thankful he'd had the sense to hide the bulk of his cocaine underneath the sofa.

'I wasn't born yesterday. Look at the state of you. You're still going to that police station even if I have to drag you there. I cannot believe you've got this drunk, knowing your son is missing. You should be bloody ashamed of yourself. Say one of the kids had walked in and seen you snorting that crap? I used to think you were a really good parent, but you're not. You're a fucking shambles.'

Kneeling on the floor, Little Vinny replayed the song on the DVD. 'This was Molly's song. It was played at her funeral,' he said, tears streaming down his face as he joined in with the chorus of 'You Are My Sunshine'. The faces and voices in his head had been torturing him all night again. 'I forgive you, Vin. Best pals forever, eh? It's good in heaven. Me and Molly hang out together a lot, but she hasn't forgiven you,' Ben Bloggs had told him. Then Molly had appeared by Ben's side wearing the same pink tracksuit she'd been murdered in. 'Tell Frankie the truth, tell Frankie the truth, tell Frankie the truth,' she cackled viciously.

'Tell the police that when you get there. Go and have a shower, get ready.'

'I can't do it, Frankie. But I've written 'em a letter for you to take to the station.'

'You will do it! Your son is in the hands of some nutter.'

'I can't. You don't understand. Nobody could, only Ben,' Little Vinny slurred.

'Why do you always stick up for that monster? There's something wrong with you, there must be.'

Little Vinny's expression became twisted. 'Ben wasn't no monster, OK? You didn't even fucking know him. He was a good person, kind. Heart of fucking gold. He should still be alive. He got me better than anybody, you included.'

Wondering if the beating Little Vinny had received had

left him brain damaged, Frankie shook her head in despair. 'Tell the police Ben had a heart of gold and see what they say. They'll know he was a monster too.'

Little Vinny picked up a bottle of red wine and greedily slurped the dregs. He then smashed the bottom of the bottle against the glass coffee table so hard it cracked it. 'You know nothing, you. Fucking nothing. People make mistakes. Accidents happen. Not everyone who has ended a life is a monster. I'm not one, am I?'

'No. But you only helped cover up a murder. That's different.'

'You don't get it, do you? You think you know fucking everything, but you ain't got a clue. It was me, OK? Not Ben. I killed Molly.'

'That's a sick thing to say. You need to give up drink, you do. It's making you imagine things.'

Little Vinny repeatedly punched the wall. 'I'm not imagining things, you stupid bitch. I did it. I killed Molly. It was an accident, OK?' he screamed.

'How can you accidentally throttle a child to death?' Frankie asked, bewildered.

'I dunno, but I did. It was a prank that got out of hand, I swear. You have to believe me, Frankie. You do believe me, don't you?'

Thinking how deranged Little Vinny must be, Frankie was suddenly scared. Gut instinct told her not to show her fright and instead play along with him. 'Of course I believe you. And of course you're not a monster. But you must tell the police the truth. If I believe it was an accident, then why shouldn't they?'

'Because they're cunts. Always hated me and my family. They'll lock me up and throw away the key, that's what they'll do. I've said in the letter that Ben did it and that's the story we must stick to. My dad and nan must never find out what I did. They'll kill me stone dead. Please, Frankie, don't tell anybody. Swear you won't tell a soul, not ever.'

Realizing she'd been living with a raving lunatic and was way out of her depth, Frankie thought of Brett and Georgie's safety. If Little Vinny was capable of throttling Molly, then he was surely capable of anything. Especially in the drunken, drugged-up state he was currently in. His bright green eyes suddenly seemed evil, like those of a serial killer.

Kneeling on the floor, Frankie reluctantly squeezed Little Vinny's hand. 'The truth is our secret. I won't tell anybody, hand on heart. You still need to go to the police and tell them Ben killed your sister though. Otherwise, Regan might never come home again.'

'OK,' Little Vinny mumbled, before replaying 'You Are My Sunshine', and singing along to it in a sincere tone.

'I'll run you a bath,' Frankie said.

'Thanks, babe.'

Once outside the room, Frankie leaned against the wall for physical support. Her father was barely speaking to her, so she daren't call him. Joey would help her in her hour of need though, surely?

'Morning, boy. You OK?' Jamie Preston asked Regan Butler. He'd let the lad sleep in his bed and he'd spent the night on the floor in a sleeping bag. Too much had been going through his mind.

'Yeah, I'm all right. Did you think I would try and escape during the night?'

'No. And even if you'd tried, I would have heard you. I'm a light sleeper, me. One of the pitfalls of spending many years in prison. Gotta be alert all the time, have eyes in the back of your head, so to speak. You hungry? What do you normally eat for breakfast? I haven't got much in the fridge and cupboards, to be honest. I usually live on takeaways.'

'My favourite breakfast is McDonald's egg and bacon McMuffin with hash browns. But I don't mind Marmite on toast again.'

Jamie smiled. 'Nah, bollocks to that. You, young man, shall have your favourite breakfast. That's my fave and all, ya know. I'll call a cab; get the driver to pick it up for us.'

His dad had been acting so strange of late; Regan was rather enjoying the company of a cool older male. It reminded him of how his father used to be when his mum and Oliver were still alive. 'Sweet. Thanks, Jamie.'

'Morning, Ed. People were surprised and a bit disappointed that you didn't show your face last night. I got a message via Terry saying you were ill or something. What's the story?' Vinny Butler asked suspiciously.

'Sorry, mate. Got on the piss with an old pal after I left you yesterday. I weren't so much ill, just unable to stand up properly. You know what it's like, while the cat's away an' all that.'

Still suspicious, Vinny asked, 'What old pal's that then?'

'Nobody you know. David Burke, a lad I went to school with. Not seen him for years. Lives in Australia now, but over here visiting family,' Eddie fibbed. After spending a few hours with his Auntie Joan, he'd gone on to a swanky bar in Mayfair with his eldest son. They'd discussed ways of ousting Vinny as his business partner, but had unfortunately been unable to come up with a viable plan. Gary's parting words were, 'Stay calm, Dad, and act normal. Vinny's bound to dig his own grave sooner rather than later. Men like him always do.'

'So, how did the party go? Antonio enjoy it?' Ed asked chirpily.

'I think so. Antonio isn't one to show enthusiasm about anything, mind. But yeah, it went OK. The youngsters all disappeared when the singer came on late in the evening. That's when my mother and Joycie got up dancing. Showing off in front of David and Patrick Fraser. Tragic, it was.'

Eddie chuckled. 'I can well imagine.'

Brett Mitchell rubbed his tired eyes. 'Why you up so early, Mum?' he asked. The bath being run, then the shower, had awoken him.

Frankie plastered a false smile on her face. Her son had only come home yesterday evening after spending a week with Joey and Dominic, and she hadn't yet explained to him about Regan because she didn't want to upset him. She also felt guilty. Since Stuart's death, she'd spent little time with Brett, had palmed him off with others. 'Mummy's got lots of things to do today, sweetheart. You go back to bed for a bit and I'll call you when breakfast is ready.'

'Why didn't Regan come home?'

'I've already told you, Regan's staying at his friend's house. Back to bed you go; else you'll be tired at school. There's a good boy.' With his dark hair and big puppy-dog eyes, Brett looked more like Jed than any of her children. Thankfully, though, he had a completely different nature. He was kind, giving and so very sweet.

When her son did as he was told, Frankie quickly got dressed. She'd already run Little Vinny's bath. Even if he only told the police the Ben story, they were bound to keep him on remand. Covering up the murder and helping to bury Molly was a heinous crime in itself. She could not wait to see the back of the despicable lowlife, but felt sorry for Calum and Regan. They were bound to be distraught over their dad's behaviour and she was happy to look after them for the time being, if their family agreed.

'Vin, get in the bath now,' Frankie said, opening the lounge door. There was no sign of him. 'Vinny, where are you?' she yelled, opening the door of the downstairs bathroom.

Frankie learned the answer to her question when she spotted the letter addressed to her on the kitchen table. She was barely able to understand it; such was the state of the handwriting:

Frankie,
So sorry but I cannot face the Old Bill. Brings back too many awful memories and I'm not in the right frame of mind to deal with them arseholes.

I have left a letter by the cooker for you to hand in at the station, saying Ben killed Molly. Preston will let Regan go then and I know you will look after my boys until I find us all somewhere safe to live.

Will be in touch soon and then we can all live together like one big happy family.

All my love,

Little Vinny xxx

PS I know I can trust you. I didn't mean to kill Molly, I swear I didn't. I don't even know how it happened, it was a freak accident.

PPS Burn this letter in the garden as soon as you've read it and don't worry about me, I'll be fine. xxx

Putting the letter on top of the kitchen unit, Frankie picked up her mobile. 'Joey, it's me. Something awful has happened. Can you come over to mine ASAP, please?'

It had become a ritual after a big night out that Queenie and Joycie would meet for a pub lunch the following day and discuss all the gossip and happenings of the previous evening like two giggling school children.

'Look on your face when Patrick Fraser said he was happily married was priceless,' Queenie guffawed.

'Oh, you can bleedin' well talk. You were all over his brother like a rash. "David, you really remind me of Dirty Den back in the day,"' Joyce laughed, mimicking Queenie's posh voice.

'I was only messing. If you can't have a laugh in life, no point in bloody living, is there?' Queenie said, feeling highly embarrassed. She had got a bit merry towards the end of the evening. The driver had even had to help her up the path.

'Was your Camila there last night?' Joycie asked.

'No. Michael reckons she was busy with her acting, but I don't believe that. Put money on it that Italian slapper didn't want Camila spending time with her real family. I rarely get to see the child, but she's always being sent on trips to Italy to see the whore's parents. Not fair, is it?'

'No. It ain't, Queen. I never get to spend any time with my Raymond's little 'un either, but I'm thankful for that. Horrid child.'

Queenie laughed. 'Glad my Ava has found herself a good 'un. I wonder how much he earns per week? Did you find out what team he played for?'

'No. You told me not to say anything about Tommy being a footballer unless he did.'

'Well, didn't you ask what he did for a living?'

'Yes. But he just mumbled something about being a sportsman. Not a big-head at all, nice boy.'

Remembering the hype that surrounded the Beckhams' wedding, Queenie said, 'I wonder if he plays for Manchester United like David does?'

'David who?'

'Becks, you know. I'm going to ring Ava now. Find out who he plays for and invite 'em both round for dinner.'

Joycie chuckled. 'You do make me laugh. You didn't even like the boy at first, 'cause he was dark.'

'I never called Tommy a darkie! How dare you say I said such a thing?'

'I never said darkie, you bloody did. Don't put words in my mouth. You called him tarbrush yesterday.'

Ignoring Joyce, Queenie dialled her granddaughter's number. 'Hello, darlin'. So wonderful to see you last night, and Tommy. Me and Joycie thought he was a lovely boy. Very polite and handsome. So what does he do for a living?'

Joyce put her hand over her mouth to control her giggles as Queenie exclaimed, 'He's a footballer! Really, dear? That's wonderful! You must bring him round to mine for dinner soon. When are you free? I'll cook one of my legendary roasts. What team does he play for, by the way?'

'Well?' Joycie asked, when the call ended. She could sense the reply wasn't what her friend had wanted to hear as her expression had turned from happy to dismal within a split second.

'Charlton bloody Athletic, Joycie. I can't understand it. My Vinny said he was tipped to play for England an' all. Surely he weren't winding me up?'

'I don't know much about football, Queen, but I'm sure Charlton are bigger than my Stanley's team. Leyton Orient, that silly old bastard supports. Used to go and watch 'em all the time when we first courted. Until I put me foot down.'

Realizing she might not appear in full wedding regalia in *Hello!* magazine after all, Queenie shrugged dejectedly. 'I can't stand football. Let's talk about something else, shall we?'

Frankie Mitchell opened the front door to Joey, then continued with her phone call. 'I'm sorry, headmaster, but I can't go into any more detail than I already have.'

'What's that all about?' Joey asked, when his flummoxed sister cut the headmaster off without saying goodbye.

'Calum's headmaster is threatening to involve the social services as he has been absent so much since his mum died. I had Brett's headmistress on the phone to me yesterday as well, saying similar. I can't take much more, Joey, I really can't.'

Frankie looked awful. She'd put on weight and had dark bags under her eyes. 'Come here,' he said, giving her the kind of hug only twins could understand. 'I thought something really terrible had happened when you called me. Is this what you're stressed about, the kids?'

'I wish! Something far worse has happened. But we can't talk here. Let's go for a drive.'

'Where's Georgie?' Joey asked, wondering if the child had run away again.

'Georgie, Calum, I won't be long. Just popping out to get some shopping,' Frankie yelled. 'Answer the phone if anybody rings. Take a message or tell 'em to call back after one.'

'OK, Mum,' Georgie yelled back.

Once in Joey's car, Frankie ordered him to drive to the nearest pub.

'Isn't it a bit early to start drinking, Frankie? You really don't look very well, sis.'

'Neither would you, if you were in my fucking shoes, Joey. Do you remember how shocked I was when I found out Jed had killed our granddad?'

'You didn't tell me straight away, but I remember you acting strange. I take it this has something to do with Little Vinny?'

'Oh, Joey, I'm in bits. It was Vin that murdered his own little sister. Put his evil hands around her throat, then throttled the life out of the poor child. I know how to pick a decent bloke me, don't I? Never again. From now on it's all about me and the kids.'

Joey was astounded. He put his hand over his mouth. 'No way! Jesus wept! Where is he?'

'No idea. And I don't know where Regan is either. That poor little sod has been kidnapped. I need a large glass of wine before I tell you anything else, Joey, I really do. I can't believe this is happening. I'm at my wits' end, seriously.'

Desperate to know the whole sorry story, Joey Mitchell put his foot down on the accelerator.

Georgie O'Hara made herself a cup of tea and sat down at the table. Calum was refusing to speak to her still and today she felt lonely and sad. Not only was she desperately worried about Regan, she missed her brother immensely too. Harry had always been a comfort to her, even in the darkest of times.

Deciding to defy her mother's orders, Georgie picked up her new mobile phone. It was in a pretty pink case and had been given to her by her mum a day after her return. She'd stored Nanny Alice's number in it under a pseudonym. 'Hello, Nan. I'm sorry I left the way I did, but I really wasn't happy at that new site. I still want to keep in touch with you though. How are you? And how's Harry Boy?'

The grandmother who'd always adored her shrieked, 'You're a disgrace to the O'Hara name, and your poor fiancé, whose heart is broken. You're a gorger, a whore, a backstabber and a shitcunt, that's what you are!'

Stunned, Georgie O'Hara ended the call.

Joey Mitchell had sat in silence as his sister explained about Regan being snatched, and how Little Vinny had admitted to killing Molly.

'Say something, Joey. What am I going to do? I don't give a damn about Little Vinny any more. He can rot in hell as far as I'm concerned. But Regan is a good lad and Georgie idolizes him. Will you come to the police station with me? I have to get Regan home in one piece. Would never forgive myself if anything bad happened to him.'

Joey held his hands aloft, palms facing his sister. 'Slow down a bit. If you want my honest opinion, this is way out of our league to deal with, and I don't think you should go to the police with that letter. Have you kept the other letter he left, the one where he admitted killing Molly himself?'

'Yes. But the writing looks like that of a six-year-old. He was out of his nut and drunk. Nobody is going to believe Little Vinny wrote it. They'll probably think I did.'

Joey grabbed his sister's hands and squeezed them tightly. Throughout their childhood and even their teens it had been Frankie who'd been the strong one, the protector. But since that shootout with the O'Haras, Joey had changed. He wasn't proud of what he'd done, but that night had somehow turned him into a man.

'None of this is your fucking fault, Frankie. You're a good person and a brilliant mum. I will stay with you at that nutjob's house in case he comes back. In the meantime, let me speak to this Jamie Preston when he calls next time. I can make him see sense and get Regan home. Once that happens, Dad has to be involved. There is no other way to end this. Little Vinny needs to be out of your life for good.'

CHAPTER TWENTY-EIGHT

Jamie Preston looked at his watch. Georgie had answered the phone earlier and Regan had been thrilled when he'd allowed him to chat with his girlfriend briefly.

'Do you reckon my dad and Frankie were at the Old Bill station when you rang?' Regan asked Jamie.

'Dunno. We'll soon find out when I ring back in a bit. How long you and Georgie been dating for then?'

'We've not been on any proper dates yet, not had the chance. But she's definitely my girlfriend,' Regan beamed, before explaining all about their blossoming romance. 'When I get home, I'm gonna take Georgie out on a proper date. Like to Nando's and the pictures. Do ya think she'll like that?'

Jamie Preston put his hand in his pocket, pulled out a wad of notes and handed Regan fifty quid. 'Yeah, I do. Take that and buy her a red rose as well. Women love a bit of romance. Don't be too soppy though. Always stand your ground with 'em. They'll walk all over you otherwise.'

A grinning Regan pocketed the dosh. 'You got a girlfriend then, I take it?'

'Nope. Biding my time, me. Waiting for the right one to come along. I learned a lot about women and the power they have over men from the lads I was locked up with.

A few geezers I knew topped themselves over birds messing 'em about on the outside. Some proper weirdos out there an' all. I got some strange letters off women I'd never met who were obviously only interested in me because they thought I was a child killer. How fucked up is that?'

Regan's eyes widened. 'That's well freaky. Did you reply to them?'

'No. We gonna finish this game of Scrabble or what? And no more cheating using dodgy words,' he added with a wink. In prison, the library had become a comfort and source of information to Jamie. Especially in dark times, he would lose himself in a good book and visualize the beaches, woods and wonderful places that were mentioned. Then he'd got into Scrabble. Glen had been sent a mini-version and they'd spent many a day playing it.

'But wank is a real word,' Regan laughed. 'Let's play Scrabble again later. Tell me about Glen. He's the man that keeps ringing you, right? What was he in prison for?' Jamie's stories fascinated Regan. No matter what or who he spoke about, Jamie had a way of making whatever or whoever sound interesting.

Jamie told Regan about all the abuse and beatings he'd got before Glen had taken him under his wing in Chelmsford. 'Then when Glen got released, it started all over again. That's how I got another lump added to my sentence. I retaliated, purely self-defence. But the geezer unfortunately died. I had no choice other than to do what I did. I'd have been dead otherwise.'

'But why did you get picked on again? You said by that time everybody including the screws believed you were innocent,' Regan enquired.

Jamie smiled. He knew now that Vinny Butler had paid that particular inmate to terrorize him, but he wasn't about to admit that to Regan. The lad had enough weight on his young shoulders at present, having learned his father was a wrong 'un. Also, time was a healer and Jamie could fully understand now why Vinny would perform such a trick. In Vinny's eyes, he'd deprived him of a wonderful daughter. Jamie could not wait for Vinny to find out the truth. How was he going to feel? Gutted, stupid and very sorry, probably. 'Give us your phone. I'll ring your house again.'

Not recognizing the voice that answered, Jamie asked to speak to Frankie.

'I'm Joey, Frankie's twin. Little Vinny disappeared this morning, but not before leaving a confession. We need to meet, speak sensibly. You give us Regan, and we'll give you the letter. Then you can take it to the police yourself, Jamie.'

Apart from Regan, nobody should have a clue who he was. Jamie was immediately on red alert. 'Who the fuck do you think you're dealing with? I'm the organ grinder, not the monkey, prick.'

'Listen, my sister and I are on your side, I can promise you that much. It must have been awful to have spent all those years behind bars for a crime you did not commit. Please meet me and Frankie. We'll give you the letter, then you can clear your name.'

Jamie's forehead was creased with frowns as his usual laid-back expression vanished. 'You don't know me from Adam, neither do I know you. Your sister has been shacked up with that no-good shitbag, and for all I know is harbouring him while setting me up. Well, you can both go fuck yourselves. No way is Regan going anywhere until I have proof my name is in the clear. And if you're thinking of grassing me to the Old Bill, be very careful. I've spent virtually all my life behind bars for a crime I had no part of. Do you honestly think I'd be bothered about spending the rest of my days serving time for something I did? Mess with me and I will slit Regan's throat in a split second, understand?'

Regan did not feel remotely unnerved when Jamie ended the call. Neither did he bat an eyelid when Jamie battered seven colours of shit out of his phone. 'So what's the plan now?'

'We're going to stay by the seaside until your family wake up and smell the coffee. Don't worry about your phone; I'll buy you a new one. I just don't want 'em tracing us. That cool with you?'

Regan grinned. 'Yeah, fine. As long as you don't slit my throat.'

Michael Butler's heart lurched in his chest when Charley Rideout informed him she'd changed her mind. He'd treated her to lunch at Langan's in hope of softening the blow, now all he could think of was why him? And not again.

A tall pretty woman with the toned physique of a gym-class addict, Charley stood her ground. 'Please don't look at me with hatred, Michael. As I said, you don't have to be involved at all if you don't want to. My parents are willing to support me and the baby.'

'But why the sudden change of heart? When we spoke the other day, you told me you were happy to abort the kid.'

'No, Michael. I didn't say that. What sort of woman would use the expression "happy" when getting rid of their baby? All I said was I had never set out to trap you and whatever you decided I would go along with. But I then told my sister and parents, and I've changed my mind.'

Michael stared at Charley's recently dyed blonde hair. Bar the freckles on her nose, she looked a bit like Nancy had, back in the day. Was that what had attracted him to her in the first place? 'Brilliant! So you've told every bastard it's mine, I take it?' he sneered.

'Of course not. I promised I would never tell anybody about us and I haven't. My mother and father would seriously not be happy if I informed them of your age and track record. They'd probably disown me.'

Michael knew he was being brutal, but no way did he want another secret family. 'Cheers for that. Make me feel better, why don't ya.'

Infatuation was probably the best way to sum up how Charley felt about Michael. He was a character, very handsome, generous and extremely good in bed. But as she stared into his cold green eyes, Charley wondered had she known the real him at all.

'Does your sister know it's mine?' Michael enquired.

'No. I told her the same story as my parents. That I'd stupidly got drunk one night, had a fling with a young guy whose surname I don't know and I am not in contact with him. Don't panic, Michael. Your sordid secret will be safe with me. I'm not a bunny-boiler like Katy is, and I have no intention of bleeding you dry financially.'

'But you're only young. One day you're bound to meet the man of your dreams, get married and have children. Why lumber yourself with a kid by an old codger who can't be with you?'

'Because I love children, Michael. I'm a loving aunt to my sister's two, and both of my best friends have babies that I regularly see. It has to be fate that I became pregnant while on the pill, it's obviously meant to be. I'm hardly a bloody teenager, am I?'

Aware his phone was vibrating in his pocket yet again, Michael pulled it out and glanced at it. Five missed calls from Katy and two from Bella. Another tart up the spout was all he was short of right now, not. Plus he had the not-so-pleasant task of killing his own brother to plan. Why was his life so shit at times?

*

Frankie Mitchell was furious. 'Told you not to mention his name, didn't I? Now he knows we know who he is there's no telling what he might do to Regan,' she screamed at her twin.

'Look, I'm sorry, OK? I thought I was handling it the right way by speaking directly to him. Let's ring Dad. He'll know what to do,' Joey suggested.

'No way. Like a bull in a china shop is Dad. Don't you remember him accidentally blasting our mother to pieces?' Frankie mocked.

'Ring Big Vinny then. He has every right to know his coward of a son has done a runner and his grandson's being held hostage.'

'Don't talk daft. How are we meant to explain the truth to him? Oh by the way, Vinny, it wasn't Jamie Preston who killed your daughter; it was your notright psycho of a son. That sound good to you, does it, Joey? We're going to have to take the Ben letter to the police station ourselves. It's the only way to get Regan home safe and sound.'

'Jamie's going to want proof we've done so – and how we meant to prove it? The Old Bill aren't just going to let us walk out after handing 'em a letter like that. They'll probably keep us there and question us for hours. Have you even looked inside the fucking envelope? For all we know, Little Vinny might have put a blank piece of paper in there.'

'Of course I've bloody well looked. I'm not totally stupid. I just have a habit of attracting and dating murderers.'

'Show me it,' Joey ordered.

Frankie handed it to him and Joey studied it for ages, trying to work out what it said. The handwriting was slanted and you could tell whoever had written it was probably pissed. Either that or illiterate. Finally, he got his head around it.

Jamie Preston did not kill my little sister Molly Butler, my mate at the time Ben Bloggs did.

I was only young back then and I did want to tell you, but was too scared of getting into trouble myself.

Me and my dad hadn't been getting on, and he'd ruined my relationship with a girl called Shazza from Dagenham by turning up at her house and blurting out my real age. I hated my dad for that, but I never hated Molly. I just wanted to teach my old man a lesson by pretending Molly had gone missing for a few hours when Ben was in fact looking after her.

I was there when Molly died and I swear Ben didn't mean it, so please don't tarnish his name. Ben was a good lad who'd had a tough life and he adored children. He even raised his own brothers and sisters because his junkie whore of a mother was incapable of doing so.

I swear on the bible what happened that day was an accident. Ben was only playing with Molly when I heard her neck snap. It was a game that went wrong, nothing more, nothing less. But Ben was traumatized over the mistake he'd made and that was why he killed himself.

I'm very sorry for not telling the truth before now. But if I'm interviewed no way am I speaking to that bastard Terry again. He's a Chief Inspector now I think, but he's a nasty piece of work.

Yours sincerely,

Little Vinny

PS Please don't show my dad this letter. I owe it to him and Molly to tell him the truth myself.

Joey put the letter back in the envelope. 'What we gonna do, sis?'

'Wait until Jamie rings back. But next time I'll be the one to speak to him, not you, you dickhead.'

Regan Butler grinned as Jamie drove inside the entrance. 'Is this a holiday camp? We staying in a caravan?'

'It's a caravan park, but yeah, it's like a holiday park too in the summer. The clubhouse isn't open this time of year, but if we're bored later, we can find a pub with a pool table, if you like?'

'Yeah, I'd like that. We got a pool table indoors and I'm much better than Calum,' Regan bragged.

Jamie looked at the numbers and pulled up outside plot twenty-one. The caravan belonged to a pal of his who he'd met in prison. Not wanting to involve Glen, he'd rung Toby earlier asking if he knew of a safe haven, and his pal had come up trumps. Apparently, lots of retired people lived on these premises all year round and when Toby had handed him the keys all he'd said was, 'I don't care what you're up to or why you need a safe haven, but just keep the noise down, OK? The old couple in plot twenty-two are in their late eighties.'

Having never been inside a caravan before, Regan explored the layout curiously. 'Can't believe it's got a toilet and shower. Big, ain't it? My dad's car wouldn't be able to tow this, would it?'

Jamie chuckled. 'This ain't one of them diddy little tourers you see being dragged along the road, Regan. It's what they call a static caravan. You'd need a lorry to move something this size. Charge your new phone up, eh?' Jamie urged, tossing the box at him.

'How we gonna ring home again? The number was on the one you smashed up.'

'I'd already stored it in my phone. How about we find a shop, stock up on necessities, then find a boozer that serves good grub and has a pool table?'

Apart from missing Georgie, Regan was having a great time. His dad never wanted to do anything these days. But being with Jamie was like one big adventure. 'So are you my uncle, if Albie's your dad?'

Jamie ruffled the boy's hair. He'd washed the blood off and thankfully there was only a small cut underneath. Regan hadn't suffered any more headaches either. 'Well, I'm your granddad's half-brother, so I suppose, yeah, it does sort of make me your uncle.'

Regan smiled broadly. 'That's well cool. Can we still hang out when I go back home?'

'If your family agree, 'course we can. I'd like that very much.'

'Thanks, love. They're beautiful. Antonio get off all right?' Queenie asked her eldest son, cutting open the cellophane around the enormous bouquet.

'As far as I know, his flight's not until this evening. Bella's driver is taking him to the airport and she wanted to go and wave him off. Keep out of it, me, don't I? Put money on it he don't even ring to thank me for the party or say goodbye. Only time he'll be in touch while away is when his bank account needs a top-up. I just hope he meets a bird on his travels. Might straighten him out a bit,' Vinny said.

'He'll be a prime target for those ting-tong birds. They go for weirdos; me and Joyce watched a programme on Thai brides recently. Oddballs and silly old bastards like your father, those are the ones they get their claws into. Desperate for a better life, I suppose. Poor little cows.'

'So what did you want to talk to me about that you couldn't say over the phone?'

'The police have been 'ere, asking questions. Hadn't been back five minutes from lunch with Joycie when I heard the tap-tap on the door.'

Gesturing for his mother to put the vase down and follow him into the back garden, Vinny waited until they had reached the shed at the bottom before asking, 'What did they say?'

'More than you bothered to bastard well tell me. That young floozy of yours is missing, isn't she? I recognized the name, of course.'

'They had no right to tell you that. I didn't tell ya, because I knew you'd bloody worry. So they checked out my alibi an' all, I take it?'

'Yes. And they asked me about Michael. Is that why you and your brother aren't talking? You told me it was over with Felicity weeks ago.'

'It was. Her disappearance has sod-all to do with me or Michael. We had a different bit of business on last weekend, hence needing the alibis.'

'So you're telling me you've got no idea what's happened to her?'

'None whatsoever.'

Queenie pursed her lips. 'You're a good liar, Vinny, I'll give you that much credit. Let's just hope the police don't see through you like I can though, eh?'

In a restaurant in central London, Eddie Mitchell had just been mistaken yet again for the actor Craig Fairbrass. This was a usual occurrence since Craig had joined the cast of *EastEnders* a few years ago, and one that Gary Mitchell found highly amusing. 'No, sweetheart. I can assure you my father isn't Dan Sullivan, neither was he ever a fireman in *London's Burning*. Off you trot,' Gary chuckled.

Eddie raised his eyebrows when the starstruck woman

finally left them in peace, then got straight down to business. 'I'm up town tomorrow. Thought I'd poke my head in and have a chat with Michael Butler before I head home,' he informed his son.

'And say what to him, exactly?' Gary asked.

'Just have a general chat about business. Ask him some questions about his casino, and try to force a few drinks down his neck so I can find out the truth.'

'The truth about what?'

'Felicity. If Vinny has done her in, he wouldn't have done it alone. Seems funny that he and Michael fell out around the same time as she disappeared. Gotta be wrong 'uns, those Kelly brothers an' all. Your granddad was never overly keen on 'em. Not many old school out there who'd give an alibi when it involved a young woman's life. I fucking wouldn't, that's for sure. They obviously ain't got no scruples. Evil pair of old bastards.'

'You're becoming a bit obsessed with this Felicity turnout, Dad. I doubt she will, but she could show up yet. As for going to see Michael, that's a dumbass idea if ever I heard one. He and Vinny'll probably be talking again by next week and just the fact you popped in to see Michael will be enough for Vinny to smell a rat.'

'No, he won't. I'll mention to Vinny I had to pass Michael's casino and poked me head in just to be nosy. I'm not brain-dead, son. I know how to be discreet.'

Gary smirked and shook his head. 'Discreet or not, don't underestimate Michael Butler. Unlike Vinny, he hasn't got a screw loose. He's the cool, calm, collected one. Your call. Do what you want. But always remember, blood's thicker than water. If Vinny and Michael did kill Felicity and know you're on to 'em, they'd stab you in the back within a split second.'

*

Frankie grabbed the phone out of Joey's hands, ran into the bathroom and locked the door. 'Jamie, it's Frankie. Now please don't freak out because I know your name. Little Vinny guessed your identity and only recently let it slip to me when he was drunk. Apart from Joey, my twin brother, nobody else knows. My father and Vinny Butler know nothing. We haven't even told them Regan is missing. Is he with you? Can I talk to him?'

'A quick hello and that's it.' Jamie handed the phone to Regan.

'Hello, Frankie. Yeah, I'm OK. Say hi to Georgie for me. I'll pass you back now,' Regan said.

'What do I have to do to get Regan back home, Jamie? Little Vinny has admitted everything to me. He was meant to be going to the police this morning, but being the weak bottle-job that he is, left a written confession for me to take to the station instead. As you can imagine, now I know the truth, Little Vinny and I are no longer a couple. Letting you take the blame for something you did not do is unforgivable in my eyes.'

'Cut the crap. What does the letter say?' Jamie hissed. Frankie sounded sincere enough but for all he knew she could be the biggest bullshitter going.

Deciding not to tell anybody other than Joey that Little Vinny had confessed to murdering Molly himself, Frankie said, 'That Ben Bloggs killed Molly and he panicked and helped cover it up. He also describes it as an accident and says you are innocent.'

Jamie Preston paced up and down the caravan. It was possible this letter didn't even exist and Little Vinny was at this moment hiding in the loft, but at least Frankie seemed to know the truth. He wasn't used to dealing with women though, far from it.

Sensing Jamie's apprehension, Frankie said, 'I'm willing

to go to the police station this very second, if that's what it takes to get Regan home. But I'm not sure whether they will keep me in for questioning. I won't mention to them that you've got Regan, obviously. That's why I haven't told anybody other than Joey. None of this is your fault – far from it – and I don't want to get you into any more trouble. If the police get wind you've taken Regan hostage, they'll probably lock you up again.'

Jamie put his hand over the mouthpiece. 'What's Eddie Mitchell like? Do you get on with him?' he whispered to Regan.

'Yeah, Eddie's cool.'

'Right,' Jamie said to Frankie. 'I want you to tell your father what's happened. Explain all about Little Vinny's confession, but under no circumstances can he tell Vinny Butler anything at this stage. I trust that bastard about as much as his son, get my point?'

'Totally, Jamie. Are you going to call back this evening?'

'Yeah. In a couple of hours. Get your dad round there and I'll arrange a meet with him. Regan's fine, so don't be worrying about him. Mess with me, though, and I'll burn your house down with you inside, Frankie. Fucking despise liars, I do. Cost me my freedom already.'

CHAPTER TWENTY-NINE

'Well? What did he say?' Joey Mitchell asked, his tone impatient. Frankie had a bloody cheek, talking to him like a fool earlier. Little did she know he was responsible for the deaths of Jed and Jimmy O'Hara.

'He wants to speak to Dad, then meet him. Can you ring Dad, Joey? I've barely spoken to him recently and I know he's got the right hump with me. If he thinks it's another drama of mine, he won't come round. He'll listen to you though.'

'What shall I say to him?'

'That something terrible has happened and he needs to come round ASAP. The more I think about it, though, we've got to keep Little Vinny's second confession to ourselves. Ben's dead, so it can't affect him, and they're bound to lock Little Vinny up anyway, just for burying the body and lying to the police. That's perjury.'

'No, Frankie. There's been too many lies already. We need to tell Dad everything,' Joey argued.

Having been strong all day, Frankie's eyes welled up. She was thrilled Georgie was home, but still worried about Harry, and couldn't think straight at present with all this Little Vinny rubbish going on. She sat opposite her brother.

'If people find out Little Vinny strangled that poor child, how does it make me look? The press would have a field day, like they did with Mum. I can't handle that again. It's not fair on the children. Not only do I need to protect mine, Calum and Regan don't deserve that either. They're good lads, Joey.'

'But Dad won't tell the press. He'll deal with things his own way.'

'No. Just tell him about the Ben confession,' Frankie insisted. She knew her father had no time for her at present. She also believed he would always blame her for her mum's death. If it hadn't been for her running off with Jed, her sweetheart of a mother would still be alive.

Joey dialled his father's number. It went on to answerphone, so he left a message. 'Dad, it's me. Call us back as soon as possible. It's urgent. Something bad has happened, and me and Frankie really need your help.'

Oblivious to his daughter's plight, Eddie Mitchell was having a beer in the Blind Beggar with Albie Butler, of all people. He'd been to visit Auntie Joan in hospital again and because of a bad accident, the traffic around Whitechapel was at a standstill. 'Let me get you another drink, Albie. Want a pint and a brandy chaser?'

Albie sadly shook his head. 'Not as steady on my feet as I once was. Been giving me a lot of gyp of late, my legs. Michael reckons it might be gout, but I ain't going to no bleedin' doctor. Too old to be pulled about. Best I just have a pint, I think. Got to get a train home.'

Eddie returned with a brandy chaser as well as a pint. 'I'll drop you home, save you arsing about with trains, Albie.'

'Thanks, Ed. Very kind of you. I don't venture up this way much any more. But today would have been Big

Stan's birthday. A few of the lads we played cards with for years wanted to toast his memory, so I felt it only right I paid my respects too. Lovely bloke was Big Stan. Didn't deserve what happened to him,' Albie said bitterly. Along with Oliver, Sammi-Lou and Stuart, Big Stan was another whose body had been peppered with bullets at Vivian's wake.

'Terrible turnout all round, that. Absolutely shocking. No date for those bastards' trial yet either. Top lad was Stuart, who got killed. Worked for me. Such a waste of life.'

Albie's eyes brimmed with tears. 'Breaks my heart just thinking about it. Oliver was a great lad with a big future ahead of him too. And I adored Sammi-Lou. She was the making of Little Vinny, God rest her soul.'

'You spoken to Little Vinny lately?' Eddie enquired.

'No. He used to ring me a couple of times a week, but he hasn't been in touch lately. I have called him, but your daughter or one of the kids usually answers. They always say he's resting. Is he OK, do you know?'

Eddie shrugged. 'Between me and you, I don't think he is. He's changed since he got that pasting. They're a couple now, him and my Frankie. I keep out of it, me. Always been headstrong has my daughter. Caused me no end of grief over the years.'

'Little Vinny's nothing like his father. He will take good care of your daughter, Ed. He's a decent lad with a kind heart,' Albie insisted.

'You and Big Vinny never seen eye to eye?' Eddie asked.

Albie shuffled awkwardly in his seat. 'I'd rather not talk about him, if you don't mind. As my old mum used to say, "If you can't think of something nice to say about someone, you're better saying nothing at all."'

'Fair point,' Eddie mumbled, taking his ringing phone

out of his pocket. 'What's up, Joey?' he asked. 'Why? What's she done now?' he added, raising his eyebrows at Albie.

Seconds later, Eddie Mitchell's face turned a deathly shade of white.

'What you looking so happy about?' Queenie Butler asked her pride and joy.

Even though his mother had since informed him she hadn't allowed the police to cross her threshold, had instead kept them on the doorstep, Vinny still urged her to follow him into the back garden again. He wouldn't put it past those nosy bastards to break in and plant a bug while his mum was out. Better to be safe than sorry had always been Vinny's motto. 'That was a pal of mine. Mehmet Malas has been got at in Belmarsh. Boiling sugared water, right in his boat race. They reckon he's gone blind. That'll teach him to fuck with our family, eh?'

Mehmet Malas was one of the Turks responsible for the carnage at Vivian's wake. 'That's brilliant news, Vin. Did you organize for that to happen?'

'No. Eddie did. He put out the word amongst a few lads in there he knows. Told 'em there'd be a five grand reward for each Turk who was got at. One down, two to go,' Vinny chuckled.

Queenie smiled. 'A good friend is Eddie Mitchell. One of our own.'

Unaware his plan to get revenge for Stuart's death had paid dividends, Eddie Mitchell drove along the A13 in a stunned silence. Joey's exact words were 'Jamie Preston never killed Molly Butler. Little Vinny was involved.'

'I don't like to pry, but is everything all right, Eddie?' Albie Butler asked. He knew what it was like to receive bad news, had had more than his fair share in his lifetime.

Convincing himself there must be some mistake, Eddie smiled at the elderly man. Albie was a gentle old soul who always seemed so forlorn; Ed could not help but feel sorry for him. 'You know what life's like, mate. Always some drama going on. Bit worried about that missing girl, if you want the truth. The Old Bill keep sniffing around The Casino, and that's no good for business, is it?'

'What girl's that then? Did she go missing after a night at your gaff?'

'No. Not at all. She was in a relationship with your Vinny – but keep that under your hat. I thought Michael would have told you, but perhaps he doesn't know Felicity is missing yet,' Eddie explained, studying Albie's reaction.

This time it was Albie whose face turned deathly white. Not again, he thought sadly. He pictured Joanna Preston. Lovely girl, she'd been; Jo deserved so much better than getting involved with his lunatic of a son. She'd always been kind to him, and a good mother to little Molly.

'You OK, Albie? Not got the DTs, have you? Your hands are shaking, mate.'

Compared to Vinny, Eddie Mitchell was a thoroughly nice bloke and if Albie wasn't so scared of his eldest son, he would have warned Ed to sever all ties with the bane of his life. Albie Butler was a gutless man though, so he said nothing.

The Kelly brothers were already in the pub car park when Vinny Butler pulled in. He'd guessed when they'd contacted him and asked to meet in person that they'd had a visit from the police.

Gesturing for them to get out of their vehicle, Vinny walked towards the pub entrance before offering both men a cigar. The Old Bill were certainly on his case far more than they'd been over Karen and Joanna's deaths and he was starting to feel a bit edgy. 'Well?' Vinny mumbled, lighting Johnny's cigar first.

'Filth turned up lunchtime. Wanted the names of everyone who was involved in the card game. They asked what time you arrived and left, if you popped out at all. We stuck to what we agreed: that you popped out to get some cigars and was gone for about fifteen minutes. Billy piped up that he could remember you moaning about a parking ticket when you got back. I played dumb, said I couldn't remember that conversation,' Johnny told Vinny.

'Good. Nosy bastards. You sure the others are all as clued up as yous two?'

'Yes. They'll be fine, but it probably wouldn't hurt you to part with a few more grand, Vinny. We never told the others it was a woman, you see. Billy's gonna tell 'em that you sorted out a passport for the Doris to start a new life abroad as she was in shit-street over here. But the old judge especially might be a bit funny, we reckon. Nothing that an extra few grand won't sort, though.'

'But I already told you I was giving you extra dosh, Johnny.'

'Yeah, but we mean on top of that, Vin. Listen, you're not silly, neither are you short of a few bob. Not everybody is like us and you,' Johnny explained. 'Billy and I couldn't give a flying fuck if it were royalty you'd done away with, but other men can think differently when they learn a Doris is involved. Billy and I discussed this situation on the way here and we reckon an extra five grand per man should keep everybody sweet, the bent ex-copper and judge included.'

Extremely pissed off, Vinny Butler bit his tongue and stamped the life out of his cigar as though it were a tarantula under his shoe. The Kellys had always assured him the men they used for alibis were as sweet as a nut, and that included the bent ex-cop and elderly judge. 'I'll get you the money by tomorrow. Five grand per man, yourselves included. A word of warning to your pals though. If any of 'em is thinking of taking the piss out of me, warn 'em to think again. I'm not a cunt, lads, never have been and never will be.'

When Vinny stomped off, Johnny turned to his brother. 'Do you think we stronged it a bit?'

Billy Kelly shook his head. 'Not at all. We've been bloody good friends to that man over the years. Some of the crap we've sorted for him would turn people's hair grey. Deserve a bit of bunce at our time of life, and he needs us far more than we need him at present, Johnny. Believe me.'

Eddie Mitchell could barely believe what he was hearing. It must be twenty-odd years since Molly Butler was murdered, but he could remember it like it were yesterday. It still brought a lump to his throat what had happened to that poor child. One of those murders close to home that he'd never forget. 'Show me the letter,' he demanded, his voice no more than a stunned whisper.

Joey glanced awkwardly at Frankie as he handed their father the evidence. He'd been insisting all day that their dad should also be shown the other letter, but his sister wasn't in agreement. She was far too embarrassed and scared to want the whole sorry truth rising to the surface.

Eddie stared at the childlike writing and shook his head in a state of utter disbelief. Vinny would completely lose the plot when he found out; there was no two ways about that. 'What time is Preston ringing back?' he asked.

'Soon, hopefully. He said a couple of hours. Don't lose your rag or anything with him, Dad. None of this is his fault,' Frankie pleaded.

'He hasn't threatened you, has he?' Eddie spat.

'No. Of course not,' Frankie lied. Even though Jamie had threatened to burn her house down, she could tell he was only bluffing. She genuinely felt sorry for him and could sense he'd been treating Regan OK.

'Is this the first you knew of this?' Eddie asked, pacing the room, letter in hand.

'Tell him the truth, Frankie,' Joey urged.

Admitting that she'd known for a while, but had been at a loss as to who to tell or what to do, Frankie added, 'But I did tell Joey recently.'

Eddie glared at his son. 'When? How long you known?'

'Not long,' Joey replied sheepishly. 'Frankie begged me not to tell you, was worried all hell would break loose.'

Unable to control his temper, Eddie pushed Joey so hard in the chest his back hit the wall. 'And now it has, you fucking idiot. Disappointed in you, lad. I really am.'

Jamie Preston ended the call and crouched in front of Regan. The lad was happily munching on a bag of crisps while watching a Western on the small TV. 'Can I trust you to stay 'ere alone and not kick up a stink of any kind while I go and meet Eddie? You know all that crap I've said on the phone was bollocks, don't ya? Obviously I had to clump you one to get you in my motor, but I swear, whatever happens, I'll never harm you again.'

'Yeah, you can trust me, Jamie. How long will you be gone, do ya reckon?'

'An hour, tops. And I'll bring us a takeaway back. What do you fancy?'

'Can we have pizza again? But this time can I have extra salami on mine, please?'

''Course you can. You're gonna have to give me your phone though. No point me giving it large to Eddie while you're chatting happily away to Georgie, is there?' Jamie grinned. 'All being well, you'll be back home tomorrow anyway.'

Apart from his desire to see Georgie, the thought of returning home made Regan feel quite sad. Today, he and Jamie had played pool and darts in a quiet little pub, and even the fact they were sort of on the run felt exciting. Better than being stuck at home with his dad and Frankie drunkenly arguing, or Calum walking around with a face like a smacked arse. 'We will still see each other when I go home, won't we?'

Jamie himself felt sad as he replied to that question. He very much doubted the Butlers would ever allow him to be a part of Regan's life. 'Fingers crossed we will, mate. I'm gonna make a move now. Won't be long.'

Eddie Mitchell strolled inside the Admiral Jellicoe on Canvey Island and glanced around. He remembered seeing photos of Jamie in the newspapers after he'd been convicted of killing Molly, but he didn't have a clue what he'd look like now. Dark, with bright green eyes like Albie's other offspring, Ed supposed.

The pub wasn't that busy, neither did any of the baseball-cap-wearing, scruffily dressed lads even remotely resemble a Butler, so Eddie ordered himself a Scotch and sat down at a table. He wasn't that familiar with Canvey Island, but could remember his Auntie Joan bringing him here with his brothers not long after his mum died. He'd played on a small beach with a bucket and spade and found a dead crab, if he remembered rightly.

Suited and booted, Eddie stood out like a sore thumb in such an establishment, and aware that the bar staff were studying him, he began scrolling through his phone. Jamie had insisted on meeting here. Said he'd been to the pub recently and hinted that if Eddie was thinking of pulling wool over his eyes he wouldn't be able to do it there.

Jamie walked in half an hour late and Eddie immediately knew it was him. Wearing a dark hooded tracksuit and trainers, he was dressed similarly to most of the males in the pub. But there was something about his stance and entrance that made him stand out a mile. He oozed class.

Jamie ordered himself a pint of orange juice, then sat down opposite Eddie. He'd been lurking outside, had watched Mitchell walk in, but had wanted to ensure he was alone before making his own grand entrance.

Jamie held out his right hand. 'Shame it's not under different circumstances, but cheers for meeting me alone.'

'Ditto. Right, let's get to the nitty-gritty. Frankie's told me everything. Apparently, Little Vinny confessed to her before you snatched Regan, but apart from trying to convince him that going to the police was the right thing to do, she was too scared to do anything – understandably. Which is why she never told me. He's still not been in contact, that gutless little prick, but we'll find him, don't worry. This is the letter he left.'

Jamie was unimpressed as he studied the letter's content. 'Looks like a fucking four-year-old's written this. How do I know if it's even real? You could be hiding Little Vinny, for all I know, playing me along until Regan comes home. Then you and your sidekick'll come gunning for me.'

Eddie stared intently into Jamie's piercing green eyes. He most definitely looked like a Butler, but had a rounder, softer face like Michael, rather than Vinny's more chiselled features. 'You're just going to have to trust me, I'm afraid. My word is my bond; anybody who knows me will tell you that.'

Jamie sneered and shook his head. 'Not being funny, but I've just spent most of my life banged up for a crime your daughter's current beau committed. And you're business partners with a geezer who had my cousin bumped off. Why the hell should I trust you?'

For the first time since Jessica had died, Eddie Mitchell felt like a complete and utter fool.

Back in Emerson Park, Frankie had tucked Brett into bed and was now comforting Georgie. Calum had been as miserable as sin, so after pleading with her, she'd allowed him to go and stay at a pal's house. What could she say or do to stop him? She wasn't his mother and his father could be anywhere.

Joey Mitchell sighed. His sister had been upstairs for ages so he'd popped up to make sure she was all right. It was clear from the snippets of conversation he'd overheard that Georgie had rung Alice O'Hara and been verbally abused. Frankie was a good mum at heart, just like he was a good son, which was why Joey knew he had to do the right thing. The shove in the chest and harsh words his father had given him earlier had reminded him of such duties.

Creeping down the stairs, Joey decided to text his father rather than call him.

> Can't say anything when you get back here later, Dad. But text me early tomorrow and we'll meet somewhere behind Frankie's back. There is something important I need to tell you.
>
> Joey x

Regan Butler sat up and rubbed his eyes. 'You've been gone ages. I was so hungry, I fell asleep.'

Jamie handed the lad a pizza box. 'Sorry, Regan. I don't know the area that well and thought Canvey Island was only down the road. Turns out it wasn't. It's poxy miles away.'

The caravan they were currently holed up in was on Mersea Island. Having been stuck in prison most of his life, Jamie's geographical skills were not great. He only knew of the Admiral Jellicoe because Glen had dealings with a bloke who lived in Canvey and he'd remembered passing that pub and thinking what an unusual name it had.

'How did you get on with Eddie?' Regan asked, scoffing his pizza like a starving animal.

'OK. You're not gonna be going home just yet though. I need to make sure I can trust Eddie first. That cool with you?'

'Not if you forget my extra salami again.'

Jamie smiled. 'Sorry, lad. I'll buy you another pizza tomorrow with as much salami on it as you want. Deal?'

Trying to take their mind off matters, Joey and Frankie were watching repeats of *Only Fools and Horses*. Neither of them was laughing much, mind. Not even when Granddad smashed the chandelier on the floor in one of their favourite episodes.

'Surely Dad will be home soon, Joey. He's been gone ages. Georgie is going to be so upset if Regan isn't with him. What a horrible old witch Alice O'Hara is, eh? Fancy calling Georgie all those terrible things. Disgusting.'

Joey Mitchell put an arm around his sister's shoulders and adjusted the throw that covered the two of them. The weather had been bitterly cold today. 'Alice is history now, and good bloody riddance. At least Georgie's learned for herself what a nasty person her grandmother is. As for Dad, he probably don't want to speak on the blower. You know what he's like when a drama occurs. Always thinks MI5 are bugging us,' Joey joked, trying to make light of the whole torrid situation.

The knock on the door made both Joey and Frankie jump out of their skins. The gates were closed and anybody entering the property needed to press the buzzer first.

'No. Don't open it,' Frankie ordered her brother. 'It might be Little Vinny, and if he's out of his box, he's capable of anything.'

Joey turned the TV down. The slats on the blinds were closed so nobody could see in. 'You got a bat or a hammer or something? I'm not scared of bloody Little Vinny.'

'It's me,' a voice shouted out.

'Harry!' Frankie exclaimed. She ran to the front door, flung it open and threw her arms around her son. 'Harry, you're home!' she cried.

Harry O'Hara screwed his face up. 'Yeah. Get off me now, Frankie. I'm starving.'

CHAPTER THIRTY

Unable to sleep, Michael Butler got up in the middle of the night. He kept getting these crazy nightmares which forced him to relive the awful day of Felicity's murder. Then he couldn't nod off again.

Filling the kettle up, Michael thought back to the previous evening. He'd been sitting in his office when he'd heard the local news presenter say, 'Tearful grandmother appeals for information regarding the disappearance of her granddaughter . . . ' Felicity had then been mentioned by name.

Felicity's nan was a smart blonde lady with a posh accent and Michael was fixated as she spoke about her granddaughter and pleaded for her safe return. An image of a sports car the same colour as Felicity's had then been shown and the newsreader had read out the registration whilst informing the public that the car could hold vital information regarding Felicity's whereabouts, and the public should keep their eyes peeled.

Watching Felicity's nan sob her heart out had brought tears to Michael's eyes and any doubt he'd had over purchasing that gun was gone. His brother was mentally ill, a danger to women, and no way would Michael allow another to suffer such a traumatic end to their life as Felicity had. Raping her, then cutting the baby out of the poor woman's belly, was confirmation that his brother was beyond control.

Michael opened the back door, sat on the wooden bench and lit a cigar. Vinny had rung him again yesterday, left a couple of messages asking to meet up. 'I love you, bruv. You know that. Let's chat face to face. Call me,' he'd urged.

Michael ran his hands through his hair. In his heart he would always love Vinny, but that didn't mean he liked him much. Lenny, Roy, Oliver and Sammi-Lou had all lost their lives thanks to his brother's wrongdoings. The entire Butler family were targets, thanks to Vinny. The time had come for Michael to put his own safety and that of his children first.

Thrilled to have her son home, Frankie was in a buoyant mood and up with the lark the following morning. She'd been disappointed when her father had turned up shortly after Harry's return without Regan, but he'd reassured her everything had gone well with Jamie, and Regan would be home soon.

'You're up early. Couldn't you sleep?' Joey Mitchell yawned, plonking himself on a kitchen chair wearing his sister's bright pink dressing gown.

'The kids'll take the right piss out of you in that,' Frankie laughed. 'Go and put one of Little Vinny's on. There's one in the bedroom and another in the en suite.'

'No, thank you. Don't want anything that's been in contact with his skin. Anyway, I can get away with pink. I am gay, remember,' Joey added with a wink.

Frankie poured her brother a coffee and sat opposite him sipping her own. Georgie had been ecstatic when she'd run down the stairs and laid eyes on her brother. It was the perfect ending to an otherwise traumatic day.

'Did Harry get a train home, like Georgie?' Joey asked.

He'd made himself scarce after his father had left the previous evening, had lain on the bed chatting to Dominic so Frankie could spend some quality time alone with her children.

'Yes. But he hasn't said why he left, and I don't want to pry. Perhaps he heard what Alice said on the phone to Georgie? That would roughly fit with the time he arrived. I was sure he'd come back to me. That's why I'm up so early. Thought I'd cook us all a big celebratory fry-up and do some planning for the future. Do you think Dad'll rent me another house? I know I've messed him about in the past, but after this Little Vinny turnout, I'm off men for good. It's all about me and the kids from now on.'

'Until you fall in love with the next loser,' Joey mocked.

'No. I'm serious. I'm sick of waking up feeling sluggish too. I want to join a gym and perhaps do a little part-time job of some kind. I need to start standing on my own two feet rather than always relying on Dad. And I want to be a good example to my children. I've not been a great role model for them so far, have I?'

Joey put his right hand on top of Frankie's. 'Don't beat yourself up. You've been through a lot with Mum dying, Jed, prison, then losing your kids, and Stuart. Of course Dad will get you another property. I know you and him clash, but you've always been the apple of his eye, Sis. You're too alike, that's why you rub one another up the wrong way. Having said that, I very much doubt he's gonna let Regan and Calum live with you once you move, so you might have to re-think that one.'

'But when Little Vinny gets locked up, who else is there to look after them?'

Joey shrugged. 'Once the shit hits the fan, a clean break will be best all round. Not your problem, are they?'

*

Gary Mitchell stayed silent while his father explained the situation. He'd known something was amiss when his dad had ordered him to drive to his gaff in Rettendon before the rush hour. 'So what now?'

'You don't seem very shocked,' Eddie remarked. 'Had you already spoken to Joey or Frankie?'

'No. Not spoken to anybody. The Butlers are as fucked up as families come, Dad. That's why I warned you not to get involved with 'em in the first place.'

'Well, I'm going to sort it out once and for all now. We're gonna need to know where Little Vinny's hiding. I'll need your help, obviously. And if we need a third man, Raymond's the obvious choice. For now, though, this is just between us.'

'OK. But if I was you, I wouldn't be fucking around doing deals to get Regan home. Preston might set you up and Glen Harper'll be waiting in the wings with a shooter for your next visit. Why don't you just tell Vinny? Let him deal with it?'

Eddie shook his head. 'No way is Vinny gonna allow that letter to get into the Old Bill's hands. He's bound to go fucking ballistic and deal with his son himself. Lose face otherwise, won't he? Enough to kill poor old Queenie, learning that her grandson helped bury her beloved granddaughter. And you know what a mummy's boy Vinny is. Be the end of the Butlers for good if the press get as much as a whiff of this, which is why I know Vinny's bound to hush it up. Preston's insistent he wants his name cleared, and I don't bastard well blame him. The stretch I done for accidentally murdering Jessica was bad enough, but at least I did do it. That poor fucker did a much bigger lump than me and will be labelled a child killer for the rest of his life if I hand the evidence over to Vinny.'

'I don't get where you're coming from. But you barely

know Preston, and seeing as he's Albie's son, he's also a Butler. They're all wrong 'uns, I don't trust any of 'em. Bad genes.'

Eddie clenched his fist and pounded it against his chest. 'Sometimes in life, Gal, you got no option other than to go with your gut instinct. This happens to be one of those times. Vinny Butler'll kill his own son, and then I am gonna ensure me and him part company for good. I want him outta my business and life. How's that sound?'

Gary Mitchell sighed. 'Dangerous, with a hint of fucking madness.'

'Glen, I gotta go now. Promised I'd take my aunt to the shops and I'm running late,' Jamie Preston lied. Glen was forever checking up on his whereabouts, or turning up at his gaff unannounced, so he'd bluffed it yesterday and told his ex-cellmate that his nan's sister had got in touch out the blue and he was visiting her.

'That your mate again? Was it him who kept phoning in the night?' Regan asked.

'Yeah,' Jamie replied. On the inside, he'd thought the sun shone out of Glen Harper's arsehole. But on the outside, Glen was very different to what Jamie had expected. He was like a Peter Pan type, the boy who'd never grown up. Glen and his cronies were all in their late forties or fifties, yet they would party as though they were still teenagers. Snorting cocaine, then sitting up talking bollocks all night was the norm. As was going to clubs and raves, and shagging call girls.

'Is Glen your best mate?' Regan enquired innocently.

'Yeah, I suppose he is,' Jamie responded. He wasn't into the lifestyle yet, but would always be indebted to Glen for being such a good friend to him in prison. That's why he'd tried so hard to join in with the lads. But it wasn't for him and he was finding it harder to hang around with them by the day.

'So what we doing? Can we get some breakfast soon? I'm starving.'

Jamie smiled. 'For a skinny whippet, you eat like a race-horse. Let me have a shower, then we'll go grab some munch.'

As the none-too-warm water invigorated him, Jamie's thoughts turned to Eddie Mitchell. Ed had insisted he deal directly with him from now on, had told Jamie to call him again today. He'd seemed genuine enough, but if he was one of the good guys, why the hell was he in partnership with Vinny? Something didn't add up and Jamie was determined to find out what.

'Show me that racing car game you got then, Brett. I'll beat you though, 'cause I can drive real cars and trucks. I even drove my uncle's horsebox recently, didn't I, Georgie?' Harry O'Hara bragged.

'Yeah, but you won't beat Brett 'cause he's a wizard with computer games and you're a dinlo, Harry,' Georgie laughed.

When both her sons scarpered upstairs, Frankie smiled as she loaded the dishwasher. Harry and Brett seemed genuinely at ease in one another's company at long last, which made her heart melt.

'Do you want me to do anything, Mum?' Georgie asked.

'No. You're fine, love. Harry seems happy enough. What do you think?'

'He's fine. He did have a go at me for not telling him I was leaving though. He hated it on that new site too, said he would've come with me and was upset 'cause I just abandoned him.'

'Did you explain your reasons?'

'Yeah. But he was still angry with me. I had to promise him I'll never leave him like that again.'

'Of course. Did Harry overhear what Alice said to you on the phone?'

'No. But he did steal her purse yesterday morning so he could get here. He saw Billy give her a hundred pounds the night before, so he got up early and ran off with it. He's such a dinlo though. He got on the wrong train first and ended up in Scotland,' Georgie chuckled.

'Oh well, he got home safe in the end, bless him. Bet Nanny Alice is fuming, mind,' Frankie smirked. She loathed that evil old cow.

'I'll answer that,' Joey shouted, when the buzzer burst into life. He was surprised his father hadn't already been in contact, seeing as he'd sent him that text the previous evening.

The CCTV that had been installed was no longer working, thanks to Little Vinny having a meltdown a couple of days ago. He'd ripped all the wires out and smashed up the indoor screen. 'That you, Dad?' Joey asked.

'No. It's Vinny. Open the gates.'

Joey ran into the kitchen. 'Shit, it's Vinny Butler. What we gonna say? I answered it, so he knows we're in.'

'Georgie, go upstairs with the boys. Make sure nobody says anything about Little Vinny or Regan. I will make up a story,' Frankie said.

'OK. I'll clue Harry and Brett up,' Georgie replied.

Frankie pressed the button that opened the electronic gates.

'Your mobile's ringing. It's Finn,' Joey informed his sister.

'Answer it and see what he wants. Little Vinny's probably been in touch, but say nothing until Vinny's gone.'

Frankie opened the door, false grin on her face. 'Long time no see. You all right, Vinny?' she asked, as casually as her voice would allow her to sound. Her heart was thumping so loudly in her chest, she wondered if he could hear it.

'If the mountain won't come to Muhammad, I thought I'd best come to the mountain. Where is he? And more importantly, how is he?'

'Yeah, he's good, Vin. Not in at the moment though, gone out with the boys. I would offer you a coffee, but Joey's here and we're about to go out too.'

Vinny had a good sense of when people were flustered and speaking bullshit. 'Well, I haven't driven all this way not to be offered a coffee. Neither have I done so to be lied to. So best you let me in, eh sweetheart?'

Two women who loved nothing more than shopping until they dropped, today Queenie and Joycie were looking for something glamorous to wear in Hornchurch.

'I could've told you there was only a few clothes shops here. Pleased with that top I bought though. Look fabulous with my black culottes, that will,' Joyce announced.

'Oh yes. Stunning,' Queenie lied. The top Joycie had bought was bold, brash and leopard print. Queenie loathed it almost as much as she did seeing a woman of Joycie's age swanning around in culottes. Mutton done up as lamb sprang to mind.

'Shall we have a coffee? Or an early lunch? Not many more shops here to look in,' Joyce suggested.

'You heard from Frankie recently? Only, since she got with Little Vinny, I've been blanked for some reason. Not so much as a phone call, let alone an invite. My Vinny hasn't heard from him either. To think I gave up the bulk of my life to bring up that ungrateful little sod. No respect these days, is there, Joycie?'

'None at all. Not like the old days. Nope, not heard

from Frankie recently either. Joey always rings me, so does Eddie. But other than that, I might as well be dead.'

Queenie glanced at her watch. 'Seeing as it's a bit early for lunch, why don't we pay our ignorant grandchildren a surprise visit? They're only down the road, aren't they?'

Joyce grinned. 'Yes. Let's shove a firework up their ignorant arses.'

Frankie Mitchell leaned against the hallway wall. Her father had insisted if any of the Butlers got in contact, she and Joey were to tell them nothing about the Molly revelations. He'd ordered them to act as normal and carefree as possible. However, Vinny Butler was a scary bastard, especially when he was asking question after question and his eyes started to bulge. 'Do you think he believed me?' she asked her twin.

'Yeah, but the problem is, he's gonna be sniffing around all the time now. Why didn't you just stick to the story Little Vinny had gone go-karting with the boys?' Joey asked.

'Because he didn't bloody believe it, Joey. Telling him me and Little Vinny had argued and he'd stormed off with the boys was the only way I could think of getting rid of him. What did Finn say?'

'Little Vinny rang him twice in the early hours of this morning. He wouldn't say where he was staying and was out of his box, by all accounts. Finn feels ever so guilty for getting him that cocaine now, and is desperately worried we're going to tell Big Vinny or Dad. I told him we wouldn't, providing he plays ball with us. I said you'd call him back. But I do think you should inform Dad of everything that's happened today first. Probably best he contacts Vinny and Finn. He'll know how to handle all this better than us.'

'Has Vinny gone, Mum?' Georgie asked, followed down

the stairs by her brothers. 'Brett knows now about Regan. He isn't a dinlo, knew something was up, so I told him.'

'Yeah, he's gone,' Frankie replied chirpily. Obviously, she hadn't told her children Little Vinny had murdered Molly yet. They would find out the truth at some point though, same as poor Calum and Regan.

Frankie hugged her daughter and youngest son, before turning her attention to Harry. 'Leave it out, Mum. I don't do cuddles,' he informed her.

If a smile could have ever lit up a hallway, Frankie's would have done in a split second. Harry had said the one word she'd been longing to hear him say. He'd actually called her 'Mum'.

'Yes!' Regan Butler exclaimed, punching his fist in the air. He and Jamie were playing pool in the pub again and he'd just won two games on the spin.

'I'm gonna ring Eddie now. Be back in a tick,' Jamie informed the triumphant lad. Little did Regan know that he'd chucked both games on purpose.

'Well? Is my dad home yet?' Regan asked on Jamie's return, his mouth full of dry-roasted peanuts.

'No. But he's been in touch with a pal, so he's OK. Eddie wants to speak to you,' Jamie informed Regan, handing him the pay-as-you-go he'd purchased under a false identity. 'Be honest with him, but don't say where we are,' he mouthed.

'Yes, Eddie. I'm fine, thanks. Being well fed and looked after. Will you tell Georgie I miss her and that I'll see her soon?' Regan asked, before handing the phone back to Jamie.

Agreeing to meet Eddie again at the same pub they'd met at the previous day, Jamie flatly refused when he was asked to bring Regan as well. 'No way. Sorry, but you need to come up with a proper plan before the kid goes home. I haven't gone to these lengths to hand him back without being sure my name is cleared. We'll talk more later. See you at six.'

The last thing Frankie Mitchell needed was her grandmother and Little Vinny's turning up on the doorstep interrogating her, but that was what she was currently dealing with.

'I know there's something you're not telling me, Frankie. You won't look me in the eye,' Joyce insisted.

'If you and Little Vinny have had a row, we won't judge, will we, Joycie? All couples argue. Is that what has happened? You had a barney and he's sodded off somewhere with the boys?' Queenie pried.

Aware that his sister was becoming flustered, Joey put his two penn'orth in. 'Just leave it, will you. It's not what you think, put it that way. Georgie and Harry coming home is what we're celebrating today.'

Joyce pursed her lips. 'Come on, Queenie. Let's go for lunch somewhere. Nothing worse than being made to feel like a nosy old bat, is there?'

Determined to obey his father's orders, Joey decided to crack a couple of jokes to lighten the mood. It was obvious his nan and Queenie could sense something was wrong. 'No way are you unwanted or a bat, Nan. Old, yes, very,' he quipped.

Not impressed one bit by her grandson's humour, Joycie slapped him around the face. 'And to think I went to the trouble of finding you a surrogate mother to have your baby. You'd make a terrible father. Worse than your granddad, and he's the most disappointing man I've ever bastard well met.'

*

Michael Butler felt a bit queasy as he neared the house where Katy lived in Tunbridge Wells. The police had paid him a visit early this morning, asking questions about Felicity Carter-Price and his whereabouts on the weekend she'd gone missing. He'd been dreading such a visit, but had managed to act as though he hadn't a care in the world. 'Truth be known, Vinny and I aren't exactly in one another's pockets. Obviously I love him, he's my brother. But we got our own lives now and separate businesses. We still hang out when we have time, but I've not had a proper catch-up with him for a while. So I have no idea how long he's been seeing Felicity for, or how often she stayed at his. Vinny's never been one to speak about his love life much,' Michael had informed the police, while trying to blank that poor woman's awful screams and ordeal from his mind. What Vinny had done to her was haunting him.

'Michael! What a lovely surprise! Worried I'd started packing for my move to France, was you?' Katy asked sarcastically. She was intending on spending the entire six weeks of the school summer holidays in the South of France, but had no wish to live out there permanently. It was good to keep Michael on his toes though. He rarely came home any more, but still kept her and the children in a life of luxury.

'Kids at school?' Michael enquired.

'Yes. Where else do you think they'd be?'

'Good. We need to talk. I've put this house on the market today. I thought it was high time we went our separate ways. You'll get half of what it's worth, even though you've never put a penny into it, and there'll be a monthly allowance for the children. From now on, you can keep yourself in that life of luxury you're accustomed to. In future, when you want to spend thousands in beauty salons, you pay for the treatments yourself – get my drift?'

Katy stared at Michael in shocked disbelief. She was thirty-seven now; she'd been twenty-one when she'd fallen pregnant with Nathan, and had been a kept woman ever since. 'You can't put my house on sale without my permission. That's against the law.'

'Tough shit, and no it ain't. My solicitor reckons the same as me: you've taken the piss for far too long. Had enough of your constant demands now, so you can fuck off to the South of France or wherever else you fancy living. Nathan'll be sixteen soon; he can choose to live with me then, if he wants. As for Ellie, she can visit me whenever she likes.'

Katy flew at Michael, her long fingernails scratching at his face. 'You absolute bastard! You've got another woman, haven't you? Is it Bella? You back with her?'

'Nope. I'm done with women, sweetcheeks. You're enough to put any man off for life,' Michael said, grabbing hold of Katy's wrists. 'Cried wolf once too often, haven't you, eh? Board will be up at the entrance tomorrow. Property'll be on the internet by then too. Your unlimited credit card's also been cancelled. I'll ring the kids later and explain it all to them myself. Take care, Katy. I'd like to say it's been nice knowing you, but that would be the lie of all fucking lies.'

When Katy chased him down the driveway, standing in front of his car screaming abuse, Michael reversed, then opened the window. 'You wanna ask for a refund from them health farms and beauty salons. Be more beneficial if you can find a new hobby that cleanses you on the inside rather than the out. Laters, darlin'.'

Katy was livid as Michael's new Range Rover zoomed off. Hoping he could still hear her, she screamed, 'I hope you crash and die, you bastard.'

*

Jamie Preston hung around outside the pub first to check Eddie arrived alone again. Mitchell seemed a straight-talker, a what-you-see-is-what-you-get type of guy, but he was still Vinny's partner and Jamie wouldn't trust Butler as far as he could throw him.

'Bar staff have been giving me funny looks. I reckon they think I'm the Mr Big of drug dealers,' Eddie joked as Jamie sat down.

'Probably,' Jamie replied, drinking the pint of orange juice Ed had got him. 'So what's this plan then?'

'I'm gonna be straight with you now, Jamie. Your pal Glen Harper I am not a fan of. You know as well as I do what he does for a living, and that ain't my bag. People who sell and take drugs I tend not to trust, so I need your word that anything we speak about is just between you and me. I'm a fair man and like to think of myself as a nice guy. But cross me and you'll see a different person. You get what I'm saying?'

'Yes, and ditto,' Jamie held Eddie's gaze. 'Fire away then.'

Vinny Butler bowled into The Casino like he owned the place, which he did. 'D'ya know if I left my phone here earlier, lads? Can't find the poxy thing anywhere.'

'Not seen it, boss,' Paul the doorman replied.

'Me neither,' Pete added. Both men had worked for Vinny since he'd opened his first-ever club in Whitechapel.

Bursting into his office, Vinny was relieved to see his phone on the desk. Very unusual for him to have left it there, but accidents happen, especially when life dumps so much shit on your poxy plate.

Pressing the answerphone, Vinny grinned when he got to message number three. 'Hi, Vin, it's me. Yeah, I'm up for a meet. Let us know when you're free and we'll sort something. Take care, and I'll see you soon.'

Vinny breathed a sigh of relief. He knew his brother would come round, and needed him on his side right now. His family might not be perfect, but they were loyal to the core when push came to shove. The Butler bond was unbreakable, like steel.

CHAPTER THIRTY-ONE

Gary arrived at his dad's cottage early the following morning. 'The Old Bill turned up at work last night. Carted Vinny off in front of all the punters,' Gary told his father.

'Over Felicity? What, they actually arrested him?'

'Not exactly, but it was about Felicity. He was his usual cocky self, happily trotted off to the cop shop for questioning. They didn't handcuff him or anything, though. Where were you last night? I thought you were coming to The Casino?'

'Yeah, I was. But I ended up going for something to eat with Jamie Preston and went straight home afterwards. I wanted to have a good chat with Gina while the kids were asleep. Barely spoken to her since she's been in Ireland. I managed to convince her to stay a bit longer. Don't want her and the kids at home with all this crap going on. She reads me like a book, does Gina. She'll know I'm up to something.'

'How long was you with Preston for then?'

'Couple of hours. Preston is adamant Vinny bumped off his cousin, Joanna – Molly and Ava's mum. And those dead creatures that turned up at The Casino were aimed at Vinny. Jamie had no knowledge of it until recently, mind. A pal of his thought it would be fun to wind Butler up while Preston was still behind bars.'

'Don't be telling him too much, Dad, or falling for his blarney. He might be a Preston by name but he's still a Butler by blood. Sweet-talkers and liars the lot of 'em,' Gary warned.

'I get where you're coming from, but I've had to trust him to an extent. And to be fair, he's been honest with me too. Turns out Jamie was behind both the Butler beatings. He sort of ordered the attack on Vinny, and he did over Little Vinny himself. He's no mug, the lad.'

Gary Mitchell was wary by nature. 'You haven't told him what we're planning, have you?'

'No. The truth coming out and his name being cleared is all he wants. Well, that and Little Vinny getting his comeuppance.'

'I still think you're wrong in thinking that Vinny is going to kill his own son. Wanting to do away with someone is one thing. Doing away with your first-born's another,' Gary warned.

'Nah. He'll be up for it, I'd bet my gaff on that. He'll blow a gasket when he learns the truth, I'm telling you. Worshipped the ground Molly walked on, did Vinny.'

'I'm not so sure. He might just force his son to do one and never come back.'

'Any more obstacles you want to put in the way, Gal?' Eddie snapped.

Gary held his hands up. 'Point taken. You know the bloke better than me, thank fuck.'

'He's done that poor cow in, without a doubt. I'm gonna tell him later I found out who was sending that crap to us, just to see the look on his face. Not mentioning Preston, of course. I'll say I found out it was to do with the gypsies and aimed at me.'

'Cool. That your phone bleeping?'

Eddie read the text. It was from Joey, asking why he hadn't replied to his urgent text. Eddie dialled his son's number. 'Urgent what?

'The plot thickens,' Eddie said, ending the call.

'What did he say?' Gary asked.

'Not much. Just that he has some new info, and I mustn't let Frankie know.'

'I wonder what's occurred?'

'Dunno. But we'll soon find out. He's on his way over.'

'Boys, what you up to? Your breakfast is getting cold,' Frankie yelled. Calum was back home from his friend's house and she'd heard him, Harry and Brett playing computer games late into the night.

'Won't be a minute, Mum. Brett's teaching me *Pokémon* and it's ace,' Harry shouted out.

Frankie grinned. Sod the breakfast; she would put that in the microwave. As long as her son was happy, getting on well with his brother and calling her 'Mum', she could deal with any other crap life threw at her.

'You OK, Mum?' Georgie O'Hara asked.

Frankie Mitchell was more than OK. It had been a long, hard stretch, no doubt about that. But finally, she felt she had her children back.

Eddie and Gary Mitchell were both taken aback by the latest revelation. According to Joey, Little Vinny had since admitted to killing Molly himself.

'When did he tell Frankie this? Over the phone?'

Joey Mitchell handed his father the letter. 'He told her just before he ran off – the night before, I think. Look, it's there in black and white.'

'Jesus fucking wept! I gotta keep hold of this,' Eddie mumbled. Even he was stunned by the latest turn of events.

What sort of family had he got himself involved with? One he would be parting company with in the none too distant future, that was for sure. Eddie might not be an angel, but he adored the ground his wife and children walked on. Which was why he had to do now what any decent man would.

'Go easy with Frankie, eh? She's very fond of Little Vinny's boys,' Joey urged.

Eddie Mitchell was in no mood for taking advice. 'And so was I, until I found out their father killed little children.'

Michael Butler switched on his pay-as-you-go mobile. It wasn't registered in his name and only Vinny knew it existed. It rang seconds later, as expected.

'You OK, bruv?' Vinny asked, his voice one of concern. When he'd rung Michael on his regular mobile a few minutes ago, his younger brother had insisted they only chat on their untraceables.

'Yeah, but we need to talk, somewhere private where there are no ears or eyes. Remember that dirt track in Hanningfield, the one we were gonna use for Clever Trevor?'

'Rings a bell, but not sure I'd find it now. That was ages ago.'

'Stick Pan Lane in your satnav. Pick up the lane, the dirt track is five minutes past that on your left. I'll meet you there at nine tonight.'

Guessing the Old Bill had paid Michael a visit, Vinny OK'd the time, then said, 'We'll go for a bevvy afterwards, eh?'

'Yeah, but don't tell Mum we're meeting. I don't want her worrying,' Michael replied, feeling awful. There wouldn't be any afterwards.

Jamie Preston switched the ignition off and turned to Regan. He couldn't keep the lad forever, had to trust Eddie Mitchell at some point.

'Keep out of trouble, boy. And don't forget to buy a rose to give that girlfriend of yours on your first proper date. Be bowled over, Georgie will, I promise ya.'

'Can I ring you later?' Regan asked. He felt sad, knew he would miss Jamie's company.

'Not from here or your phone. If you need to speak to me, just call from a payphone, OK?'

'But you don't really see payphones any more. Everyone has a mobile these days.'

Eddie Mitchell got out of his Range Rover. 'You all right, Regan?' he asked, ruffling the lad's hair. 'Get in the motor while I have a quick word with Jamie, please.'

'Has he been in touch?' Jamie asked.

'Sure has, with Finn again. He's promised to ring Frankie later, so fingers crossed. I'm gonna get Vinny to come over to mine once I've dropped the lad off. Not looking forward to telling him, but it's got to be done,' Eddie said. He'd decided not to inform Jamie of the latest twist in the tale. Frankie's wishes and welfare needed to come first, but Ed would secretly have loved Jamie to know that Little Vinny was in fact Molly's killer.

'Will you keep me informed with what's going on?' Jamie asked.

'Yeah, sure. Your name will be cleared sooner rather than later, I'll personally make sure of that. So keep the faith.'

'OK. Speak soon.'

When Eddie started the engine, Regan wound down the window. 'Bye, Uncle Jamie. Hope to see you again soon.'

Feeling emotional because he'd been called 'Uncle' for the first time in his messed-up life, Jamie Preston trudged back to his vehicle.

Vinny Butler was a worried man. Eddie only ever asked him to come to his gaff in Rettendon if there was something important to discuss, and he just hoped this wasn't about Felicity's disappearance again. Two and a half hours the Old Bill had grilled him the previous evening, and although he could tell they had sod-all on him and were just fishing, it was giving him the heebies to keep talking about her now.

When Roxy Music's 'Dance Away' blasted out of his CD player, Vinny turned it down. One of his all-time favourite songs, today for some strange reason it reminded him of the good times down at Kings Holiday Park in Eastbourne. What a brilliant place that had been, until he'd got the whole family barred. Every weekend there'd be top stars performing, whether it be comedians or singers, and his mother and aunt would get glammed up to the nines. In their element they were in that plush clubhouse and so was his little Molly. She'd won the talent competition there not long before that bastard had ended her life. Jamie Preston was going to get his comeuppance big time, once all this Felicity stuff had died down. He was the next on Vinny's hit list. He could still visualize Molly even now, standing on that stage belting out 'You Are My Sunshine' while twirling around and having the audience in fits of laughter. If ever a child was born to be a star, that child was his first-born daughter.

The sound of his phone ended Vinny's reminiscing. 'You all right, Mum? Got a couple of hours to kill later. You out or in today?'

'Not sure. Me and Joycie are still fuming, boy. Got treated like shit when we visited Little Vinny and Frankie yesterday. He weren't there, but that poofter brother of Frankie's was and he all but told us where to go. Bloody cheek! Joyce has been a bleedin' good grandmother, same as I have. Makes you think what they'd do if we ever got forgetful and incontinent. Probably chuck us straight into some shitty council-run home and sell our properties to pay for it, if yesterday was anything to go by.'

Vinny smiled. He'd noticed his mother's soapbox rants increase as she'd aged, and he could never imagine her mellowing. She certainly had an old school way with words. He hadn't heard the expression 'poofter' for years. 'I think Little Vinny and Frankie have had a big kick-off and split up or something. Her and Joey were cagey with me yesterday an' all. Look, why don't I take you out for lunch, then we can both pop round there together? Don't invite Joycie though, as I want to chat to you about some other stuff too. Got questioned by the Old Bill last night. Barking up the wrong tree as per usual, but that's why I never called you back as promised. I've spoken to Michael as well. Will explain all later.'

'OK. What time you picking me up?'

'Shouldn't be long. Eddie's summoned me over to his for some unknown reason, but I doubt it'll be all that time-consuming. I'll bell you when I'm leaving Rettendon.'

Cranking up the volume of his stereo, Vinny joined in with Bryan Ferry as he sung the words of 'In Every Dream Home a Heartache'. Little did he know that when he reached Eddie's cottage, his own heart would be destined to ache forever more.

Pacing up and down his newly laid wooden floor, Eddie Mitchell kept sporadically glancing out of his front-room window. He'd done a lot of thinking since speaking to Gary earlier and had now come up with a definite plan of action. It was for the best all round. Eddie was a family man, would walk on hot coals to protect Gina and his children.

Ed had no way of summing up in a nutshell how he felt about Vinny Butler now. He could never hate him; they'd been pals for years and had experienced some great times together. He felt dreadfully sorry for Vinny over what he was about to tell him, knew the news would break the man's heart. But when Eddie glanced at the other side of the coin, he'd obviously made a mistake setting up business with the bloke. A rumour had been going round the underworld for years that trouble followed Vinny everywhere, and Ed should have listened. But the thing that preyed on Eddie's mind the most was how Butler had callously disposed of Felicity Carter-Price. No way was that woman going to turn up now. And she'd been pregnant with Vinny's child. Knowing Vinny as well as he did now, Eddie would bet a random stranger ten grand that Felicity hadn't got rid of the baby and Vinny had tricked her by pretending they were going to keep it and play happy families. Eddie remembered meeting Joanna Preston, Vinny's last girlfriend and the mother of little Molly, back in the day. She was a lovely girl, but rumour had it that Vinny'd only got with her as some kind of sick payback for her father shooting his brother Roy. While in prison, Vinny apparently found out through the grapevine that Joanna had given birth to another daughter, but she'd chosen not to inform him about her existence because she didn't want Ava to grow up in the same world as Molly had died in. Then, Bob's your uncle, Vinny gets out of nick and not long after Joanna is killed by a big red truck down the Dengie Straight near Tillingham. Her killer was never traced and Vinny of course had the perfect alibi.

Although the truth was crystal-clear to him now, Eddie still felt like total shit as Vinny's motor pulled up outside. He'd get no satisfaction breaking such news, was dreading telling him.

Vinny grinned as he stepped out of his motor. He was in a good mood because Michael had contacted him. 'Just been having a boogie on me own to "Virginia Plain". Love that tune. Reminds me of the early days, back in our Whitechapel club. Came out in 1972 and Champ used to blast it out the DJ system after our singers had finished. It was Roy's favourite song at the time, I think. Having one of them melancholy days for some reason, pal. Been playing some tunes that reminded me of the good old days on the way 'ere. Auntie Viv and Molly sprang to mind especially. So, what's up? And if it's about last night, the Old Bill turned up at The Casino and wanted to ask me some questions in the office. I've got nothing to hide, Ed, but needed to get them off my back once and for all. So, I told 'em in front of the punters to take me down to the station instead. Everyone laughed as I winked while walking out with 'em.'

Eddie took a deep breath. 'Sit down, mate, and drink that brandy. You're gonna need it, trust me.' The fact Vinny had been thinking about Molly on the journey here made this even harder.

'No booze. Got a lot of running about to do later and I promised to take my mum out for lunch. What's going on, Ed? I don't like mind games, you know that.'

Puffing his cheeks out, Eddie shook his head. 'I'm so sorry, mate, but there's no easy way to say this to you. The reason my Frankie and your son have split up is because Little Vinny confessed to killing Molly. He reckons it was some kind of accident. I don't really know what else to say to you other than I think we should keep it to ourselves and deal with—'

'You what!'

'It's hard to take in, I know, Vin. In bits, Frankie is. We all are.'

'You gone off your fucking rocker?' Vinny sneered.

When Ed handed him the letter, Vinny stared at it with a look of total confusion. His son had slanted, distinctive handwriting and even though it was badly written, Vinny could tell it was his son who'd penned it. Screwing the letter up, Vinny leapt up and grabbed Eddie by the throat. 'Is this some kind of sick joke, you cunt? Who gave it ya?' he bellowed, eyes bulging with fury.

Eddie grabbed Vinny's wrists. 'It's no joke, mate. It's the truth. I'm really sorry, but I couldn't not tell you. Little Vinny confessed in person too. He originally told Frankie Ben Bloggs had done it, then changed his story before scarpering.'

Heart beating faster than ever before, Vinny shook his head repeatedly. 'Nah. There's got to be some fucked-up explanation for this. No way did my son kill Molly. Someone must've forced him to write that. Probably that cunt Preston, what's the odds on it being him? Kill him with my bare hands, I will. Rip his heart out of his chest and feed it to the pigs.'

'You're in denial, and so would I be. But it's the truth unfortunately. Your son spilled his guts good and proper. He reckons he never meant it, said it was a game that went wrong. Your daughter wasn't abducted from the club that day, Vin. Your son had the hump with you, wanted to scare ya, which is why he arranged for Ben to collect Molly from nearby.'

Picking up Gina's cherished potted plant, Vinny flung it at Eddie's head, narrowly missing. 'Shut up, you mug. He didn't do it. No fucking way. He had the same blood running through his veins as Molly, you fool.'

'Getting upset with me isn't going to change what's happened. I'm just the messenger boy here. It's Frankie you really need to talk to. I'll drive you over to hers now, if you like?'

Vinny slumped on the armchair, necked the brandy in one and smashed the glass down on the coffee table. 'I know my own son. Don't need anyone telling me anything about him.'

'Your reaction is totally understandable. I'd probably be the same if it were one of my boys. Think back to when it happened, that day Molly went missing.'

'But Preston was caught red-handed. He was identified as being outside the club that day by witnesses, and the Old Bill proved that he'd made those phone calls.' Vinny was trembling now, felt sick to the stomach.

'Yeah, I know all that, mate. Preston held his hands up to being outside the club and making those hoax calls. He didn't kill your daughter though – your son did,' Eddie replied, handing Vinny another brandy.

Vinny put his head in his hands. Flashbacks of that horrendous day came flooding back. Joanna had gone out shopping with a pal and he and Molly had been huddled up on the sofa eating Marmite soldiers while watching *Sesame Street* when his son had rung him from the club to inform him there was a flood in the cellar and he thought it was the washing machine. He'd taken Molly to the club with him, and Little Vinny had promised to keep an eye on her while he was down in the cellar. When he'd returned, his son was asleep on one of the leather sofas and Molly was nowhere to be seen. Half an hour tops, he'd let Molly out of his sight, and that was the last time he'd ever seen her. 'The pipe, the arguments, Shazza,' Vinny mumbled.

'What's that, mate?' Eddie asked.

Tears streaming down his face, Vinny barged past Eddie. 'I gotta go.'

'Vin, come back. I'll drive you over to Frankie's. Little Vinny's meant to be calling her later. Nobody knows where he's holed up, but we can find out, go visit him,' Ed bellowed.

Vinny was in no fit state to be reasoned with. He turned the ignition, then zoomed off like a man possessed.

*

Queenie Butler was catching up with *Loose Women* when her son's car screeched to a noisy halt on her drive. 'Don't tell me, your phone battery died, you daft ha'porth,' she joked as Vinny let himself in with his own key.

Queenie turned the TV off. 'Whatever's wrong?' she asked, when her strapping son sank to his knees on her new shagpile rug.

'It's Molly,' Vinny wept.

Queenie kneeled in front of her son. 'Molly's headstone hasn't been trashed, has it, love?'

'No. Far worse than that. Little Vinny's admitted to Frankie he killed Molly. Didn't believe it myself at first, but now I've thought about it, I know it's not bullshit. The pipe on that washing machine didn't pull itself out that day, did it? Little Vinny was the only one at the club when that happened, and he was looking after Molly when she disappeared. I'll kill him, I swear I will. I'll make him look me in the eye and tell me the truth, then I'll put a bullet straight through his skull,' Vinny spat, snot running from his nose.

Queenie went as white as a ghost. 'Vinny, no. It can't be true, son. Someone's pulling a fast one, they have to be. Who told you this? Eddie?'

Vinny nodded, then handed his mother the letter. 'That is Little Vinny's writing.'

Queenie put on her reading glasses and perched on the sofa. 'Never believe everything you read, boy. He could have been forced to write it.'

'What, like he was forced to confess the same to Ahmed that time, you mean?' Vinny shouted. 'Even on his deathbed, Ahmed was adamant Little Vinny killed Molly. Laughed in my face, he did.'

'Wouldn't surprise me if Eddie wants you out of the business and this is his way of achieving that. No way would Little Vinny do such a thing, neither would Ben

Bloggs. That poor little fucker might have been a bit simple, but he adored Molly and was brilliant with kids. Brought up his own brothers and sisters while that stinking whore of a mother of his was stood on street corners hawking her mutton. And Little Vinny's a brilliant father himself – far better than you and Michael, may I add.'

'Eddie wouldn't pull a stunt like this. He's my mate.'

'Where's Little Vinny now? It's him you should be talking to.'

'Nobody knows where he is.'

'Well, best you find him. And as for those Mitchells, blood is thicker than water, boy, never forget that.'

CHAPTER THIRTY-TWO

Queenie Butler lifted the doll out of the shoebox. 'Molly Dolly', Vinny had named her, after the pretty little angel she'd belonged to. Molly had taken a real shine to her, carried her everywhere, even to her death. Molly Dolly had been found covered in mud, not far from her granddaughter's lifeless body.

Tears rolled down Queenie's cheeks as she lifted Molly's favourite toy towards her nose. She thought she could still smell her granddaughter's scent. Or was that just wishful thinking? Pears soap she'd used to wash Molly with, had never been able to use it since. Too many memories, heartbreaking ones.

A lone tear rolled down Queenie's cheek. She had always known in her heart. That's why today wasn't as big a shock as it should have been. She had prayed she was wrong, but a tiny part of her had always wondered. Vivian had sensed it too, had made insinuations, but Jamie Preston's arrest put an end to all the gossip-mongers pointing their fingers at her grandson, and at the same time allowed her family to grieve in peace.

Little Vinny had been a rebellious teenager back then with not the nicest nature, but as he grew up, settled down with Sammi-Lou, then became a fantastic father and husband, Queenie's seed of doubt faded. It never totally vanished though and she'd been ever so scared when the police got their hands on a confession Ahmed had taped. Little Vinny had apparently admitted to killing Molly, but insisted Ahmed had held a gun to his head and forced him to say what he did as a ploy to get even with her Vinny. Queenie had always thought how far-fetched that sounded, but once again had convinced herself her grandson was innocent and Jamie deserved to rot in prison. What was the alternative? She'd already lost too many close family members and had no intention of losing another. Especially one who'd turned his life around in such a positive manner.

Queenie picked up the phone. She'd already tried to call Little Vinny four times, but his phone was switched off. Her Vinny had always drummed into her not to leave any incriminating information on answerphone machines, but for once Queenie had to take a risk. 'Boy, it's me. Now listen and listen carefully. Your father has heard rumours it was you who murdered Molly. He's on the warpath and out looking for you as we speak. When he finds you, you swear on your kids' lives that you didn't do it. If he doesn't believe you, he'll do away with you, boy. Killing your own blood is the biggest sin. And I know my Vinny, that little girl was his world.'

Vinny Butler placed the flowers in the vase at the base of his daughter's headstone. 'How are you today, sweetheart?' he asked, kissing her photograph. With her mop of blonde curls, sparkling eyes and amazing smile, Molly truly had resembled something angelic. She'd have been in her mid-twenties now, might have been married with kids of her own had some sick individual not denied her her future. 'I came here to apologize to you, Princess. Please forgive me. I know it was him now, your brother. So sorry I didn't protect you like I should've done,' Vinny wept.

'Aww, what a pretty child. Beautiful headstone too. I always notice how nice this plot is kept. I'm over here most days, you see. My son died at ten years old and he's buried just over there,' the woman pointed.

Not in the mood for exchanging pleasantries, Vinny wiped his eyes with the cuff of his Crombie and glared at the woman.

'Meningitis. You never get over it, do you? Just have to learn to live with it. Was Molly your child?'

'Yes, you nosy old cow. Well, she was until her older brother decided to put his hands around her throat and throttle her to death. Strange what life throws at you, isn't it?'

Shocked and not knowing what else to say, the woman mumbled, 'So sorry,' then scuttled off.

'Vin! How are you? I've missed you so much and been ever so worried about you,' Frankie Mitchell gushed, waving her hand as an indication for her father and brother to leave the room. She was shaking so much; she could barely hold the phone.

'Not great, Frankie. But I am going to get better. You alone? Where are the kids? Finn said Regan's back home, but I don't believe that. I think he's lying to me.'

'Finn wouldn't lie to you, Vin. Regan is home and he's absolutely fine. Harry's home too, so we can move away now. That was all that was stopping me upping sticks in the first place. I had to be here for my kid's return, you get that, don't you?'

'Put Regan on the phone. I don't believe you.'

Having pre-warned Regan this might happen, Frankie called him.

'Hello, Dad. We all miss you. Where are you? Can we come and visit?'

'Was it Jamie Preston who snatched you? Did he hurt you at all? Was his mate there too? It's so good to hear your voice.'

'I'm fine, Dad, honest. I don't know who took me, but there was only one man. I was scared and missed you all, then Georgie's granddad rescued me and brought me home,' Regan said, winking at Frankie. She'd told him to spin this particular yarn.

'OK, son. I'll see you soon. Put Frankie back on the blower.'

'See, I told you he was fine.'

'What happened to Jamie? And how did your dad get Regan back? How did he know where to find him?' His paranoia was spiralling out of control.

'It's a long story, Vin, but to cut it short, my old man tracked Jamie down and sent him packing. We won't be hearing from him any more, put it that way.'

'Is he dead?'

'I'll tell you more in person. Dad's told me not to say too much on the phone. Are you in Lincolnshire?'

'No.'

'Where are you then? I need to see you to sort out this move. I'm not living in some rubbish house. We'll choose something nice together.'

Having been sceptical at the start of the conversation, Little Vinny was now starting to trust and believe Frankie. 'Finn said you got rid of the letter. Where is it now? You didn't tell him what I wrote did you?'

Frankie's heart was beating like a drum, but she had to keep the façade up. 'I burned the letter because nobody needs to know now, do they? You were young, Vin, made a mistake, end of. It was an accident and accidents happen every day. I believe everything you've told me, although many wouldn't. But I love and know the real you, which is why I'm willing for us to make a fresh start. I never mentioned anything about what was in that letter to Finn or anybody else. Let's just forget about it now. Jamie's been dealt with and won't be bothering us no more, so we can move on with our lives as one big happy family.'

'I'd like that, and can you give my dad a message for me? It weren't Felicity at the police station with Terry. I remembered, the woman who was kind to me had dark hair. I think I recognized his girlfriend from dancing at his club.'

'You sure?'

'Yes. Just tell my dad Felicity ain't Old Bill. I got it wrong. He'll understand.'

'Will do,' Frankie continued to chat to Little Vinny as though everything was fine before asking the all-important question.

When Little Vinny happily reeled off an address, Frankie had tears in her eyes. If only he hadn't performed such a despicable deed in his youth, they probably could and would have been happy together.

'Let me make you a cup of tea, boy. Thanks for coming at such short notice,' Queenie Butler said.

Michael Butler yawned. Since Felicity's murder, he was suffering from insomnia and permanently felt knackered in the daytime. 'I can't stop, so don't worry about the tea. Got to be somewhere soon. What's the problem?'

'It's Little Vinny. I think his life's in danger.'

'What!'

Failing to mention that the allegation might well be true, Queenie told Michael what she wanted him to know. 'Not a cat in hell's chance Little Vinny did such a dreadful thing.

You've seen with your own eyes how wonderful he is with children. You need to get in touch with your brother and stop him from doing anything he'll regret.'

'Sorry, Mum, but I'm not getting involved. I've had enough of Vinny's dramas to last me a lifetime,' Michael spat. Vinny obviously hadn't told their mother he was meeting him later and he hoped this latest revelation wasn't about to balls his own plans up.

'That's not the way I brought you up, is it?'

'Unfortunately not.'

Queenie pursed her thin lips. 'And what is that supposed to mean?'

'It means I'm done with all this madness. It's time to forget about family business and concentrate on myself. My whole life has been a charade. Our family is like one big pantomime. Death, destruction, arguments and violence. It's over for me. I'm moving on.'

Queenie was shocked by Michael's harsh assessment, but was still determined to make him see sense. 'Your brother needs you right now. Those Mitchells are behind all this – I'm sure they're planning to stab Vinny in the back. You have to watch his back, be there in his hour of need. That's what brothers do.'

Michael stared defiantly into his mother's eyes. He loved her, of course; always would. But he could now see her for what she really was. A trouble-making, bitter, manipulative woman who always put herself and Vinny first. 'Vinny ain't my problem. He's your problem now. Oh, and I'd take my head out the sand, if I was you. Best thing I've ever done.'

When Michael turned his back on her and sauntered towards the front door, an incensed Queenie grabbed him by the back of his jacket. 'I brought you into this world, show some bloody respect. Don't you dare say such awful things, then walk out on me.'

Determined not to show his true emotions, Michael turned, kissed his mother on the cheek and uttered the words, 'Until we meet again.'

Vinny Butler listened attentively while Frankie Mitchell told her version of events. He'd turned up acting calm and politely asked Eddie and Joey if he could speak to Frankie alone. 'What exactly can you remember him saying while having these nightmares?' Vinny asked.

'He just said stuff like "Sorry, Molly" and "I didn't mean to kill you". He was such a good dad when I first met him, Vinny, the best. Nobody could get through to Georgie and Harry at the time, but Little Vinny connected with them. I know our relationship was odd because of Sammi-Lou and Stuart dying, but I truly fell for him and could see a big future together for us.'

Vinny ran his hand through his hair. Frankie had told him so much that could only have come from his son; any doubt or hope he'd had that it was all a misunderstanding, or that his mother was right and the Mitchells were in fact out to get him, had now vanished. 'So sorry he's ruined your life as well as mine and his sister's, Frankie.'

Frankie had fully expected Vinny to act like an arsehole towards her, but instead he'd been kind and considerate, which made her feel even sadder. 'If it makes this any easier, he swore blind that it was an accident. He said he was dangling Molly upside down when he realized she'd stopped breathing. He then tried to resuscitate her, but couldn't. I'm sure he was telling the truth, Vinny. I know that's not much of a consolation, mind.'

For once, Vinny Butler bit his lip. It was clear to see what an effect this had had on Frankie and how traumatized she was. His son was a liar, a born evil liar, because he remembered the coroner's report. Even the police had told him she'd been throttled to death on purpose. 'Tell me what he said about the day Molly went missing. I can't take hearing any more about her actual death, it breaks my heart. Did he say anything about why he took Molly in the first place?'

'Yes. He said you had split him up from his girlfriend by turning up at her door and telling her and her mum he was younger than what he'd said he was. I can't remember her name. Little Vinny was rambling when he told me all this.'

'Shazza. Her name was Shazza.'

'That's it. I remember it now. I think that's why he had the hump with you. He said he'd run away after that, but he couldn't forgive you for spoiling things for him at the time. He was also jealous of your relationship with Molly; I know that for a fact. He hinted on many an occasion, especially when he'd been drinking, that as a child he felt unloved, unwanted, and when Molly was born he felt like he didn't exist far as you were concerned. That's why he gave his sons equal attention, so he reckoned, although he did admit to me once that Oliver was his favourite. Sammi-Lou told me that too. She said he'd always doted on Oliver.'

'The day Molly went missing, did he say anything about a flood at the club?'

'Erm, let me think. It's all a bit blurred, but, yes, he did say something. I remember asking him how he'd managed to hand Molly over to Ben, and he said something about pulling a pipe out of the washing machine so it flooded the cellar. I might be wrong about that though. He could have said indoors, but it was definitely something to do with a flood and a washing machine. Does that make sense to you?'

The turmoil and loathing Vinny felt were overwhelming, but he managed to keep his emotions in check in front of Frankie. 'It makes perfect sense. Thanks so much for your time. I'll get out of your hair now.'

When Vinny stood up, Frankie did the same. 'The moment he gets in touch, I'll let my dad know.' Her father had told her not to tell Vinny his son had already called.

Vinny kissed Frankie's right cheek. 'Thanks, love.'

Frankie's eyes welled up. 'I'm so sorry.'

Vinny waited until Frankie was out of earshot before mumbling the words, 'Not half as sorry as that evil cunt of a son of mine will be when I get my hands on him.'

The cold February air chilling him to the bone, Michael Butler was shivering, yet sweating at the same time. Beads were forming on his forehead, but no way could he take off his crash helmet. Too risky with DNA so shit hot now.

'Hurry up, Vinny,' Michael mumbled. The lane was desolate, a dirt track that ended at a metal gate. The fields behind probably belonged to a farmer. Would it be that farmer who found Vinny's body? Michael wondered. Only he couldn't imagine many people walking down this particular dirt track, not even dog walkers. There was something eerie about it, and it wasn't too dissimilar to the one Vinny had ended Trevor Thomas's life in. That's how he and his brother had come across this spot in the first place; they'd driven around trying to find the perfect place to commit the perfect murder.

Finally, hearing the distinctive sound of an approaching vehicle, Michael's heart rate went into overdrive. Roxy Music's 'Jealous Guy' was blasting out the speakers. That was one thing Michael had never been: jealous of Vinny, or anyone else for that matter. What he was about to do had sod-all to do with envy, it was purely about wanting to lead a normal life, keep his family safe, and ensure no other woman met the same fate as Felicity. Nothing wrong with that, was there?

Michael stepped out of his hiding place among the trees

and lifted the plastic front of the helmet. His brother had already stepped out of the car to light a cigar.

'Bruv! You shit the life outta me then. Where's your motor? I'm so pleased you called.'

Hands trembling like leaves in the breeziest of winds, Michael lifted the gun. 'I'm sorry, Vinny, I really am. But I've got to do this before you bring us all down.'

Vinny was stunned, but after the day he'd had, he just laughed manically. 'And there was me thinking you were auditioning to be Evel Knievel.' He held his hands up. 'You can't be serious, Michael, not after all we've been through. This is a joke, right?'

'I wish it was. I love you; always will, but I don't like you. You're the bane of my life, have been for a long time.'

Realizing his little brother was serious, Vinny's eyes welled up. 'You're not thinking straight. What about Ava and Mum? I can't believe you would do this to them. I found out only today that Little Vinny killed Molly. Can you believe that? It's fucking true, I swear, bruv. Can you imagine what I'm going through right now? Drop the gun please, Michael. We can sort this another way.'

'No. I need to sort this once and for all. Champ, Roy, Oliver and Sammi-Lou are all dead because of you. Who'll be next to suffer while you end up walking away scot-free? My kids, perhaps?'

'Look, I know I've been a cunt at times, but from now on I'll change, I promise. I love you, Michael, and if you shoot me now you'll spend the rest of your life behind bars. Both Mum and Eddie know I was due to meet you here at nine, so how you gonna get out of this, eh?'

Sweating like a pig, Michael shook his head. 'You're lying. I've got an alibi.'

Vinny slung his phone at Michael's feet. 'Ring them. I'm not lying, I swear. I rung 'em both in the past hour,' he lied.

Michael raised the gun again, hands trembling.

'First time I've seen you in a crash helmet since you were a Mod. Remember me and Roy clubbing together and turning up on your sixteenth birthday with that Lambretta, do ya? Skint us back then, that did. But do you know why we went without ourselves for a few weeks to buy you it, and all those Mod clothes you wanted? Because you were our kid brother and we fucking adored you. Always had your back, I have, Michael. Please don't do this. You'll break the spine of our family. Don't you think they've been through enough already? Especially Mum. How's she gonna cope, losing me so soon after Auntie Viv being murdered?'

It was at that point that Michael Butler dropped the gun . . .

CHAPTER THIRTY-THREE

Having ordered Gary to take an early morning trip to Stock, Eddie Mitchell waited impatiently for his return. He'd told his son not to call him as he was worried the police might be tapping the phones because of Felicity's disappearance.

Ed had just put the kettle on to make himself another coffee, when he heard the crunch of tyres on his gravel. He bolted outside. 'Well?'

Gary shook his head. 'Gonna struggle to pull it off. Looks like a pokey little council house, and it isn't detached.'

'Oh, for fuck's sake! He told Frankie it was a big gaff, detached.'

Gary chuckled. 'Only kidding.'

Eddie clumped his son around the head. 'Grow up, will ya? This is hardly a laughing matter.'

'Sorry. Just thought I'd lighten the mood. The gaff is absolutely perfect, Dad. Got a long drive, plenty of trees and there are no security gates.'

'How close are the neighbours?'

'He hasn't got no neighbours. Very secluded. You wait until you see it. No cameras, nothing, just plenty of trees, bushes, and a long narrow drive. The perfect setting to commit murder.'

Eddie was a relieved man. He wasn't looking forward to later this evening, but sometimes in his world, things just had to be done.

Bella D'Angelo flipped the omelette with a big smile on her face. Michael had been distant with her recently, hadn't been coming around so often and, on the occasions he did, would insist he was too tired to make love.

Yesterday evening, Camila had been out with friends so Bella had cooked Michael a romantic candlelit meal. He'd turned up hours late, after ten o'clock, but they'd still had a wonderful evening, chatted and laughed like the old days. Then they'd ripped one another's clothes off and had passionate, wild sex. Their lovemaking had always been like that once upon a time, and Bella felt joyous today as she was sure they'd turned a corner. Antonio being around had never helped matters. But now he had gone off travelling, Bella secretly hoped Michael would move back in with her permanently, especially after last night.

Camila Butler grinned as her father came into the kitchen. 'Mum tells me you had a lovely romantic evening last night.'

Michael kissed his daughter on the cheek. 'Yeah. How was your evening?'

'Good. I went to Prezzo's, then back to a friend's house.'

'What would you like in your omelette, Michael?' Bella asked, handing a cheese and ham one to her daughter. She'd had a Spanish housekeeper when the children were growing up, but now liked to cook herself.

'I'm not hungry. Cami, take your omelette upstairs and eat it, babe. I need to have a chat with your mum.'

Wondering if her father was going to finally do the honourable thing and propose to her mother, Camila skipped happily up the stairs. Having said that, if her boyfriend ever proposed in a similar way, he'd be wearing the omelette, not eating it.

Noticing that Michael had an odd, deadpan expression on his face, Bella turned off the frying pan, sat at the table opposite him and held his hands. 'What's the matter?'

Michael snatched his hands away. 'I'm sorry, but I can't do this any more.'

'Do what?'

'This. Us. It isn't working for me.'

Bella's eyes glistened. 'How can you say that? Last night was amazing, just like old times. Now Antonio's not around, we can make this work, Michael. I know we can.'

Having mugged himself off in front of his brother last night, Michael was determined to redeem himself.

'But it ain't like old times, is it? And you know as well as I do, it never can be. I'll always love you, Bella, but I unfortunately can't forget. I have tried, believe me, really tried. But what happened just won't go away. It's imprinted in my brain.'

Bemused, Bella begged: 'Please don't do this, Michael. We can't change the past but we can change the future. We'll move away, if you like, start afresh somewhere. As long as I'm with you, I don't care where we are. I love you dearly, always have done. You and I are soulmates.'

Tears brimming, Michael smashed his fist on the table. 'Do you know what I visualize every time you're naked? Ask me, go on.'

'No. But I can probably guess what you're going to say. Please don't go over old ground, Michael. We need to move forward.'

'My brother's cock up your cunt, that is all I can think of. Big, was it? Suck it an' all, did ya? Now can you see why I've got to call it a day?'

'That's a disgusting thing to say, Michael. No need for that. Way below the belt.'

Michael stared Bella in the eye for what would probably be the very last time. 'But it's true. Look, I'm sorry, I truly am. But it's over. This time for good.'

Vinny Butler sat up and put his thumping head in his hands. After holding it together so well yesterday daytime, he'd got completely obliterated last night after his own brother had tried to kill him. He truly couldn't understand how Michael could hate him so much. Not when he'd always loved him. It was confusing, to say the very least. But no more confusing than Little Vinny killing Molly. How could his own blood do such a thing?

Most of Molly's things were at his mother's house, but he'd kept a shoebox of memories himself. He'd never looked at them as the thought upset him too much – until last night. That's when he'd found the poem Little Vinny had made up and read out at Molly's funeral, and it had literally sent him over the edge.

Spotting the poem lying on his bedside cabinet, Vinny snatched at it.

I miss you more than words can say,
and blame myself every single day.
As your big brother I should have protected you more,
But I fell asleep and you walked out the door.

I hope that God will take good care of you,
and love you as much as your family do.
Life will never be the same without you Molly,
and I hope you are playing in heaven with your favourite dolly.

That wicked boy who took you away,
will pay for his evil sins one day.
Until that time I want you to know,
that me, Dad, Nanny, Auntie Viv and Uncle Michael all loved you so.

Vinny screwed the poem up in his hand. 'Well, you were right about one thing, you evil little shitcunt. That wicked boy who took Molly away will pay for his sins, sooner than he fucking thinks.'

Gary Mitchell stuffed half a rasher of bacon in his mouth. 'So what's the plan of action?' he asked his father.

'I'm gonna ring Vinny in a bit. Tell him Finn's been in touch and Little Vinny's promised he'll ring Frankie today before seven. I'm worried he'll go on a bender otherwise. He'll stay alert and off the sauce, see, if I give him that news early doors. Was there any lighting up that driveway?'

'Not that I saw. Obviously there might be some up near the front door, but I didn't venture that far.'

'Nobody clocked your car this morning, did they?'

'Yeah, I parked it right outside the gaff,' Gary said facetiously.

'Stop with the comedy act, Gal. Today of all days, you prick. None of this is funny, lad. It's serious stuff.'

'Heard and understood. Did you and Vinny discuss how you're gonna do the deed?'

Eddie nodded.

'Silly man,' Gary uttered.

Eddie pushed his virtually untouched breakfast to one side. 'I'll give him a call now.'

Queenie Butler was beside herself. She'd rung Vinny, Michael and Little Vinny numerous times, but none of them had answered even though she'd left messages ordering them to do so.

With Michael's harsh words still ringing in her ears, Queenie stared at a photo of him, stony-faced. She could remember the day that photo was taken so clearly. Michael was a Mod back then and for his sixteenth birthday, Vinny and Roy had clubbed together to buy him a Lambretta. It had been snowing, and she'd found out the day before that womanizing old wanker she'd married had been servicing Judy Preston on the side. It hadn't stopped her from smiling in the photo though, and Vinny and Roy looked so fresh-faced and handsome in their smart suits. Vivvy was in the photo too, so it must have been Lenny who'd taken it.

Turning the page, Queenie felt melancholy. There was a photo of Daniel, Lee and Adam sitting on her lawn eating ice-lollies. The elder two were pulling funny faces, but Adam was beaming, bless him; he must have only been about four then. Another one whose life was taken far too soon, under the wheels of a District Line train. Of all the ways to die, Queenie thought bitterly.

The next page cheered Queenie up no end. These photos were taken at Kings Holiday Park in Eastbourne. The opening night of the upstairs club and Prince Charles and the Three Degrees did the honours. So funny that was, especially when Vivvy had lunged at Prince Charles after too many sherries in desperation for a photo with him. She'd nearly knocked the poor man flying. He'd looked at them in horror after that, had Charles. Even though Queenie informed him, 'Excuse me! I'll have you know I'm Whitechapel's equivalent to your mother and Vivian is my sister.'

The next page made Queenie laugh even louder. Viv was in a deckchair and Chester the moggy she'd loathed who belonged to that awful Baker family next door was staring at Viv, giving her the evil eye.

Turning the page again, Queenie mumbled, 'Ahh.' Ava was sitting on her conservatory step hugging Fred the dog. Inseparable, those two had been. Viv had loathed the creature. She used to call him 'Ratpig' and a 'bastard nuisance'. Queenie smiled as she recalled some of Fred's antics. He had such a funny character, but was a little sod at the same time. She'd never forget that day when she took him over the park and it took her over two hours to catch him. He hadn't run away, just refused to go back on his lead. Would sit twenty yards away with an evil glint in his eye and a catch-me-if-you-can expression on his smug little face. A neighbour ended up catching him with a hot chicken fillet, and Queenie gave him such a kick up the arse when she got him indoors. She'd never let him off the lead after that. But it thoroughly annoyed her when Vinny or Ava did and he'd trot back to them like a little angel. It was as though he took the piss out of her, knew he had her right under his little paw. Fred Butler, what a legend. Queenie would do anything to give him a cuddle again now, and her Viv. Life changes in a blink at times and you don't realize what you had until it's gone.

The doorbell made Queenie jump. Hoping it was one of her boys, she looked out the window. There was no car. Hating uninvited visitors, Queenie huffed and puffed her way into the hallway. 'Yes,' she shrieked, yanking open the front door.

Standing on the doorstep was a stunning blonde girl with dark shades on. 'Queenie, it's me.'

Queenie put her hand over her mouth. She looked so different. 'Roxanne!'

'Yes, can I come in?'

'Of course you can.'

Roxanne smiled and turned her back. In that split second, Queenie's heart lurched out of her chest. The reason being, she'd spotted a pram . . .

Frankie Mitchell handed her father a mug of tea. 'Do you reckon he will kill Little Vinny?'

Eddie shrugged. 'It's none of my business, love. Well, obviously it is my business to an extent, as you got caught up in it. But how Vinny intends to deal with his son is his call.'

'Are you going with him tonight?'

'No,' Eddie lied.

'Why not?'

'Because it's family business, Frankie. I never involved Vinny in our feud with the O'Haras, did I?'

'No. I suppose not. He was really nice to me yesterday.'

'Who was?'

'Big Vinny. I wasn't sure about him at first, but I genuinely like him now. I would hate him to get arrested for killing his son after all he's been through.'

'I couldn't agree more. Excuse me a sec, darlin'. Need to make an important phone call.'

Eddie left the room and gently tapped his head against the hallway wall. He just wanted this to be over with now, quickly.

Queenie gasped as she took the baby's woolly hat off. 'Oh my God! The resemblance is uncanny.' The child was a boy and already had a mop of thick, black hair. It was curly, which was also unusual. Queenie scrutinized the child and put her little finger inside his tiny hand. Thankfully he looked and seemed to be reacting normal. 'He's a beauty, Roxanne. How old is he?'

'Three weeks and five days. He was a big baby, weighed over nine pound.'

Queenie sat on the sofa. Whatever the circumstances, she was already besotted. The child was a Butler. 'Look at you, you're a little belter, aren't you?' she smiled.

'I'm finding it difficult, Queenie. I do love him, but I don't know how to be a mum. You were the only person I could ask for help who I trust. You won't tell anybody I'm here, will you?'

'No, lovey. Not if you don't want me to. But your dad's been worried. So we need to tell him you're OK at some point. But not now. How did you know where to find me?'

'I rang Alex and she told me your address. She said she'd bumped into you in some shopping centre and you'd given her your new phone number and address in case I got in touch.'

'That's right. Bumped into her in Lakeside last year. Your hair looks nice by the way. Suits you blonde.'

'Thanks. I am a natural blonde, but I dyed my hair to disguise myself not long before I met Daniel. How is he, Queenie? I'm so sorry for telling porkies about my age and identity, but I was only trying to protect myself. I didn't have a clue Michael was my father or that I had an older brother. My mam lied to me all my life, so did the man pretending to be my dad, and my nan and granddad. I couldn't believe it when my mam burst into that registry office. I was gobsmacked.'

Queenie cringed. Just the thought of that occasion made her feel sick to the stomach. In a nutshell, fate had brought Daniel and Roxanne together, then ripped them apart in the cruellest way possible. 'Nobody has heard from Daniel since the day of the wedding, love. All we know is he's gone abroad somewhere and Lee followed him out there.'

'Has Lee left his wife?'

'Yes. Right in the lurch. She couldn't afford that house on her own. Michael told me she's moved back in with her parents. Still, not his problem. A blessing they never had kids, I suppose.'

'Unlike me,' Roxanne said sadly.

Queenie moved seats. Cradling the baby with one hand, she put the other around Roxanne. 'I'm your nan, here to help, and you can talk to me about anything. Does the baby seem normal to you? You know what I mean, don't you, love?'

'No. What do you mean? I've never had a baby before, have I? It seems weird, you being my nan. And it still hasn't sunk in that Michael's my dad yet. I barely know the man. What's he like, Queenie?'

'Hold this beautiful boy of yours and I'll bring out the photo albums. You're not in a rush to get off, are you?'

'No. Actually, I was hoping I could stay with you. Not for long, just a few days. I've been chucked out of the accommodation I was living in.'

Queenie stroked her granddaughter's beautiful blonde hair. She was still a child herself, bless her. Poor kid looked anxious and lost and obviously had no idea that her own baby could turn out to be very abnormal. Joyce had looked it up on the internet for Queenie. Children born in incestual relationships tended to be backward and look odd. 'You can stay as long as you like, sweetheart. And I won't tell a soul you're here, I promise. Be our little secret, eh? I'll tell you all you need to know about your family an' all. And my, oh my, back in the day we were such a big family. A real force to be reckoned with,' Queenie bragged wistfully.

Roxanne kissed her nan on the cheek. 'Thank you. I'd like that very much.'

Vinny Butler was sitting in his office, impatiently tapping his fingers against the table while watching the news. He'd heard nothing more from Eddie yet and just wanted to get this over and done with. There'd been no word from Michael since he'd driven off last night like a Barry Sheene wannabe.

'For fuck's sake,' Vinny mumbled as news of yet another terrorist attack was brought to the nation. Since that attack on America last September when planes had flown into the Twin Towers and other targets, you heard little else on the news these days. Today's attack was a bomb left in a sports bag at a train station. It had killed thirteen people and injured numerous others, some critically.

Debating whether to ring his mother back, Vinny decided not to. This whole Felicity saga had made him paranoid that all his phones might be tapped, and he was pissed off with his mum for leaving lots of stupid messages earlier referring to Little Vinny. She hadn't said anything too incriminating, but if the Old Bill were listening they were bound to guess there was some kind of drama going on. Time and time again, Vinny had urged his mother not to leave messages unless they were asking questions such as what he wanted for dinner. With what he was about to do, he really did not need her interference. Eddie had come up with a great plan and he'd square things with his mother afterwards. She'd believe him too, he was sure about that.

His phone bursting into life made Vinny jump. He'd had adrenalin pumping through his veins all day. 'Well?'

'Meet me in half an hour, mate. Where we arranged,' Eddie Mitchell replied.

Vinny Butler ended the call and took a deep breath. 'Gotcha, ya cunt.'

Little Vinny stepped out of the shower and studied himself in the mirror. His hair was growing back now, but had no style and he'd yet to sort his teeth out. But Frankie still loved him, so that's all that mattered. Now Jamie was out of the equation and he, Frankie and the kids were moving away, he would spruce himself up again, be the kind of man he'd been while with Sammi-Lou and forget about the past once more.

Cutting the labels off the clothes he'd purchased earlier, Little Vinny smiled. Tonight was going to be a special evening. He could feel it in his bones.

Eddie felt uneasy as he hung around in the quiet lane near his home. It was literally a stone's throw from where Tony Tucker, Patrick Tate and Craig Rolfe had met their makers in what was now described as the 'Rettendon Murders'. Eddie hadn't known the men involved personally, but he'd known of them. It gave him an eerie feeling that what went wrong that night for them could also happen to him. They'd met their deaths in a dark Range Rover, and that's what Vinny Butler drove.

When Vinny pulled up minutes later, he was surprisingly jovial. 'Those bastard terrorists want stringing up. Been another attack with thirteen dead. This one weren't a suicide bomber, it was an unattended bag. Dunno what the world's coming to, do you? Gone are the days when we were young and you could look at an unattended bag and think "Result!" Be frightened to pick the fucking thing up these days, eh?'

Eddie chuckled falsely. ''Ere, I've got some news for you. I found out who was sending us that crap.'

'What crap?'

'The bible quotes and dead creatures.'

'Dave Newton?'

'No. Turns out it was the pikeys. Harry overheard his uncle talking about it,' Eddie informed Vinny, studying his reaction carefully.

'No fucking way! You sure? I was positive it was Dave Newton. I reckon Harry's winding you up?'

'Nah, he ain't, Vin. So it was nothing to do with Felicity after all, poor cow. Hope they find her soon. Oh, and when Little Vinny spoke to Frankie on the phone, he mentioned Felicity too. Said something about he got it wrong – she ain't Old Bill. Told Frankie to tell you. Weird shit. Has he lost his marbles perhaps, d'ya think?'

'More than likely,' Vinny mumbled.

'I bet you're dreading this evening. You're much chirpier than I expected you to be, if I'm honest, mate.'

Vinny clenched Eddie's arm. 'I'm telling ya, pal, if you'd have found that poem that horrid little cunt made up and read out at Molly's funeral, you'd be chirpy too, trust me.'

When Vinny turned on to the main road, Eddie stared solemnly out of the window. This was going to be far more difficult than he'd anticipated.

Queenie was eaten up with worry, but was trying to take her mind off the inevitable by talking constantly. The baby was so bonny, she'd fallen in love with him. But that didn't alter the fact his parents were blood relations. It was sickening, and so bloody sad. What hope in life would there be for that poor little mite? And Roxanne didn't seem to have taken to motherhood at all, which was hardly surprising, considering her age and the circumstances. What Queenie couldn't understand though was why the girl had gone through with the pregnancy in the first place. Not only was it terribly wrong, it was so unfair on the child and the rest of the family.

'Show me some more photos, Queenie. Daniel never told me much about our family. I've learned far more off you already,' Roxanne grinned. She was captivated, listening to stories about a family she was part of, and was already beginning to understand herself a bit better. No wonder she'd always had a fixation with the East End of London and the underworld, even though she'd attended a school in the North East. It was obviously in her genes.

Squeezing Roxanne's arm, Queenie said gently, 'I think we need to have a little chat about your situation first. You've not even told me this bonny lad's name yet.'

'He hasn't got one.'

'What do you mean, he hasn't got one?'

'I was going to call him Daniel, then I changed my mind. I can't register him, can I? They'll find out my real age and identity, then they'll take him away from me and send me back home. I don't ever want to go back home, Queenie. I hate my mum. This is all her fault.'

'What name did you give at the hospital?'

'What hospital?'

'The one you gave birth in.'

'I gave birth at my friend's house. She helped me and cut the cord. It was so painful; I thought I was going to die. I never want any more children,' Roxanne said, tears rolling down her cheeks.

'Oh, lovey. Poor you,' Queenie replied dismally. 'So you've not had him checked over or anything yet?'

Roxanne shook her head.

'Oh dear Lord. Why didn't you just choose the easy way out, love? You must have known things were going to be difficult. Surely a termination would've been a more sensible option, wouldn't it?'

'I couldn't, because I love Daniel. I know we can never be together, but I will always love him, Queenie. This child is his.'

Little Vinny poured himself a glass of red wine. He'd been good today. This was his first drink and last night when

Frankie told him she still wanted to be with him, he'd poured the remainder of the cocaine down the toilet. That stuff didn't agree with him anyway; messed with his mind.

Today, Little Vinny had busied himself by going to Lakeside. He'd felt a bit paranoid at first, but was determined to overcome his fears. He'd bought dinner and drinks for this evening in Marks and Spencer. Then he'd shopped for a couple of new outfits and, most importantly, the ring.

Opening the small velvet box again, Little Vinny smiled. Sammi-Lou was his past, Frankie Mitchell was his future, and he could not wait for them to be married now. Perhaps his sons could be best men and Georgie and Harry could be bridesmaid and page boy? Now that would be the perfect wedding.

Eddie Mitchell urged Vinny to slow down a bit. Although he'd taken a drive out here earlier to get his bearings, he made a show of looking lost. 'I don't know this area too well, do you? I hope we haven't gone past it,' he lied.

Vinny had chosen not to use his satnav just in case of anything going wrong and the police tapping into his history. 'Nice round 'ere. I fancy moving out this way. Nearer work and me mum. I might ring some estate agents tomorrow, start the ball rolling. Pal of mine lives in Stock an' all. Good lad is Mad Mark.'

Knowing they were nearing the property, Eddie took his phone out of his pocket.

'I think that's it there. Gotta be, I reckon,' Vinny announced jovially. He was still reeling over Michael trying to kill him, but determined to put on a front. No way could he ever tell a soul that one, Eddie included. Mugged him right off as a person. People saw the Butlers as a force, for fuck's sake. As for what Little Vinny had done, yesterday had to go down as one of the worst days of Vinny's life without a doubt.

'Yeah, that's it. Ashbourne House. Right, drive down the road and pull over somewhere while I ring Frankie. Keep schtum 'cause I haven't told her anything other than to ring him.' Eddie punched in his daughter's number.

'You all right, Dad?' Frankie asked. She was on edge this evening. Something bigger was going down than her father was letting on, she was sure of that.

'Call him in five, love. Just say you can't find the gaff and you're lost. Ask him to walk down to the bottom of the drive so you can see him.'

'Where are you, Dad? Is Vinny with you?'

'Don't ask questions, Frankie, just do as you're told. Any problems, I'm on the spare phone.'

Vinny's breathing became more laboured. He'd tried not to think about it all day, but the time had come to say farewell to his first-born. Loved that boy, he had. But there was no forgiving what he'd done. Molly was his little angel and kill for her, he would.

Little Vinny put on his trainers and opened the front door. There were no lights along the drive, which was a pain. It was a shame he hadn't thought of buying one of those heavy-duty torches while in Lakeside.

Nearing the entrance, Little Vinny's initial thought was that Frankie had borrowed her father's car as a big four-by-four came towards him with its full beam on. Temporarily blinded, Little Vinny put his hand across his eyes to protect them, then screamed as his father leapt out of the car, grabbed him and put his hand over his mouth. 'Dad, what you doing? Where's Frankie?' Little Vinny spluttered.

'Walk nicely, you little cunt,' Vinny hissed.

'Good luck, mate. I'll be waiting out here for you,' Eddie

said, as Vinny grabbed the sports bag out the boot. Vinny had wanted him to go inside the house as well, but Ed had flatly refused.

Little Vinny's eyes resembled that of a startled deer. Had Frankie tricked him? Or was she still coming?

Once inside, Vinny ordered his son to sit on the scruffy-looking armchair. It was so tempting to put his hands around his son's throat and choke him to death, just as the shitbag had with Molly. But that would implicate him, and Vinny was far too clever for that.

Little Vinny was petrified. It was obvious his father knew about Molly. 'Where's Frankie?' he asked again in no more than a stunned whisper.

'Indoors. You didn't honestly think she'd want to spend the evening with a child killer, did you?' Vinny spat.

Little Vinny put his head in his hands and rocked to and fro. 'I'm so sorry. Loved Molly, I did, and I wanted to tell you for ages, even when it happened. But I was scared they'd lock me up as well as Ben. He didn't mean to kill her. I was there and saw it. It was an accident. Ben loved Molly too.'

Unable to stop himself, Vinny grabbed his son by the neck. 'Don't fucking lie – I know it was you who did it. Tell me the truth, you owe me that much at least.'

When Little Vinny burst into tears, Vinny paced the room rambling and shouting. 'Gave you everything, I did. You wanted for nothing. How could you do that to any child? Let alone your own little sister. You're vermin, the scum of the earth. Then you try and blame your mate. No wonder that poor fucker killed himself. Hanging from a tree is preferable to knocking about with you. You disgust me. I fucking loathe you. You're sick, weak and evil, that's what you are. And you let another bloke do life for a crime he did not commit.'

Little Vinny was inconsolable. This truly was his worst nightmare. 'I didn't mean it, Dad, honest I didn't. It was a game that went wrong. I loved Molly. She was my sister.'

'Game! I'll give you a fucking game,' Vinny bellowed, punching his son in the face. 'Now for once in your sorry bastard life have the decency to tell the truth. I wanna know how Molly died and why you did it.'

Little Vinny could not look his father in the eye and instead stared at his feet. Then Ben and Molly's voices appeared in his head again, so he told his father what they were saying. It was better coming from them rather than him.

'So, you throttled the living daylights out of your beautiful little sister because you was jealous. How did I create such a monster, eh? What did I do so bad in life to be blessed with such a son?' Vinny bellowed. He had never felt so sick in his whole life. Was gobsmacked, totally.

'I can't tell you how ashamed of myself I am, Dad. You have to believe me.'

'You didn't tease or torment her, did you? You know, just before she died.'

Little Vinny shook his head.

'Answer me properly,' Vinny screamed, clouting his son once more. He was crying now, couldn't stop himself. The thought of how scared his little princess must've been as her evil brother ended her life was far too much for him to cope with.

'No. It was quick. Molly never knew anything was amiss until I put my hands around her throat. I swear she thought it was a game. But then she did look scared. I've never been able to get that image out of my mind. I was out of my nut when it happened, had been drinking, puffing and sniffing glue. Something inside me just snapped. It was like I had these voices in my head, telling me to do it. I'm so sorry. I look back now and can't believe what I did. It's like I was a different person back then.'

'Once evil, always evil, boy. Now you're going to write a letter for me.'

'What! Why?'

'Don't ask questions! Just fucking do as I say,' Vinny spat, handing his son a pad and pen.

'What do you want me to put?'

Little Vinny had tears rolling down his cheeks as he put pen to paper. His number was up, he knew that much. All he could think of was Calum and Regan. They'd be fatherless as well as motherless and they didn't deserve that. Orphans, with nobody to take care of them. He didn't want that turncoat Frankie anywhere near them. That bitch could rot in hell now for all he cared.

'Read it back to me,' Vinny ordered.

Dear Calum and Regan,
If you are reading this letter it means I am dead. I am so sorry to you both for choosing the easy way out, but I just couldn't carry on living a lie. The truth is, I cannot get over losing your mum and Oliver. I tried to be strong for your sake, put on a brave face, but inside I was a heartbroken wreck suffering from severe depression. I want you to remember I will always love you and be looking down on you every day.

Until we meet again,

Dad xx

PS Tell my dad, Nan and Uncle Michael I love them and I'm sorry too.

Vinny marched his son around the house looking for the perfect spot. There wasn't one, so he picked up the sports bag and settled for the garage. 'Right, this'll do.'

'No, Dad. Please don't. I'm still your son, and I've changed.'

Vinny Butler was devoid of emotion as he tied the rope on to the large hook that hung from the ceiling.

'Dad, don't kill me. I'm a different person now. A good person. My boys, they mean the world to me. I'll never see them grow up. I'll move away, you won't ever have to see me again, I promise. Please, let me live. Not for my sake, but for Calum and Regan's. Please, Dad,' Little Vinny wept. 'Mean the world to me, my boys. I want to see them get married and have kids themselves.'

Taking no notice of his son's cries for forgiveness, Vinny coldly ordered him to climb up the ladder. He had worn latex gloves throughout, and doubted the death would look suspicious anyhow.

'Dad, noooo,' Little Vinny screamed, as his father pushed his backside up the ladder.

'Walk,' Vinny spat.

Little Vinny sobbed as he reluctantly put the rope around his neck. 'I love you and I'm sorry, Dad,' he genuinely told his father.

'What goes around comes around. Remember your sister winning that talent competition, do ya? Singing the chorus to "You Are My Sunshine"?' Vinny callously kicked the ladder away from under his son's feet.

Hearing his son's neck snap, Vinny crouched on his haunches. Visions of Little Vinny in his first school uniform, playing happily with his toys at Christmas, and singing at the street party in Whitechapel they'd held in honour of the Queen's Jubilee came flooding back as Vinny stared at his son hanging lifeless on that rope, a lone tear running down his cheek.

Vinny stayed frozen for a minute or so before picking up the sports bag. 'Goodbye, son.'

*

Eddie Mitchell was having a hot sweat. Vinny was taking far longer than he'd anticipated and he just wanted this to be over with. The wait was prolonging the agony.

Finally, the garage door opened and Vinny came walking towards him. Eddie stepped out of the Range Rover. 'All done?'

'Yes, mate. Was tougher than I thought it would be, to be honest. I did love him, you know, I suppose part of me always will. He was my first-born.'

Eddie felt incredibly emotional as he pointed the gun in Vinny's direction. He'd put the headlights of the motor on so he could see clearly.

'Ed, what ya doing?' The shocked expression on Vinny's face was clear to see. Yesterday Michael and now Eddie. Were they having a laugh with him? Trying his patience, or what?

'I'm so sorry, pal. I thought the world of you at one point, really didn't want things to end this way, but you dug your own grave, unfortunately.'

Rooted to the spot, Vinny held his hands in the surrender position. 'Is this some kind of sick joke? Only it ain't very funny, Ed. What the hell am I meant to have done?'

'I know what you did to that poor woman. I know every single, sordid detail.'

'Dunno what or who you mean,' Vinny snapped brazenly.

'Yes, you fucking do! Don't lie to me. Makes you no different to your son. I had a chat with Michael, forced the truth out of him.'

Realizing very quickly by the look on Eddie's face that he was going to be far less of a pushover than Michael, Vinny came clean. 'All right. Look, I'm sorry, mate, for lying to you. I honestly thought her bloke was behind those threats and she was Old Bill, that's why she had to go. I went too far, I know that now. But Michael got the wrong end of the stick when he accused me of trying to rape her. I was on top of her, I'll admit to that. But I was only trying to pull her teeth out.' No way was Vinny going to mention the baby, as whatever Michael had blabbed, he very much doubted he would mention that.

'And what about Ava's mum, Joanna? And Little Vinny's mum, Karen? You see, I know about those an' all, mate. Michael can be quite the chatterbox at times, you know.'

Absolutely stunned by his brother's betrayal, Vinny sank to his knees. 'Once a Butler, always a Butler',Vinny could hear his mother's voice as clear as a bell, 'A grass is worse than a sewer rat', 'Whatever the stormy weather, you boys stick together' – the sayings his mother had drummed into himself, Roy and Michael as kids were ringing in his ears. She used to make up her own bedtime tales and quote them regularly. How could Michael do this to him? Vinny knew he'd never truly forgiven him over Bella, but he'd never had him down as a backstabber. Not his brother. 'What you done to Michael? Did you force him to put a gun to my head last night? Where is he now?'

'Answer my question first and I'll tell you.'

'Yes, I made 'em both go away. Karen was a fucking junkie and Joanna denied me years of knowing Ava even existed. Now tell me what you've done to my brother?'

Eddie crouched ten feet away from Vinny, gun still firmly in hand. 'As if your Michael would ever snitch on you. I've not even seen the bloke. And if he really did put a gun to your head last night, it's a shame he never pulled the fucking trigger. As I said, you've dug your own grave, Vinny.'

Fire in his eyes, Vinny Butler leapt up. 'You cunt. You backstabber. This been your plan all along, has it, Mitchell?'

Vinny coming towards him as bold as brass while he was holding a gun wasn't something Eddie had prepared himself for. 'Never. Unlike you, I've got some morals.'

Laughing manically, Vinny Butler held his hands in the air. 'Kill me then. Go on, shoot me. What you waiting for, Christmas?'

Eddie Mitchell felt sad. It was clear now that Vinny was a madman. He couldn't even see that he'd done wrong, felt no remorse whatsoever for the things he'd done to those poor women.

'Backstabber,' Vinny hissed, as he edged closer, waving his arms in the air.

Things not going to plan, Eddie held the gun aloft, positioned himself as best he could to aim where he wanted and mumbled the words, 'Sorry, mate.'

Seconds later, he pulled the trigger.

CHAPTER THIRTY-FOUR

Three Days Later

Eddie Mitchell shut the office door and sat at his desk. A few days had passed since he'd unfortunately had to end the association with his business partner, and as far as Eddie was aware neither Vinny or Little Vinny's bodies had yet been found. That didn't worry Eddie. It wasn't as though a postman would be delivering letters for Little Vinny, was it? And the gaff was in a very remote area.

Eddie considered himself to be handy with a firearm. But because Vinny had shown no fear when staring death in the face, he hadn't been able to pinpoint the exact spot he'd hoped to. The side of the head was where the bullet should have lodged, but with Vinny coming towards him like a madman, waving his arms in the air, Eddie had no choice but to shoot there and then. The bullet had entered the side of Vinny's neck and he'd immediately gone down like a sack of potatoes. Before losing consciousness, he'd managed to utter two words: 'Backstabber' followed quickly by 'Mum'. Eddie had then checked his pulse and, satisfied he was a goner, placed the gun in Vinny's right hand. The plan had been to make the crime scene look as if Vinny had found out about his son murdering Molly, forced him to write a suicide note, then hung the lad and killed himself. Whether the police would now see it that way, Eddie did not know. But even if they suspected Vinny had been gunned down, the filth had no reason to suspect him. That's why he'd been so determined not to go inside the house; his DNA could easily have been found. And he'd been clever with his outfit too. He'd told Vinny he was dressing casual and he should do the same himself. Unbeknown to Vinny, he'd worn a pair of size twelve trainers instead of his usual size tens and stuffed the front with scrunched-up socks. That would cover his arse if any footprints were found. It had rained heavily the last couple of days too, so Ed very much doubted any evidence would be discovered. Only in Vinny's Range Rover, and that didn't matter. They were business partners and, in the eyes of the police, best pals who were always travelling around in each other's motors, so of course his DNA would be inside the vehicle.

After the shooting, Gary had picked Eddie up in a prearranged spot. He hadn't used his own vehicle but a hooky one that had since ceased to exist. Ed's tracksuit and trainers had gone up in flames that same evening too. You could never be too careful when committing a crime. And even if the Old Bill did suspect foul play, Vinny had upset so many people over the years it could have been any bastard taking a pop at him. The police loathed Vinny with a passion, would probably want to shake their hand and congratulate his killer rather than arrest him. Eddie doubted very much the police would put too much effort into this investigation, and with a bit of luck, even if they did, they'd tie Felicity's disappearance in with it too. They might not be able to prove it, but they knew that Vinny had done that poor woman in – another reason to take his own life, perhaps? He knew the net was closing in on him so to speak, so chose the Vinny Butler way out.

Pouring himself a Scotch, Eddie stared at the photo of himself and Vinny that had pride of place on the wall. It had been taken out the front on opening night. Knowing it was time to put the final part of his plan into place, Eddie picked up his phone. 'Hello, my name is Eddie Mitchell. I'd like to speak personally with Chief Inspector Terry, please. It's regarding the murder of Molly Butler. I know it's a case he worked on in the past and some new information has come to light that I'm sure the Chief Inspector will be interested in. I'd also like to report a missing person. My business partner hasn't been seen for three days now. His phone's been switched off and he's had no contact with his family either. It's very unusual behaviour. His name is Vinny Butler.'

Queenie Butler was beside herself with worry. She'd always promised Vinny not to involve the police if he went missing, but the not knowing where he was was driving her insane.

Debating whether to contact the police for the third time today, Queenie decided against it. 'Mum, if I ever go AWOL and I haven't been in touch with you for a week, seven whole days, you know I'm dead. But under no circumstances do you ever involve the filth before that time,' her son had always insisted. And nobody knew her eldest as well as Queenie did. Chances are, Little Vinny had admitted the truth and Vinny had him holed up somewhere, torturing him slowly day by day.

'Queenie, you know when I first arrived and you picked the baby up and said the resemblance was uncanny, did you mean Daniel?' Roxanne asked.

Queenie sighed. Her granddaughter's obsession with Daniel hadn't faded. She'd been bombarding Queenie with questions about her brother since first thing this morning. 'No, love. I meant my Vinny. He was born with black curly hair. In fact, I've never seen a baby before that looks so much like my Vinny did. It's the Butler genes, I suppose.'

'Oh, OK,' Roxanne replied, her tone one of obvious disappointment.

Queenie had the number of a private doctor that Vinny used. He was very trustworthy; a lot of villains used him for bits and bobs, so Queenie had invited him round to check over the baby the previous day. Thankfully, everything seemed fine with the poor little mite. 'He's crying, lovey. Wants his mumma. Why don't you pick him up, give him a cuddle?' Roxanne hadn't shown any affection whatsoever towards the child since she'd arrived and that worried Queenie immensely. What sort of life would that poor little sod have when he left hers? And how the hell was Roxanne going to cope alone? She was only bloody fifteen herself. Vinny would've known how to handle this, Queenie thought sadly, willing the phone to ring.

Roxanne stood up and gave her grandmother a hug instead. 'No. You pick him up. He likes you, Queenie. I can tell.'

Queenie pursed her thin lips. It had been a good distraction, having Roxanne and the baby present, but she was losing her patience slightly now. The longer it went without hearing from Vinny, the harder she was finding life. 'I know how tough this must have been for you, sweetheart, but please start calling me Nan instead of Queenie. Because that's what I am, isn't it? And Daniel isn't your boyfriend any more, so you have to forget about him as such. He's your brother, isn't he?'

'Yes, I suppose so,' Roxanne replied sadly.

Queenie picked the baby up and held him to her chest. Never had she seen a baby who looked so much like a child of hers. She turned to Roxanne. 'Seeing as this little bruiser doesn't have a name yet, I think we should call him Baby Blue.'

'Would you like any drinks or snacks, sir?'

Michael Butler smiled at the pretty air stewardess. 'Scotch on the rocks and a packet of plain crisps please, sweetheart.'

'There you go, sir. Enjoy your flight.'

Feeling happier and more relaxed than he had in ages, Michael stared out of the window. Charley Rideout had been the last bird he'd had to dump, and she'd taken the news reasonably well, all things considered. She was still adamant she was keeping his baby though, which was a pain in the arse. But Michael had offered to pay maintenance, although he doubted he'd see much of the child. Not now he'd decided to up sticks and move abroad.

The letter had arrived last week and since then Michael had been running around like a blue-arsed fly, trying to tie up loose ends. Vinny was the one loose end he hadn't managed to tie up, but he was relieved about that in a way. Whatever Vinny's faults, he was still his brother and killing him could well have tortured his soul for many years. Michael smiled, he truly couldn't wait to see Daniel and Lee again. Had already promised he was going to move out there permanently so the three of them could set up a business together. And he'd already sold his share of the West End casino he owned to his business partner, which was a bonus.

Thinking of his family, Michael felt no remorse. His mother had bombarded him with phone calls these past few days. Vinny was on the missing list, by all accounts, but Michael was done with the whole Butler drama thing. It was like an ongoing soap opera, but instead of watching it on TV, he'd been forced to live it. And the death of

Felicity Carter-Price would live with Michael forever, along with the guilt. He'd come to the conclusion that Vinny was Vinny, and if his past had finally caught up with him, then he only had himself to blame. Perhaps someone had been gunning for him the same time as he was? Or he was sulking? Whatever, Michael no longer cared.

Vinny had ruined so many people's lives over the years, his own included, and Michael knew that this time there would be no going back. Apart from keeping in contact with his dad and his children, it was time to distance himself from his troublesome family for good. Cleanse himself and his life.

Michael hadn't yet told his mother he was leaving the crap weather of England behind to start afresh in sunny Majorca. He'd thought about sending her a postcard when he got there but had already said all he'd needed to. She was bound to be furious with him, but Michael was past caring. All his life he'd been taken for granted, whether it be by his mother, Vinny, or the women in his life. Well, not any more. From now on he was putting himself first and in future when he introduced himself to people, he wouldn't be holding out his right hand and saying 'Michael Butler' like his mother had forced him since he was two years old. He would introduce himself as just plain old 'Michael'.

DCI Terry wasn't convinced. He'd read the letter Frankie Mitchell had given him explaining Little Vinny had been present when Molly Butler had died and it was in fact Ben Bloggs who'd killed her. He'd also listened intently to every detail Frankie had told him. DCI Terry was a very clever man. He had the knack of knowing when people were either lying, hiding something or trying to protect themselves. That's how he'd risen through the ranks from a young PC to the position he currently held.

Sitting next to his daughter, holding her hand, was Eddie Mitchell. He'd explained to DCI Terry the time and date he'd delivered the awful news to Vinny at his home in Rettendon and Vinny's reaction to it. He'd also said how worried about his best pal he was, revealing that the last thing Vinny had said as he'd left his cottage in a blaze of fury was: 'I'm gonna fucking kill him.'

The Chief Inspector sat back in his chair. He'd only just joined the police force when Molly Butler was murdered. That poor little girl was the first dead child Terry had ever seen, and he'd never forgotten the sight of her tiny body in that shallow grave. 'Something here isn't quite adding up to me to be honest,' he said loudly.

'Why? It's written down in black and white,' Eddie reminded the man.

Terry leaned forward, placed his elbows on the desk and rested his chin in his hands. Looking deeply into Eddie's eyes, he then focused on Frankie. 'I think we all know who really murdered Molly Butler, don't we? And it wasn't Ben Bloggs, was it? It was Little Vinny.'

When Frankie Mitchell mumbled the word 'Yes', DCI Terry felt a warm glow inside. He had always vowed to get justice for that poor defenceless child. It might have taken him twenty-two years, but finally Molly Butler could rest in peace.

EPILOGUE

Quentine Butler was [illegible]
passed [illegible]
heart [illegible]

Staring at her [illegible]
Quentine's [illegible]
cuddly cheeks [illegible] black [illegible]
to stop her [illegible]

[illegible]

[illegible]

Oh [illegible]

[illegible]

child [illegible]

who [illegible]

[illegible]

I'm sorry that I'm not [illegible]

[illegible]

[illegible]

[illegible]

You [illegible]

I [illegible]

[illegible]

EPILOGUE

Queenie Butler was in pieces. Today, a whole week had passed since her Vinny had gone missing and she still hadn't heard a word from him.

Staring at her beloved son's baby photos, tears poured down Queenie's face. He'd been such a beautiful child with his chubby cheeks and black curly hair. So much so, people used to stop her in the street and gaze inside the pram in awe.

Hearing the baby wake up, Queenie walked over to her great-grandson and held him in her arms. 'Shush now, it's OK, Baby Blue,' she whispered.

It was two days ago Queenie had woken up to the poor child screaming its head off. She'd shouted for Roxanne, who never replied, then she'd found the note in the kitchen.

Dear Queenie/Nan,
I'm sorry, but I'm not ready to be a mum yet. I want you to take care of Baby Blue for me until I'm older, please.

You'll make a far better parent to him than I will. You're a natural.

Love you and thanks for telling me the family history,
Roxanne x

Bar the doctor, Queenie still hadn't told anybody about Baby Blue, or Roxanne's visit. All she could think about was her Vinny. 'If I don't get in touch within seven days, Mum, then you know I'm dead. Only call the police after that,' her son had always insisted.

Queenie walked over to the record player. It had once belonged to Lenny, Vivvy's son, and she'd kept his record collection too.

There was one record Queenie had been playing all week. She'd even placed a framed photo of Vinny next to it. Looked so sweet, he did, in his pale blue romper suit. Had she done the right thing, encouraging him to be what he'd become? But she knew in her heart that, even if he didn't contact her by the end of today, she wouldn't change a thing. Her son was an East End legend, just like the Kray twins, and nobody would ever forget him. Her Baby Blue, that boy she'd given birth to, would be talked about for many years to come. Surely that was better than being a nobody, wasn't it?

Queenie put the needle on the record. The song was by Them, a famous group from back in the sixties.

Dreading tomorrow and the reality of never seeing her beloved son again, Queenie dropped to her knees and rocked her great-grandson. She then cried a thousand tears while singing along to the words of 'It's All Over Now, Baby Blue'.